THE BACKSLIDER

The
BACKSLIDER

{Knowing Deception as a Virtue
or...
Knowing virtue as a deception...}

a novel

Seán McGrady

DZANC
BOOKS

For
Cecília

&

my children

Maria, Joanna, Joseph
Nina, Michael
& Simon

DZANC BOOKS

1334 Woodbourne Street
Westland, MI 48186
www.dzancbooks.org

ISBN-13: 978-1936873043

Printed in the United States of America

First edition published by Dzanc Books / November 2011

Book design by Steven Seighman

10 9 8 7 6 5 4 3 2 1

The eye with which God sees me is the eye with which I see Him. My eye and His eye are one. If God were not, I should not be. If I were not, He would not be either.
Meister Eckhart

To pretend is to know oneself.
Fernando Pessoa

PROLOGUE

When we all get to heaven what a day of rejoicing that will be,
When we all see Jesus, we'll sing and shout the Victoreeeee...

When we eventually meet Jesus, what a day of awkward encounters that will be. All the new faces. The new beings made from old beings. Salvation is the promise to become what we are not. In backsliding you may become what you are. Getting to heaven then becomes a worrying thing. No gain, all loss. I tossed and turned in my bed at the notion. Maybe Heaven was not for me. That encounter I would like to forgo. An inner impulse led my soul, back in its sixteenth year, in a rather different direction.

CHAPTER 1

The very first thing that happened was... well, insofar as I am recording the events, and the qualifications and restrictions are mine, the very first thing that happened was my idea to commit a petty crime. I suppose, with a different designation, a different perspective or intention, the whole thing would be described differently, and even the first event—if there is such a thing—would be different, and maybe by the time I have exhausted myself in telling it, I will see that my story—yet it is barely a story—is merely to benefit me and in a manner of using the language I know and knew best. The language of me and my world. Now and then.

In reality there are limitless ways to do it. There is simply too much of it, not too much *reality* but too much language with which we describe it. Furthermore, I am right in there, in the story, embedded amongst others. I am not the detached observer. So, be warned, the story will have a ghostly quality, a sense of indefiniteness. Unreality. But please, remember, being a fake is not my nature.

Yet, the beginning is merely an edge. As indeed is the end. If we stick to these coordinates it would be a mere surface circumnavigation without penetrating to the depths. If it's only a story that is required, the beginning may be possible, as stories are merely edginess, tiptoeing around the horizons, effect to effect. People like a story. It is *the* place of an illusion. The history is a different story.

What happened? Take a leap. The baptismal water is plumping everywhere except perhaps at the edge. That's how you'll find me: I'm never at the edge.

*

The day, a spring Saturday, beckoned, like white whale obsessed Ahab on the back of the monster Moby Dick. Deadly day that it was. Big day in my dreams, sucking me in, into its body, into its entrails. No resistance offered up by the day; it was, in fact, invitational.

I ignored the sadness and madness descending on the city. The lamentable lunacy of the unpredictable. 1972 was to be the year of supreme sadness. This was the full effect. It led to a body of badness declared as the cause in all its glory, exploding here, there and everywhere. Destruction, despair, misery and madness. The proclaimed cause therefore was merely an *effect*. The green light went on, and all were dazzled in the glare. Yet they proceeded apace in their temporary blindness.

No day to be sat idly or to pray wildly. Let loose the wiles of the will. Speed, accuracy, organisation. The plan was plain enough. Establish myself in a manner of a racehorse in the stalls. Speed was what counted to this steed. Only the course was before me.

Rise early before all else. Hoodwink the forty winks. Ease the body from rest to motion, kinetic not frenetic. To E-motion. Expression. Drum up some speed. Feel the beat. Ignore all early arousal to diversionary and deceitful pleasures. Like the lying full hard-on that rises with every dawn. Bury the risen Lord. Fill the empty vessel with initial self-intoxication. Nil nourishment to calm the nervous belly. Just chew the fat. Inspect the crime scene, clear the mind of residual doubt, and commit the act. Exit the crime scene, leave the house by the front door, not like the thief by the rear. Pick up sidekick and accessory-to-the-fact-to-be, Linus Larkin. Suggest that we make our way to town via the main thoroughfare.

Ease Linus Larkin into his accomplicity. Lay the foundations. Remove obstacles to conscious participation. Unfold the crime. Just like an act, a drama, the proceeds will take their part, a production certain to be greater than mere need. The intention, to make something of myself.

The deed done, head home in anticipation of triumph, my body aching to achieve more success. Survey the family of faces, full or fallen. Listen to the chat, cheery or chastising.

Would I be chased by accusers or be able to eat lunch in peace?

Then out to green acres to play afternoon football. To boldly and bodily enjoy the criminal reward. The sense of a successful sin. Then to church to praise the Lord and pray. Admire the beauty of evangelical Eva, Eva Angelic, coming and going from her distant pew. Beauty out of my grasp. Then home to put the feet up and watch *Match of the Day*. Up to the crow's nest at the midnight hour to feel above it all. To look down, to bend down for bedside prayers. Bed itself. In curled up foetal warmth. Sleep soundly, undisturbed by guilt.

This was my organised encounter with what was agreeable to me: judgement by God is a failure to understand things, so no guilt can possibly accrue.

CHAPTER 2

It seems that it never occurred to me, Marius Moonston, of the south Belfast Moonstons, not to commit the crime. It opened up to me as if there was no alternative. It was just there to be done. To be followed. A sense of dynamism prevailed. Self assertion gripped me from the brain to the bowels. Beelzebub's harmony. Composed in a sinful commitment.

But surely I must have considered the alternative, for a voluntary act must involve the apprehension of its contrary, must it not? I must have envisaged not doing it. Somewhere in my head there was the not doing it. Yet, I felt compelled to act. Compelled to see in prehension.

What is decisive is not known, maybe never known.

Therein lay my bondage and perhaps the bondage of us all. So, I did the bad, but somewhere there was still the good. I transgressed, but I wasn't full of badness. Only partly full, like right now, only partly myself. A diminishing persevering self. Obeying my dying sense of my very own badness. Am I right? Maybe I was just badly infected by the Ulster consciousness, like the effect of damp in houses near the river, slowing people up.

Badness. The Irish from the black north, black cloud country, like the word, badness. It's in the Ulster mouth at birth. They place it upon you by word of mouth. It suits their mode of expression and indeed their mode of being in general. The mode of mood. Some folk I know say *mut* for mood. Like *he's in a good mut*. Country folk. The Germans, I learnt, say *mut* for a movement of the soul, the centre of ourselves, the heart, and *mood* in English has, I think, the same origin. But the Irish have a mode of linguistic expression they can get their teeth into or, more accurately, their jaws into, as false teeth or no teeth are common. The firming up of the jaws, the tightening up of mouths and the twisting of faces.

There is the Belfast badness. Get that word by the scruff of its neck and you have *bawdness*. *He's a bawd egg!* they say. Foul smelling ovum of evil. You can smell badness, it is claimed. It's in the wind.

The wind bloweth, said the mother, when announcing the approach of badness. You can smell it even before it's cracked open. It's in the begetters from the very beginning. They are a foul lot. There's plenty of it about, stinking up the province, and the province of their thinking is that badness and evil, badness and sin are the very same thing.

There is the badness you can see and the badness you cannot, and the latter is often confused for goodness.

The mother especially loved to hate it, and she put all her facial muscles to work, self-taught tautness to snapping, when she said something of the sort, *He's full of bawdness that one! So he is. Bawd!* From her moral crow's nest, she was always on the lookout for real badness.

She wanted to protect us, her wee things, from the big badness. She wanted to see it for what it was and do away with it before it infected us. Except, that is, for the badness in herself, which she thought never existed, and so she never saw it. She never looked sufficiently well at her own self, yet her self was her problem.

What, then, is badness? Where is it to be found? Is it in the immanent otherness of dishonesty and deceitfulness of character? The will to deception. What is badness? Is it that within us that is not us? And goodness for goodness sake? Is it that within us that is us? To call someone good is to say they do not deceive people by making them think they are what they are not. They have the will to truth. They are open, they avoid concealedness, they are unhidden, they are undeceptive. The totally good person, if there is or was such a person, would be so distinctively open that, if we could be equally perfect in conception, we would be directed to the form of goodness itself. Goodness is to reality what badness is to unreality: one is that which makes the thing what it is, the other that which seeks its destruction. And reality is to perfection as unreality is to imperfection. There are names for us as creatures of badness. The *backslider* and the *hypocrite* are two such names.

*

One cloudless spring morning before the dark clouds inevitably appear, there was a knocking on our front door by the uncoated Ulster constabulary men, whose knock was like no other. They were blown up the short distance from the Donegall Pass constabulary fortress to Botanic by one of those wicked winds the mother said she could smell. Badness brought right up to her clean doorstep. All concerned were sealed inside the pristine parlour, the mother, father, and constabulary men. Ructions followed in barely a moment of time. I was standing at the hall table outside the door, in a barely disguised state of extended curiosity, when the mother, in a dramatic parlour exit, exclaimed to all available ears, *They've murdered your Uncle Patsy! The hypocrites and backsliders! The bad eggs!* This was the badness not seen, the badness she once was blind to, but now could see. She could see it clearly, lying in state, all at once, with Uncle Patsy cold in the dustless parlour, in a solid state of unmoving parts. The man at a dead rest quickened her to the new form of badness and a new deadly sadness.

*

Ma Moonston didn't have time for actors. She dramatically shunned them. The old Uncle Hughie, the lodger in her precious house, was an actor of the sort she deeply despised. His daily performances of begging and borrowing and pretending to be ill made her sick. Through the theatricals she could see only laziness, filth and habitual self-humiliation. And hypocrisy in his flagrant flouting of faith: idols in rows by his bedside, gambling in his head, and booze forever in his belly.

Actors need alternative names and in the Ulster tradition of renaming she attributed to him a new title to go with his performances: *Slippy Tit*, she called him and laughed with the name still in her mouth. It took several efforts to get it out. But the laugh itself was an act.

The backslider and hypocrite are indeed actors, not by profession, but by deep personal intention. It's a conviction. The law of their nature convicts them. The rules immediately present. I myself was more familiar with the rhyme, reason and rules of being a backslider, not that perplexity was ever far away.

The backslider is rarely easy with his disposition. He is denying something massive. The backslider is the evangelical hypocrite. He has slid away from the path of the truth and goodness of God. Often, he is bodily, but no longer spiritually, in the community of believers. This is his deception. The backslider wants both worlds. He sits there in the midst of the believers and knows his own deception and knows they do not.

They think I am a representative of the truth. Part of their truth. I endeavour to be part of it, but I am not and so endeavour anew to pretend to be part of it. Therein lies a task. A performance of resistance on one front, persistence and perseverance on the other. In it, but not of it, but not detected to be not of it. He is filled with himself. Behold, your sins will find you out, says the scripture, but the backslider says they won't. He mingles comfortably in both worlds, with his main virtue, his falseness in freedom. Ineffable. In the world he denies the Church, in the church he denies the world. In the world he affirms himself.

If he could set up a church of the backslider he would. *The Assembly of Evangelical Backsliders*, he would call it, and they would gather to testify to the merits of deception. Deception would be cultivated; no one would know who was who. The basis of it would be disobedience to all openness, and they would have Oscar Wilde as a saint, and his declaration, disobedience is man's original virtue, would be written above every entrance.

Would you be free of your burden of sin? Oh no, for the burden of sin is no burden at all. Those evangelicals would have us in bondage to the unsinful. And the unsinful is what? Anything not on the long list of sinful things. They say it is following Jesus and anything that diverts the mind from that singular path is sinful. The world would be some shite heap if that was the case. A bigger shite heap than it is now. The big sin is living a life. Living for yourself. Being yourself. Unsubmissive. But that is the most unsinful thing I can think of.

The fundamentalists pretend to take self-denial to new limits. Self-denial is their very own self affirmation which should be off limits. In fact, the total servitude to the Lord was all a bit of a subterfuge to promote the self, particularly by the officers of the church, the Pastor, the elders, who are stotious with the elder spirit. The ministering without ministerial garb, administering the plain clothes card, is an assertion of self, and captures me in the dead of night when unconscious clarity cuts the cord with which we cleave to all illusion.

Neatly-tailored Elder Berry was a nice enough elder, almost feminine in his approach, unctuously cordial as he shook your hand with his own limp paw at the church door, his way to slip past your barely-working critical attention. Playing his electric guitar with his eyes closed and with nodding head movements, he clearly thought highly of his talent. A church man with a guitar of the electrical sort was an undoubted assertion of himself. He strung along the church girls with his mathematical melodics and said they could call him Karl.

But the likes of elder Cord, Billy Cord by name, in the suit of smooth beige corduroy, attached assertively to style—thus nicknamed umBillycal Cord—and the slickly greased enthusiasm of Deacon Jimmy Fox, greasy of hair and silky of tongue, conducted themselves more brashly, taking military charge of all and sundry, on Sundays and all other non-Lord's-Day days. They didn't care to court your favour, theirs was the highest court in the church. They had the authority of God almighty in their mouths and searchlight sin-senses to continually remind you of your saintly state of sin. Yes, the saints were free of sin but they could still sin and there was always a watchful elderly eye looking for the signs.

Watch them jostle for position. I did. With a mixture of amusement and bafflement. I watched them demanding undivided attention. You could see their countenance of control. I saw it. The deception was at work in those who declared it to be a sin. Their wandering eyes of ambitious authority cast governing glances over signs of disobedience, disobedience to their acts of deception.

The message from the high pulpit was always in your ear. There was no hiding place. *Beware the backslider! He is in your midst to destroy your faith. He is not what he seems. He is the servant of Satan the Deceiver. The backslider, with a demonic will, will drag you back with him, will drag you to Hell where you will roast with him on the bubbling, eternal, satanic spit. We spit on the backslider with our spiritual spit, and he will sizzle. A purifying spit, like Christ's spit in the eyes of Blind Bartemaeus. We deny Satan's divisive disobedience.* So saith the Pastor, the shepherd of his flock, leading them all in his direction, to sit at his feet and worship. His words are always very clear and near. Or is he the mad barking sheepdog in *Far From the Madding Crowd*, pushing them over the cliff to destruction?

His propositions are elementary, powerful mind medicine. Fire medicine from a live wire firebrand. Boiling balm. Electric enlightenment. Shocking. Cauterising. A spiritual surgery, singeing the submissive soul, leaving an abiding sacred scar. The backslider will always feel its pull, its itch. And he will feel his backsliding badness. His disobedience. When he feeds, more and more, on the idea of his own being's importance, he still senses the discomfort of the disfigurement that rests somewhere within. When he stretches his mind in directions new and fruitful, the scar will extend with it and painfully bind the present to the past all for the sake of the future, the future coming.

An assertion, from the nifty-minded Nietzsche, I believe, may give the backslider hope in the face of all this, and even offer prestige, the assertion that falseness might be the very thing that is the essential condition of *life* inspired. Denounce the deified falsifications. Defy with the noble lie. Fight lie with the courageous lie. To effect a love of life. Not to love the life of effect. A life affirmed in spite of all infirmed. A life of clear vision, undistorted. You must keep both your eyes open for the tyrant or the priest, but also you must see, through your overseeing eye, the whole spectacle. If you are looked upon falsely by false prophets, humiliated, threatened, lied to, maligned, what can you do?

Ask the question *In practice what does this deceit consist of?* It consists of occupying bolt holes of convenience and taking refuge in creative characterisation, ultimately in order to defy real badness. The truth is, deception can be deceiving, what matters is whether it is a mere effect or whether it is productive.

The path of my spiritual deception was born in this evangelical free for all. To renounce false judgement is to affirm life. Life beyond good and evil. *Disobedience is man's original virtue.* Dear Oscar. Who am I? I am who? Who was I then? Marius Moonston. That's who. With feet firmly in the Ulster firmament.

CHAPTER 3

There was no alarm clock, just a special inner excitement that was especially alarming. Disarming. Awakening. It just kept on ringing in my lazy head, keeping me alive to things, courting the crime to come. It had imaginary strength. In the night, it manifested itself every half hour or so until it was really time to wake. To wake from a weak sleep fully, formally resigned and ready for the day. But this was not to be resignation day; it was assignation day. Everyone was tired from the business of mourning. If I had any doubt about my deed, I would think of Uncle Patsy in the parlour, dead as a dodo, now nothing for being nothing.

The deed done I took my light and lean sixteen-year-old self out on the iniquitous walk, the body much in mind, the hand that reached and grasped, the legs that transported me away. Pounding to the pounds in my possession was an initial heaviness of heart. Strong for the absence of food. A starving strength. Appetite, continuous conscious desire for the day dissolving the weight of guilt. The walk was waking, wondrously loosening. A waking walk on wet pavement with an unpleasantly stiff, bad Irish wind cutting up the face. A powerful reek straight from the arse of MacGillacuddy's way down south somewhere. It's an elemental annoyance. A Presocratic element. The fundamental connection to nature. An energetic exposure. Getting wind of it between streets and open entries. It blows its cold nuisance in through the inadequate coverage of your clothes. The fragmented mother did something inadequate with my clothes, fragmenting the form of the upper apparel, miniaturising them in boiling water or some such domestic treatment. Always inadequacy in the length. In short, short. Riding up the body with even minimum movement. Complaints of this shortcoming were blown away in family laughter. *My shirts are always too short and tight, look at it!* I shouted. I demonstrate with the loose shirt ends. Tight is fine, but not the constriction combined with lack of adequate dimensions. That points to the nature of tailoring. *And my knickers too massive.* I refrained from demonstration of the monstrosities here, but bent my knees slightly for no known reason. *What gives?* My bollocks, that's what gives. Laid loose they were. Never the twain shall meet, knicker waist and shirt tails, leading to an irritating sense of bodily imbalance that I found difficult to tolerate. An awareness that was itself somewhat uncomfortable.

All started off just fine, an even feel, between top attire and bottom. Then, on one fine freezing day, I couldn't tuck the shirt into my trousers. I raised my trouser waist with a powerful tug but, with a single stretch, out came the shirt again. I tucked it back in time and time again. Pulled up the bags until it looked ceremonial, ritualistic. No good at all. The cold air got right in there, onto the skin. The sensitive skin on the hip.

The early sun was low and blindingly bright. Its ninety-three-million-mile rays stabbed me in the eyes. I squinted, briefly entertaining the idea of my peepers confronting the sun full on, and of the sun blinding the sight out of them. I thought of becoming a church celebrity, a blind boy restored to sight by the ministerial healing thumbs mediating God's mercy. I'd seen them praying for the blind in the church, with formidable hands clasped on wondering heads and the thumbs pressing ever in, like great clamps on the eyelids. The blind grimaced, but received no sight, and stumbled back bewildered to their seats.

But could I trust God on this one? Was I up to that test of faith? An absolute faith was required. I would surely fall short. Even an immeasurably small margin of failure would leave me with unseeing eyes. I saw the scene with my third eye and I shuddered. Eyeballs rolling in search of sight. Not even light. The sun could have its way with its long rays, and I would bow to its power by resigning myself to sight by squinting.

I soon found myself in some strange fella's slipstream some ways down Great Victoria Street, the street that leads me straight, without any deviation, to town. To the very centre of the town, its heart, where the Saturday shoppers beat their way.

But I did deviate. No sooner was I on the main thoroughfare that I found myself, even with squinting eyes, taken by a sight, indeed the sight of a site, of a pair of trousers, incredibly loosely tailored around what was undoubtedly a diminished Ulster arse. An immature arse, a farce of an arse. A sorely sight! A sorely sight even to blind man McHawky from across our street, who was said to see by some vagary of the vision all unsightly things that passed within his sniff.

An arse before me that would not be out of place in an African famine. The poor African male arse was a case in point when talking of failed arses. A suitcase in point maybe. Full of donated clothes. I'd seen them on TV, performing for the camera with their perverted sartorial swagger. Co-ordinated with a wide smile as if all was well within the world of all co-ordinates. In someone else's trousers, indeed in all manner of garb that had been picked out of a mountain of clothes by thin, black, picking fingers. All I could see were underdeveloped bodies in over-sized outfits. The outfits out-fit the wearer. But we were a long way from that undisciplined place of African apparel *unawearness*.

I was thinking too clearly, not paying sufficient attention to what was around and about. Conceiving adequately is a severe joy but not recommended on a big busy street with roaring traffic. Adequate thinking can get you killed; it takes you to a place that is not the place you're in. It wasn't a time for meditation, or meditation on meditation which could lead to the precious unconscious.

Back here in busy Great Victoria Street, via the deviating conceiving of the fashion of Africa, the endeavouring, fully conscious mind fell again on what was immediately to the fore.

This bringing to the fore is foreknowledge. We have it. This is a mind that knows what is coming and going in front of it. What is on the horizon. And even what is far to the rear. What is immediate in the realm of encounters. What is fear and what is fortune. A mind credited with a capacity to deal with the instant. My contentment in confinement, in solitude I quickened to it, as much as I failed in all thought behind thought.

Maybe you wouldn't credit it. I did. I gave it great credit. I credited it even in my incredulity. Credit to a massive swathe of faded blue jean material, between the lower back and the upper thighs of the stranger, folds in a void surging up to this or that particular fold shape by tectonic-type hip movement. An eerie emptiness resided within those abundant leggings, a void, a vacuum sucked up as an idea, deep into my demanding mind, into a suitable processing point that churned out the annoying formal idea of inelegance.

An abandonment of refinement was what it was, of definition, a retreat from pleasing style symmetry. Looseness was not an idea I liked. Like a loose idea. A bad definition. An idea separated from the thing. Its thing. Intentionally. A notion out of control.

An indefinite article was before me. *A cheeky article*, said Ma Moonston. The definitive indefinite. The unrestricted who required strictness. Strictness as in the stick that is used for discipline. There was an arse to whack into shape here. The mother would move heaven and earth to whack an arse out of its disobedience. But first it needed to be found and revealed.

So much has foundered on the rock of indiscipline. Parmenides over Heraclitus. The One. Mind over sense. Talking sense is not sense. Changeless over ever-changing. Socratic substantial solidity of wisdom in place of sleaked Sophism. The ideal over the practical. The singular substance over the modal many. Spinoza's obsession, his Substance abuse. The substance of it all is form.

The mother's word for all slippery thoughts and acts was *sleaked*. A form in her head of badness. A word that sneaked out of her mouth like a serpent. A word that was poisonous in its use. A great word.

The whole area of looseness was as uncomfortable to the mind as it was to the body. Some body. The body as an example to us all. I knew not the identity of the occupant of these ultra-baggy pants, in whose wake I walked, but it seemed necessary to attach a name to it, and indeed a fitting name for the ill-fitting idea soon and with some surprise came to mind.

So, Les Buttocks was christened, in his blissful ignorance of the mental event that was wholly mine. And though I only encountered this Les Buttocks just the once, and from behind, never seeing his face, never knowing a single idea of his, his idea was always with me as an aesthetic beacon. I felt my own buttocks for comfort. Flesh that had been whacked into shape.

I allowed myself to laugh at Les Buttocks and the appropriateness of the name, but it was laughter that ultimately resided heavily in the heart as sorrow. It made the heart's nucleus heavy, because at the root of it was something I deeply despised.

The misunderstanding at the bottom. Right there before me in his human, masculine skinniness was the misunderstanding of what the body is capable of. The light scrawny frame of a lad that couldn't fit into his own clothes. I condemned his failure to seize the idea of fitness, to make it fit in his mind.

It was all such brazen ignorance. To display it, a deliberate denial of form. No attempt to find any approximation to it. An insult to the mind's proper function to freely find the proportion in things. The proportion that conforms to the power of the mind and the potential of the body. Movement entirely in the realms of the active. His was an eminent example of the inactive, of weakness, powerlessness. Slowness too. He moved like a no-action replay. Inattentive to the body's commands. He was to be his eminence Father Meek, the demon Christian Brother, shrouded from head to toe in those diabolical black duds. He was a forger, for here was an attempt to make ugliness and untidiness into a thing of fashion, and thus a thing to be followed.

The world had become lazy in the fashion department. Les Buttocks was lazy and no good. He needed to be hooded and hidden. I gave birth to a healthy spite for him. I could spit on him, such was the extent of my spite.

I extended my vision of his life. I saw him getting up to no good. He declared his intent in his dress. He wore himself. He was hostile. He was virtually a venomous presence. Barren in virtue. A baron of the estate of corruption. He entered the streets from a hovel of adulteration, from a family of filth, born from the seed of seediness, cocooned in ancestral crap. He needed to be sobered up in a uniform, in the army maybe. Privately. As Private Buttocks he needed an uniform identity to express his nonentity. In that case, the uniform of a loin cloth, like Mulvaney in Kipling's *The Incarnation of Krishna Mulvaney*. Then we'd see what his body said.

He had set out this day to further his badness, beyond his relations. His intention was to foul up other lives. Poison and destruction was in him. I had him in my sights and had the supreme determination not to be his victim, the victim of his sneakiness, of his treachery. Of his skiving, of his intention to loaf, and have people loaf with him until they grew bored of loafing and took to slicing up life around them. He would lead weaker minds than his to bondage and ultimately to hell. I would keep my eye on him. Not just now but in time to come. It might even come to a fight with him. That area of thought was uplifting.

CHAPTER 4

Les Buttocks was an apparent distraction from my definite purpose that day, but lessons were to be learnt from that dander in a daydream. Those lessons lay in wait, in the eventual comparison and conflict of powers. Here, I saw only that his deceit was merely self-deceit.

I immediately felt superior in my close-fit dandy charcoal jeans as we moved steadily ahead down the road. I stretched my legs on every stride to tighten the muscles on my thighs. Close fit made closer. I reflected on my reflection in glass. How splendidly my legs were sealed in the heavy denim. I thought how well they must look to the outside observer, a notion that instantly raised my spirit of self-esteem. Esteem that comforted in the case of contamination of doubt. Doubt that was lingering over the continuation of my crime.

I turned my mind back to closing the door of the Moonston house behind me, thinking that the firmly-closed door and what lay inside did not contain the crime, as I first thought. I wasn't free of it. It was carried with me on my route to the Linus household, to walking with Linus and beyond. I thought as I moved on, that the crime had only been partly committed, the centrepiece, so to speak, but the extension of the crime lay ahead. Just ahead.

Do not crimes continue beyond the discrete event, no matter how discreet they are? A crime needs its minimum space, to take its very own minimum time to make it what it is.

I inched forward in thought, to an increased edginess at this annoying self examination, an unpleasant endowment to those meditations that stood as a counterweight to the erection of a recently rising self-esteem.

Wilfully burying those meditations, I found firm ground. Real ground, that which takes the soles of your shoes. I felt firm steps. I had stepping with me in the thoroughfare my chosen accomplice, brain-box Linus Larkin, who, with all his heightened ability to ease to the abstract, knew not that he had the displeasure of criminal complicity. His understanding was elsewhere. His view of what lay ahead a mistaken one. That knowledge decreased my edginess, as it was amusing to know he didn't know, and that I knew *for* him. That my motivation was completely private to me was also something of a joy.

Linus seemed not to know crime itself, that is, as an active committer of it. At least insofar as I knew him and I thought I did. And with this knowledge, I pointed out to *Linus the accomplice* the empty arsed trousers that lay directly ahead of us—which somehow he had managed to miss—to divert him. I then administered the name Les Buttocks just as Linus's eyes met the majesty of the formless rear, but I never expected him to convulse in laughter in the manner and extent to which he did.

In Linus's mind, the order and connection of the idea met perfectly with the order and connection of the thing, and when that was the case, it was the illuminating idea, the concrete concept, in full familiarity. You know it because you already knew it. That was why Linus was wobbling like a harmless, joyful drunkard, this way and that across the broad pavement of Great Victoria Street.

I cannot control my body, Linus warbled, unable even to control the pitch of his voice. Normally, the only reason for such a high-pitched hullabaloo would be some bastard grabbing you by the bollocks.

I'm all loose-like. Loose like Les Buttocks! Like his trousers. My own buttocks are weak as jelly bitsers. And he held a flabby jelly bitser of his own between his fingers.

Control yourself Linus boyo, I said. *Your dignity. Your body has to be kept under control. You'll end up in the road to nowhere. Under a big Ulster bus and then it'll be up at the City Hospital which is the same thing as nowhere. That's where'll you'll die in agony.*

I can't stop. I just feel loose. I think loose, and I am loose. Is that the looseness you feel when you're dying, I wonder. First loose, then stiff. Too loose to care. I think I'm going to wet myself well and truly, Marius. Through looseness. Through my Y-fronts. Wet my trousers. Wet my gusset, and it'll be all sticky and uncomfortable down there in the gusset.

My name isn't well and truly Marius. Just plain Marius. It well and truly is.

My gusset, warbled Linus. *My damned gusset. Say gusset!* He grabbed my chin with a firm hand, and turned my face to his, and insisted I say it.

Gusset is a grand word, said I. *Gusset, gusset, gusset.* I give him his gusset thrice to his face. And even more for his appetite for delecta-tion. *Gus Set. Good name that. Like Les Buttocks. Lay Bootocks, by the way, is the French of Les Buttocks. Lay Bootocks,* I said again with an overly-accentuated Frenchness and repeated it several more times.

Lay Bootocks, Lay Bootocks, Lay Bootocks! I said it as fast as I could manage.

This gargling mock-Gallic repetition was bad for Linus's weak wobble, which was threatening to take him right off the pavement, onto the road, and under a rumbling Belfast trolley bus. I held him back and we both wobbled.

I shuddered at the idea of being crushed under such a monster. I had imagined it many a time when I had rushed out madly in front of one, just to make myself look as though I was nimbly and athletically in control of the body I dwelt in, and that was mine. In fact, so nimbly did my body work that it *was* me, only under a different aspect. The body aspect. You cannot really be anything without a body. Even God knew that when He placed the soul in it.

I could feel the dangerous weight of the machine beneath my feet as it rumbled on the concrete before it and about it. The earth itself shook. Shops all around trembled. What would it be like to have your skull run over by such a vehicle? An ostrich egg under a sledgehammer? What would a mind be thinking in that moment of head cracking? Would it hear the cracking inside its own head as it was crushed? The badness in me wanted to see such a head cracking, to know for sure what it really was like. But, the thoughts, they would be a private affair.

God help me! said Linus in his distress. *Lord take this weakness away from my loins! Firm up my loins! O Lord, giver of loins, be merciful!*

What words are these? He decomposed me with his magical composition. Linus didn't know the Lord at all, even as much as he didn't know crime, and yet he was praying to Him in his moment of trembling need. In a moment of temporary circumstantial removal, I thought the Lord would be full of His wrath at such a trivial mocking prayer and would lay His heavy hand on us. A mocking petition to deliver bodily normality, when what was required was a simple sense of gravity, lest we float off into a lofty spiritual wilderness. But if Linus didn't know the Lord, his ignorant mocking wouldn't have been half as bad.

Mock not lest you should be mocked. Out of my mouth, by God, shot one of the mother's articles of faith. I almost felt her inside me saying it. Like demon possession. It was irritating that there was a Bible text in my head for almost everything, and sometimes they just spilled out of me. I mocked nevertheless, took the risk and took the high ground in active mocking, a mood from whence issued new and inventive forms. In full flow, I never thought of the moments of being the victim. The temptation to this devilish disposition was usually triumphant. Override and hide the weakest moments of will. Will should never be weak and disabled. Being able to mock the Lord was a powerful thing; it required massive will power, but it made it easy to mock the rest of creation. Yet, only human creation can be mocked, an animal cannot be mocked, nor a flower. You cannot mock nature.

Before I knew better, I had often tried to mock my dog, but I could see that he was not in the business of mocking. After that failure, I reasoned that if you cannot mock a dog, you cannot talk to one either, so why have one? I was in that mocking business with the rest of the human race. That was exclusively our game. I was a mocker like strong drink is a mocker, one drink leads to another just like one mocking joke leads to another, and one mocker usually leads to another (*mocking is catching,* says the mother) just as Linus was led by me. Intoxication to *inmoxication.* Mocking is toxic. And Belfast was one poisonous place. Solitary mocking is never as good as mocking in a pair, or in a triumvirate, the Father, Son and Holy Ghost of mockers. Stimulation in triangular fusion, in harmony of horsing around. But ultimately you have to know that you could handle being a solitary mocker or else you are no better than a coward. Like the individual members of a lynch mob. And mocking is dangerously close to doing a lynch job. Being on the wrong end of a mocking is a powerful education to that end. Lynch is an Irish name and lynching an Irish game.

Mocking is mickey taking, mickey mockery, a mock is like a frock, I said to Linus. Linus roared like a Lionus lioness. I felt mad with the mocking. Mad drunk. *Drunk as a lunk!*

Put on a frock and you get a mock. This was me with a nervy serving. Linus often lent me his formidably attentive ear here on the first class delivery of these words. If his head is turned up to the heavens, as it was, something good is customarily on its way out of him. Or he might be about to fart of which he had no fear.

But, if you wear a frock you can mock, as you will not be recognised in a frock by the mocked, he declared out of a minuscule hiatus of hilarity.

If you can stand up to the mockery in a frock, you can never again be shocked by the mock. Frock is a type of dress, a Vicar who is defrocked is in distress. In dis-dress. I confess! And I mocked with a Dublin accent which was itself mocked by its very use.

For frock's sake Linus, fruck up!

Tick tock are you timing me by the clock? I am not to be timed.

Time and motion, I muttered. *Time and motion at work.*

What's the mutter, said he.

My mother? I muttered, *Why mention the mother?*

Mutter not mother, uttered he with a grin.

Discarded words that mattered. Misheard words that mattered. Linus did not say mother. For the mother's ultimate threat was the frock. The threat of a treat of a frock that covered the cock. She'd have all boys in a frock at one time or another if she could. Teach them their place. Remove the old codding clutter from their heads.

She likened a boys head to a batch of bread, all blown up out of a lowly lump of dough. What was the sense?

Mocking is catching, says that mother. I pretended I heard her. She pretended to fear a world where mockery becomes normal. Here it comes again. *Mock not lest you be mocked.* The motherly mouth uttered that, and I remembered it. That very mother whose mocking capacities exceeded the majesty of mocking in the very empire of mocking. Flocking souls to the mocking empire knew not of the Queen Mother of mocking. But nothing held back the tide of mocking; it lures us as if it was in us by nature.

Linus lad, Les Buttocks is in need of the Lord's help with his loose loins if anyone is, not you. Anyway, God won't listen to such useless rubbish.

You never know.

No! You never know…you you you never know! I shoved Linus with a decent amount of force to correct his course. He was never easily disposed to a change of direction. I thought of the word dispensation as we passed a chemist, which seemed for an instant like an inconvenience. I wanted to classify the loin idea.

Ever heard of a dispensation? I asked Linus.

No, just loins, he said. *And diarrhoea!* We parted thinking ways for a short time: he still engaged with loins and Les Buttocks, whilst I departed with dispensations.

Dispensations are not just what you got at the chemist: God Almighty, we were told, divides history up into them. Not chemists, dispensations. Great chunks of time are divine dispensations. All history is God's history. That's how he rules his creation. By decree. Not just spiriting along. The body is His temple. I reckoned loins needed one dispensation all to itself, as did amusement, whilst I half-listened to the bellowing Pastor in his pulpit going on about the dispensation of prophecy. In that era they knew all that was going to happen but never said so in plain language, dispensed only in code.

But even if the Lord once attended to loins, that dispensation of Lordly loin intervention is surely over. The Lord created us with loins and should give some sort of warranty, but eventually we have to tend to our own loins, for which we are held to account. One day, He will return to inspect them—the dispensation of inspecting—and hold us responsible for the shape of them. The dispensation of loin judgement that will be called. Neither can we hide our loins under a bushel, as bushels are scarce in cities like Belfast. Anyone who tells you differently is not a wise man. Nor even a godly man. But maybe a devilly man.

The Devil surfaced to work his will on loins all over the city. No one's loins felt at ease. Looking over your shoulder fast became an occupation. Men lost their loins left right and centre, which accounted for everything of the loins, for being traitors to the *cause* of this, that, and the other. Does not matter what cause, if you are a turncoat, it's off with your loins. Turncoat is a great word. The Preacher said that it was all most definitely the Devil's work, though he didn't have a good word to say for Protestant turncoats which made me think that he turned a blind eye to their loss. I was interested to know if Uncle Patsy in the parlour had been tampered with in this way. In order to find out, I asked the mother if he was a turncoat. With unusual immediacy, she stood in a stillness that appeared threatening, with eyes rolling and lower teeth jutting out of a jutting chin, giving off a fierce and murderous intent.

CHAPTER 5

*B*ehold *your sins will find you out.* There she blows again. *I have been crucified with Christ,* the inner voice shouts, *it is no longer I who live but Christ who liveth in me.* A truly terrible Biblical bombardment.

But I did live, and I did say, *Let not your heart be troubled, Marius lad,* to fight the Christ within. I said this like the times tables as I left the house, with the crime left half inside and half out. I knew this was a Bible text, but I had taken to corrupting the original to suit my backsliding purpose. Backsliding is not just denial, it is an assertion of something else, and my corruption of verses was an affirmation of me. These variations of verses were spilling out of my mouth unhindered. So, I had to watch myself or I'd be spouting out the alternative holy stuff in far too free a fashion, and I might soon become the subject of discussion, or even the object. I just had to catch myself on.

There was a fly in the ointment known as Rob, my older brother who was now becoming fly and fast flowingly full in his own ways. He would know things even as he knew himself, all sorts of things, and he would know if I was going beyond the pale and occupying a place of impurity. I needed a more disciplined way. His knowing was annoying. He took account of the day's goings on and stored them in his head. He classified them as urgent or not urgent, and the former were laid before me the night of the same day, usually as we hopped into bed. The non-urgent came out in dribs and drabs to make me uneasy.

Watch yourself, he'd say. *It's easy to lose your way. Even in just what you say. Don't wed yourself to the Devil with your words.* Here he caught me off guard, mockingly mimicking Holy Communion, saying, *Body of Christ,* as I placed a chocolate button in my mouth. I had a whole packet of buttons, and I said the magical words after every one that was placed precisely on the surface of my tongue until the body of Christ began to mean something. I thought of the buttocks of Christ and a wedding with the Devil.

The brother's own words became stranger and stranger. He used to say things like the rest of us, still did, but he was adding things that came from another place. He attended more and more to his secret meetings. Whenever I asked him to play football, he would say, in a routine manner, that he had a secret meeting.

His current pretension, or should it be preoccupation, was to be a pastor. He was two years older and had grasped the idea that to look after yourself was also to command other people. He commanded me to a certain extent, with words and looks. He had a wide range of commanding behaviour. It all boiled down to admonishments and teasing. Belittling was a speciality. He allowed himself lots of leeway and was thus good material for the preaching and pastoring job. At about this time, his talk gave prominence to denouncing life and the things of the flesh, overtaking talk of normal things.

*

Leaving the house on the momentous morn, I dandered along at a steady pace to 33A Agincourt Avenue. I kept repeating *Let not your heart be troubled, believe in yourself,* whilst thinking of any possible reason that the brother would have to attach the name backslider to me. Me, him, me, him, until I reached the front door of Linus's house where the conflicting notions concluded.

On the Larkin doorstep, the imposing Larkin door prompted impositional thoughts. In that small distance from my house to Linus's, I routinely passed two churches which, in my mind, always resembled chambers for the dead more than houses of the living Lord. The Botanic Presbyterian Church, a Gothic fortress, I imagined, possessed me in a demonic fashion, its tall watchtower, with a distant and dark open gallery at the top, displayed on no occasion a watchman, unless he was a ghostly night watchman, never seen. *Watchman, what of the night?* Words that scared me.

The second in order, but only yards away from the first, appeared out of the architectural gloom like a white Mediterranean villa, palatial in proportions, but with something of the sepulchral about it. Despite its stainless, perfectly whitewashed walls, it too possessed me, in cold isolation. It appeared to me as an abandoned monument, from where God and all orders of creation had in an atom of time vanished. I never saw a soul enter or leave. I thought of the brother going there to his secret meetings in the dead of night. I thought of the secret rapture. Had some already been taken?

I passed these two churches morning and evening, to and from school, hurrying out of the vicinity of each one. An idea sustained itself through the possession: if I stood still there, the world would be seized by an awful presence.

The Larkin address was a quick sniff away from the far-from-fragrant Lagan River and the adjacent realm known as the Holyland: Palestine Street, Jerusalem Street, Cairo Street, Damascus Street. British Israel, the father said from above. I couldn't make any sense of that, except that the British were special to God, just like the Jews were.

Damascus Street, my usual route to Agincourt Avenue, was not the site of any major spiritual intercession in any man's life, as was Damascus of old, but there had been a recent spate of hellish activity with the flames of Protestant petrol bombs illuminating the front rooms of Catholic houses. Lately, loutish lads stood about at the top and bottom of the streets. They'd give you a look and a half, stirring the defences. I put my head down and walked. Sometimes I spat as I walked, just to look hard.

The door of number 33A, the Larkin family home, was there to be rapped, so I rapped. Linus would be there waiting, ready, as always, to play his part. He'd be my sidekick for a spell. I intended to put him under a spell. Make him mine.

CHAPTER 6

*B*lessed assurance Linus is mine, oh what a foretaste of committing the crime, I sang softly to myself, a blasphemous backslidden destruction of the beloved hymn. I sung it in the continuing sunshine of the morning. Nothing overcast in view. Linus, beside me, was my sidekick at large. The stuttering clot Chester to my manly Marshall Dillon. Chester was not the man to be, not if you wanted to be a man, but someone always had to be him or his like.

The noble character always has to have an obliging helper who is simplicity itself. Same as loyal Tonto to the Lone Ranger. *Me Kemo Sabe,* says Tonto. Me who knows. But what does he know? Tonto can read tracks in the dust like no other but needs further instructions. A bloodhound can do that, but he doesn't know what it all means.

Linus was he who was under instruction. Linus said what you wanted him to say, and Linus always said, *What are we going to do?* or, *Where are we going to go?* Just what I wanted him to say. So, when I spoke, I led him in a particular direction.

His encounters were in my hands. In that sense, he followed the nature of dead Uncle Patsy when he was alive, but I didn't want to think that Patsy stuff here and now, his face like a petrified church gargoyle, his hands frozen in a twisted final grasp on life, so I shook myself up and didn't think it for long. Linus didn't know our future

direction, he always assumed I knew. But at least he was there and
there I wanted him to be.

Being there is more important than you'd think. As is *not
being there.*

Being somewhere else was a chief characteristic of so many friends,
and it is a travesty of the idea of friendship. Being somewhere else
totally daft. Off to town shopping with their ma, off to their granny's
or their auntie's house for tea, somewhere completely out of reach.
Off to the Catholic mass, off to confession on a Saturday night, off
to a music lesson, off to wash their da's car parked miles away at his
work, off to somewhere on the endless list of uninteresting out-of-
reach destinations.

I despised it, and the lie that lay at the root of it. I despised
the disappointment in the slender deception. I hated the idea of
disappearing off to relatives, because I loathed going anywhere near
mine, and what was worse, mine coming anywhere in the direction
of me. I hated it partly because I knew something about the nature
of deception.

Why? Why did friends always have to go off somewhere? Didn't
they make a fuss about it? Didn't they stamp about loosely with
their bodies and rhyme their parents' heads off to make them
change their minds? Linus had no such list of places and would
be there, in his abode, in a state of readiness. Billy McCandless,
an alternative friend and possible candidate for poll position in
my plan, spent large tracts of time in his bed. Whenever I called,
there he lay, and even when awake and in the world, his face
displayed that fullness of sleep that told you he still occupied
the bed.

Punctuality, readiness, it all meant something in the mind of
Linus. I admired him for that, in the implicit way a boy admires
something of another boy of a similar form. I was always there in
my fashion, with food eaten, shoes on, hair combed, teeth cleaned,
and when the door was knocked, I didn't delay or disguise my
enthusiasm to open it. Readiness and steadiness.

The Linus family door was opened by Linus himself on my first
rap and closed behind Linus before the second rap was even born
as an idea in my head.

Linus stepped outside with a fully awake unMcCandless-like countenance. His step was more like a dance, practically a pirouette, as if he'd been listening to *Swan Lake* before I had arrived and was still in the spirit of it all.

I said, *I thought we could take a dander to town.*

CHAPTER 7

Which way? said Linus.

Pawn to queen four, I said. Notations for life, directions and mood. Speed and slowness of movement. We played chess. Usually on the pavement on dry days with my wooden Staunton set, when we weren't lying on our backs studying the movement of clouds and their ways. *Clouds are like people*, says Linus on occasion. Occasions I laughed. *Like black people, you mean?* I said, owing to the general dark nature of our Ulster clouds. *Like Red Cloud, the Indian*, he said. Another occasion to laugh.

We used the traditional P-Q4 opening as the innocent deceit to suggest that we knew exactly where we were going in chess, so we adopted it as shorthand for going somewhere by the main route. Linus sometimes played the pawn to king's rook three variation which was a clear indication he has no plan and no idea how to continue. In fact, it just reflected his mood for mooching about in no particular direction, so that notation became code for general uncertainty of direction.

In 1972, a ridiculously remote place called Reykjavik rallied our attention to chess. I was forever Bobby Fischer, Linus solidly and soundly Boris Spassky. *The biggest battle since World War Two*, said the father from a short socialist distance. His socialism was immanent, his sympathies clearly with Spassky. I called Linus Boris, and he called me Bobby with a faint and funny Russian accent, to put me off. I didn't want to be Fischer at first, as I was not in love with the Americans, but Fischer was immediately different. His own indifference to other things was what I saw. He played chess as a backslider, but play was not the right word. Like you don't play boxing. He denied chess and affirmed it. He was probably closer to Spassky than he to his own country. *But you love the cowboy, the man of the west?* Yes, I loved the wild west. The west that was not yet the US west. Every man for himself.

We sometimes played a game when there was a whole pack of us on the street or in the entry. It started with everyone shouting, *Every man for himself!* Then we scattered at exhilarating speed. Immediate direction unknown. Movement at maximum speed initially, then slowing, at rest in a hiding place, then movement of mind to trap, to wrestle the victim to the floor and kick the shite out of him. It was what it was. The game has no name. It was all activity even when nothing seemed to be moving.

By playing chess, Linus and I made a swift move to acting and thus to backsliding. Chess, in dynamic terms, is a manifestation of growth of mind. An outgoing of something within. The best players are called grandmasters, achieving as much mastery of themselves as of the game.

I found playing chess scary. Inattention was always threatening, like losing yourself, forever on the edge of an abyss. It brought me closer than most things to my pure thinking self. Sometimes, in thinking of a move, I moved to thinking all about myself. Approaching that was as scary as not knowing. Sometimes, it was easier to hide behind others and let them do the knowing.

Revolutions are like that, said Pea-head Purvell, our history teacher. One cause, one movement, a tyrant in fact, moving a multitude of ignoramuses in one direction. That was what it was like here in Belfast. The mob of the unknowing.

Linus took to the serious Spassky seriously. He was attracted by the gravity of the man, the gravity of the unsmiling expression and sober sports jacket. Linus had some gravity himself somewhere. Not easy to pin down though. Like gravity itself. I hoped I had gravity. The backslider should. We touched each other through attraction but this was offset by properties that repulse, keeping us separate in our movements as bodies.

Immediately present to me was the property of a domestic circumstance that separated. Linus stank of tea, milky tea. I didn't get sea sick but I did get tea sick. His words came with the sickly aroma, impairing them, the receiving spirit foundering on a rising tide of bile. It kept me apart. The pleasure of tea had long departed with my desire for the baby bottle, the baby bottle filled with that tan brew.

Linus was a solitary boy. His head was not filled with the common notions of boyhood that might have made him popular or simply acceptable. He didn't run with the crowd nor did he walk with them or stand still with them. He didn't seem to possess the features characteristic of everyday friendship. He was teased and taunted at school for his simplicity but not sufficiently to change his general direction.

This was partly down to some of the particulars of parentage. The Larkin parents never had another child for him to speak to or of, or be eternally annoyed by, a form of life that seemed so natural to the rest of us, strangled in small spaces with loads of siblings at our necks. He didn't experience the daily brutal honesty of brotherhood and sisterhood that stood as good practice for self preservation in the outside world. He had none of those battle scars that steadied the rest of us with sneaky half-friends and outright enemies. Nor weak points in his mind as a result of constant cruel teasing, but at the same time, there was no evidence of the ready artillery of abuse with which to retribute when that moment of conflict arose, as it surely would.

The enthusiasm with which his parents always agreed to farm him out to any offer of temporary adoption, by any outside element of humanity, registered itself, in my imagination, as wonder, envy, and quandary. He had a seemingly no-hassle life with no one to hassle him. I thought: this lad needs some protection.

When Linus left his house, was it a case in the minds of those he left behind, that he ceased to exist for them? His parents asked no questions. Whereas, all other parents I knew, including my own, started to fry themselves with frustration, modulating themselves into madness, desperate to get you back home for those inconsiderately conceived and unnecessarily circumscribing events. What then emanated from parents to son? Joyous participation with the Prodigal son? Or was their anger their donation? And perhaps the gift of violence.

Where were you when your tea was here waiting for you? was a regular emanation from enraged red adult faces.

Out enjoying myself, replied innocence with filthy pale face.

Enjoying yourself? erupted the red face. *I'll make you enjoy yourself with a good skelping round the legs.* That was also an occasion to laugh, but not the same sort of laugh at all. Some boy at school informed me that some people liked to be skelped. That got a universal laugh from all who had ears to hear. Whispered inaccurately in my ear in a line outside the science room.

The masochist people, he said, *that's the name of them,* as if they were a tribe. He read it in a magazine, he said, in Skinner's barber shop, after which he took his knowledge, and the magazine, and went about the school yard skelping legs with a wooden ruler to find the tribe's members.

Most legs were not welcoming of the skelping, and mouths shouted, and swore and there was ample laughing and crying that sounded like forest people wailing in a foreign tongue. He had a joke about the masochist tendency that I never really understood until later. It seemed important, and I held suspended in the mind the idea that there were people who liked to be skelped and people who liked to skelp.

Another absence of normal parental behaviour in this Larkin case, was the fact that they never came searching with the same perverted mad love of other parents, ready to skin him alive for not reporting absence and whereabouts outside the times and places previously agreed. We never saw the Larkin father or mother chasing the son around with the caring weapon of punishment— in the case of the rest of us, usually a swiping or whipping object picked up casually in a rage, to curb disobedience. Disobedience was the norm of course, as was being punished in the normal, old fashioned way.

A common sight in the street was of a mad parent dashing from a doorway with an instrument of skelping. They'd skelp their very own child in public, in front of friends who'd look on, laughing their heads off at the spectacle. Futile attempts were made to escape, lots or wriggling and goose-stepping, and, combined with the indignity of much wailing, it was a monument to misery and merriment. Onlooker laughing, done in full awareness of their own experiences of punishment, bordered on hysteria.

Linus never felt the skelping whip for not obeying the imperatives of time. He never witnessed his parents shamelessly blowing a gasket at his disobedience or heard the queer words shouted down his ear, *I'll give you disobedience!* He was confused by the spectacle. He gazed upon the whole sorry business of punishment in astonishment. He never laughed in panic at the prospect of a good hiding, with the parent bearing down, nor yelped at skelped, or experienced that limbo laughter combined with crying, a sort of temporary madness.

He entered and left his house when he liked, and those wonderful parents of his were always impressively absent from view. For all we knew, Linus could've been running his own life, and his parents could've been under the floorboards rotting away, having been affected into alternative existence by Linus himself. Was that possible? In my eyes, Linus had never tasted the bad apple. Never stood stiff-necked against a prohibition.

With a species of slowness that could've possibly been dangerous, Linus had an easy manner that made such a scenario believable. He had a pre-historic face, hard to read, nothing much written upon it. He had the basic skull, fatless, skin tightly stretched over bone that made him appear either pitiful or menacing, depending on where you happened to encounter him. *Concavity, concavaceous.* Great words. I chanted these constructions when the images were before me and the ideas urged me into speech.

Starving skinny people were far more frightening than fat well-fed people who were just comical. Linus at times looked like a starving sinner, bringing with him the death he wanted to share. Not unlike the dead face of Uncle Patsy, but if Linus's living face had come out of the blackness of our coal house when I was midnight shovelling, it would have administered to me my worst fear. To this menacing idea of Linus, I privately attached the name Golgotha, the face of the skull, a suitable perversion of the original meaning. Golgotha Larkin would have been some stormer of a name.

Yet such looks could also transmitted a powerful sadness, and at times, I saw that in Linus. Mostly though, in the light of day, in lighter thinking, he was straight as well as solitary. Straight? Yes, a straight thinker. Right down the line. The unimpeded Linus line. No bendyness. No ambiguity in his talk, no double dealing, no recognised irony, no sarcasm, no innuendo. No Devil's elbow. No U-turn back to a place he was not before. Despite my continuous efforts to introduce him to a more permanent state of flexible thought, craftiness in longitude, he remained, in the main, steadfastly straight.

Straightness in a bendy world and there was an abundance of bendy thinkers in this Belfast place, like the little man from number twenty-six on our street, who stood at his back door in a heavily-stained string singlet, warding off the world with wayward comments. Heavily bearded like a barbarian, he looked like a Kerry Blue peeping through a hedge. Words came from inside and beyond the beard.

He sought to ward me off one fine morning. He asked, without an introductory expression of misty clarity, if I had a bird up my nose. I was kicking my heavy, rain-soaked leather caser ball up against his backyard door with annoying power and precision, the repetition intensely rhythmic, when the whole of him came leaping through the doorway and marched me to the beat of his drum. He approached me in a crouched capacity, in anticipation of a flying ball that lay ready at my kicking foot. He came to an uncomfortable proximity, so the ball couldn't be kicked such a short distance, asking, *Do you have a bird up your nose son*?

Thinking literally and not ridiculously, I offered him up a squeaky, quivering, and confused, *In what sense?*

In what sense? In the sense of a human being being afflicted and effected with nasal feathering, he heaved back. *Feathering your little nest, I say. So answer. Either you have or you don't have a bird up your nose. By God's holy necessity.*

I said back, with a nervous laugh blown as air down my bird-less nose, that I was pretty sure I didn't. He had his foot on my ball at this point, pressing his sole firmly, and squeezing small amounts of air out of it. His raised voice of insistence and impatience, whilst pointing to his precious backyard door, said I bloody must have. I assured him with unequal venom that I didn't. There was nothing up there that shouldn't be. But that was private.

If you're bangin' that bloody door of mine like that with that missile like a hawk out of hell, you must have something against me. I have to think you have a bloody bird up your nose. Then I was told to take myself off to my own back door to annoy my own parents with my pecking nose. That, just there, was all bendy thinking, something like madness but not quite, and there was lots of it about in this town. And more to come with the great Ulster talent for inventing new ways of it and venting it all over. It was tiresome for a straight thinker, until I realised its worth and then bendy thinking became all the rage.

I told Linus about this bird-up-your-nose encounter, and he creased up with laughter, but then, when it dried up, he asked me what the bird-up-the-nose thing really meant. This seemed to suggest that, somewhere in his mind, he was thinking in a bendy fashion.

I didn't really tell him what it meant, because I couldn't put it into words. I just said, *tweet, tweet, tweet.* But then sometime later, when it was mentioned again, I said that it means whatever it was that was funny about it.

Linus fell about with occasional bendy thinking but never fully adopted it himself in its full form. I wondered what he laughed at, if he didn't know what it meant. I raised my eyebrows. It was just a picture in his head, of a bird and a nose, and the bird coming together with the nose. Or was it? Did it signify something else? Did he give it some other significance? Signifying was a funny business in its own right, as was the word. The sort of word that was being encountered more and more.

Like noses. Noses were pretty funny anyway, and there were lots of them about that were funny, and the more you thought of noses and the nature of the nose, the more hilarious they became. If I met someone, the nose was the first thing that came under consideration. If I said nose loads of times, it sounded very un-nose-like. If I looked and looked at the word nose, it even looked more like another word than nose. If I thought about the operation of my own nose by sniffing up and down and not using my mouth to breathe, it became a strange thing indeed. Apart from nearly choking in panic with the idea that the nose was not sufficient on its own for breathing, the nose breathing itself was a peculiar thing.

Feeling my nose, gently up and down, up and down, led to a very disorientating, not to say a very disturbing, experience. If I rubbed gently on the bridge, holding it gently between forefinger and thumb, I could have a nose spasm, which was the slowly bringing forth of a pleasurable sneeze. Once I tried to get Linus to do it, but despite considerable effort, he never quite made it. He was always on the edge, head back, ready to plunge forward, but then lost it somewhere and ended up with only an annoying irritation deep in the nasal passages. I asked him to explain what he felt, but he said it was private. I said, *do you have a bird up your nose?*

On occasions, I would rub his nose to show him the precise way of it. I made him pay close attention to my own technique and my juddering sneeze at the climax of it all. We were caught in the act once by an adult woman, the pair of us participating, rubbing away at our noses. She squinted at us, a confounded adult squint it was, and eventually gave us the icy eye of dark-cloud suspicion. It was the eye that transmitted the idea of contravening a divine law. We continued in the act of nose rubbing but never without the idea of its wrongness which reduced the pleasure of the whole enterprise. The moral of that story was nothing moral but something purely practical, practically moral perhaps, if good and bad are separated from good and evil. It was the sad affair of keeping your eye from roving, paying attention to others in case the dark eye of sad suspicion that transmits wrongness catches you in the act of something you might not as yet know is wrong.

What religion are you anyway? I asked Linus out of the blue one day; he looked up at the clouds but didn't say.

CHAPTER 8

Linus's freedom from parental restriction of movement continued despite the emergence of great, threatening forces. It was almost magical: people appeared and disappeared. There were transformations, reincarnations, visions, a new awareness was required. At the very time, nine-thirty on that sunny Saturday morning, as we sauntered down Great Victoria Street in our own separate awarenesses, a young lad of ten years old was swinging happily amidst the glorious green acres of the Ormeau Park, not fifteen minutes from our footsteps on the road to town, about to be lifted off the swings to be butchered up and burnt down to a small crisp. When I heard the news later, I immediately thought of a small crisp butcher.

This was not the world of terror that Belfast was to be burdened with for three decades and more but the other world of diminished accountability, debauchery, depravity, and seedy decadence let loose and camouflaged in the wake of the primary terror's awakening. The small crisp butcher was never found, and those responsible for many like it still walked the city streets.

With Les Buttocks still in sight as we reached about half way down Great Victoria Street, and with his new identity, imposed from without, making him different, the absent buttocks and rolling hills of denim captivating, in full, the mind of Linus, I considered putting my plan into action. It was simple. The consideration involved firstly, the said deviation of Linus; secondly, a satisfactory spot to perform the act in the shadow of the deviation; and thirdly, a convincing piece of acting from me.

It was hard to say whether I took to acting or acting took hold of me. Whichever it was, this was where I became different from myself, where backsliding itself became something else, a stand, and not merely a falling away from something that stands and is understandable only if you stand with it. Initially, it was all the acting externals mind you. The demeanour of taking a part. I partook of various forms of Belfast hardness. I confronted the hard men of the city in perfect privacy. I took the role of Uncle Patsy that was not Uncle Patsy at all, but what Uncle Patsy should have been. I fought for my life, I didn't plead for it. I didn't have a frozen, pleading dead face on me. I even took the role of the preacher and damned all sinners.

Acting, all part of learning the ways of participation. Participation being a way of violence, rooting yourself in another society or the society of another. Partner was a word I liked, torn from the western: being part of someone else, and the something else becoming a part of you.

Time was passing. Passing, Linus and I, did the time. I should already have completed the part of the deed that involved Linus before I did, I wanted it over with, but the most unwelcome of uninvited mind-guests, guilt and shame, appeared to slow me down. The always active internal tribunal demanded a judgement, all annoyingly and powerfully present, a conflict, a form of violence, making me waver with the weight of it, making me consider the nature of the act and the consequences of it to my character. But the right moment came, and I could not let it slip by.

The act I had in mind was a sleight of hand in the context of trust. A hand job. An inside job to boot, the inside of it already completed at home, and locked behind the front door. The outside job, the cover, remained unlocked, an open work.

Linus walked and wobbled with laughter beside me. I had in my trouser pocket that stolen five pound note, neatly and constructively folded. How that note exceeded itself. In the neat folding of the note, there was a folding and formation of a thought. Take note, in that folded state, was my world at that moment. I looked forward in excited fashion to its eventual unfolding. The event unfolding as it would any moment now. Through this folded note a special world was opening up to me. Almost a new idea of me, or a new idea that I had of myself. A point of conversion.

A crisp, newish note it was, hadn't been circulating all that long in the filthy thieving hands of others. Now firmly and comfortably in my pocket but it should not have been in my pocket at all, nor in my possession in any way, but in the note money compartment of my sister's purse, as it was owned by her, owned by her as payment for her job as a tippy tappy typist and shorthand writer.

She spent a whole week taking squiggly shorthand and madly tapping a huge keyboard for just about that sum. A blue note and some small change in a small brown packet represented her labour for eight hours a day, five days a week, and all the shite you can take from the shallow people in the office workplace. She came home with tales of the silly shallowness. Sobbed as she shared the stories. The sobbing was worth a private laugh. And when, after the weekly work, she was given her pay in a packet, she put it in her small purse in a handbag of white patent leather and carried around until it was transported and deposited in the home, apparently safe.

The neat small pink purse lay temptingly open on the big brown settee in the well lived-in living room, on a patch worn bare by ever shifting arses. Left open with a corner of blue paper peeping out offering up its indisputable identity as currency and its denomination as five pounds. This was not premeditated theft. The item simply offered itself up at precisely the moment I entertained the idea of myself desiring an object for which it could be traded. The act followed the appearance of the thing. A creative coming together. Theft was never itself a single thought. When offered up however, there was a moment of meditation. The thing, the object, a significant moment. Then, the thought of her sobbing with the thought of her steeped and surviving in the silly shallowness of her work. And the notion of something being stolen there, in that office. Her sobbing was testimony to that. In the midst of my meditation, something weighty and deep of voice told me to take it. *Take it,* it said, *make it yours.*

I don't know, I said, imagining the sisterly sobs.

Seek out your own ways, it said. *Have the courage to possess it.* So, I possessed it but not in a cowardly way. It was the act of a backslider.

In a recollection that can only be divine, and in richer and deeper meditation upon it that continued well after the act, I can see that the crime was in me from the beginning. It has its origins in the beginning. Perhaps from the beginning of the world, as the Bible says somewhere about sin. Sin is in the foundation of things. Not maybe at the very beginning but sin coming onto the scene seems to make sense.

Sin as the rupture between God and man, man and man, man and himself, sin must be, as everything else must be. Or, if existence be, then let sin be. The crime is such a rupture, but also a sign. For a sign is what I seek, a sign that sin itself is not such a sad affair.

In my thinking heart, in my seated restless soul, the rupture was there waiting as a courageous act emanating from that part of me that wanted to know the good and the bad. That required an encounter, a conversion, a conceit of a deceit. An emanation is something inseparable from its cause; it turns back upon it and accuses it. From the very early stages, I felt that accusation upon myself. Emanation became *immanation*. It dwelt within. Fermenting. Fomenting. Forcefully coming to fruition. And then my expression in the world as the possessor and deliverer of the demonic gift. What I received here was to be given back out. Who was there to receive my gift?

The evangelicals, who had a stranglehold on the Protestant mind in Belfast, always talked of the gifts. It was God the giver, His magical gifts and man the receiver and disposer. This was the nigger in the woodpile for me.

Solomon said in his song, *the backslider in heart shall be filled with his own ways, and a good man shall be satisfied from himself.* The inner voice continued to say, *Seek out your own ways.* A backslider must deviate from God's ways to find his own ways; he must fill himself up to full capacity and spring forth. I felt the full filling. Full of active personal affection. In the words of Nancy Sinatra, I was *a lyin' when I should have been a truthin'*, and the entire untruth about myself poured out. Lying in all the best blessed circles.

But without a doubt, I wanted to be an actor, for in the essence of the actor is the hypocrite. The true actor does not seek solace in real tears. I acted daily, and it became so convincing that at home, I was loved for the act. I was loved for the things I was not. Because the acting was both bad and pleasurable, goodness and badness cohabited. In the mirror on the wardrobe in my room, there was a reflection of the lies. I practised my lies. I performed them. I committed to them.

CHAPTER 9

One thing I made sure of: I was not going to follow the form of Les Buttocks. I did not want to be a backslider to form. I wanted to be true to form which was backsliding to the uninformed. At the same time, I did not want to become obsessed. Obsession is not the way of the backslider. Obsession is a form of idiocy. It separates us from personal power. Like my uncle, Johnny Ratchitt, who was slave to the idea of flushness. He could not see a thing in this world unless he first saw how flush it was to another body. Flush is something like form, but the mind of Uncle Johnny, unlike a true form, was not to be followed, nor in fact was the example set by his grotesquely obese body that was not at any time flush with anything.

That the body was understood and not merely attended to was important. I was not going to drown it in the unseemly. Or in seams loosely sewn. I listened to it, not as a still form or an unmoving thing. A person of status must do that. Feel the power of body. Reactions, speed, space, vitality, energy, excitement, strength, endurance, demonstrable dexterity of one's material autonomy. The body is as an affecting force to be reckoned with. The physical correlation of the thoughts about it. The bodily will, not a thing, but an activity.

Initially my external appearance was indeed the obsession. I made sure I was not a weak empty pants, that my buttocks were never so much less than my trouser arse material to exhibit unattractive looseness. Pert, not impertinent buttocks. So, I continually felt around to my rear to make sure they were filling any void, and that when I stepped out, whether slow or fast, one foot in front of the other, there were no unsightly ripples to disturb the mind pleasing rounded proportion.

That buttock feeling became a nasty little habit, and my mother, when she caught me with her beady eye touching the area, kept asking me, with debasing tone, what in God's name I was doing? I eventually told her the lie that my knickers were too tight, and I had to keep pulling them out of my buttock crack. *That's a dirty habit,* she told me.

I was educated in perverse ideas of body awareness and was affected by their power to bodily truth. Women of the day knew what they wanted from a man by way of a body, and my sisters, as growing women of the day, embarked on a regime of education to improve the understanding of this young male mind on what it lacked, pointing out anything that failed to measure up. It seemed important to know what a woman's mind was directed to. Women were the measure of quite a few things. To me that measure was all about the body, but it was really a mind game, a mind game about the body. The body of truth. Mind and body, I soon learned, were one and the same thing really.

The body of Les Buttocks was still striding out in front. Linus was thinking his way, and I was thinking mine. I had my thoughts on the hands of Les Buttocks. Though I couldn't actually see them, I detected from his hunched posture that they had been thrust deeply into his front pockets. Why? He wasn't playing with his balls or warming his hands, though these might have been compensatory pleasures. It was because he was fully aware that he was coming up short in the backside zone and also aware of the probability of a discerning following gaze. His hands were in his pockets to reduce the abundance of material at the rear, to force the excessive fabric forward, and give the rear a form, and the form an appearance of content. It came to me in a flash that my annoyance with Les Buttocks was the fact, the fact for me that he was pretending to be what he was not. He was lying through his trousers. He was acting.

This legacy of lies lingers in the legs. It's an observed truth, that men, who persistently have hand or hands in pockets, are seriously concerned about their lack of lower body physique. To take those hands out, thus releasing the surplus fabric, is a source of great anxiety. The hands immediately become redundant and the awareness of body underdevelopment is reflected in the mind as general weakness in a world where weakness is an open invitation to humiliation.

Negative body awareness is a cruel state of mind because it corresponds perfectly to the negativity of mind. It is a gateway to sadness. So, I was not only excessively aware of my own body, I was constantly scouring the horizons for those who had that negative awareness and exhibited it in the unmistakable disguising habits.

I saw that even the great film actors were guilty. Cary Grant invariably had his right hand slipped casually into his right pocket, in a vain attempt to conceal his underdeveloped match stick legs. The hand in the pocket assisted self-deception. Humphrey Bogart had the habit of hitching up his pants to get the seat of them back into place, though the place being itself very limited, was very hard to find. Alan Ladd did exactly the same, forever pants hitching. Bogie and Ladd, two small men with a big fear of drowning in the huge amount of pant material that was the style of the day.

I pointed this out to Linus, but he didn't know what I was talking about. I squinted into his little sunken eyes, past the dark shadows cast by his eye sockets, and he wasn't there. With his wide open mouth, he swallowed, in vast quantities, his very own plankton of place and time. His thoughts were buried deeply in the arse of Les Buttocks. He didn't have a television set. He knew nothing of the big film stars. It was useless.

CHAPTER 10

My crime. A fine thing, I thought. A crime in line with fine thought. Finely tuned in line with what a body is capable of and which few know. A sin and a sign. Mostly it was mine. An expression. A possession of a transgression. A repossession. A form of growth, a movement. Not artful, but crafty. With purpose. A revelation. A geometrical shift. A denunciation. An overpowering It all came back to backsliding. With this crime I was taking giant strides to backsliding maturity.

In a broader context, it might be thought that it involved a measure of payback for the type of body/self consciousness that gripped me, a theft indeed of my own thought. Not so. Retribution may be considered a wrong step for the backslider. A backward step. The backslider slips back but only to move forward.

The sisters who were responsible for this implant should be given credit. They felt free to play the game of names, and what was free was considered to be good. Destructive to some, but now I see not to me. It was creative comic-cruelty, cradled in the unkind cunt, a process of assigning names. The boy was named to put him in his place. Grand mastery over Master Marius, downsizing him, intending to beget an idea of physical insignificance.

In tandem, the two set about their task. Starting with one applying the label *empty pants* to the skinny form before them, then the other responding with *sunken chest*, then *empty chest* and *sunken pants*, until the chant soon resembled a magical incantation, the aim to place me under a spell. By emptying me of my ways, they tried to improve their standing A form of stealing itself.

I tried to repay them by issuing insults of my own, announced like Papal bullshite, drawing detailed attention to their mountain ranges of pimply teenage faces and unmanageably wobbly arses, but their dull minds seemed infinitely insensitive. Whatever happened to the insults once inside their heads was never disclosed to me in any outward sign as painful. Not until later, when I increased my creative capacity to divine more precise areas of insecurity, did some affects become known. Needling was an art that needed mastering. There was a place for it. When I was a novice, I thought like a novice. They were sister superiors in every respect. All I needed was a surplice. A vestment that exposed my innocence. A totemic tunic fitted and fined tuned to my beaten body.

However, the game was not played to a finish. I played another game entirely. When the five pounds was firmly in my possession, I never thought of retribution. I thought of me, me on my feet in Great Victoria Street.

CHAPTER 11

I had in mind a shop, just ahead, in forethought. Firearms & Tackle by name was a no-shop shop. It simply seemed to lack any proper essence of shopness. The name bore—in large bore lettering—the word *tackle* which has sporting associations, though this particular tackle was just a reference to the accoutrements of fishing. *Tackle* was also a term used by men of maturity and boys who thought they were men of maturity, for their private manly parts. More commonly used are *bollocks* and *balls*, but tackle seemed to be reserved for talking about discomfort in that region, or drawing attention to the importance of the area. Old Hughie, our lodger, would say it when he was wrestling with the front of his massive trousers. *My bloody tackle's all over the bloody place,* he'd moan, whilst fixing himself. Fixing involved a degree of squirming from the waist and twisting the trousers whilst moving the hips. Sometimes the hand was put down the front of the breeches to sort out more complicated discomforts. *Once more into the breeches,* old Hughie would say proudly on these occasions.

Firearms & Tackle sold guns and tackle, but all the goings-on inside of that shop were out of bounds to minds not fully appreciative of firearms and fishing, which meant the minds of kids. In a kid's logic, there was no natural link between retailing and hunting stuff. The same sort of mental leap applied to those strange shops that sold medical supplies, their unimaginative window displays advertising folded-up wheelchairs, deluxe crutches, hearing aids, false limbs and a host of other items that were not naturally considered the sort of things you buy over the counter. Like uniforms for priests, butlers, maids, and cooks. Even old Hughie had a menagerie of scary idols on his bedside table. Where did people buy statues of the Virgin Mary or the saints? Where did he get them? In the statue shop?

In smaller lettering on the Firearms & Tackle sign it said, *the sporting man's shop,* but the clientele stumbling in and out fell well short of my idea of the sportsman. These wheezing, wank-weary, overfed, old red-faced rascals in green padded jackets paraded themselves like prize warthogs. Snouts grunting their joy, feet fouled up with gout. If they could have exposed their warthog tackle to public view, they would have, but I imagined them to be limp and withered specimens, not worthy of the attention they craved. Fishing was a no-event sporting event. No sport at all, just a pass the time pastime and a pastime is no sport. All those fancy reels, and rods, and hooks meant nothing.

Guns, glorious guns did have some attraction, though perhaps not a sporting attraction. They had a power, they were for real. Guns had gravity. Guns could talk. The gun spoke with sound and smoke. Guns could replace your mouth in anything you wanted to say. Have guns, will travel. The Colt Peacemaker in particular will take you further, with its long, slender barrel. Elegance calibrated to kill. Forty-five calibration to be exact, to blow all the fat, wheezing wankers away. Hear them grunt their final grunts on the way to the happy hunting grounds. Or in combination with the word, the gun could offer a wonderful freedom of expression.

But such a power they were well known to have, and they were placed outside the bounds of a boy's possession in order to limit his power. I loved cultures determined by the idea of guns: in westerns, the fashion to follow, the fashion of the leather holster, held high or low by hide gun belt, creaking with every turn of the waist, weighed down by heavy metal, fully loaded pistol, hanging slickly and slackly from the hip. What pleasure in the sound of the heavy gun pulled from its mooring, slid with hollow suction sound into full view. But gunplay I never regarded as sporting, as sporting activity was something unreal, a sort of play-acting, whereas gunplay was very real. You could play with guns alright, and we played with imaginary guns, with toy guns, but that is not what sporting gunman did with guns. They went out and shot things, like birds and rabbits, just as the fishermen hooked real fish. With their guns and rods they had killing on their minds. Not that I objected to the killing. It simply wasn't sporting.

*

The shop window was familiar as it was passed often enough but alienating to a boy shopper. Orange cellophane on the inside of the window tinted all the merchandise on show. Like the world seen through those colourful sweetie papers. As a shop it was a troublesome idea. Would it change if I bought something? Would that be decisive? Somebody at school told me that Firearms & Tackle sold steel catapults for just ten bob and that interested me. A steal for ten bob, a mere tenth of the value of the fiver I had in my pocket. One fine day I looked through the orange cellophane and there it was, outside and displayed on its box. Another fine day I walked in, and among the gasping gentry standing, with my orange ten bob note, I bought one. All without a question being asked or even minimum attention paid to the purchase. As I handed the money over, the big barrel of a man behind the counter took it whilst conversing with another blubbery skitter at the other end of the shop. He handed me the weapon in the same casual manner, without even a caring look at me. And out of the shop I went, shaking with excitement, with a beautiful piece of weaponry firmly in my hand. I felt like loading it with a stone and firing it through the fucker's orange window and then scramming up the road laughing for my life. Or aiming it, full power, between the ignorant bastard's eyes. Seeing his unsporting frame keel over, like Goliath at the receiving end of the boy David's slingshot.

All authenticity was in my grasp. Steel frame, thick rubber and a neat leather pouch for couching the ammunition. It was a powerful thing to hold and behold. Not a toy thing at all. I couldn't wait to load it up with a smooth round stone and fire it at full stretch to feel its power. I dreamt of knocking birds off their telephone line perches. With it in hand, I could stand up to the bird up your nose man. When he comes out with his bendy idea, I'd just produce my weapon and he'd beg for forgiveness. *Speak the Queen's English or else*, I'd tell him. Powerful! Power was everything. Is everything. The essence of things.

*

Firearms & Tackle pertained to the final part of the plan I had in my mind. Linus' eyes were watery and he claimed he couldn't see, his nose running with laughter-induced, free-flowing, snattery solution. Why does all that stuff start flowing when you laugh? Why are these things thought in situations that need undivided attention? That didn't occur to me then at all. Linus was barely open to discourse, he was still flirting like a drunk with the idea and image of Les Buttocks, who still strode ahead of us. Communication that came in laughter-hyphenated phrases was all very annoying when you were straining to understand something somebody said. All you get are the lumps of chewed and garbled language.

I had gone to bed the night before, excited by the fact that the plan in mind was in place. It was hard to get off to sleep, the thinking over-active with the cornucopia of extended imaginings, small, precise, confined ideas, little buds expanding to a nightmarish bloom, all stemming from the idea of this particular five pound note. Money, what was it? Exchanging hands. The hypnotic pound symbol. The magical business of money. It was a thing for investing, a thing between men, essential to men, but here I was investing my whole self in *it*. But the money was not yet in my possession, it lay beyond me, below me, in limbo, and so the crime remains merely a matter of thought. I was last to bed and the purse was there safely on the settee, but how safe was it until morning?

I considered placing the note in my possession then and there in the sitting room before bed, but that would have created a problem of unknown proportions. Burgeoning little black babies were vomiting up their bile in the timber pile, eager to keep me alarmingly awake. The old skitter Hughie was known to wander the landings whilst we slept, his aching barometrical feet, he claimed, could predict small meteorological variations, whilst being the cause of insomnia. Those two indicators drove the mother to wall climbing and war dancing. He was an addict to sugary tea, which he made for himself in the middle of the night on his wanderings, and he was under suspicion for many a missing bag of sugar and other items.

On another front, from bitter experience I had learnt that practically nothing and nowhere in this house was safe from the mother's tendency to expert tidiness. It was a tidiness divination that knew no bounds. Tidy to the normal mind was not tidy at all if they had known her concept of tidy, and, even in her own mess of a mind, she was forever pushing the frontiers further and further from the normal idea of it. An artefact of tidiness, she contemplated again and again and for some reason considered it not tidy and then re-tidied it. Even an almost invisible speck of dust made a whole tidy area untidy. It was the extra-sensory perception of untidiness. What a habit! And what a mind to inhabit!

The house itself annoyed the life out of her, because it was a house of nooks and crannies that gathered dust. An old house. Victorians valued hiding places in houses as much as they held in high esteem the creative concealment of vice in their own ostensibly sober characters. They had safe deposit boxes in their minds. In their houses, they had recesses, recesses in recesses, vaults, basements, spaces under floorboards you could stand up in. The mother hated such architectural invention. It paid little attention to the practicalities of the domestic cleaner. She desperately desired a new house, a small house of perfectly square spaces with no secrets.

Every secret place I could think of, however, no longer seemed secret when I considered the mother's searching knowledge about how to locate crevices. Possible hiding places in my mind were, in hers, only areas of possible untidiness. But a fiver was slim and could be slipped or forced into the smallest crevice.

After several minutes of half-sleep, in a half dream, dreaming that I was perfectly flat like a bank note, folded and unfolded so often that I began to fall apart at the creases, I considered slipping downstairs for the money before Slippy Tit, the tea maker, made a midnight journey to the kitchen.

First, I ruminated on a safe area of concealment. I stood in my room and looked around for one. *Where, where, where?* There was the rest of the house, but I didn't want the money to be beyond arm reach. That was almost as bad as leaving it where it was. In my immediate possession maybe, simply under the pillow or in my pyjama pocket? No, not in the bed. The violent manner of my sleep could transport the note to an unknown destination. I had lost things before in the bed. Socks were notoriously difficult to find.

No, I fully felt the fear of getting up in the morning in the routinely forgetful haze, staggering to the toilet and returning to the room to find that the mother had already made the bed to tight perfection. And the dangers of removing night wear. Throwing off the cutesy and comfy, softly-napped, flannelette pyjamas had its perils. Forgetfulness is common as one divests. Seeking minimum time in bare skin and in the distracting desire for the warmth of the day clothes, one can easily fall foul of the thing that will give you away. Pyjamas thus tossed aside and left for a second unattended in untidiness would be madness. The mother in her own madness would be in there amongst them, folding them and checking the pockets. And if I tidied them, that would raise her natural suspicion.

Morning came and the realisation of a significant day. The first significant thing I did in the morning—always—was to jump with crazy haste into some fresh underpants. Though they were massive, the underpants felt immediately and relievingly tight in relation to the utterly intolerable laxity of the pyjamas. When I got downstairs the purse was still there.

My underpants, once tight in the immediateness of the early morning exchange for jammies, were now, with the abundance of movement, loosened and my nest of testicles hung uncomfortably abandoned as I walked. My awareness of this was always close at hand and my hand was always not far away from taking the tackle in hand to tidy up. How comfortable were Les Buttock's testicles? Did he have tight underpants below the acres of loose denim? I shared the thought with Linus without divulging anything of my own private problem. I just mentioned underpants specifically in relation to Les Buttocks, and Linus apprehended the idea with such immediacy of interpretation that it occurred to me we were representatives of a universal privates problem amongst boys.

CHAPTER 12

Firearms & Tackle was in sight. It was set well back from the road, beyond even the pavement, by an open, un-walled, stone forecourt. Outside the shop door was a small, restored black cannon, the sort we saw regularly on warring galleons in swashbuckling films. *Captain Blood* and all those. Errol Flynn in tights, shouting at his hearties, tight on his tackle. I was sure he must have been comfortable in his tight tights, and it amused us to amazement that all these ideas seemed to come together. Loose tackle, Firearms & Tackle, cannon balls, balls and tackle, and Errol Flynn tights and tackle. Linus was fully responsive despite not knowing exactly who Errol Flynn was. I kept feeding him with more and more associations. Rubbery-bodied and grunting like a pig with the laughter, he could barely spit out a sensible word. He was trying to compose his own variation, but I couldn't understand a word he said. But that was funny in itself.

Hey, look at that! For God's sake Linus, look what it is I see!

I took off like a purged whippet in the direction of Firearms & Tackle. Linus sobered up to this assault on his relaxed equilibrium, abandoned his rubbery gait and stiffened. A smile of simple idiocy took grip of his countenance. He looked in all directions with perplexity spelt out on his face like child's scribble, and it was precisely the perplexed face I wanted to see. I looked back as I ran and the distance grew between us. I was already halfway between Linus and the gun shop, making sure I obscured Linus' field of vision as much as possible. I zigzagged and waved to keep his attention upon me. My exclamation had already confused him. *What has he seen, what has he seen?* he was saying into himself. *What is he seeing, what is he seeing? What is he thinking?* I thought to myself. I looked back at Linus as I continued to forge ahead, and I pointed ahead of me like a mad discoverer of a treasure island, treasure trove. Linus began to trot after me and then quickened into a run. I increased my pace also, trying to keep well ahead.

What, what! hit the back of my head. *What do you see Marius? Gold, I see Gold! Treasure!* I shouted back. I heard laughing.

Here, just here with the word *gold* in and out of my mouth, I encountered a counter to my strategy. I was still running but disturbed by a nasty little rogue thought, a little nugget of pure annoyance. Not entirely new but more powerful. Linus Larkin, my dear simple friend Linus, was being used. I, his friend, was deceiving him. What he saw in front of him was I, his friend, declaring a state of affairs as one thing whilst I knew them to be something wholly another. Something was wrong. It was a simple sense of wrongness. The deceiver in me was not compatible with the soul-saved Christian or the friend I claimed to be.

God had claimed my thirteen-year-old soul in a gospel service three years before this sinful event, with His irresistible grace applied to my total spiritual inability, transforming my antenatal forfeiture of wilful goodness. I had been regenerated. My essential nature had been overhauled, changed, not just modified, but substituted, so much so that I was not even the same person I was before. I was a new I, and as I closed my eye to pray the prayer of salvation it was the closing of an I and the opening of a new I. My eyes were fully opened. Seeing the glory.

And so I read the reformed theology books, the books now stacking up on brother Rob's writing desk, trying to make sense of the whole business. But I had no mind for it. Words high, and almighty, and over my head. In fact, there was no sense in the whole business, but there was sense in the partial business. Everything awkward to the understanding was eliminated except for something that seemed certain.

That time. Certainty in the stirring, in the bewilderment, in the grip, in the frenzy, in the ecstasy, that was taking hold from without. Doubt in the resident dubiety about demonic or divine. There was a trembling, a dread, no ordinary dread, but rather the shaking dread that grinds your bones to dust. The dust of the earth from where we came. The tongue was loose, spitting out words that were no words, the breath a faltering wheeze from within, a breeze of icy cold on the brow from without. Such a snarling beast that rages inclined the mind immediately to the Devil. Had God forsaken me? Nothing here but me, not even God. I chant: *God is nothing, I am something, God is nothing, I am something... praise be to God!* Knowing then that it was I.

Sitting on that Pentecostal pew, the usually blind pew of a singular sheep following the flock, there was the unambiguous, the quickening, the accelerated awakening to alarming self awareness. The body illuminated. The body filled. Estrangement from the common notions that guaranteed security of tenure in life. Annihilation of all need. The life that we cling to. Irresistible in momentum. A grace in gravitational abundance conquered all resistance.

It was like a madness. My arm shot up heavenwards in an apparently unwilled movement, almost taking it out of my shoulder socket. My fingertips tingled as they touched an invisible elementary power. I had a natural erection that followed an assault on the body, a body about which I had no previous knowledge, where every nerve crackled with extended sensitivity, and every particle produced an effect that generated infinite affects. It was not hidden behind a burning bush, it was open and here, the burning was inside. In its openness, it asked a simple, burning question, accept or reject? But, in this void, accept or reject what?

Unavoidably, I looked around. Drawn back to life. Inevitably. That place smelled. It was church after all. A congregation of smells. What was evident was the ludicrous nature of the surroundings for such a touch with ultimacy. All around, God's people celebrated the act of arm lifting like those crazy intoxicated drunks spilling out of Mosey McGlibb's pub in Sandy Row on a Saturday night. They welcomed me into the big, buxom, thronging bosom of the chosen. The state of not being I was a special knowledge, and I welcomed my inclusion by being an active disciple, back in the world, doing everything a saved by grace soul should do because *faith without works is dead*—though works without faith are even deader.

I showed my faith to the cold world, inside and outside the warm, holy bosom, to the bosom's titular heads and to the family of the faithful who suckled daily from the bigger bosom of the titular big heads, who themselves, being above suspicion, admired the bouncing tits of buxom beauties who swelled the ranks seeking hands-on healing. I learnt here that faith was indeed the *substance of things hoped for and the evidence of things not seen.*

What I did not see, or foresee, as soon as the saved seeing stopped, was the veil of ordinariness being placed upon my eyes, so I that I had no manner of understanding other than the account from those around me.

The *other* was snuffed out by the earthly idolatry the faithful cherished more than their original mysterious encounter. God died in solitary salvation and then was resurrected by the lynch mob. Some would say they reverted to a primitive witness, but in a sense the opposite was true. Their delusions were sophisticated attempts to preserve what they said they detested. What they said they detested is this world. Like those who, in a temporary state of sophistry, convince themselves that some evil action is good in order to justify performing it. Their interest was in the outward showing of the signs rather than the private, inside conviction. Thus the church was a permanent parade of show-offs, the ritual ratified justification. Emotion was just plain emotion. Emotion more of feeling than motive. That single solitary act, that act of loneliness, was transformed by the congregation into a collective enthusiasm which could not hear any longer the inspired individual voice.

So I, the soul-saved confused Christian, who loved the world but said he did not, was deeply unhappy with the present act of deception, because it seemed to indicate that the will to badness within had not been eradicated. The arm that was raised may have been an uncertain certainty. Was I not really the new I?

Of course not. I already knew that. But it comes back to haunt me. Just like the Devil is continually taunting the saint, the Lord taunts the backslider.

Get thee behind me Jesus! Fuck! I, the saved and sanctified, swore into myself. *Fuck, fuck, fuck, FUCK! What fucking luck is this?*

Wedged uncomfortably in my mind between my fledgling scheming and the idea of my self-respect, was the vision of the innocent, smiling-in-perplexity Linus. But, was Linus really *that* good? Was he *that* innocent? Was that innocence, if it proved to be really there, in itself a form of goodness? What goodness did Linus impart to the friendship? I know I said that he hadn't an ounce of badness in him, but that was possibly a surface thing, merely an unformed impression, not a real thought. A feeling. So the mind, in a geometrical shift, settled on a plane, and risking considerable confusion, circled in its off-centre recesses searching for any immanent badness that was attached to Linus Larkin. It revealed that Linus was more active than I gave him credit for, not the purely passive soul his vacant expression proposed. Was he active through passivity? Isn't it possible to allow yourself to be acted upon in order, when the right time comes, to do? Composing yourself. Enjoying being the host until the always-giving guests have been sucked dry. The word to describe this is, I think, scavenger. Not a nice word, not a nice thought, not a nice thing. The hyena, the vulture. Yes, I was using him here, but was he not on occasion trying to use me? And for what reason? Spiralling out of this hasty hermeneutic were instances of his unfriendly behaviour, acts that quite possibly marked the emergence of an unruly independence.

On this very morning I gave him a series of pleasurable ideas that spawned the joy of side-splitting laughter, but something in his mode of acceptance made me think of it as theft.

There was also Linus the cheat. He cheated at every opportunity. Petty cheating. Clumsy cheating. He cheated at games. Every game we played, I caught him cheating. He was moving a counter, countering the throw of the dice, to an advantageous square or to a locale that freed him of a penalty. If we played football, he claimed he had scored more goals than he actually had. He lied and cheated, because he knew if he didn't he would always lose. He was a clumsy cheater, and I had little respect for that. If he had

been good, that would've been something to respect. Good cheaters
are never caught, and so they are not recognised as cheaters. Like
good thieves. It's not that I never cheated, I did, but I regarded it
in itself as a means of reducing someone's arrogance in the business
of game playing where every win is milked to the maximum. So,
cheating had its place as a sort of mechanism for combating an even
worse crime, gloating. That, I thought, was not Linus's motive.
His motives were linked to specific acts. All along, I knew Linus
cheated. I saw him, but I just couldn't tell him in a cold blooded
way that I had. I thought it would be too devastating and tactless.
Neither, deep down, did I want this to seduce me into thinking that
cheating made you a cheat. Backsliding might, after all, have been
considered a form of cheating.

What other spectre of troublesome nonconformity did Linus
resurrect in the midst of our simple friendship? There were
recognised rules to follow, most definitely so, rules governing our
form of life. Following a rule is tied up with the idea of making
a mistake and he made such a mistake when he introduced into
our simple ways a forbidden fancy. Linus had eyes for one of my
sisters—the one that had the complexion of a mountain range on
a relief map with high pimple peaks—and, the instant I heard this,
was the moment I feared for our friendship. It was a total mystery
to me and created great moments of boredom when he ranted
on about her all the time, incessantly asking me daft questions.
I tried to sweep it immediately into the mind's arctic regions, to
be frozen out by the censor that dispenses with destructive and
contaminating ideas.

Does she fancy me? he said, to which I returned no answer. *Do you
think she fancies me?* No answer. *Does she ask about me?* Nothing.
Does she...

Give my head peace! I don't know! I exploded and walked off. Such
an engagement took me to the edge of a precipice where I could
barely breathe. Like Jesus on the pinnacle being diabolically tested.
Friendship teetering. Was the Lord, in his mysterious ways, using
Linus to taunt me?

If she doesn't fancy me she must be a lisbian, he said with a little
laugh. Lisbian? And laugh he should at that word, as it seemed to

make no sense. But it pulled me back. Wasn't *lisbian* a reference to
those beings who hailed from that ghastly Belfast suburb, Lisburn?
The Pastor in the church used to rant, red-faced, about the
unconverted perverted *lisbians*, but the logic of it all didn't make
any headway in my head. I began to feel sorry for all the queer
folk from Lisburn. What had they done? *They are perverted,* said
the Pastor. Like the Lurgan people who were called Lurgan spades.
What was their crime? *Thay are a dull people,* said the father. I let
on to Linus, through various signs, that the whole talk about sisters
was not welcome. Sighing, grimacing, rolling my eyes, walking
away from him when the subject arose.

Linus had his way with language. A maddening way. His
mispronunciation of words hit a certain delicate point of the mind
like a sledgehammer. Words that sent you reeling about your being
with displeasure the more they were mis-said. He said *nucular* for
nuclear. *Vadil* for *valid*. Nobody really used this word *valid* anyway
as none of us were in the logic business, but *he* did, as a favoured
expression, in place of the word *true*. So it was strange. *It's totally
vadil,* he'd say. Some smart arse called him an invalid. Oh, they
all come flooding back! *Pelanty* in place of penalty. *Deuteromony*
instead of Deuteronomy. *Pineumonia, Irrevalent.* I suffered them
all in strangulating silence and refused to view them as simple
instances of innocence.

Was it a confirmation of something about him that none of my
other friends were well disposed towards him, mistrusted as they
were? They called him a *wee soak*. Now, I knew that a *soak* was a
drunk, but nevertheless, they said he was a soak out of his wetness.
Soak was wet and being wet meant sissiness, and the wetness idea
was extended to mean greater wetness, soaking wetness, and there
a big sissy. The word soak was now adopted and used freely for a
selection of big fat sissies that roamed around our way and who
were bantered mercilessly.

Linus, dear God only knows what he did in the privacy of that
home of his. Frustration abounded. The ignorance of it placed
a perfectly private fear within me. The imagination grew in the
fertile ignorance, and all types of sinister scenarios blossomed.
Ignorance is a dangerous thing. I needed something of an idea, an

image, an impression of the actual internal workings of the Larkin house. I invited myself many a time by saying, *let's go to your house and play*, but we never did, even when it was raining and within the Larkin vicinity. He always had a preference to come to mine instead, despite the mother's audible objections to me bringing in *wet dirt* from the street. She talked with a forked tongue, but he listened with a forked ear, so he didn't hear.

Who was the real Linus? Linus was something else, something to me, something else to himself. He was loyal company, but I could have got that from a pet doggy. As I raced ahead to Firearms & Tackle with the sleight of palm and digits to cover the discovery of the fiver uppermost in mind, I was thinking on some remoter level that Linus was operating on the dog-loyalty level. I was treating him like a dog, but doggy-type loyalty was precisely what I required that day, and I reasserted to myself the correctness of the choice that was Linus.

I disposed temporarily with this rather gnarled nugget of doubt and continued in relatively resistance free thought on my run towards my target, which I expected to reach in a second or two but never seemed to do so as quickly as I desired. Linus was just behind as I reached the little black cannon, but I stood in his way, thus preventing him from viewing my hand movement down the side of the artillery, the side that flanked the small wall dividing Firearms & Tackle from the next shop. Like a magician, I opened my hand with a flourish, the magical fiver in it. I said not a word. Linus said not a word, his face just as I would have desired it if I had thought about it beforehand. His look was one of total delight and unquestioning acceptance of the whole event. He beamed joy in my direction.

I kept my hand open and thrust it closer and closer to him in discrete jabs, displaying the increasing reality of the fiver, bigger and with greater reality, to dispel any reserve of incredulity he may have harboured. *There*, said the open palm, *there it is*. And, if he had doubted that display, I gave him my face, for on my face I showed him proof. Eyebrows lifted high, eyes bulging, mouth and surrounding lips in a rather stupid, upward, orange, segment-shape of a smile, all convincing him of the genuine truth of the find. The evidence was in my hand. The display of it meant to tell him that the discovery was not mine alone, but *ours*. With my other hand on his shoulder, it further confirmed it was not my find, but *our* find, and the thing shared made him a greater accomplice. Then his words of excitement came spilling out.

You jammy swine, he said. *I saw it as well. I saw it, but I didn't see it as a fiver. It was just a piece of paper. How did you know it was a fiver? I must have been half asleep. You got it just because you were ahead of me. But I saw it as well.* There, here, here and there, you see? There was Linus in those words of his in a new light.

But you didn't see it, you lying turd. He hadn't seen anything because there was nothing there. I couldn't say that, but I almost blurted it out. *If you saw it as a piece of paper, you didn't see a fiver,* is what I did say. *And you wouldn't have run to pick up a piece of paper. I saw it as the fiver.* This turned out better than expected. He said he saw something when in fact he saw nothing. Now he was a witness to something he said he had seen but hadn't. He could not deny now that he had seen something blowing in and around the cannon. Linus looked down at his own hand and the front door key he held in it.

Can you look after my key? I haven't got any pockets in my trousers. What sort of trousers didn't have any pockets, was my line of wonderment. I looked down at them and partly round to the back and sure enough pockets were absent. Now the trousers looked massively odd. A Dickensian snugness and density that suggested tights, and placed my thoughts, for an uncomfortable moment, in Linus's mother's underwear drawer. A sense of helpless fascination rooted my gaze. Plain pocket-less leg coverings! Pocket-less trousers were unacceptable to the discerning spirit. Open to general ridicule. Were they home-made? If so, that was also unacceptable. Were they worth a laugh? Indeed so, but the overriding matter of the money transgressed upon the less pressing matter of the pocket-less trousers and trampled it down until it allowed me no more than a light snigger.

I took his key and dropped it into my back pocket but wasn't happy about it. It was a massive piece of metal, the sort that might unlock a door in a medieval castle. In my pocket, it would be forcing the material of my jeans into all sorts of shapes. I didn't like looking after things for people, but I thought I owed him.

So, through the over-valued idea of a fiver, a whole world of purchasable things beckoned. A list of favourite retail outlets was drawn up privately in the mind. All my immediate wants were satisfiable and, something like the song said, money was in my pockets and I wasn't gonna want no more. Actually, the money was indeed in *my* pocket, and it was held firmly there by the hand that had shown it to Linus. It was felt to be there, and I didn't want to abandon that touch until it was exchanged for the so-desperately desired things. I didn't judge that I wanted these things in an idle fashion. Nor just for fashion which was, itself, considered idle. Just to have things or just to have for appearance sake. Like a woman wants diamonds to adorn the body. Or those nonentity males, whose essential requirement in life was to have the fancy car to show off. Somewhere, they met in the middle, the girls with the diamonds and the blokes with their wheels. Invariably, the blokes were nothing but big sacks of loose uselessness who needed to be encased in moving metal to be admired. They didn't play football, just idled in their cars and waited for the attention to reach them.

If someone happened upon a large rectangular area of mud and puddle, they may have seen me. I played football in these Belfast bogs we were informed were football pitches, the white lines having sunk without trace. *When does the tide go out?* shouted some smart mouth of a fly boy. I strutted about in the mud with two giant turds on my feet, generously given the name football boots. Other boys had sleek boots, and they mercilessly ridiculed me and called me clog feet. I thought of the footwear as ballast boots, or bondage boots, holding me back, denying me speed and betterment as a footballer. I was wearing indecent sporting footwear. Where had my football boots come from anyway? Some second-hand shop in Smithfield Market, rooted out of a big cardboard box of other discarded boots? Who knows?

Aye, he's a great wee footballer, the mother would say in her boastful liaisons with neighbours. A woman of almost complete consciousness and therefore ignorance and delusion. A woman of stories.

I continued to strut, in spite of the boots, in the land where strutting was a declaration of false fortitude.

Something of a troublesome idea came to mind. The head that entertained mighty ideas of personal betterment was gleefully heading for a spending spree with stolen money. Were there not excusable grounds for his crime? In mitigation, I offered up to myself the idea that I had been unjustifiably denied betterment and this was seen as a sort of trade-off to allow me to avoid being a nothing. Use the money to be something and pay it back later when success had been achieved. But where does that line of behaviour stop? What crimes can be committed with this logic? Was it not in line with backsliding, backsliding as betterment?

We bounced out of the Firearms & Tackle frontage, as if on springs, and back onto the main thoroughfare with a new intent driving us on. But, the entertaining phenomenon that was Les Buttocks was nowhere to be seen. I looked down the street that had a new active intensity. Saturday morning shopping people stormed past and headed towards us. Freed from their weekday work, they appeared as nothings and nothing to us. A crowd of nothings out to spend the something they had earned on something that was nothing. Les Buttocks was among them somewhere, hidden, perhaps entertaining some other critical spirits, but no longer us. We had lost him in the herd, lost him in our minds which were flush and fresh with the joy of affluence. Mammon was well and truly possessing us. We skipped to its tune, quivering with our excited talk and the thrill of new and wanted things about to be in our possession. All other thoughts were like nothing, and we were the only people in existence with value.

Except for the proprietor of Harry Black huckster world, Harry Black himself, the big-bellied bastard. You could see the badness in his big, well-fed smile. The mother seemed to link being well fed with badness for every time she went beyond a simple statement in reference to their badness, she attached to the term *well-fed. Big, bad, fat, well-fed Harry Black.* Food also figured in other insults of the mother. He was also called a *bad egg.* The ideas passed to me. Yes, indeed, with Harry Black it all corresponded. He was fat with food and badness. Money made Harry Black smile and was his main motivation for rising out of a warm bed to the day. He was a liar, for his smile was only there to get you into his shop. The lying smile. If you went out without a purchase, he lost the smile, and you feared him and his non-smiling face.

He was not satisfied at having any old shop, only a shop that he claimed sold everything. He used to tell the father never to ask him if he has something as he can get anything. *Anything from a single brass tack to a twin-engine bomber,* he said. He certainly had the tacks, a drawer full of them. He charged a penny for each one and would even throw-in the paper bag, which he habitually said was not free for him. I didn't think there was much call for the bombers, so he could claim he could lay his hands on those with a high degree of confidence, a confidence trick, as with all the other unlikely things. I wanted to ask him for a bomber some day. Twin engined. Put him to the test. All his weight on the back foot. I often sat thinking about what other things I could ask for that he could never get in a million years. He would have to say those words, *no, I can't get that.* And his big, lying smile would disappear. I would then smile at him. There were stacks of things I could think of, and I wanted to expose him as a liar in front of all those who thought he was great because of his boasts. He would probably say he could get the bomber, but it would take a long time. And then I would say, it doesn't matter. It was the thing my teasing Uncle Patsy used to say to us. He'd say, *Do you want a penny now or sixpence later?* If we said the penny now, he'd say you couldn't have it because you were too greedy and impatient. If you said the sixpence, *later* never came. He was a needler. The mother said so, and she hated such needling.

The mother always used Harry Black's emporium for all sorts of purchases. She liked the merchandise and the prices. The mother bought everything she could from his deep drawers. Attire for the whole family. Suits, shoes, shirts, and even our underwear were all from Harry Black's. Harry Black always smiled at her coming in, and going out, and even more when she was loaded down with bags of his stuff, even if it was all on approval. He knew she would be tempted by some of it in the inspection process. And the mother's inspection was governed by the need to buy. The mother behaved as though it was a gift, but he was not a giver, only a taker. He was also intimate with the mother, as there was nothing more intimate than the apparel we wore private to our skin, that he handled and sold to her.

Harry Black's caused family friction. Money disappeared into his pocket from the housekeeping cash, and the father held the mother to account. Harry Black's name filled the air, Harry Black this, Harry Black that, until we thought Harry Black was there. Arguments spilled over past the point of origin to a field of accusations of the most uncalled for sort. They publicised the disagreement in big dramatic shouts. Thrombosis didn't seem far off for either, due to a Harry Black-inspired clot in the blood supply. They were listened to in different parts of the house. Rarely was it original, rarely was it unfunny. Rarely did it improve my appreciation of the Max Bruch vinyl violin, the mounting rhythm and climax entirely destroyed by the father's base abuse of Harry Black. The father was a gentle soul, though occasionally quick to easy provocation, and, due to that disposition, was not long unaffected by the mother's externalising malevolence. Sometimes he was the direct recipient of it, and the longer they remained in each other's company, the more venom she distilled within her system especially for him.

He loved to go to work to be out of her poisonous presence. He extended his time at work whenever possible, taking longer shifts whenever offered. It didn't take long for the mother to realise he didn't want to be around her and her unpleasant little world. She soon became jealous of his work and his time spent beyond her. She engaged more and more of her own time in undisciplined imaginings, inventing worlds of pleasure and amusement she thought engaged him on the outside. He worked in a large bakery complex, had started as a simple labourer and worked hard to get promoted to foreman, but to that promotion she assigned her mark of displeasure, as she equated it only with his enjoyment. She sought to depreciate the position, as it conflicted with her idea of him as subordinate to her control. The result was a rapid deterioration of the healthy and happy family environment.

One day, the father and I sat in the car on a side street near Harry Black's, whilst the mother slipped out to get her man some new underwear. *I'll only be a wee minute*, she said. The *wee minute* hit the father's delicate patience inhibitor like a lump of swinging lead, and a flood of impatience swept aside all but surface composure. In her absence, as the moments ticked slowly by, he shifted about restlessly in his old, well worn Harry Black knickers. He had told her to hurry herself up and not mess about or keep looking at the articles of clothing until they were worn out by the looking and feeling. She always checked them thoroughly for their soundness.

She was a woman of feeling. The garment elastics were stretched hundreds of times. They were held up to the light, held down to the light, held sideways to the light. Fat swollen fingers felt every particle of the cloth. They were held at arm's length several hundred times. *All they are are underpants*, he said in her absence. Beyond that, his thinking was private to himself, but he moved his lips without making a sound. Not just underpants to her, however. They were a purchase, and a purchase had to be given due process of examination. A trial. A judgement.

When she returned about forty-five *wee minutes* later—about six hours in car waiting time—he wasn't happy, especially on the surface. The man was forging new horizons in self control. The *wee minutes* she had spoken of had ticked by, and we had said bye-bye to them in our frustration, knowing she would not just buy, but that she would buy time and risk the father's wrath to purchase some precious pleasure in Harry Black's. She eventually came, smiling, exhibiting perverted excitement. He boiled and bubbled, grimaced and wriggled like his arse was shitting darning needles. She was ignorant of the discontent as she produced and exhibited her prize purchase. Out of a free, brown Harry Black's bag and up in the air, pinched between her forefingers and thumbs, displayed to the outside public via the windscreen, the biggest white Y fronts I'd ever seen. Man-mountain size that may have fitted the large arse of Big Johnny Ratchett. Fully flush to his ample buttocks. I envisaged the label stating *H* for huge or *MA* for massive. An unrefined undergarment, basic for the needs of a sophisticated man and unsupportive of his most sensitive regions. Wearing such things made one body-aware and then, being aware, want to become, once again, unaware. But there was no getting rid of body awareness.

The wifely, womanly display of this article was without words, merely a smiling face of pleasure that issued forth all the meaning. *What do you think of those for a bargain? Are those alright for you? Only.* As the bargain price was spilled from her lips, the word *only.* Isolated in the sound waves, the father's immediate action was to stop the garment from being advertised to the whole Sandy Row community of bargain hunters. With his powerful labourer grip he rolled them up in a tight ball and held them, unbeheld, in his firm fist before stuffing them back into the brown Black's bag.

Rage issued forth into the world in vicious tightness of everything corporeal. A supreme effort of suppression. Skin strained on his face like a corset. He then started the snout sniffing, the pleasurable release of tension when he got annoyed and excited. She hated the snout itself and the frenzied snout-sniffing with an aggressive passion. An active passion which seemed contradictory. But, the father maintained the momentum to restraint, refusing to engage in a verbal slanging match. He simply engaged first gear to get us home and away from Harry Black's.

The mother was mad. An absurd madness. She liked mad word games and inspiring others to partake of her madness. And her mad world. Within this world the mad mother made the father an ill man, ill with an unforgiving ulcer, the pain particularly searing in those moments of irritability. He soon withdrew as he realised that these games couldn't be won. He would often retreat to his bedroom to lie on his side on the bed, raise his knees to his chin and wait for the ulcer pain to subside. *Go on ya big babbee*, the mother said as a going away present. And to anyone who would listen she added with increased venom and considerably more annoyance at his strategic disappearance, *If you want to know real pain you should have a babbee come out of you.*

We all sniggered knowing what was essentially funny, and indeed essentially tragic in these scenes. Imported underpants and other sundry relics of previous embarrassments that the father seemed particularly predisposed to, escalated the need to laugh. But the laughter was also entirely ignorant, unaware of the pain he always privately suffered. (How do we know pain that is privately suffered?) The father's mind was in turmoil, and inside the body, he was scarred by the acid eating the lining of his stomach after the dreaded H Pylori had done its terrible best. He wriggled about in the form of the unborn to get some relief whilst we, in another room, paid attention to a different interpretation of events and could barely relieve that other pleasurable variety of discomfort, the pain of uncontrollable laughter.

That laughter remains within me because the ludicrous nature of those events are still in me, conceived as they were then, to see and to think, and when the fog of other ideas is cleared, there is a flow of disturbed feeling corresponding to something contained within the idea itself, and the result of it is a discomfort that not only points to the particular thing but to the universal.

Belfast, as I recall, was full of this discomfort that makes us all take a form to lessen it. It informed us to understand and obey it. It was also full of Harry Black-type emporiums run by Harry Black-type shysters. He was a Prod who didn't need excessive prodding to sell to the Fenians. He was a man of the free market, whose constitution was unwritten in his abundant flesh, there, as testimony to the higher calling of making money. What was not made a mere artefact in his mind was the idea that religion should not interfere with commerce or smiling. He smiled his lying smile at the enemy, even though he hated their Fenian guts. Money was his religion, re-formed over and above his reformed religiosity. His was the cult of the black market, the Black market for a big bargain, for a big bargain-hunting public that had the intentionality for a bargain built-in as standard and didn't give a damn about the origin as long as the price was right. Everything was sold loose, loose like the big, loose, Y-fronts in the car, no fancy packages or brand names. Not even bogus brand names, merely brand-less articles. If there was a brand at all, it was the price that was branded in the minds of buyers. Out of such markets, I got my jeans, and suits, and shirts, and all the stuff that hung on my lean frame, as well as my first winkle pickers and elasticated Chelsea boots.

The whole emporium idea was largely adrift in the wild ocean of unconnected notions, but it seized my attention now and again. It brought to mind Firearms and Tackle as well as Harry Black's, but there were more questions than answers. How would you go about embarking on such a venture? Where do you get the stuff to sell? Can you open one anywhere you want? I was drowning in confusion, but I kept afloat with the strong idea that having something other people wanted must be a good feeling. That they would have to come to you to get it, was an even better one.

I wanted the parents to open a shop in our completely wasted front parlour. It was currently made by the mother into an untouchable and largely unoccupied space. Dust free. A vacuum regularly vacuumed. Made so by the mother's fussy hands. For her it was not a matter of *if you are Irish come into the parlour*, but rather, *if you are a clean stranger in a stiff suit come into the parlour.* The Mormons managed to get in. They were squeaky clean and stiff enough in their suits. As was Uncle Patsy, who was murdered and in a wooden suit. She had always wanted a parlour for people not to be allowed into. The houses she was raised in had no such luxury. Straight off the street into the living room. *Living room?* The room for living that had no room for living. Everybody piled in, with all their dirt and germs, and lived happily amongst them.

I had ideas I considered creative, and they connected to a degree. To transform the parlour into a shop, it was just a matter of knocking the bay window out and putting a giant flat glass window in its place, with a glass door to one side so people wouldn't have to come up the hall and in through the normal parlour door. Get rid of the piano against the back wall and put a counter there. The sister played the piano on a Sunday morning prior to church and, as that was one of the great annoyances of my life, it would not be a loss. Rip out the mother's precious, fake fireplace and put up shelves. Next, put the good settee into the living room and throw out the old piece of brown crap we sat on whilst watching TV. Nobody else in the street had the idea, so it would be great, even though my imagination did not entirely affirm the idea of my street with a shop in the middle.

Just think, I thought, doing Harry Black at his own game. Wiping the lying smile off his lying face. But, the idea of that our street didn't seem to be a shop street was a constant annoyance to me. For a start people didn't come up and down it in their droves like in the city centre streets. The enigma of shops also existed in the mind of one of my friends. Ginger McArkle was his name, a lad

of powerful logical latitude in most thinking things under his hairy
red bop, who nevertheless couldn't quite grasp the idea behind the
logistical goings-on in a petrol station. On each occasion he passed
a garage and in the privacy of his own company, he spun into slow
and careful cogitation and considered the nature of petrol pumps
and the petrol storage. One day, he unloaded his bewilderment
onto the minds of an assortment of us hanging loose in the entry,
looking for a laugh. What he arrived at was a question; *How is
it that they can store so much petrol in those wee pumps?* It was an
intimate moment indeed. A precious moment. The ins and outs
of retail-dom in general were the cause of great and annoying
perplexity. What we knew for certain was its necessity in the way
of things. As was hilarity. And that won the day in the entry. As it
often did on other days.

Linus and I stood, grasped by the junction being Hope Street
and Bruce Street, with the aspect of retail-dom we actually knew
something about firmly in mind. Hope Street to our right and Bruce
Street to our left. Hope Street would take us through to the Dublin
Road and then, with hardly any left turn at all, on into the town
centre. Bruce Street would take us away from town and west to
Sandy Row, where Harry Black's empire was located, as well as a host
of peripheral shops squeezed to the margins of major retail-dom,
selling delightfully dodgy merchandise and hosted by shifty shysters.

We also had the option to go straight ahead down Great
Victoria Street, which also led through to the town centre, but
our preferred P-KR3 route was via the Dublin Road, which had
an interesting shop window, displaying the wonderful world of
cigarettes. A smoker's paradise. A whole window devoted to the
puffing desire. Beautiful packets of fags all spread out. Tens and
twenties. Stupendous names. *Will's Whiffs*! Stimulating the desire.
Capstan Navy Cut. Wild Woodbine. Senior Service, with an old
navy galleon printed upon it. *Aladdin Turkish*, with a mysterious
tanned, turbaned Turk taking your attention. *Swingstyle 41* filter
tips, with an almost naked blonde woman, undoing her bra in mid-
air, and standing in the loftiest of high heels. Jesus, what a world!
Always the ignorant lusty eyes were drawn back to the *Swingstyle
41* woman, to the further details of her bounteous beauty. This

was the sort of bounty the saints should be rewarded with by God. The proverbial *bounteous eye shall be blessed*. What was the bounty of this *Swingstyle 41* woman? A big satin bow on show in the high and mighty blonde hair. Luscious red lipstick on closed, pushed-out, pouting lips. Blushed cheeks. Smooth, tanned skin with a sheen. A seriously seductive look in the eye-lined eyes. Holding the bra clasps: long fingers with long, varnished finger nails. Silky, satiny, skin-tight, see-through cami-knickers. High heel mules with the instep thrust up into a painful looking cramp, enkindling calf curve. The light given by the informing inner eye could just see her elegantly slipping one of those slim filter tips into her mouth and with head held back, releasing it with an upward puff of smoke to follow. It was a long journey in the imagination from the crummy clients who entered and exited that shabby shop door, but as it was a trip that was being made, and made in the imagination and not the intellect, the advertisers had their success. Great ideas of self were imagined whilst a cigarette was held in hand, and the chemical high elevated it to further absurd greatness.

*

The choice before us was familiar enough, and with it a familiar feeling of force, standing there with the directions just there, there for us, and the freedom to choose one, the excessive weighing it all up, the possible pleasure in stepping out to reach it. As if we had never made it before. Always the choice of this way or that when the junction was met. We called this junction Bob No Hope junction. It was a funny and dangerous junction, for many a life was united to eternity as a result of indecision or bad judgement, as they stepped out into a raging traffic. I had no tolerance for bad judgement that was really, to me, annoying clumsiness, so I had little sympathy for the clumsy dead people who should have had *R.I.P the much loved and clumsy clot etc.* etched on their gravestones. I, on the other hand, was nimble and could dodge through the traffic without the aid of a favourable traffic light.

So, this way or that? I had Harry Black and his shop in mind, for the mother had mentioned to me in a breathless barrage in defence of Harry Black, when I said Black's stuff was duff and dire, that he had some sporting goods at good prices, hanging up outside, or in cardboard boxes at the door and in his drawers inside behind his counters. I didn't want them in the drawers, because that would mean asking Harry Black himself, yet I wasn't sure to trust the mother on sporting goods. If the boots I had were anything to judge by, then her judgement had to be judged faulty.

With the ideas of this way or that waiting for a decision, other thoughts hovered in mind, messing up the whole simplicity before me. Behind the door at home, things were going on. Things of the Saturday morning variety. But, the goings on would be circumscribed by the future event that was powerful in its potential to rearrange the usual events and, if it was encountered as actual, would determine what happened for the rest of the day. Saturday was essentially a buying day, a frantic, mad, parting-with-cash day. A day that dawned with the joyful anticipation of new possessions. When all early morning routine is exhausted - the waking, the cooking and the eating, the washing, the grooming, the arguing - buying entered the mind for real, though it hadn't really been out of the mind since it drove the mind along in low gear. In fact, it was the mind in overdrive. A mind without the means of buying was on its way to madness, for it had the drive without a place to drive to, a desire without a means of satisfaction.

There would be that moment, that point in thought, when the idea of buying replaced all else, the purse sought, found, and opened to disclose an absence of funds. I knew very well how this would effect mood and action. The disclosure would be followed by a desperate disordered search, first by the discovering mind, the sister whose money it was, then by the rest of the pack in the confines of our domestic enclosure. The father, the mother, the other sister, the brother. The purse would be clicked open and clicked shut time and again, the fingers feeling inside that miniscule space for what was quite obviously not there. Each would take it in hand and one by one undertake a demonstrably more extensive search of the tiny vacant lot. I could envisage the mother snatching it out of the father's grip to assume authority on the matter. There would be blank stares of bewilderment. Stares that stared at the other stares who stared back. Stares that marched up the stairs to the landing ground of stupidity. The quietness of ignorance would be punctuated by sighs and little laughs of disbelief, all of which would soon gave way to outrageous questions to dispel the mysterious nature of the happening. Was it, it would be thought, ever there at all? Had it been spent? Something resembling logic would soon replace the chaotic questioning. Retracing the steps. The steps would then be re-stepped. All going on in my absence.

I imagined it all and foresaw the various ways in which this future would become real. The thing I most feared, I imagined most. I feared they would search all over, within and without, and then, by their very own process of elimination, postulate that it was most likely someone had taken it, someone in the family. I feared my being the very last suspect in their line of investigation, having eliminated all other alternatives, to which all attention and intention would be drawn. I feared the relentless interrogation. I would eventually be thought of as the perpetrator of this crime. The youngest with the most fickle mind. I had lied and cheated routinely over small matters. And if it was thought that that someone was me, what would they think of me if I didn't crack under the questioning? If I was seen as guilty but never admitted it? What form of judgement would they arrive at? It was all going to be about me in their minds. That they would be forced to think about me, about the being that was me, the being that was not me, the being that was for me the being I was going to be, and the being that was for them and others. Yet this would, would it not, also be a conversion point in the moment of backsliding? The idea of *me*, taking flight.

In the street, at the junction, a decision had been made. Who made it? *We* did. What did we decide? We headed off, Linus with freezing fishy hands under his armpits, his thoughts private to himself and mine to me, but apparently without alternative intervention, we decided the same thing, going in the same direction together.

CHAPTER 13

Lordly intervention, the shouting preacher said, *is very much still here in our midst and never listen to anyone who says anything contrary to that.* It was an additional ingredient to the recipe of rights and wrongs in the place of interventions. He scared the holy shite out of us every Sunday night. Beyond the doors of this little church hall, in the dawn, in the day, in the dark, a world of madness awaited. An assassin or a demon might steal us away. He would then burst into song, *Steal away, steal away, steal away to Jesus* was a favourite. Everyone joined in. I lodged my attention in the word *steal.* His stolen sheep bleated back in fearful desperation to his plaintive plea for their souls to persevere. There was no denial permitted here, all was safely affirmative, and there was even an ounce of courage evident in their bleats. The shepherd said the Lord had given him the gift of *oversight.* God saw through his eyes. He wore spiritual specs. Massive eyeballs rolled behind high prescription, long-sighted lenses. That was in itself frightening. Like the man with the x-ray eyes.

Every day there is blood being spilled in the bucketful on the streets of the city, he said, *but only Jesus's blood has the power to save us.* Then he would hit us with his latest bold superstition which masqueraded as spiritual science. *There's chemistry in that precious blood*, he said, *that transmits motion to the soul, so the soul can move toward everlasting life.*

The Lord won't always be waiting around with the blood, he warned us, *even though he is a waiting God who excels at waiting*. It could be a once and for all offer, like with the man who sold his sets of towels at the Lamas Fair in Ballycastle. Selling towels from a stall and selling salvation from a pulpit offered interesting and even comical comparisons as the sermon got longer and the listening mind wearier. Worthy of a fanciful dander in the midst of inexhaustible Christian fervour. Down the lanes and down the aisles of the sacred and the profane. All this was mind-broadening, but only if you were a backslider, or a potential one. In straight thinking and in wayward imagining. There's nothing quite like it when you mix serious matters with the idle or what, at first, may appear idle.

In the serious matter of the holy soul-cleansing offer, it isn't like everyone gets the same square deal. It isn't square deal Surf washing powder. Man is not the measure of fairness. Nor is TV advertising. He is at the mercy of a wanton eternal will. No time like eternal time, which is no time at all. Time to accept or reject is allotted before time. Jesus has already said, *That's it, I've had it with you, I'm not going to strive with you any longer. My spirit will not always strive with man.* Man can strive all he likes until he looks ridiculous in his striving, but there'll be no one on the other end of the line. No amount of coaxing and crying or tugging on the Lord's holy raiment will convince him to reconsider your case. No new evidence will be permitted. Case closed. That soul will spend eternity in that infernal place.

When I was supposed to have my eyes shut, I looked around at the striving, to see if I could discern the degree of it in a posture. Buttocks shifting uneasily in a pew was a sign.

And on and on the preacher droned, painting with his inadequate words his picture of Hell. *Dante's Inferno, that's not Hell*, he said, *that's a playground compared to Hell.* His inadequate words found adequate responses in inadequate minds. I saw the body aspect of these minds leaping out of their seats Some, I swore, I saw going forth more than once. They moved just like old Uncle Hughie when he dashed from his room to the bog with the onset of diarrhoea. Hands outstretched, angled forward, desperate for relief from loose living or just plain loose shitting. The sinners needed to shite their sin. *The last chance saloon or salvation?* bellowed the increasingly purple-faced preacher. *Do you want to sit forever in the lap of Satan?*

Pressed in my pew, in the midst of all the fearifying, I had regular visions. Before me, this whole circumstance was transformed into the television quiz show *Take Your Pick*. The Pastor was the unctuous and ever-smiling quizmaster Michael Miles, who offered you increasing amounts of money for your precious key to the box that might hold your fortune. He could keep increasing the offer, but he could also just halt with that first paltry sum and give up offering any more. And all you would be left with is the key that might just be for the booby prize. You'd stand there looking sheepishly ridiculous, smiling like an idiot, regretting holding out for more. The big booby prize in the great game of life was to have the key to Hell in your hand.

It seemed a fearful, cruel message, but the preacher said it was all about love. He loved love and abysmal stories about love. The divine hand of love reaching through eternity to the sinking sinner in the abyss. But this love was tempered by the divine justice. He was full of stories about salvation that was inspired by God's love. He liked to make it personal. In my backsliding doubt I thought he was lying. He told us of a saved man, who phoned him up in the middle of the night, worried about the eternal status of his unsaved wife's soul. She had died of cancer, but she was a lovely woman who had not an ounce of badness in her and who did well by everyone. The preacher said he asked God for strength and the right form of words to tell the man that his dear, all-loving wife would be in Hell forever, whilst he would be in heaven forever. They would be eternally separated by the love of God. Her undying expression of loveliness here, there, and everywhere was neither here nor there. In fact, it was there in Hell.

It doesn't matter, said the preacher to his congregation, *if you are loving or good by man's measures, because man is not the measure of all things. If you haven't been saved you are lost!*, he blasted at us like a nuclear wind. *It's also no good if you are married to someone who is saved. It does not rub off like boot polish!* It occurred to me that the man wouldn't or couldn't be happy in Heaven if he knew his lovely loving wife was roasting in Hell. Or, is the memory erased in Heaven? Do we not need our memory to know who we are and if it wasn't actually *us* being saved what is the point? These were backsliding thoughts.

It all got very complicated and people were not encouraged to think too hard about it. *Stop the philosophising,* shouted the preacher, *you either have to trust God or you're lost.* He hated the man who thought from premise to conclusion. Here, with these words, he looked directly at me, just as my mind flirted with the questioning doubt. I shook to my most cowardly core, and immediately abandoned every idea that was a seed of the sceptical. Then I moved my mouth to say *Praise the Lord,* hoping he would see my utterance with his long sight and pass over me in his oversight. Or would he see me afterwards in hindsight? In his dreams perhaps. I had no keenness to think beyond the waking world.

For a certain period of time, I felt happy with the abandonment of a larger reason, replacing it with the smaller religious rationale. There was undoubted contentment to be had there. God's not going to have to explain himself, I thought. Not the same as questioning your da. Questioning itself was as good as signing up for the fiery furnace. Abraham obeyed God's command to kill his son Isaac without a single objection. Yes, it was all about love, the love that passes all understanding.

The one thing questioning does above all other things is to reveal something of the *I* that questions.

CHAPTER 14

To where goes the I? I have to know where I am going. The lack of certainty is unnerving. People can't take advantage if you know exactly where you are going. Not led by primary blunder of desire but by knowledge.

We were assured and confident as we approached Harry Black's, heading into a ridiculously bright, low sun, when a big lumbering funny thought most assuredly shat upon me. About me. A confidence trick. What about me? The thing me. But not a thing. Entirely. Like me as a *causa sui.* Myself causing myself. Almost. Jesus was there. The Lord of hosts, but I refused to host him. He was like holy tinnitus, background pealing of bell ringing in the gospel message. The thought moved on swiftly without him, at least in the foreground. *What makes me me?* Just me. Marius. It is unnerving to think such a thing as the self and its own cause. The phantom nature of it. Phantom like no other phantom. A withdrawal in thinking. The real nature of it. Nature both nominal and real in awareness.

It's a bully of a notion that bunks the mind queue, depositing itself, like big lumps of fat do on the body, and sitting in its essential heaviness ahead of dainty, timid, light notions that seem to be me and define me most of the time. How is such a thought made manifest? I have a body in mind, my own body. I have a tendency of thought in mind, standing out, objectified. Like an outside body. I feel free. But not free as I have to be me.

Then another big lump of a heavy thought deposited itself like the other one. *Never mind what makes me me.* I uttered. *The thief is me. Am I really a thief? I steal away, not to Jesus, but to me. I steal for me.* Then this, *I am not what I think I am.* I protested! *The thief is not the real I. The thief seeks to steal my real id entity, but if I am a thief, if I admit to being a thief I can still conceive of myself without the idea of thief. If thief was removed I would not be removed. I am greater than the thief. Deeper than the thief, wider, higher, I am better than the thief.* So, I repeated, *what makes me me, the me that is not to be removed without removing me? Is there something about me that, if removed, would see me removed? And if posited it would posit me? Is that what to de-posit means? The removal of that which is posited. Or the placing of a posit. An entirely strange word, posit. Pose it* That's how I said it. And thought it. *A poser. One who seeks to be seen as something special.* The world then was full of posers positing themselves. Seeking desperately to be what they were not. But that was a body thing as well as a mind thing. A mind posited and a body posed.

Compose. Compost. Like shite. I compose. Effort! My particular effort. That was it. That's the word that came forth as we strode forth. The composition of effort. That was what we were in our very own aspect. I sensed my own effort. Not merely a thinking thing. There was of course *my* body. If my body was destroyed I would be destroyed—would I? The preacher in the church said not, with all his being. All this postulating soon dissolved into inadequacy as Harry Black appeared in big body with an essence of boldness intrinsic to him. His posing began. He would depose the shoppers from their lofty perches.

The thing that was Harry Black agreed with my idea of him. I posited him and there he was. In full posit. Posing in retail fashion. Affecting both myself and Linus with our illuminating eyes, as he lined up in our sights. What we didn't want was for the both of us to be in his illuminating eye. Harry Black's was encountered at a moment of chaotic business. His goods were fluttering in the breeze from wooden Harry Black clothes hangers attached to a deep

un-taut awning. The hangers marked with Harry Black & Sons—
how strange to think of him as a son—also had the address of his
shop in smaller letters underneath, all carved into the wood in
black. Black lettering for Harry Black. Maybe not carved so much
as branded with a branding iron. I thought of Harry Black's titanic
arse being branded, as he put me in mind of a big heifer. Not the
heifer of the cow species, but a heifer, including the cow species.
The word *hefty* must have come from the heavier word *heifer* and
he was all of hefty. He should have been named Heffernan instead
of Black. Harry Heffernan sounded just right.

So, Linus and I called him that from time to time. We had
loads of those hefty hangers of his in our house. Almost like
having the man himself there. In his real world, Harry Black was
easily distinguished among the throng. He was like a queen bee in
amongst her attending hordes of endless droning bee-ings. He was
a man, but he was really a big woman, understanding a woman's
wants and talking the common woman's talk, just the way women
talk. He was a fat sissy, a big girl amongst the girls.

Linus and myself, in un-discussed planning, planned to avoid
him. We didn't want him to grasp us by our fragile attentions
and brow beat the money off us with his powerful vending will.
We wanted to browse freely, as though we were free to do so,
but browsing was not an easy mode of shopping in Harry Black's
establishment which was cultivated by him as a space for buying
only. He didn't want mere eye browsing. Browsing wasn't in his
language. Why wasn't there a *No Browsing* sign then? It was natural
for people to browse but he wanted to change that and make it
natural to buy. He didn't like browsing at all, but, within his low
brow, he didn't like the word *no* either. He didn't want to give the
slightest impression that there were no-go areas in his shop. *No* was
a negative he wanted not. It was a psychological intuition of his
that he didn't want any signs at all that had the word *no* in them.
Nobody wants *no*. Other shops around had *No this, No that* signs
all over and that was no good for Harry Black. Written sign with
no were quickly picked upon by shoppers and repelled them. He
personally determined what the areas of customer activity were,
and that was the key to his success. He implanted in the heads of

his customers the idea that they were active and not passive, and did not rely on signs to direct them.

Once there inside, even outside with the fluttering clothes on hangers, he was there like a big bluebottle fly buzzing around, orbiting the scene, landing on this customer and that customer like they were fresh and benign tasty sweet-smelling turds. As turds, they simply could not act in defiance as turds by nature are passive. A passive by-product. I never ever heard anyone saying, *oh, I'm just browsing*, for that denial would have cut no ice with Harry Black. In his ice-cold being, it would have been as if the words had never been spoken. He nailed the attention of possible deniers with actual goods until he had them buying the goods just to get out of the shop. You'd think people would be put off by this sort of pressure, but the truth was, they were persuaded that he was able to satisfy the needs they never knew they had.

The shop cut the street in half with goods on rails well out onto the pavement and, as the crowds slowed to get passed, Harry Black pounced with his broad Belfast sales talk. If, on the rare occasion, someone was going out the main door without something, boldly and adamantly denying him, he would offer items to view at home at their leisure. *Take these with you lady, just look at your leisure. Don't for God's sake worry about money; we'll work something out for you.* Not leisure when they had Harry Black in their very homes, him in the form of his goods hanging in there, and a good bit of their consciousness was consciousness of Harry Black and his world.

So, his shop extended out to the points of the compass, way beyond the pavement to the hearths of Belfast houses. Husbands cursed their wives for their foolish devotion to Harry Black, but Harry Black had them where he wanted them. Harry called himself the *Bargain Buddy*, and there was a sign to this effect in his shop somewhere, but the terms *bargain* and *buddy* were not conceptually friendly, a friendly shopkeeper there was, but not a shopkeeper friend, as the shopkeeper was the keeper primarily of his own interests. And this was especially true of the huckster and Black was most definitely a huckster. A fuckster as well, as he fucked up more marriages than all the fancy men Ulster could produce.

The power of a presence! The limited thing acting to the limit, a boundary beyond his body, but the power of the idea of his body and mind expressed to great effect in the head of another. He was like a God. Not an infinite one but a powerfully finite one expressing his spectacular finitude with all his being.

We wove ourselves through the throng, not as gods, nowhere near, but as small finite modes, moving between the mesh of material, and married women, and the material of married women. Who they were was immaterial. Women of material interests. Our thoughts were intuitive, independent but the same, modulated mutualising modalities, so much so we could have been considered as one being for the action was for the same end. A dead end. Just like different parts of our own bodies, down to the most basic bacteria at work inside, acting according to their own nature, but in doing so coinciding with the interests of the whole. With some exceptions.

Linus slipped one way, without the aid of slippers, myself the other around clothes rails and people, and we were, with unexpected suddenness, in the holy of holies of Harry Black's shop without the presence of the most high Harry Black himself. We needed hoods to hide our selfhood. He was a big mode, like a traffic island, but, fleet of feet, we dodged him. In Heaven we were, not seventh Heaven, not quite bliss, but a lower higher element. The truth is we didn't feel assured that we had gone unnoticed, so our demeanour was tailored—unlike his crap clothes—and conditioned by the thought that we had been picked up by the extraordinary Harry Black retail radar and so had only limited time to see the merchandise unhindered. Being nabbed in the nobblers by Harry Black was a fearsome prospect. Mesmerism by bigness. He would corner us with his big blubbery body, swathed in rucks of casual raiment, his big being, big softness, big smell of sweat, big in the way he would mesmerise us with big authoritative retail talk, big in the presentation to us with stuff, and big minded to see right into our souls, to see our inner joy of prosperity, that we had money to spend.

He would not offend us or fend us off. The light in his eye would be there for us. He knew the skiving presence of children without money, he saw it in their furtive demeanour and their slinkingness, and he would chase them off unhesitatingly with big, hefty, sweeping movements of his arms in conjunction with irrefutable words of dismissal. But he would surely divine with his trained divining mind that we had money in our pockets, and the same divining process processed the idea that the money would soon be in his pocket. Linus looked edgy to me as I must have to him.

I felt for the fiver in my pocket as if it was in immediate need of protection and kept my hand there, the folded note firmly between forefinger and thumb. I rubbed it with the end of each grasping finger. It was a smooth experience to my sensitive, young finger tips, so I kept moving my fingers back and forth over it, and it presented to me an idea of what was smooth and what a pleasurable thing smoothness was. The word smooth was good as well. It suited what it described. Smooth was itself smooth. Some foreigners couldn't say it.

A Portuguese plumber in India Street said *smood*. I heard him say it to the father once when he came to fix a leaking pipe. *Nice smood finish,* he said after a job in our house. I couldn't help saying it over and over again until it didn't sound like itself, but still, there was a pleasant sensation in its saying. It occurred to me that some people took delight in the way they said words. The sound came to the ear in such an agreeable manner. Neither the mother nor the father said things in a refined way at all. The sounds they made were harsh and forced out either in anger or over-excitement. The father boomed bounteously and spat out the words whilst the mother hissed and screeched, both paying no attention to the aesthetic of speech. Power was what they had, power of the vicious representation, but only to us and each other. They showed their fawning faces to the world and spoke and acted with meekness and mildness. Performances in passivity but the passive act is really no act at all. Rather the absence of act. A fading away into an area of weak existence.

I discovered the pleasurable feeling of smoothness in the loose balls of material pulled from the inner seams in my pockets, which, once felt, were felt obsessively. Even when unfelt, the idea itself provoked pleasure. Those bits of material, usually excess trouser substance of cloth. Sometimes so much material came off and a hole appeared, not appeared, as it was not seen, only imagined with a finger feeling it for information as to its dimensions. The mother kept saying to me to get my hands out of my pockets and to stop picking at them or a hole would appear. And she insisted with her vicious representation that such fiddling was a *dirty habit.* She prophesied it like the best of the ancient Hebrew Nabis, for holes did eventually appear. The ball of dust had to go somewhere, she said. And it was the picking that was dirty. Like nose picking. Like picking scabs. It was the picking habit, and a habit is generally bad.

The mother waged a war on habits as she did on dirt, yet her own life was nothing but a series of habits. There was, however, a whole lot of truth in the hole thing. Holes did appear but pockets were there precisely to comfort the hands, and the hands could not be still in a pocket. And we were not allowed things in our pockets as they would make holes or misshape them. She said that she was going to sew up all our pockets. It had to be thought, though, that, even if there was a hole there, the hands could still feel comfortable in them, even beyond the hole where the fingers could poke through to touch the bare leg skin. Not when the fingers were freezing, though. That was unbearable. Unless there was a pimple head to be scratched off on the thigh, then it was bearable. It was the presiding pleasure of pimple-head picking that beat all.

A habit is a rest. At each stage of our lives, we should cultivate some form of habitual sensuality that is appropriate for our mind at the time. A sensual rest is the best rest of all. Like a mind massage. The proviso is that it should be consistent with dignity. There are always those, however, who would deny such experiences to themselves and others. The denial can be camouflaged by some practical motive, but there are more sinister ideas at work. Destructive ideas, because the motive is really to destroy the self and other selves. The moment you become aware of this in someone who you think loves you, is the moment that all ideas you have of them change. And if viewed adequately, then ideas of the world change too.

We continued to move modally in the confines of Harry Black's store. My eyes, independent of the fingers, were particularly active, roving around the Harry Black merchandise, up above on high rails, straight forward in glass counters, and they scanned the labelled drawers behind the counters for the goods that were craved. Football shirts, shorts, socks, boots. Anything with a football connection. If I had thought that was a possibility, even for a second, I would have grabbed the first items that matched the names and reflected the function of the names in performance. On the edge of my hearing, I felt Linus mumbling something or other, but I let his mumbling slip by unattended. They were just mumblings that went straight through me without touching me, like a powerful physic of fine salts. Two big and almighty questions occurred to me and captured all my attention: *What am I here for?* came first and was quickly followed by, *What am I doing here?* Fleetingly I thought the abbreviation; *What am I?* and, *Who am I?* I feared it, the debilitating nature of it, but there was a sure-fire way of conquering it: reason it out of existence. I didn't nick that fiver that I was feeling between my fingers to be tortured by the fear of spending it, to completely waste it. It was taken into my possession for a purpose; the act was justified by the purpose. The purpose was good and all the decks of everything else were swept aside. Ditched! All peripheral piffle. The previous owner didn't need it. She would waste it on things that were not needed. She bought things and then discarded them. Her room was a mess of those discarded things. And the discarded things caused disharmony between the sister and the mother, a disharmony that spread like wildfire throughout the abode. The mother waged a war on discarded things discarded in the wrong place to make a mess. Furthermore, she would go back to work and, in only a week, have that money back in her purse. I could only beg for money. I could rant on at the father for hours for some small amount and still not get it. Pocket money was pitiful, as pitiful as the fluffy bits in the pocket. And what I wanted was not just some stupid trifling fashion thing; it was a thing that would make me something. An essential thing. I really needed to leave school soon to go to work and get the things that were essential for my being something. Education was important, but the last place you would get that was at school. What was on offer at school was a messy mixture of imaginative ideas, wholly inadequate as understanding, and a group of incapable people who circulated them. Teachers were an ignorant bunch. Indications of idiocy abounded. A formal fount of incapacitation, theirs and ours. It was hit-or-miss what ended up in our heads as constructive or destructive. These ideas masquerading as knowledge functioned, in different circumstances, as either sources of highs and lows, entertainment or sorrows, darkness and light. Out of it came all our fears, all our dubious pleasures for when we were pleasured in a state of the imagination we were not sure if we should be. We had a passive relation to events and to our actions. School, I concluded, wasn't natural.

Imagination was indeed running riot in my head at high velocity and tracing queer geometrical patterns. A headstrong head. A head heady with desire. Desire, that essence of man insofar as he seeks to sustain himself. But the desire depends on the disposition, which can be weak or strong. Imagination or intellect defines the weak and the strong.

I desired in desperation, desired in wonder, desired in distraction, desired in participation with unconnected vague notions, so I desired in weakness. White football garments. I wanted an all white kit. Shirt, shorts, socks. I wanted to be an angelic footballer, and white was appropriate. Harry Black's had a preponderance of things white, especially undergarments, but I couldn't distinguish one thing from another as it all tended to hit me in one block of white. White raiment everywhere. Was the white mass above me football wear or underwear? It looked like a row of T shirts but it could as well have been vests, old men's vests. Into my mind leapt the terrible thought of pulling on one of those old men's vests just before a match and realising that it was not a football shirt. Too late, I'd have to wear it. It scared the shite out of me. I didn't want a football vest that masqueraded as a proper shirt. It would fool no one. It would amuse everyone. I didn't want to be invested into the ranks of the ridiculous. The whispers on the sidelines would say, he's wearing an old man's vest, and inspire laughter at large. That was the sort of thought mothers had, an amateurishness of thought, a way of thinking that tried to get away with garments of one type that resembled another because they were cheap.

That'll do you, she would say. Like a motto. *That'll do you for a football shirt.* She never said that about dirt and dust where one speck was too much to bear. Cleanliness was never a question of *that'll do*. The *that'll do* motto only applied to what *we* wore. That's why I took the fiver: so I could choose for myself something that wouldn't simply be a *that'll do* thing.

There in that shop, I detected a form of self-hate at a time when I strove desperately to love myself. Entering into my way of thinking was a whole set of new ideas about my actions. Second-order thoughts that analysed the value of actions and the thoughts that inspired actions. These reflections became longer and longer and more and more troublesome to a previously trouble-free mind.

Crossing my line of vision and into focus was a face familiar. Its familiarity disturbed my concentrated efforts and was connected with an excessively acute sense of irritation to both the face and the name attached to it. Tommy Binney! He straggled behind his bargain-hunting mother with that limp and crouched gait of the thwarted appetite to be somewhere else. Binney lived somewhere around here in the streets near the shops and went to Park Secondary School, just like us. But as soon as he crossed the academic threshold on his first day he was directed to the lower streams for lower minds. He swam in those streams for his whole school life, with a whole school of other fish brains. His name was a stumbling block to friendship. I didn't realise that names played such an important role in determining who you chose as a friend. I simply couldn't bring myself to be a friend to someone with a name like Binney, which was silly to even say. Reminded me of pinny. An apron. Binney in a pinny. It was comical. It also sounded like binman which was not a nice thought. Some boy I knew at school had a binman father and all the half-wits shouted after him, *Your da's a binman,* knowing it to be a powerful idea to have over someone. Like saying to the face of someone who is ugly that they are ugly.

Better to have your da on the dole than emptying the bins. There was some prestige on the dole. It was only tough men who were on the dole, tough enough to refuse work, refuse what the state demanded of them, and therefore considered themselves victors over the state. Work was being a lackey to someone else. Dole men asserted themselves on street corners where they performed pose smoking, waiting for the bars to open. They held themselves high in their own minds. The minds of such men informed themselves that they were above a moment's work, never mind a day's work, and you were a fool to do it if money was there without having to work for it. And when you went to get your dole, you illustrated your manhood with a surly swagger that was passed on efficiently through the social network and from father down to son.

I kept saying Binney over and over again to myself, and it never got any better. It was a phenomenality somewhere on the intuitive level. There he was in all his Binniness in Harry Black's, in all his particular blackness of ignorance. He had all the facial features of the mother Binney in masculine form. These features were the expressive front to a Binney mind that was slow and stupid and roguish and disobedient. His mind was not on full gas, burning on the pilot light only, but if the word *pilot* suggested a sort of inner controlling presence then that would be far from the mark. It was gas mark zero. Low light, using minimum power. Merely a little spark of inner light that illuminated a small area of mind to its limited capability. I always saw him in the caning line outside the head's office suffering for his unruliness, a hilariously daft smile preceding the painful grimace and the unstoppable tears. It gave full meaning to the name Binney. Prominent teeth were the first port of call to the idly-observing gaze. They rested firmly on the lower lip with the upper lip pouting out and up so his teeth were always on view. It looked as if the word *fuck* was made for that mouth. His head rested far back on his neck, and there was an expectancy that it would lurch forward at any moment as if about to sneeze. The Binney eyelids were large and lazy, the eyes themselves oscillated from side to side in some fruitless, purposeless search. The sounds of Binney were of equal unattractiveness. He snorted through a snatter-filled nose like an excited swine.

Who would not find all this annoying? Only someone with equally annoying features and idiocy. I considered the horror of being confined somewhere with him. I had a hope that he wouldn't set his lazy eyes on me here in Black's, but I had to depend on luck for there were no hiding places. I could only remain still. In fact, Binney was still in his usual half-asleepness, the state he normally arrived to school with. That, and the boredom which

Saturday morning shopping with old mother Binney would inspire, meant that it was as though he was sleepwalking. My guess was he was being force-marched in the direction of some desperately dull purchase, some sort of under-attire, knickers, or vests, or school footwear perhaps, and the singularly numbing effect of that would be my saviour. He had probably been pulled and shoved around any number of stores already, probably been to Welsh's just directly across the road from Black's, which specialised in Y-fronts for the male loins and advertised them, in their massive extensivity, extensively in their window. The fountainhead of the father's underwear was to be found in Welsh's well-stocked drawers. My mind wandered momentarily in the realm of underwear until it edged back to football raiment.

Linus hadn't noticed Binney at all. His attention had been taken and deposited weightily elsewhere. If I transmitted the word *Binney* to him in its singularity, just *Binney* all alone, perhaps in a whisper, he would surely crack up in laughter as he would also if I mentioned the word *trunks*. *Binney*, all alone, was sufficient, as sufficient as *trunks*. *Binney* and *trunks* might have been too much. I had it under control in my own head, carefully keeping all those explosive associations under a veil of serious thought, but Linus was not so much in control, and serious thoughts were few and far between in his head. I was tempted though. and it was hard to resist. I had this small power over Linus, and it felt good to watch the effect as I released an idea. I could feed him words that moved around in his mind, moved him this happy way and that.

The Binney duo disappeared into a changing room with ma Binney, holding a fat armful of Black's merchandise. It was going to be a long morning for young Binney with all that trying on, with his old ma twisting and tugging him this way and that in the new clothes, telling him to straighten up, to make sure of a complete and sure fit. That would make Harry Black's fat face shine. A woman with a haystack of clothes heading for the changing rooms.

Harry Black wasn't honest. He wasn't Harry Honesty. He tried to get away with duping dopey people, and that was dishonest. And that he did well and often, as there was a big vicar's surplus of dopey people. I didn't want him to think I was a dopey person. He slipped over to me like a fat slug, his slimy sales pitches lingering in the air behind him like silvery slug tracks. He handed me a shirt which he took off the rack on the ceiling with a long pole with a brassy hook on it. How did he know I had my eye on that shirt. I wasn't even sure myself. He must have, at some point, tracked my line of vision. He had great peripheral vision to add to that devilish divining mind.

Take it in hand young fella. It's top quality stuff. Feel it. Inspect it. Put it on, it looks just your size, he said. It had a little hole in it; I saw it immediately, right in the middle at the front, almost covered by his Havana cigar of a thumb. It was a pin prick size of a hole but a hole nevertheless. A fault. And I saw it. Immediately. I took it in hand. I brought it closer to my eye to make sure and then placed a finger over it. I could feel it and see it, but the feeling of it was more powerful. Like when I felt the hole in my trouser pocket. The mother always said that a hole would just grow bigger unless it was mended properly, and if there was a hole left unmended, a finger would find its way into it eventually and find it irresistible not to fiddle with it until it got bigger and bigger. *Holes don't get smaller by themselves,* she said. It was true enough. And stupid enough. Experience confirmed it. The truth and stupidity of it. I remembered finding holes in clothes with a finger and then making the holes bigger by boring my digit into it. I could not help it. But they never got smaller. Black, even with his divining mind, didn't realise that I had seen or felt the hole.

Are you sure it's OK? I said to Black.

Of course I am sure, Black blasted back.

Is it perfect? I said, *Like you said.*

Of course it is. All my stuff is premium quality. And perfect for you. Are you not sure about my honesty? Am I a liar? He was quick to take this tone.

I said that I just wanted to know it was all OK. That's all. From his mouth. For my money I wanted it to be all OK. I didn't want to pay for a hole.

Are you questioning my honesty? he repeated. *Do you think I am a dishonest soul?* It was in a deep voice out of the depths of his fat neck somewhere, from high above me as he withdrew to a straightening-up, in order to give over godlike authority. It was one of his techniques to diminish the denial power of the buyer.

No, no, but do you know it for sure that it is OK for quality?

He told me he never makes mistakes, and everything in his shop is perfect, and that is why people buy the things he sells and why they come back again and again. I asked, did he inspect everything and was he absolutely sure everything in his shop was perfect? He said he did and he was.

In that case, I said to him, *I do question your honesty.* Did I actually say that? I might have. Sometimes I think I did and sometimes not. How are we to know? Why is my memory so weak? I know that I thought it, at the very least, just as I am thinking it now, in *that* way, and I am sure that he saw that I thought it. I just cannot picture myself actually saying it. Is it a fact that I said it?

Black hadn't yet opened his big salesman's mouth, the mouth that declared and set forth the ideas that made people buy, but I had the measure of him. Having the measure of someone is a grand feeling. Black always had the measure of people. With his tape measure and his mind measure, he sized them up and made them smaller. Nobody was their proper size in the presence of Harry Black.

Harry Black was a real creature of the surface and therefore a bad egg, but he disguised his badness with his friendly selling act. I would have found it less of a problem to kill Harry Black than a slug, which I hated more than most things. I had a nightmare of sleeping in a bed full of slugs and then another nightmare of waking up to find limpets in the bed. I called out that there were limpets in the bed, and my brother Rob leapt up from his bed, out of a deep sleep, demanding to know exactly where they were. The idea of killing Harry Black was an idea that I never had then in any distinct way, but I have now. I should have had it then. Killing insects is a problem for me, but the idea of killing a bad human being is not. Maybe because we humans are in the same game as each other and insects are not. There's no cheating with insects.

In Harry Black's big surface shadow, I offered up to his possession his football shirt with the hole. My finger covered the hole, but as I released it partly into his possession, my finger uncovered the hole and held its position for a split second, as if to make the fault more apparent. I felt warm in the head area. My brow burst forth with beads of sweat. My finger tips seemed to pulsate. My extremities in fact. Harry Black looked at me, not the hole. He didn't want the shirt back. It was still in my outstretched hand, demonstrating the hole, the whole hole and nothing but the hole. But, he didn't want to have it back in his possession; he wanted it to stay in mine. He wanted an act of transfer with money passing into his possession, and a piece of formed cloth out of it. Not merely the transfer of an object though, but of power, his power over someone else. I wanted to transfer my frustration into an act. What sort of act?

I wanted to kill him. Rub him out. Remove existence from his essence and for his essence to fade away. Such was the hate for him that filled me at that moment. I wanted his fat, sweaty body dead and gone. I wanted his enterprise dead. I wanted to be the one to end it. If only I had the means. I had the will, the true idea. It was born in me then and made me into a killer. This was not a sudden, newly born idea. I realised hate was in me already.

Hate, that was it. Accumulated hate. Hate and hurt. Hate, a pain accompanied by the idea of an external cause. If I hurt enough, I would be hating enough, and if I could think enough, I could see the source of the hurt and hate. Hurt, a transition from power to weakness, from a state of some healthy equilibrium to a state of doubt as to one's adequate occupancy of one's own being. Removing the source of doubt would remove the hate and the hurt. Thinking was good enough to know the source but was it good enough to dispose of it? Was it to be an idealist or a materialist matter? Black was a large amount of matter which occupied a large amount of space, but wasn't he also just a big idea? Uncertainty was certainly prevailing. A future uncertainty. A near future uncertainty that was almost present.

I took a look down there at my feet. Don't know why, but there's a reason for everything. There's a sense in why one thing follows another. Not necessarily like one ball striking another and so on, more like one idea fitting into a particular set of ideas. Like this. A concept bearing its weight on another. There they were, my black scuffed, weighty, winkle pickers, on scuffed solid wooden floors. Solid heels so noisy in movement. I would have to walk to the exit

door in concealing quietness of step. Impossible with these shoes.
I would pound to the exit away from Harry Black and without
a purchase in my hand and without my fiver in his fat money-
grabbing hand. *Trust in the Lord,* came to me. *Wait patiently for
him.* Is that appropriate? God save me from Harry Black. Make me
strong against this fat unrepentant sinner. This money -grabbing,
pull-the-wool-and-any-material-over-the-eyes reprobate. Why are
there so many rich sinners? *Wait patiently for him.* Too much of
that in my denomination. Wait for the Lord to answer prayer.
Wait for the second coming. Wait, wait, wait. Too much waiting.
They kept saying it was going to be soon and the waiting will be
over. All the signs were there. The signs and the wonders. Wars
and rumours of wars and all that. They are still saying it. They
were saying it two thousand years ago. How much waiting can a
person expect to do? What sort of game is it? The faith game, they
say. If you can't wait in faith, you are lost. It should end now with
me in this predicament.

I couldn't wait to leave the shop, but I couldn't leave the shop
just like that. Obligation was a confining factor. Any shop owner
worth his salt would have you feeling a nasty breed of guilt if you
walked into his shop and then walked straight out. Or even if you
didn't spend a reasonable time browsing.

Tension. Strain. I felt it all in a tight bottom. The hole. That
hole. Cramping up. All my tension locked up down there. Finger in
the other hole picking, picking. Taking a single step locked it all up
even tighter, and the buttocks came into play. Drawn in. Tightly.
Awful pain. They trapped the trunks in there. The word *trunks*
wasn't quite as funny anymore when I thought it. The mother
bought them here in Black's. Trunks called out to be bought. Or
across the road in Welsh's or Stott's emporium. Depended on the
feel. And the notion of where they were going. I simply couldn't
wait. I aimed ahead to the exit. Just an aim initially, and I was
pretty good at aiming. With my bow and arrows, and darts, and a
football on somebody's back door. I could also move like a panther,
jumping and weaving through tight spaces.

Two yapping women stood at the door blocking it. Yap, yap,
yap, they yap. There was a minimal gap between the yaps. Clits chit

chatting across the threshold. Searching a rail of stuff on either side with expert hanger-shifting hands whilst they gossiped. We shoved past them on the way in, as if they weren't there. They were there for the day. Fixtures. Fitting fixtures. One woman reeked of badness. Macgillycuddy's reeks again! You'd get sweaty climbing a reek, but she didn't look as if she'd been up a reek. From her a sweaty sort of scent was on offer to the nostrils. The other hag smelled of sweet perfume, and she was all done up on the face like a big film star, a look that pulled my attention firmly towards her. Black framed eyes and big red lips, a neat nest of high hair way above me, and gorgeous, shiny, soft, smooth clothes right there before me.

To get out, I'd have to push through them, but I didn't want my nose in the sweaty smell or in that confined area where the stinking scent entered me, so I chose to push past with my nose towards the sweet woman with all the softness. Linus was close behind, almost up the back of my shirt. In the process of passing the women, Linus, in his mad undeviating dash, shunted me into the sweet woman face first, and my nose was wrapped in sheaves of cool undulating satin. Folds and folds. I found myself in wondrous, womanly wolds, where many a sinful sheep has grazed. Wolds rhymes with folds, and what are wolds but folds in the land, and, if you know how wolds seem to go on forever, you'll know that I had landed in her endless acreage. Her woldy folds were thick like treacle. Not at all flimsy. My little face was gobbled up and smothered by smoothness. There was excitement in the smothering. Oh sense of sense! Lord of holy hosts! Beelzebub and his arch demons! My mouth was immediately full of nonsense. The hallucinations of suffocation. The foundations of the world did shift and shake. The march of monumental moments gathered momentum and was upon me. Something which didn't belong announced itself as extension and idea. A memorial, a shrine. Hip, hip hooray! On her wide hips rested my protective palms, one on each powerful, heaving, resisting hip bone, there to halt my forward motion, preventing me falling fully, face-first into her skirts.

I pressed gently in order not to be known by her as a dirty toucher. I touched a woman once in a crowd. Quite by accident, my hand raised and grazed her buttocks. *Fuck off you wee pervert,* she told me. Now, face forward, eyes pulled to focus in on pale blue hills. Bearing down on me, pressed a weight, the heavy focused vision of an unknown country. I felt faint and weak, in the head and in the eyes, in the stomach and legs, but not powerless. Something within me was unfurling, unfolding, being set free.

Even the youth shall faint and be weary, the young men shall utterly fall but He giveth power to the faint, so that they shall mount up with wings as eagles, they shall run and not be weary, they shall walk and not faint.

I felt faint with the idea before me, which said, *Prepare ye the way,* and the way was a source of strength. I was in my world, but there was a horizon in view, not far off, that opened up a new order with new words and new acts. It was the eternal now sunk deep into temporal flux. It was not that I didn't want it to end; it just felt, quite mysteriously, out of the world of beginnings and endings. What does eternity do with time? It gobbles it up. Just as time gobbles us all up. All without exception and, as if we never had in the first place. But it also gives us the now; it isolates it among all that is slipping beyond us into a vast bottomless pit, a pit we constantly peer into in the dim hope of pulling something out of it. That's the dream we live in, if we live for memory. Eternity is our salvation in the ever present. Was this God speaking to me? It sounded like it, but it also didn't. At least the God I knew. New gods, however, would become familiar as experience and knowledge grew.

This little episode routed my idea of women in a particular direction, confirmed to me by the mounting desire to know as many as I could in intimacy, without ever having to commit to one only. I began to see them everywhere. When one had gone, another appeared, replacing the previous as if by eternal decree. I fancied them all with some mysterious fancy. The things that had unfolded. Something definite about them took my fancy, took it and sometimes even held it against me.

Even though Linus didn't see the woldy worldly world of the unknown country that transfixed me in Black's womanly establishment, he lived for the significant moment, his own moment, his very own eternal now. But, he didn't feel my now, the immediate pleasurable pressure, he didn't suck in the soft breeze of a breath that came from deep inside that womanly inner world. He went his way, the way his mind led him. For that *was* him. His definite him. His endeavour was in some other direction, and it seemed a fine direction, serving him well.

I felt the still-folded fiver in my pocket, and out of eternity, I leapt into the world of things, out of Black's shop and into the streaming street just behind Linus.

Linus turned to me and issued forth his very own desire to kill Harry Black. To my *why*, he said that he hated his fatness. His inconsiderate fatness. He said he was fat because he was inconsiderate to his own being and then, as a result of that neglect, he treated everything else with that negligence.

It makes you shake with anger. Raging inside. Fatness really is really aggravating, he said

How would you do it then? I said.

Do what?

Kill the fatty calf? The big black bull.

Don't know, haven't really thought that far. Starve him, I suppose. Kidnap him and put him in a wee room and starve him. Tease him to death with food he cannot eat. Slow poison him with poisoned food, or cat food for a laugh, so he can eat until he realises he is dying from it. Carve him up and feed him his own fat.

It's even more annoying to think of him in his underwear, I said. *Standing there with his big belly heaving over his slacking knicker elastic. Knickers from his very own drawers. Admiring his fat self in the mirror thinking he looks lovely. Thinking he looks lovely to the women in his shop. To that sweet-scented woman with the satin folds.* At the mention of it, I felt an immediate and powerful sense of jealousy surging through me and then rage. I felt like killing Black myself at that moment. Madly strangling the life out of him. Not keeping him in a wee room to starve. That was too slow. Hitting him on the back of his annoying skull with the flat of a spade or planting a weighty hatchet in his greasy inconsiderate bop. I couldn't cope with the idea that the satin blouse woman gravitated about in Black's orbit. They were beings together but shouldn't have been by nature.

Linus and I were beings together in the street, a natural pair, delivering, with powerful mutual intuition, our frustrations to one another. Seemingly out of nowhere. It wasn't really there before. It was serious. It was in earnest. Something had to be done. And when it was done, they would be asking, *Who did this? Why was this done?* Then they would look for motive, and they would never find a motive that was to do with hatred of inconsiderate fatness.

*

Something shited out of a brown Belfast bog was before us just down the street from Harry Black's. The bloated body of bloatboy Tanner, bouncing along toward us in his steady, unwavering state of supplication. The hate we had for him ran through us like a powerful laxative. I could see it in Linus and felt it immediately in my bowels. It was just as if he'd followed us because he didn't seem too surprised to see us. He gravitated to us as if by a natural law. The natural law of bloated shite, attaching itself parasite fashion, to free fast flowers in a one way slow speed idler. A weakling who could only become strong by attaching and moving in another's motion, slowing down others instead of speeding himself up. a girlie boy who would become a womanly man, a whiner, a yapper, a two-faced Janus bitcher. There was one thought between Linus and me. He should be shoved into the same deep hole as Harry Black. It was deadly to be alone with him, critical if you yourself were with him in his house with his parents. He would humiliate you in fast fashion.

Spell gargoyle, he'd blurt out. He was a shitty show off in front of his meek teacher parents. Rather than have a go and get it wrong, you just had to say quietly that you didn't know or that you knew but didn't want to spell it because he didn't know and wanted you to tell him. Then he would shout out the spelling having one eye on his parent's pleased expressions and the other on you, his miserable victim.

No one who knew him would shed a tear if he was no longer here, except those who always shed tears over people they never really knew, even if his baldy, doting da mourned him. There was a boy who disappeared from our street and was never seen again. It was in the papers. Him smiling at us all. Everyone said what a lovely boy he was. But they didn't know him. We did. He was a little shite and whoever removed him had done the world a good turn.

Just as we were considering how best to remove Tanner, in the immediate, not the terminal sense, he displayed in the form of a dance the sudden need to depart. His knees rubbed together, and he stamped his feet. His hands went deep into his pockets, squeezing down on his bounteous thighs. He bent slightly forward and shivered. When he spoke, he held his breath, his tight body constricting the words. His face tightened up in a grotesque red grimace, then loosened, then strained again. Clear signs of a full-to-bursting bladder. He always did that. He always waited. Then ran off somewhere for a powerful pish.

He's a nothing, said Linus. *A nothing.*

No, I think he is a something, for how can a thing like him be nothing? I said, *what gets on your goat is the something that he is.*

I mean he's nothing definite, said Linus.

No, he's something definite. Definitely something. That's what I hate about him. You can't hate something that's not definite.

Nor can you love it.

Thinking of Fatty Tanner in this way put Linus in mind of Plain Anne Barnett. We called her Plain Anne because she was *just there*, nothing definite. *She's just there,* we said when we thought of her, because that seemed just right, at least in words. If you fancied a girl, it had to be for something definite. But Anne was nothing definite in her features, and we wondered if anyone could ever fancy her if she wasn't definite, wasn't pretty nor ugly.

Tanner would fancy her, Linus said. *So you can love something that's not definite.*

No, he wouldn't fancy her. He would just be left with her. That's different. That's not fancying someone really. In any case, we are talking about a useless shite like Tanner, and he doesn't count. I'm talking about someone with a decent appreciation of looks.

But there is more to a person than their looks, said Linus.

That's true, I said. *And Anne is probably nice in other ways. Maybe*

it is concealed and has to be brought out of its hiding place. Or maybe
the looks can change according to some other inner quality.
    What do you mean?
    I haven't a clue.
    We headed in his direction as we were going in that direction and
almost forgot about Leo's. Leo's gents outfitters was a dangerous
place to forget. Leo sensed excess money off a person, or just
money, and stood in the street outside his shop to snatch them by
their weak wills and snare them with his irresistible outfitter offers.
Before they knew it, they were in there facing one of his mirrors,
wearing one of his jackets or suits. Leo wouldn't have wanted us,
but I wasn't in the form to take any chances with my fiver, and I
thought he would surely know that I had it. We quickened our
pace, but as we passed him, he had someone else in his sights. Yet,
with his powerful retailing sense, he marked me with a side glance,
perhaps for future reference. I didn't like that idea, being in his
head, in his future plans. Apart from the disturbing occupancy of
the idea of me in his head, it meant I could never walk down that
street in peace.
    That's what life was becoming the older you got. People became
obstacles to a peaceful walk. You tried to avoid them and, in doing
so, took yourself on a detour. Worry. You woke up thinking about
the awkward things ahead. Inferiority. Hatred of the encounter
with superiority. There were clever boys and handsome boys and
cheeky boys that shouted at you their injurious insults that often
hit the target.

CHAPTER 15

thought of what they were all doing at the heart of things at home. The mother and the father in a state of holy war, the silent, cold war after the usual Friday night dialectic of stupidity. Hostilities, almost to blows but not quite. The pay packet at the centre of the storm, which was the norm. It was the very eye. Who got what and who spent what and who got the upper hand in the argument. Who got humiliated. Saturday morning always dawned with a virulent violence still in the air, the consequence of the night before, with money to figure big in the coming day. Where Linus and I were standing, they would be soon enough and more arguments and fights would erupt with the spending of money.

To say I am not a clear thinker does not mean that I am not a deep thinker. Perhaps it is the contrary. Expression coming before understanding. The easy diversions—just like this one—are the ways in which I seem to dig deeper, for they are circulations, spiralling epicycles of the main area at issue, what is really paramount in my mind. Eventually, they wear the ground down around it and make it collapse into the hole, or the whole, of some meaning.

In Ulster the simple naming of things was important, it made things simple, like the mother named things and re-named them, and you had to have a name so people knew who and what you were attached to, but I never seemed to see simple things. I saw names but there were other games besides names.

It has always been the same. I read a book, and it takes me ages to complete it, if indeed I ever finish it. Finishing is not the object. I sometimes stop at a point and resolve not to go on. I can come back, even if it is years later. Something prompts me to move on. I re-read sentences over and over again. Sometimes they mean something directly or are a sign for something else. The sign is often more important. It points to where my mind really is, or should be. There are books all over the place with bookmarks in pages at various stages, where a halt has been called on reading. I go back and read a page or two and then there I go, off into another imaginative diversion. It's leaping back to life, that's what it is. Out of the still page, plunging into the raging movements of nature. The real book is the book of life. My life is the sum of such deviations, the elementary impulse never to be still.

It is the same words spoken, when someone talks to me. I fix my attention on a certain set of words and stop listening to anything else that's coming my way, though my face carries on making appropriate expressions of phoney understanding. It's intensional. That's become a bit of a craft. Craftily operating at speed on a number of different levels. It's a revelation of a way ahead.

Jackie McMaster insisted you paid heed to everything he said. He insisted on examining your face for any sign of mental flight. His beady eyes scrutinised you like a cybernaut scanner. He wouldn't let you look away, for if you did, he grabbed your chin and turned your gaze back towards his lips. He made you pay heed. It had tremendous annoyance value, and that is why McMaster was not always made welcome.

He also habitually rubbed his runny nose on his woollen sleeve and kept his sleeve pulled over the inside of his hand in order to make the habit more convenient and a little more secretive. If you tried it, you'd see. But it could never hide what he did. At the precise moment he rubbed it, his face fled to the fortune of habit, his eyebrows leapt up into his wrinkled forehead and his right cheek twitched. Guaranteed! The best you could say for it was that it made him look harmless and innocent. Which he was. Blood sometimes trickled down his nose with the rest of the heady brew, and he just rubbed that off too without ever being concerned. The rest of us did look concerned, but after the first time, we didn't bother to say anything. We just thought of blood oozing into the watery, elastic snatter and shivered with disgust. You never wanted to wrestle McMaster for fear of his bloody snatter rubbing into your face or somewhere where it would be felt as cold and wet later on. Nobody had the disposition of mind to tell him to fuck off, for he was a good lad.

I treated general experience in a contemplative fashion. I marked it in a similar way, in wandering thought. Here I was with my crime, the money being central, and my mind drifted back to the house where money was the source of all discord. I needed to concentrate on the matter in hand, but the diversions were not entirely irrelevant. They were ways in which my mind sought to resolve internal questioning of actions and motives, the very things which drive us along as moral or immoral beings.

Linus said something that just swept, without resistance, into my hearing ear. He said he fancied some sweets. That must have been something I wanted to listen to. I heard it loud and clear. Sweets were important. It broke my stiff concentration. Changed my direction to a less confined attention. He felt the loose change he had in an odd little purse on his belt, shook it about and then took it out to look at it. There were a lot of old coppers and a thrupenny bit occupying a considerable degree of space in it. He rattled it again and smiled like a baby with a rattle.

Doesn't your big door key that I'm holding for you fit into that purse of yours? I asked. In the short time that it was thought about, this heavy metal object in my back pocket obliterated every other notion, and played fast and loose with my levels of irritability.

It doesn't fit, he said with an unmistakable certitude that brought the subject to a swift close in terms of conversation. In my mind, it continued for a short while, with the thought that it may, with its weight, burrow itself a hole in my jeans pocket, aided by my leg movements, and deposit its indisputable coldness on my thigh somewhere.

Linus said that he fancied some Raspberry Ruffles. These were the very sweets that once nearly had him thrown out of the public library. The wrappers are extremely rattly, a species of stiff cellophane, and the more you try to unwrap them quietly, in a measured manner, the more noise they make. *That's because you try to do it slowly*, I said at the time. *If you do it fast the noise is less, it's a swift, slippy swish of a sound, and nobody will hardly notice it. It makes a lot more noise for a split second*, he said. *Daft*, I said, *the less time the less noise. No time no noise.* So, he tried to do it fast in the city library reference section, and the sweet shot out of the wrapper like a cannonball and over the big table where all the shooshing old men were sitting. It started them shooshing in the direction of the brown missile. It reminded me of the bouncing bomb in the film *The Dam Busters.* It made me think of them as Barnes Wallis sweets. I thought of it smashing into one of the old shoosher's teeth and smashing them to bits in his greasy gub, like the bouncing bomb did to the bricks of the Eder Dam in World War II.

At the side of the library table, Linus grieved after the swiftly disappearing bouncing sweet. They are big sweets, and you don't get many in a quarter pound. Only about five or six. He would never get this one back. He tried in vain to look for it as he passed the table on the way out. In a casual sort of way. But only a token look for he couldn't get down on his knees or crawl under the table in such a place as a library. And everything around seemed to be chocolate brown, the tables, the floor, the chairs. Even in his token attempts at a search, the men returned to him an intensively dirty glance, and there were regimented, silent shooshes on their lips ready to depart towards Linus if any noise departed from his wee being.

The shoosh to silence was a powerful weapon. How could anybody stand all that silence for so long? It was like a graveyard. The old shooshing men were not far from that fate. Church wasn't even that quiet though, it was like church because you were always shooshed to be quiet. Unless you said *praise the Lord* or something appropriate. In the library, a wee urchin couldn't say shoosh without an old shoosher saying shoosh to that. But, in church it took courage to make a loud religious declaration. And it wouldn't sound right coming out of a child's mouth. The believers would accuse you of making fun of the Lord. Only with the rank of adult could you say it. I used to mumble the various utterances to practice, then gradually build up the volume. But what made you an adult? There was a certain age that you could start saying *Praise the Lord* and *Hallelujah* and *Amen* and *Glory to God,* but there was no definite age given. Not like smoking or drinking, though everybody smoked and drank before that age, and some also said the things in church and got away with it. Unless you sniggered afterwards and then you got a stern look. Sniggering was for churches and libraries. You always saw something very funny there and sniggering was the only reaction, but it was painful to keep sniggering without bursting into a full blooded bawl of a laugh. Sniggering seemed to inspire you to think of a thing in ever funnier ways. It inspired illumination. We only went to libraries to mess about. The city library was full of echoing corridors of wood and marble. There was a lift. The grand City Hall was better. You could get lost in there. We played hide and seek and were chased around by the porters. We slid and skated on the shiny marble floors as if they were ice.

But Raspberry Ruffles were tasty and mouth-watering. Crisp dark chocolate with moist raspberry coconut inside. The chocolate cracked on the first bite. My mouth craved that. My stomach was empty and desirous of such a sweet and satisfying load. It wanted to expand. I felt my trousers loosening at the waist, and my belt required tightening. That didn't seem to stop the trousers slipping. That meant the arse in them was lowering as well. I didn't want to be a Les Buttocks. The idea of it made me hoist up my pants and tighten my belt another notch. I didn't want to be fat either, like Turner, just a little bit more rounded, so clothes would fit snugly and not hang off like the unfed Africans had them.

If you had a quarter-pound of Raspberry Ruffles in Africa, you'd be in serious danger of being attacked. It occurred to me that it was not only in Africa that this would happen, in the very streets where we stood, there were individuals who'd kill for some Raspberry Ruffles. But they did it for badness, whereas the Africans did it out of need. Need was a serious matter. Nothing was really needed in Belfast the way it was in Africa, so they would have eaten the sweets differently to us. However, even after the Africans had eaten them out of need, they would have kept the wrapping paper just like us, because when you looked through it, everything was rosy red, and Africans were said to like novelties like that. We always looked through a Raspberry Ruffle wrapping paper. Up to the sky, up against somebody's face. Firearms and Tackle had that yellow paper inside the shop window. Chemists also always had a big see through sheet of orangey yellow paper in their windows that made everything in the window orangey yellow in just the same way that Raspberry Ruffles paper made everything reddish. It wasn't really like paper. Cellophane it was called, but when it was wrapped around a sweetie we called it paper. A sweetie paper. Anything that wrapped a sweet was a piece of paper.

The paper in my pocket was no ordinary paper either. Paper money was a special type of paper. Did I take it out of badness? Or was I like the African? I needed it. I did need it. I was more like an African than a Belfast bad boy just doing things out of badness. I could feel the sharp folded edge of the fiver pricking my leg. A pleasant prick. Like a pin gently pressing on the skin with sufficient pressure to just about make you aware of the body under pressure. Occasionally I slipped my fingers into my pocket to feel it. Between my forefinger and thumb, I rubbed it to feel the pleasant effect of the raised parts. Money was lovely. Notes especially. Something more than just an exchangeable item. In the house, I had a Chinese note that I had found in the street. Crumpled up in a ball and looking like rubbish. I smoothed it out and placed them in the middle of a big book. I took it out from time to time, when I was bored, just to look at it. Not just looking at it but studying it. Its colour. Its texture. The print and the pictures. Chinese print made no sense but the pictures did. An arrogant Chinaman looked at me from out of it. Like the way a doctor looks at you. Down his nose and through the bottom of his glasses. The Chinaman was no doctor though. He had grand robes and looked like a warrior. He was looking down on his slaves. I felt I was looking up at him like a slave. Even when I was above him it was as though he was still looking down on me. He looked cruel and savage. I thought it must be worth something, but I wanted to preserve it. Kaiser's, the antique shop on the Dublin Road, had a list in his window that told you which notes and coins were valuable. Most of them were

British though. Every time I got change, I frantically looked to see if I had a valuable one. I thought I had one quite a few times. It was always a near thing. I had a 1937 thrupenny bit once that I thought was valuable, and I ran like hell down to see the list but it was a 1937 penny that he wanted. Close, I thought. But it wasn't close at all. I had a penny of almost every date at one time or another except a 1937 penny. Some pennies and thrupenny bits were worth about fifty quid. How was that? It made me wonder but not all the time, for wondering all the time would get you nowhere.

Let's have a look at your change, I said to Linus. *Before you spend it on sweets. You should always look at your change.*

What for?

To see if it's valuable.

We went through every one we had. Nothing was ever valuable. Just dirty. Dirty and disappointing. I told Linus the reason for my curiosity because he was a friend. I knew he would share the money if we found something. I thought I would deserve a good share as I had the knowledge. He only had the coin but lacked the knowledge. But I never told anyone else about valuable coins. Like the father and the mother. I always asked to look through their change without telling them what for. I dreamed of coming across one of those valuable coins. Some boy at school told me that some pound notes had different serial numbers on them, the one on the front different from the one on the back; that made them very valuable. It was a printing mistake he said, but they were worth a fortune. The mother and the father never let me near note money to check it. It occurred to me that I hadn't checked the note in my pocket. So I removed it and unfolded it. I took a look at the number on the left hand corner then turned the note over. I leapt inside. The number was different. I turned the note back over. No it wasn't, it was the same. The very same. I turned it over. Was it? Was it the same? Yes. *Shite! Shite! Shite!* I shouted. The long number was hard to compare.

That's a great fiver that, said Linus. *It must be worth more than a fiver. More than yesterday even.*

What! What do you mean?

People say that things get more valuable the older they get. Everything is getting more valuable.

It's probably getting less valuable because people are always putting prices up and the fiver remains the same.

He was speaking in ways that made me drift away from him. It made me feel tired. Heavy. In the busy, busying street, a mountain of things came to me and sat on my mind as Linus rabbited on. Noises that would normally wake you were sending me into a dream. Linus's idea of the value of things was too difficult to think about in this state of mind. It was drowned by a whole lot of other things. His lips were still moving, but I only heard the odd word or part of a word. I wouldn't get away with this sort of thing with McMaster. Did Linus see me drifting? I tried to come back from time to time, but it was like being on the settee late at night trying to watch a film, fighting back the sneaky trespassing sleep.

The sleepy idea I had in front of Linus was that of the father taking somebody's car door off whilst he drove down a narrow street looking for a parking space. The door of a parked car opened when the father was looking on the other side of the street. I think he saw a space, and he went mad on the accelerator to get it before anyone else. The mother screamed when she saw the door swing open. My brother Rob and I heard the thud, and the scraping and scratching sound of a large amount of sliding metal. There was an argument in the street. The man with no door said the father wasn't looking, and the father said the same of him. They were both right, but the father was righter as he couldn't possibly know if a door was going to open, but the other man should have seen our car. The father said to him, *Am I supposed to look inside every car to see if someone was going to open their door?* That was mad. Everybody would be crashing all over the place. He was good at arguing.

On a Saturday, as the day got older, there were always arguments in the streets of the city. Everybody was tired with the shopping. They all set off happy but went back home in a foul mood. They didn't get what they wanted, so they went in a huff. When you were in a huff, you always saw something to argue about. There were some terrible fights. Shouting and swearing in the street. *All big talk,* said the father. Ulster was full of big talkers. Ulster was always in a big huff. No one got what they wanted. That's why there was always disagreement and arguments on the news.

Linus wasn't on the whole a big talker nor a big shouter, and he rarely exhibited huff behaviour. Not much anyway. He was sometimes in a quiet mood that you could not identify specifically as a huff. He rarely said he was good at anything, so I assumed he wasn't. I knew he wasn't good at football, and despite his outrageous claims on rare occasions about exploits on the football field, and his clumsy cheating at games, there wasn't much else I thought he could be good at. Except as a friend. It's funny how you just started to think about someone in a different way all of a sudden and how it got complicated. As if you passed a point, and the way of thinking was different. The whole pattern changed.

When I was looking at Linus fiddling with his money, I saw his face in a different way entirely. It didn't look like Linus at all. Just that aspect wasn't Linus. His nose looked longer, and some other things about his features, his eyes, his lips and chin, they didn't look right. It frightened me for a second, like he was standing there dead frozen, just until he looked up, and he was Linus again. Maybe because his head was so still. I realised that whenever I saw him, when I recognised him, it was because he was always moving in familiar ways. He was never really still. I had a thought. If I saw him dead in a coffin I probably wouldn't know him. I'd say, *Who the hell is that? That's not Linus!* It wouldn't be him anyway, it would just be his lifeless body, and it's the life that you recognise as a person, not a still body. It's the smile in the eyes and all that. It's a regular pattern of motion and the mind behind it all showing through. I imagined being called to identify his dead body and saying, *That's not him and it is him*, and the police getting angry at that uncertainty. But I couldn't think of it in any other way in my imagination, so I got annoyed with it and stopped thinking it altogether.

We moseyed down to Patton's sweet shop to see what he had under his flat, glass counter. Old, bald, specky Patton and his flat, glass counter display. What a laugh! The mother called him Poker Face Patton due to his unsmiling countenance. All the sweets were down there under the glass. In rows of little containers. You had to point to what you wanted, and he slipped his arm in under the glass from his side of the counter. It was very low, so he had to bend down. He got really fed up if you chose lots of different things, and in between choices you stalled and had him crouching there waiting. And if he had bent to get something you had chosen and had placed his hand upon it, and you changed your mind, he'd express an explosive sigh. So you had to be sure what you wanted, but he hated waiting for that just as much. The pressure wasn't pleasant. So it was ideal to make up your mind well in advance. But no one ever did that. His poker face remained unaltered in its stiffness but his breathing became hurried. He sighed and made you feel guilty. He made you make a hasty choice. He had that counter made as a counter-pilfering device. The old open counter that tilted like a football stand invited theft. What made him so? I assumed his sadness. I conceived a world of sadness for him. He was lonely. There was nothing bright to cheer him up. There was only a miserable little existence in his miserable little shop, protecting his sweets in the glass counter from thieving young brats. He wasn't at all like Harry Black. He wanted you out of his shop, whereas Black wanted you into his. What would you want a shop for if you didn't have the patience?

Linus said he wanted two ounces of Raspberry Ruffles, and old Patton sighed. I said to Linus that two ounces was hardly anything, and he'd be better going for a quarter pound. *That's double your money,* he said, and I said it was double your sweets. Patton was weighing the sweets, and I was nudging Linus into action. I whispered to him to get four ounces. Patton was pouring the sweets into the wee white paper bag after weighing them, when I nudged Linus so hard he blurted out to Poker Face Patton that he wanted a quarter pound instead. Patton stopped his pouring and sighed that sigh of massive annoyance. The world stopped. Time stopped. Then back to movement and time in a seamless leap. I found that I had turned my back on Linus when he asked Patton for the extra two ounces. I had denied him. It was too painful to watch. I discovered myself looking at the door to the street, trying to find a substantial diversion. I heard the extra sweets being thrown into the scales and then poured into the paper bag. I heard Linus's money being transferred to the mechanical grabbers that were Patton's hands. Linus passed me and opened the door. I didn't want to be last out with Patton's crazy gaze staring into my back, so I tried to push past

Linus in the doorway. We both got stuck for a split second and then we tripped over each other onto the street. We looked in the bag to see how many sweets there were. Linus counted six. *Three each*, he said. *You'd only have got three if you'd only bought two ounces*, I said. He nodded and gave me three Raspberry Ruffles. I didn't want to take all three, so I offered him one back. He took it and said thanks. I didn't like the way he took it because there was barely any time between me offering it and him taking it, but I knew he loved Raspberry Ruffles better than me. I just didn't like him taking it so quickly, and I didn't like him for that short moment. And I didn't like that I didn't like him, so I tried to forget about it quickly.

We ate Raspberry Ruffles in different ways. I held mine in the wrapper and bit the chocolate off first. He stuffed two whole ruffles in at once. He said he loved to feel all the mouth space taken up with soggy coconut and chocolate. His mouth was so full at the beginning it wouldn't close. He had to hold his head back so that saliva wouldn't run down his chin, but his head gradually came back down to normal position when he got the mouth situation under control. When I had finished biting off the chocolate, I only had the deliciously sweet pink centre left. I bit little bits of it to make it last. I was nibbling delicately as Linus was frantically sucking and chewing. I tried to make him laugh so that he found great difficulty holding it all in his gob. He held his head back again to prevent the contents spilling out.

One time I said something really funny, and he spat all the stuff out all over me. Then he swore at me. I laughed out of control. I was going to say Les Buttocks to him just as he put both sweets into his mouth, but I didn't feel like it because I was still thinking a bit about not liking him. Not so much but there was something of it still there. Something annoying. I didn't feel like laughing. I remembered what I had said about plain Anne to Linus, *It's just that you can change your mind about somebody the more you get to know them.*

There is always something about someone that can make you change your mind about them. Always. And you always get to know someone more, so there is always something else to know that you didn't know before. And there is always something that will make someone change as time goes by. It's not what I like to think about because you then expect something to change. And the same applies to your own self, you might wake up one morning and discover you're not really you the way you were the day before. Not entirely you that is, because you'd have to be mainly you to recognise that you weren't. Something has changed that you don't like. Or you do something that doesn't seem to come entirely from you, but you keep it nevertheless and start being someone strange, alongside your own being. Until it becomes you and somehow you know it's you.

CHAPTER 16

Deviation. The sign posts were all around, not pointing to external directions but to places in my mind. The mother was a domestic servant and the father was a foreman labourer. She cleaned other people's houses as well as her own. She cleaned all day long. Even when she stopped the actual cleaning she still thought about cleaning. There was always with her an intention to clean, and each cleaning session was accompanied by an intense intension. The father loved his job. He skipped to work and trudged home. He was at home at work. He didn't talk about his work to the mother, but she talked nothing but her work to him. Though he talked to himself about work. I've heard him rehearsing something. Talking to himself but as if there was another person there. This drove the mother through the roof mad. After her work she yapped and yapped about nothing but work.

There was something about her work that was frightening as she turned into a raving lunatic when she talked about it. I sometimes accompanied the father to pick her up from work in the car. After school usually. In the summer it was a nice trip. To the mental hospital in the country. The windows were open in the car and the warm air rushed in. The brightness made you squint. From the start, the mother let the air rush out of her mouth and talked about all the work intrigue. She spoke without hardly taking a breath through her massively pliable mouth. There was a mountain of intrigue where she worked in the mental hospital, cleaning the mad people's rooms and changing their beds. She called the nurses and doctors dirty and filthy craters. She said that there's no one dirtier in the world than doctors and nurses. Even filthier than the mad people. She said that they in their higher than high manner expected her to clean up their mess after them. The father gave his considered opinion about all the goings on when he could find a space to speak, but she just rounded on him in a rage, detecting a defection from her cause. They were generally not sufficiently supportive of her, and she said he always defended them. He laughed—which itself ignited her wrath—and said he didn't, but that made things worse with her. He said he was only trying to understand the situation properly.

Understand! she shouted, *I'm telling you this is what happened.*

You have to tell me everything, he said.

He was a fair man. It agitated him to think she was on the verge of hating him, but he couldn't deny his natural inclination to be fair. He knew quite well in their own arguments that she was inclined to exaggeration and invention. That nervousness, that was his way, was expressed in a host of habits, most notably the fiddling with his tie. The tie fiddling involved ever increasing twisting, increased twisting directly proportional to increased irritability. The thumb and forefinger of his favoured right hand were the tools of fiddling, and they sought out every area in the upper tie, concentrating around the knot. The aim seemed to be to make the knot a perfect shape and for him to know that it was as neat as it could be. He felt and felt and fiddled and fiddled. That questioning and the fiddling turned her into rigid stone, cold silence. She gritted her dentures beyond the pounds per square inch safety limit for false teeth snapping. He continued to tie fiddle. He even freewheeled the car when he could, so he didn't have to use his fiddling hand to change gear. He said to me that he was saving petrol.

The silences were murder to stand. The silence of her and the fiddling of him. And the anger. When we got home, they never talked for the rest of the day and sometimes more. Sometimes as much as a week. She sometimes wouldn't even cook dinner

for him. We all ate dinner and he made his own. It wasn't very
comfortable when she talked to us about him. Something left me
in those situations. Something took flight. Or something withdrew.
Or something came to harness me. Something happened that set
something free to bind me.

I imagined Linus with us in the car or at the dinner table when
the mother was in a silent mood, and realised that I could never
bring him that close to our family life. What would he make of
such behaviour? I wished them departed. Departed from life. In
their tombs. Deep down within the earth, so I could bring Linus
home, and we could be free to play there. The mother would not
be there to sigh at the presence of dirty outsiders. She would not
be able to impress upon them her dissatisfaction with her life. The
mother called me her wee bird and diamond but I wasn't precious
to her. I wasn't a diamond or a bird. I didn't want to be precious to
them because they tried to rob me. She stole my pet tortoise and
threw it in the bin when I was at school. When I came home I asked
where it was, and she said it had died. She was cleaning and said
that it wasn't moving when she touched it. My little tortoise was
in the bin lorry while I was at school. Among all that rubbish. *He
wasn't dead, he was hibernating*, I said. She thought it was dirty and
should be where all the dirt was.

He can hibernate in the dirt, was what I thought she said in a low
voice. The bin was long gone and so too was the tortoise, dumped
into a mountain of garbage. He'd be trying to crawl out but his
pathetic little efforts would be without avail. I thought of his little
scaly legs trying to overcome the endless heaps of rubbish. I wanted
to steal something from them. The father was not to blame for
the mother, but he was to blame for letting her get away with her
behaviour, so I saw them both as a single problem.

When I mentioned Linus in the presence of the mother and
father, they looked at me with one of their funny looks, as if to
say, this Linus sounds too good to be true. That I didn't like. It's
no wonder they didn't have any friends. Friendship itself was a
dirty business and therefore a dirty word said with venom. When I
mentioned the word *friend,* the mother made a face that expressed
the essence of hate. *Aach, friends!* she said as if she was choking on

the idea. It was the mother who was the people hater. She assessed them on sight, and turned up her nose, and screwed her face up at most of them. She squeezed vicious words out of her mouth to express her distaste. She didn't like them near, in, or even just around the house. She constituted an unfriendly presence in her own constituency, created an air of hostility that made any friendly visit nerve wracking. She acted as a sentinel around her little queendom, guarding every possible area of invasion, moving from one outpost to the other to keep an eye. What was it she wanted to keep out? Within the domain itself, our movements were monitored. When we left a room, she entered it to assess the damage. She tidied and straightened every crease. The dust in the sunlight drove her into frenzied attacks on dirt and filth in general. She equated the dirt and filth with the outsiders, calling them filthy and dirty beings.

I didn't bring Linus to the house because I didn't want him to be contaminated by the atmosphere. They would spoil him for me. They may even drive him away completely, maybe to find a whole new cadre of friends. I wanted to bring him to my church though. That is where I felt most at home, especially with my emerging status as the backslider. At home with the contracting minds of the godly. The church came along in just good time, as did my strengthening sense of self, a compound to stiffen my mastery of circumstances. At church I felt my mind expanding.

Are we going back to your house later? said Linus with the residue of pink raspberry mush annoyingly on the corners of his lips.

Probably, I said. The thought of bringing Linus back to the house had a strange effect on my lower body, particularly my knees, which immediately felt weak, as did my shins which were usually strong and dependable. The weakness seemed to be moving south. Both leg parts behaved as though the recipients of a large and excessive pressure and weight. My stomach made noises due to the collisions of certain uncomfortable ideas, but I knew that my stomach was the principle vehicle of my emotions. Linus looked carefully at me, a clear sign that he did not like the indefiniteness of my *probably.* My indefiniteness, however, was definitely deliberate.

CHAPTER 17

Just down from Patton's sweet shop a crowd had gathered. A nosy crowd. Noisy with all their nosiness. Sniffing for signs. It's the sign of the times, they say. All on tiptoes, seeking reward for their inquisitiveness, straining at a controlled distance to see something. They had blocked the pavement so Linus and I would have to wait, and that was annoying. Even the road was being blocked by growing numbers of people spilling on to it. Crowds doing violence to a person's individual momentum was nothing less than frustrating. I was once carried post match by a crushing football crowd in a direction not to my inclination and deposited at some distance from the place that was my intended destination. And in enemy territory, a district brimming with aggressive characters. That is Belfast and its margins and territories. I found the whole experience of being leg-lynched was not in any way helpful to the suppression of fury.

This sort of disruption was becoming routine on a Saturday. The increasing regularity of the bomb scare had everyone on the street several times a day, spilling out of shops and offices, but the initial attraction of the possible presence of a bomb, like the one before us, was an indictment of a man's intelligence.

Nobody in the bomb scare was running away screaming for their lives. They all nosed in to see what the army and constabulary boys were doing. The more they were pushed back, the more they nosed

in. I wished the bomb would go off and blow the noses off their
daft faces. I said that to Linus, and he stiffened with laughter. We
thought of all the noses flying everywhere. And boozers running
away with noseless faces, their detached, bulbous, purple, senseless
snifters somewhere in the atmosphere. From where we stood, we
couldn't see anything, just the backs of overcoats and jackets, and
stupid looking hair.

The other new endeavour was that of men rooting about the city
streets, and indeed the province, shooting people they claimed were
standing in the way of them getting what they wanted. These men
were always in a bad mood, as they never got what they wanted.
The whole matter of names was important in this development,
a certain name was sufficient to have you on the run from the
gun. A personal name or a name that you were attached to as a
member. These dangerous circumstances may never have arisen
had names not existed. But a situation like that would be almost
unthinkable. Here as things stood, you had to think where to go
with your name, where your name was welcomed and where it
wasn't. Linus and I happened to live in an oasis of toleration, small
though it was, where all names were awarded nothing more than
their simplest denomination. A street or two away however, and all
things changed. It was necessary in the course of practical living to
traverse the city and move in and out of hostile districts. Looking
over your shoulder and being ready to run were fast becoming the
advisable mentality.

Uncle Patsy never adopted this mentality; he ran headlong into
the midst of the moody men.

In a predicament of no forward movement, Linus's attention
was drawn to some beer bottles resting on the kerb. We sometimes
brought empty beer bottles we found in back entries back to bars
to get the deposit money, but it was stinking in those places. We
weren't allowed into the pub but the entrance smell was enough to
make your insides convulse. But the pub men were always very nice.
Their smiles were evident through the dense smoke. Booze seemed to
have a good effect on some people. I wondered if the mother would
benefit from the frothy brew. Lots of people who hadn't drunk a
thing were just nasty to you for simply being there. *What are you*

doing there? they'd say in a nasty way. If you said *I'm doing nothing,* they would try to say something clever, but meaningless, that usually started with, *I'll give you.* Like, *I'll give you nothing!* The mother used to say when you were crying, *I'll give you something to cry for!* And there is a common saying, it is better to give than to receive, but adults did all the giving and the wanting to give. I never understood that saying anyway. It was confusing if attended to for very long.

I spent some idle time thinking about it. In an ideal world then, if by our giving we receive, there may be a group of people who are always receiving, and enjoying it, without ever giving, in which the real joy is said to consist. The logic becomes a little shaky when we consider that there have to be receivers in order for there to be givers. But if we are all encouraged to be givers there would be no receivers to give to. We would simply look ridiculous going about offering things to non-existent receivers.

Furthermore, if I am actually receiving (i.e. joy) when I am giving, I am not *really* giving at all. So, assuming that it is possible for us all to be givers (which it is not as these concepts must include one another) we would in fact all be receivers, which is in fact the reverse intention of the received wisdom, because we would all know beforehand that we were really giving in order to receive.

Boozers were a stinking breed though and were always giving in their taking. They gave off a powerful mixture of an aroma. No question about that. Like old Hughie the stinker. The drink stifled any endeavour to cleanliness. They just waltzed about in their layers of dirt, sniffing for the next drink. No place for the stinker sin in church. They would say you had the demon of dirt and pray for you to exorcise it, or just preach at you so much you got fed up with being dirty and changed your ways. Some people didn't wash or change their clothing at all, just came out to town in their festering raiment. Like the crowd before us, who stank in a seamless coalition. I asked Linus did he know the word raiment, and he said he didn't, but he didn't go to church, and that's where that sort of word was used. *In any case thou shalt deliver him the pledge again when the sun goeth down, that he may sleep in his raiment.* All the people in this crowd must have received the pledge to sleep in their raiment.

In the spirit of names, I called Raymond Barnett, Plain Anne's brother, Raiment Barnett, and every time I saw him coming out of his house opposite ours, I thought of him as Raiment. Raiment in his raiment. Linus loved it and laughed the Linus laugh. He threw his head forward and strained his neck to the limit and squeezed his breath through his tightened mouth. By throwing his head forward, he brought himself close to you, and I think that was the unconscious purpose. I always threw my head back, so was I trying to create a distance? His laugh sound was really a breath. His eyes were like a Chinaman's, all squinty with no sign of pupils. Just an eye line. In energetic laughter, tears would just sprout out of the lines and off his face as if propelled out under considerable pressure. The effort of squeezing out the laugh probably did it. It was a phenomenon, and I sometimes thought of it in his absence. Come to think of it, he did exactly the same thing with a smile. His smile was all that was his laugh, without the squeezed-out sound.

Les Buttocks and Raiment, Linus said, *what a pair they would be.* Linus continued to say raiment instead of clothes when he had the chance. *Hey, look at my fucking raiment!* he said once when I spilled some ice cream on his trousers. That was very funny.

In a monumental act of civility, the bombers always gave a warning so they wouldn't kill innocent folk. They had a secret word that they transmitted to the police when they phoned in their warning so the police knew to take it seriously. That was until some more serious bombers came along who weren't so nice about the whole thing. People said they were like animals and were mad. Why were they mad? Because they didn't play by the rules. I thought they must have their own rules, and we didn't play by their rules. Would they call us mad? Perhaps there were just lots of games with different rules. There was certainly one large game where most of the people took part, but there emerged a very small game where only a few knew what was going on. Eventually that small game became the large game.

The nicer bombers played by the rules that demanded that they only attempt to blow up policemen, soldiers and property, especially shops and offices. They put bombs under police cars, so they blew up when the car was started or the door opened. These booby trap bombs were becoming all the rage. Linus caught the phrase on the news and said that they were designed to blow up women's boobies. I swelled up and nearly bust my gut laughing. Soon enough a number of mad, untutored individuals came along in the form of a group and announced their name far and wide and even deep, said that their game was the only game in town and had to be played by everyone. If you didn't play then you would be playing no game at all. They attached their name to the game: the Provos. The Provos proved proficient, but they were anything but provisional. They soon became grandmasters and had the whole place in perpetual check for a lengthy period of time.

My cousins from a dangerous Fenian district swiftly submitted their particulars in application forms to the Provos, clearly stating their mad credentials, and said that their speciality was rooting out turncoats. They had me in their sights, the father had given us fair warning in his own capacity as a turncoat, which had named us all turncoats by proxy. Soon there was general madness, and you couldn't be what you used to be, just in name only.

You couldn't trust a soul, not even the constabulary men, who had their own problems. Being a policeman here was no life at all, a fool's game some said, yet there was no shortage of police recruits. Just a shortage of breath. Your home wasn't safe, your family wasn't safe. You couldn't relax for a single minute. You had to take handfuls of sleeping tablets, like the mother, just to get a night's sleep. Then, when you woke up, your first thought was, is this going to be the day? Is this the day you die? How will it be? A bullet to the head from a sniper, or being blown to bits? Every knock on the door is a cause for alarm, every stranger walking past the house. In the morning, look out the window. Anything suspicious before you leave? Scan the horizon. Out the door, stand there, look around. Check under the car. Turning the key to open the car door never failed to be nerve wracking. Waving goodbye to your family, knowing this could be the last time they see you.

But, it's good pay, said McMaster, the same McMaster who wanted to join the force when he was eighteen and who rubbed his snattery nose on his sleeve. I pictured him as a grown-up policeman rubbing his nose on the arm of his unadulterated RUC uniform. It made me shudder, and I had to look for another idea to get rid of it. I told him he wouldn't pass the medical test for the police, due to his sinus problem. Every time he ran fast or headed a ball, his nose started bleeding. It didn't worry him, because it stopped sooner or later, and he seemed OK. I couldn't actually believe McMaster could grow up. He was just a messer and couldn't take anything seriously. He made a joke out of everything. It was nice to be like that, but you couldn't be like that as a grownup.

People kept piling into the crowd from behind us. It was like at a football match. Just pushing, and shoving, and some people trying to climb over you. I had my hands in my pocket to protect my fiver. There was always some skiver around trying to take advantage of these situations. I told Linus to put his hands in his pockets. He reminded me that he didn't have pockets, and if he did he said that he wouldn't use them because he couldn't breathe if he had both of his hands in his pockets whilst being crushed by the crowd. It would be like being alive in a coffin under the ground. Your arms would be stuck down by your side, and you wouldn't be able to turn around. You wouldn't be able to raise yourself up at all, and the only thing you could do was panic. We didn't like to dwell on the coffin scenario for any length of time. A coffin was a dwelling for the dead. It was far too frightening on all thinking fronts. Linus said it was something to be reserved for only your worst enemy. We always said that if we were spies who were caught by our enemies and tortured for what we knew, we would sing like canaries if they threatened us with the coffin. Then we tried to think of the worst tortures possible. And the best torturers. The Spanish Inquisition was the best at torturing I said, you'd never hold out unless you were totally daft. *No, it was the Japanese*, said Linus. He told me that the Headmaster at school was a prisoner of the Japanese during the war, and they mercilessly ripped off his fingernails. And all the Japs stood around laughing. Everyone at school looked at the head's fingernails for solid proof of that claim, and even though the nails appeared normal, not gnarled or black, everyone swallowed the story whole and passed it on. Then the terrorists in Ireland started their business, and they knew a thing or two about torture. And so did the police.

Uncle Patsy had been tortured. He was a patsy Patsy, found under a South Belfast railway bridge with a black hood over his head. Lured there by loyalist lunatics who formed themselves into a gang to show they were as good at making a mess of people as the Provos. The father told us that he had to look at Uncle Patsy's dead face to make sure it was really him. It was him alright but also not him. It was his stiff body. His face was frozen at the point of most pain. There was terror and fear in his expression. It was beaten, and bruised, and swollen, and had great lumps of wood embedded in the flesh. There were tiny traces of blood from a hole in the temple. His eyes were bulging out from the sockets. His arms and hands were rigid in a pleading posture. The police said that the murderers had tortured him before shooting him. They had beaten him about the head with planks of wood and sections of discarded railway sleepers to put him to sleep. Uncle Patsy was a quiet man, a quiet sober man who couldn't keep his mouth shut whilst stotious with drink. A man who worshipped the father for his wisdom. He always came to our house to ask the father for advice. But when he went to the pub, he was a different man. He shouted and sang and got angry. He had upset some people in the pub with his songs, and rants, and temper. *Where's the peaceful man who came in*, they all asked. That's what did it for him. What is awful is that the father would carry forever in his head an idea of the dead, tortured Uncle Patsy. His very own brother. His wee brother, who he messed about with merrily as a kid in the narrow Market's streets.

I have an idea of it, but it's just not the same as actually having seen it. There is also the idea of Uncle Patsy being taken to his place of torture and execution, of him pleading for his life and receiving no mercy. No one saw that except his killers. I thought it all the time and especially at night, when darkness came, just like the night he was murdered. Darkness came to get Patsy. A dark night under a railway bridge. Into the dark tunnel they went. Then darker for Patsy under the black hood as the world disappeared to him. It was not something I liked to have in my mind, though I felt it was important to know it. So, I allowed it in, knowing that would be troublesome to rub out. The mother told the neighbours what happened in that Ulster manner that celebrated misfortune.

There was a lot of laughing and big talk among some in the crowd. They were not scared of bombs and being blown up. The police still kept pushing them back, but the mob just leaned back lazily into them. Somebody said the police wouldn't stand there if there was any danger. Then they all laughed as if they needed to laugh, or maybe they thought it was like being at a comedy show. I thought they were idiots, not because they didn't move when there was a chance they would be blown up, but because they all laughed like idiots with great gaping guffaws at things that weren't funny. What was funny was them, and their brainless faces, and their smelly lives, and their buck stupid animal nosiness, and their big talk. And they were in the way in an annoying way. Blocking our way to the sporting goods shop in Wellington Place where I wanted to spend my folded fiver. I suggested to Linus that we backtrack and cut through to Gt. Victoria Street. He said it was a nicer walk anyway and we walked off leaving them all to laugh and be blown up.

CHAPTER 18

We kept looking back over our shoulders at the buck stupid crowd for fear that we'd miss them all being exploded out of existence. We turned and walked backwards so we could see them until they drifted out of our sight. We didn't want to miss the moment. Then Linus put his arm around my shoulder as we stepped slowly backwards. That arm. It didn't feel right at all; it had a queer and uncertain effect on the body. His arm was not just lying across my shoulder in a lightly loose fashion, it fell heavily on it and gripped it. And his hand on the end of it at the far side engaged my upper arm like a hook, pressing me towards him. I think I was laughing, in some curious and nervous discomfort. How odd that I didn't like this development, this expression of his that made us look like sissies to the Saturday shoppers all about. It felt anything but natural, and natural was what I liked.

I think we make a good team, he said. I never considered the idea of us as a team or anything other than friends. It seemed to suggest we were in some competition with other teams. It also sounded very American, which immediately made me want to disengage.

Fuck the world, he whispered in my ear, *we are the team!* It was whispered at first to release the forbidden word in an almost apologetic manner. As there was no response from me, that seemed to demand a pardon, his word took the air in full freedom. *Fuck them all to hell! Fuck my parents, fuck your parents. Fuck the bombers. Fuck the crowd!* He seemed suddenly fucking mad. I laughed at something that wasn't immediately funny. It was, however, hovering and ready to go somewhere.

I placed my hand on Linus's hook hand in order to take hold of it and remove it from my arm, so I could slip out from beneath his resting limb and then away to a decent distance. A departure to decency. But his hand refused my pull and grabbed my arm more possessively, so my hand simply gripped his as if embracing it. I tried to pull a little harder but in doing this, it was as if—being not one thing or the other—I was not only embracing it, but caressing it. Why was I afraid to tell him simply to remove his arm? I felt his stare on the side of my forward-looking face and when I turned to him he was smiling into me, a great smile into me, only about an inch away, so uncomfortably close it felt penetrative. It made me look forward and pull back. Manifested in a slower pace.

A team, he said. A team of two, he meant. His eyebrows lifted themselves high into his forehead, registering some sort of a seductive solicitation to which I should respond. His words were a simple statement of fact, but his eyebrows offered up an interrogatory value. A query. It was momentarily confusing. The term *team* didn't sit comfortably with me, as it didn't sit comfortably with the idea of friendship. I played for the school football team but hated most of the people on it. It was made up mainly of a bunch of moaners and groaners and selfish slackers who just wanted all the glory all the time. There were comedy teams on television that hated each other's guts and pretended they liked each other for the sake of their act. In fact, *act* was a good word for their relationship.

I didn't respond except with that smile, which Linus took to be a favourable reply. So, he loosened his grip, and I moved away from him by at least a yard. I was happier at that distance. All was normal again. We could continue in our customary friendship, with the usual rules governing it. It was fine. It was free. But there was also a freedom of thought, and this vacancy ushered in a thought about how customs can change as ideas do.

We avoided main thoroughfares and took the empty entry route. An entry is a space of a place between the backs of houses. Entry to the backsides of Belfast life. That was where you bummed around, and where the mad men of the Provos would ditch their night's work. You cannot have an entry without houses, like you cannot have a valley without hills. We loved entries and the houses that made them. It was a city full of houses and entries as it was a city of a valley and hills all around it. We loved entries, yes. Their quietness. Hiddenness. The hidden ways to places. Always out of the sun, either simply too narrow to receive it or dominated by the long shadows of the grand houses on either side. Entries seemed to be built for play. For intrigue. For fatigue. For flight. Some were wide enough to be the ground of major football matches. Like ours at the back of our house. Full of play. Echoes. And the backs of yard walls were perfectly fitted for handball. Out of our back yards we came and entered the concrete and cobbled arena. And spent whole days there. Mooching, sporting, shouting, chasing, laughing, plotting, planning, experimenting, arguing.

Linus and I took an entry that led to another entry, and that entry had a fork in it that asked us to choose. One way was very narrow and the other was wide. The narrow one just about took us single file and our shoulders rubbed up against the walls on either side. It probably wouldn't even take a bike. What happens if somebody comes the other way? What if we met a mad brute or a crazy dog? People had mad dogs to chase you away. Their snouts pressed up against cracks in yard doors and they sniffed and growled at any movement. We'd have to shift our sluggish loose limbs and slip into a race rhythm in that little space, trying to stay off the walls so as not to slow us up and tear our clothes. Tearing your clothes was reason for the parents to go mad. The mother would go off into the rawest of rages and chase you around looking for your bare legs to skelp, whilst shouting, *Those clothes cost money!*

There seemed no end in sight in the narrow entry option so after the first few steps we turned back and took the wider route. This one was concreted, whereas the narrow one was cobbled. Cobbles were very slippery and nice to look at under a gaslight, but if you had to run, your first few steps would be running on the spot, unable to get traction. You'd be on your hands, scrambling to get off the mark.

Very often the things that were nice to look at didn't lend themselves to play. We constantly tried to play football on the College Green up by the University. It was perfectly flat and grassy like a bowling green, and surrounded by tall trees and shrubs and the beautiful college building, but the caretaker kept coming out and chasing us off. It was too good for football. He didn't frighten us; we just shouted, *Hey, there's Banana Nose!* But one day when we ignored him he went to his office and called the constabulary. When they came, we just stood our ground and listened to the voice of the law with no fear. They didn't like to be called to sort out such trivial matters as there were more serious concerns with all the murders and bombings to deal with and the constant threat on their own lives. But we had to go. As the peelers liked football and were once boys, they were sympathetic to us and gave Banana Nose the caretaker a look of contempt for being a force for spoil-sporting. Banana Nose the caretaker just kept saying he had a job to do, but he was just a fussy little man with a nickname.

CHAPTER 19

We moved on down the wider entry.

I'm Mr McKeown, he said, *McKeown of this entry. I'm often here, standing here looking for boys like you two. Useful boys. Boys that know a thing or two about being useful. And useful means good. Good is useful, I always say. And useful is always related to money. A relative of money you might say. Useful boys are always on the lookout for money.*

What's the name of this street that this is the entry of? said Linus, as if all that garbage coming from the man's mouth had passed through him like a physic of salts down his gut. McKeown shook the trouser pocket he had his hand in with the hand that was in it. A hand that was used to being in a pocket. That pocket which was used to having something in it to shake. It was deep, and there seemed to be something in it besides his hand because he shook the pocket to shake what was in it. Or else it was just a bad habit. A rule of thumb. I looked at it and so did Linus. I never saw Linus looking, but I knew he was. We were meant to look. But we didn't know what was in it. Nor in the other pocket that was unoccupied by a hand. That hand rested on the entry wall. On the brick and mortar. It held him up because he was at an angle. But he also had an angle in his head. Like a gangster asks, *What's your angle, buddy?* We knew the meaning of that well enough. Just as we knew there was meaning for us in the shaking as there was in the leaning. The empty pocket didn't really mean anything.

The total trousers of McKeown were shiny, black and massive. Wide and mountainous to the knees, then crumpled and piled up at the base camp that were the feet. Pulled up high on the belly by braces. Linus said to me that the Yanks call braces suspenders. I blew out all the air that was inside me as an expression of disbelief. The mother would want me to wear braces, but I wouldn't, unless there was the sort of motherly compulsion that was not going to be denied. I would never wear them in America, where they were called suspenders. Did McKeown's mother make him wear them, even though he was a full adult? Had he been to America? He also had, buckled around himself at a lower level, a thick leather belt. Strange on his high-waisted trousers hoisted almost to chest height. Somebody in a western film said, *You can never trust a man who can't even trust his own trousers.* No, grownup men had a preference for the braces. Some of them indeed wore a belt and braces like McKeown. The suspender idea came back to me with McKeown standing there. A man couldn't wear suspenders, for that'd be queer. Different altogether in the look and the feel. All wispy and they went around your waist. That'd be awful. Not to say unlawful. Imagine in the school changing rooms having to be seen in those. It'd be a quare old laugh for somebody.

Do you boys want to earn ten bob, ten bob in coin or note? said the leaning tower of McKeown with saliva seething through his peerless broken choppers as he smiled the seedy smile. He smiled to get us to accept his offer. Like an invitation. Like saying it was a pleasurable thing to do. With a reward at the end. He'd like us to do it. It would make him happy. It would make us smile.

What do we have to do? I said.

I've a bad back, he said, as he took his hand from his pocket and his other hand from the wall and placed both on the small of his back, pushing in so that his front pushed out extensively. He groaned, he grimaced, and out of it he smiled again. Then his front went back in, and his hands resumed their positions in the pocket and on the wall. He leaned again. But his front didn't go entirely in. *All you have to do is shift some furniture. To save my bad back.* His accent wasn't a Belfast one for he pronounced the *t* in furniture, not as *ch,* but with the tongue pressing on the palate, not unlike Ulster country folk do. *Furnityure.*

Haven't you got a wife? said Linus. I snapped a quick giggle.

I wouldn't ask a woman to do that, he snapped back with his teeth closing shut of their own accord like a hair trigger bear trap. *Are you in a rush? It'll take a minute of your time. Ten bob for a minute or two.* It was a minute, now it was a minute or two, which generally meant more than two, as adults have a tendency to minimise tasks they wanted younger people to do for them.

Where is it? I said.

In the house up the stairs. On the top floor. In the attic. The hand in his pocket took flight, and he pointed to the top of the four-storey house. Then the pocket was again occupied with it. He shook the change around in the sack again. I thought the ten bob would get me what I wanted, and I could replace the fiver in the sister's purse when I got home. Or I could say I found the sister's money and get some praise. I would put my hand down the side of a chair and pull it out. Ten bob would get me a football kit and there'd be no crime. I would chastise myself for taking it in the first place, and then all would be well. I would even pray to God to ask for forgiveness. It was just a mistake. It could all be rectified. The Pastor kept saying Jesus died for all our mistakes, all the ones he saw us making with his all-seeing mind. Strange!

Away up there? said Linus, with a bit of a laugh and a pointing finger. McKeown looked up, and in that minimum time of McKeown's upward look, Linus looked across at me to shake his head.

It's not really that far, not as far as it looks. There he was minimising again. *I can see you're altogether fit lads so there's no problem. Ten bob for the job,* said McKeown, as he returned his friendly look to us. Out came his hand from his pocket loaded with notes and change. He picked through it with the other hand that came off the wall. His foraging fingers were fat stumps. His finger skin was bitten, and dry, and cracked, and brown with nicotine. His fingernail tips were lined with black filth as if painted with black eye mascara. He gasped at the sight of his own money. A ten bob note was unravelled and placed before our eyes. I liked this note, its browny orangeness.

I had the urge to take out my five pound note and compare it. My hand was almost in my pocket when it was prevented by a thought. A notion that McKeown loved money, that he might take it from me in a sneaky way if he sees it. He could hatch a plan there and then like a big human womany hen. Plan or no plan we moved in the direction of his invitation.

Take my step as your lead, boys, said McKeown. We had walked up the four flights of stairs in the wake of his massive Belfast arse, a moving black mountain towering above us. An earthquake on a mountain must be just like that. The Black Mountain that towers itself above Belfast. Linus walked behind me like a Sherpa, like Sherpa Tensing, all tensed up. Old boy McKeown gasped on every other step. He stopped from time to time to look back at us and grin. On every landing there was a door to a room and sometimes two. It was dark when the room doors were shut and there was a powerful enclosed smell of smoke from cigarettes and damp in the whole place. On the third flight there was a marginal light from a slightly open door. As we approached from the stairs we could see into a bathroom. An icy blow surged in our direction.

You cannot heat these places, said McKeown. *They're too big, you see. You'd have to have asbestos walls to keep the heat in these places.* He reached for the bathroom door to close it, as if alarmed that it was open, his stubby mitts grabbing the handle with great firmness. Resistance set in. He pulled until his face was puffed up and red. My senses were awakened to a smell. Like shite but not shite. Not regulation shite anyway. And to a small voice within the bathroom. It squeaked, *Let me out!* It couldn't be though. It was the door creaking for sure or the wind blowing. That cold wind from high up that I felt before from the open door. For almost sure anyway. The door did creak but it seemed to creak on top of a squeak. A human squeak. Like the mother made at the news of Uncle Patsy's demise.

Where's your wife? enquired Linus with a greasy uneasiness governing his tone. It was abrupt and bold.

The wife? The wife! What's with you and the wife? The wife isn't here. She's elsewhere. Elsie. Elsie Elsewhere. That's her. And she can bloody go to hell. She's a whore, boys. You know what that is? A strumpet, an instrument that plays on your nerves, and you pay for your pleasure. You pay, you pay. A whore. A whore is a deceiver, a backslider. A seducer of Jesus and the saints, a turner of good into bad. She liked bad boys, boys. She said she'll take them to heaven but hell is for whores. A trap from a trap mouth. Burning hot for them to roast their cunning cunts off. The filthy craters. But you boys are without blemish or spot. Aren't you? Little lambs. Little lambs. Spotless lambs. Christ, you're good boys. Aren't you? Excitement underpinned his voiced words. It occurred to me that he would sound like the preacher if he hadn't done all that swearing. It all sounded very Biblical. He was now standing with his back in front of the closed bathroom door, looking down at us like a mighty preacher prophet. *It's warmer upstairs, the heat's on up there. It's hot as hell. That's where the furniture for moving is.*

In the upper chamber, McKeown had our attention. Paraffin was the source of the hellish heat, with several heaters on full wick, and with the door firmly closed behind us—McKeown had shoved it several times with his shoulder—I was racing towards a form of sleepiness. My attention was therefore easily attuned. In fact, I resembled a devotee to the hypnotic word. The word that cut in was *cunt. Crack* and *cunt. Crack in the door and cunt inside the door,* I mouthed to myself. It was the first time I heard it from an adult mouth, and something of that mouth seemed to speak through mine. The soothsayer boys at school sometimes said it, but they said anything that was forbidden. Yet they seemed to have some form of insight. *Have you ever seen a wee doll's crack?* was a common enough quip from a cheeky skitter.

Linus took to tugging my pullover from behind. A sobering pull. He pulled my shirt out of the back of my trousers, and I felt an uncomfortable vacancy around my waist area. This, however, had a bearing on my movement back to sense. I had no idea what he wanted with all his pulling. I liked my shirt well tucked into my trouser waist without any break in the tuck. Even a small inlet represented annoying discomfort. So I usually tied my belt tighter by an extra notch to keep everything in place.

Look in there, look at the space in that wardrobe, said McKeown within the room that withheld the task. *Like a cavernous cunt,* he said. It was an immensely black space alright. Until we moved closer. It was contained in a big attic room with acres of space. But not much light. Murky acres. Shadowy. Any light came through the glass of a small dormer window. The glass itself was dark with dirt. It was nobody's room. A no body room. But I knew the room because it was like my room, my bedroom. An attic at the top of a big house. It also had a dormer window but it had light. It had the possessions of a boy in it, so it was a somebody room. Its warmth was true. Here in McKeown's domain, it was cold warmth of the feverish form. *That's a space and a half,* the man said. *Look at it.* We looked. A space and a half, I thought. The half beyond the space was the unmeasurable.

You boys look sporty. Fit and sporty. I bet yous play sports. Do you want to play a wee sport now? he said.

You mean a game? I said.

Aye, just that, he said.

How do you play? What are the rules? said Linus.

Never mind the rules. What's the game? I said.

It's a game without rules, said McKeown. *The best sort, the most fun. Full of the unexpected.*

How do we know what to do then? I said.

That's a part of the game. You see, I know the rules, you don't. I'll tell you what to do when you need to know it. A step at a time. Pretend I am playing chess and yous two are the pieces. The pieces don't ask for the rules, they don't have to know the rules, now do they?

Linus laughed out loud. *I'll be the king,* he shouted out of his laughing mouth. He then made short horizontal and vertical movements with his hands tightly down by his side. He moved close to me. He shuffled, pushing me along a bit. *Checkmate! Checkmate! Hey mate, checkmate!* he said in a sort of mechanical, robotic way. It was an odd Larkin aspect. Was he under the paraffin smell spell and the spell that was spelled in words from the McKeown mouth?

The King! Indeed yes, you will be, said McKeown. *And what'll you be?* he said to me. *A knight? A rook? The all powerful queen?*

But the chess pieces aren't actually playing the game, I said with a tightness of mind at the back of the remark. My sleepiness came and went. In between there was an alertness that was like a speeding up of thought. An excitement. *People are playing the game with the pieces. If we are the chess pieces, you'll be playing with us. And we won't be playing at all.* McKeown looked like a mad professor. It sent the wind of worry up me.

But you are a human chess piece son, and that's the difference. You'll catch on when you start playing. Wooden chess pieces don't ever catch on. And it's not really chess, but you'll get the idea soon enough. His rage turned into a loony smile. A smile with wet lips, lips that his tongue continually moisturised.

So what's the game then? said Linus.

It's a language game I speak of. So to speak. I speak, you listen. There are the three of us. That's important because three is a divine number. It's in the nature of things. Everything important is three. Past, present, future. That's three. The Father, the Son, and the Holy Ghost. Faith, hope, and charity. We are made up of mind, body, and spirit. Oak, ash, and thorn, the faery triad of trees, where the faeries live. Earth, heaven, and hell. In school yous have three terms. Three dimensions define the physical world. Thought, will and deed are the three things that make up all our actions. The anti-christ is numbered six six six, three numbers and each the double of three. It was the third day that the Lord rose from the dead. It was the third hour He was crucified. What do you say to that? The three of us are magical. And there's much more.

There's three in my family, said Linus.

There's three stumps in a cricket wicket, I said.

Three in a hat-trick in football, said Linus.

Three medals in the Olympics, gold, silver and bronze, I said.

Yes! said McKeown. *Yous have it. This is the game of three!*

The blighter was infesting our minds with dizzying notions, having us speaking as if we weren't speaking at all, heavy notions that were bearing down on us like hundredweight bar bells. If we were not up in the altitude of a skylight room, I would think we were deep in the legendary Limbo. Linus and I were smiling stupidly under the strain of the strangeness. McKeown smiled back in his sleazy manner. *Sleaked*, the mother would say. We, Linus and I, had something in our grasp for an instant. But then total wonder. We wondered what the meaning of it all was. The game of three?

McKeown wandered around the room and collected three chairs. He arranged them out in a circular pattern not far apart.

Why do you want to play a game? said Linus, *I thought you wanted to shift some furniture.*

Oh I do, said McKeown, *I do indeed, but yous two are good company, and I like good company. And yous'll enjoy this. All work and no play...not good on a Saturday!*

Dark. It got dark. Gloomy. It needed light. A sight of light to dispel an emerging dread. One glance at the dirty window glass, and there seemed no significant contrast beyond. The flight of light as if McKeown had command of it.

Sit down boys. McKeown sat himself down and beckoned to us to do the same. The beckoning was like a reckoning. It felt sickening. His chair was flimsy and creaked. We sat and our chairs creaked as well, and our knees touch. *We play this in the country. On dark, rainy days. The darkness makes us get closer together. It pushes us together. And we sit. The city is different, folks are always out in the rain. There's no tight togetherness. No respect for the elements. Home is not home.* He latched on to his braces with his thumbs. His pockets were now empty of his hands. His thumbs were thick. They ran down the length of his braces to his waist. To the leather button fasteners. The buttons strained on the thread. His forefinger met his thumb and rubbed his waistband between them.

It's a word game. In the beginning was the word. One of us starts with three words. Three words starting with the same letter beginning with A. The next one continues with three words beginning with B. And then the next with C. Then back to the first one for the next letter. Think to make the words connect.

He's a nut. That's what I thought. *Up here we are in the sky with a nut.* A country nut that's fallen off his tree and rolled into the big city. Away out of reach from the world touching knees. Listening to him. Watching him feel his braces and buttons. Seeing his saliva seething mouth spit out his words. His face plumping up with pleasure. He rubbed his fat knees on ours. His gabardine on our denim and corduroy. He wanted words from us. He wanted our words to mix with his. All our words to mix together. In our heads. In our separate heads. He wanted to bring them together with words. I didn't like

games with just words. I liked doing something. Even if it was just
moving a chess piece. This was too much like school stuff, with the
teacher trying to make something very boring fun.

An animal arrives, said McKeown. *Those are my first three words.*

You go, I said to Linus.

Before breakfast begins, said Linus.

Carting coffee cups, I said after a half-huffy pause.

Dirty damn donkey, said McKeown. He smiled a grotesque smile
as he squeezed out his last word.

Eating each... each... each erection. McKeown heaved a dirty
laugh. A cough laugh.

Fucking fat farter, shouted Linus. I laughed out loud. That the
fucking fat farter was McKeown was my very thought.

Heavy hard hissing, McKeown continued immediately.

Infested—shite I can't think—in instinct.

Just Jesus Jew. Linus shrugged his shoulders.

Kill, killer, killing.

Let life live.

Man, mother, masturbate.

Need nice nooky.

Open one orifice.

Pale pure plaything.

Quote queer queen.

Randy rascal requests.

Shite sitting sithole. That black man! From Africa.

To the toilet! shouted McKeown. He sweated. He shifted on his
seat. The chair creaked. He unseated his arse and re-seated it.

Unload upper urge.

Very violent vomit.

Wanking woman wants.

No x, I'll go on to y—Yummy Yoghurty Yuck.

Zip, Zipping. Zap!

Silence.

Now close your eyes boys, said McKeown. It'll all happen in your
heads. *Blind Bart's all three. I'll close mine too. Tight to blackness.
Now say the dirtiest word you know.* We closed our eyes not knowing
if he would close his too, but we thought he would.

Bastard! blurts Linus. Was he smiling? All was black to me. With some flashing colours.

Now don't look now! shouted McKeown. *Next.*

*

I was suddenly aware of what was happening at home. Because it was so familiar. The most familiar game of all. The father was in bed after a night shift. The mother was in a giant huff. A huffy puffy, we called it. We had a song for people in a huff. *Huffy puffy, come blow your horn,* we sang it to the huffer when they were in a huff. It eventually hit a nerve, and they'd snap. But not sung to the mother. That was a different order of huff. She hated the father resting. Especially on a sunny Saturday morning. She had the language of hate. She called him a lazy louse. She set about housework, frantically at dust busting. Hunting out the day's dust, thrown up by movement. She also hated movement. She hated the sun in the house for showing up the dust that was thrown up. In her head was significant movement, a swift progress—or regress—towards annoyance. She had a map in her head, not of the physical world, but of areas of displeasure. She visited them daily. In the early morning, her attention was drawn to them and stayed there for most of the day. Divided between the inner and outer. You could see it in her eyes. Where she went. She also took things from the outer and placed them in the inner areas of the unpleasant. They often stayed there. The father was there. He was not in bed. He was embedded in her hateful mind. Like the sisters. The mother hated them growing up into women, so as young women they were placed in the inner area. As was the idea of women in general. Women were hussies. All women were brazen hussies. I laughed at the word hussy when the mother uses it to refer to the sisters. I looked it up. The word hussy comes from a word hussif, meaning housewife. Yet hussy means a whore, a slut, a tart. Nasty names. I was not entirely sure what they meant, but they had a splendid force about them. There was also the term *loose woman* in the dictionary. I laughed at the idea. A rubbery woman, I thought. A woman laughing to rubberiness. A loud cackling Belfast woman. But what was loose about a woman?

I wanted to call the sisters sluts, whores, tarts, but something always held me back. To their faces. Their pasty pimply faces. The sisters were annoying when they teased and also when they just went about their business. They were just annoying being around. Their voices were annoying. One of the sisters would sing and that would drive me mad. She thought she had a nice voice and could sing, but I hated her voice when she sang with it. It was a sign she was happy but it was the source of sadness for me. I'd tell her she had a voice like a fog horn. It was a racket in my ears and an immensely destructive thing to the smooth operation of the mind.

I needed new words of ridicule to get back at them. Some powerful ammunition to knock them back. *Singing slut* was good, I thought. *Whining whore wench. Shut your cunt cake hole, you singing slut.* I tried them out in secret. I spat them out in the way the mother spits out her insults. Through a tight mouth and gritted teeth. They had words for me that hurt. They laughed their heads off when they said them to me, and I just stood there looking loose and weak. I had to laugh at the whole thing sometimes, because I saw that the names they used were indeed funny. And I was body loose, and the looser you get in the body the more likely you are to laugh. When I gave in to laughter, I was also on the verge of tears. Names. *Twinkle toes. Bonnick face. Empty pants. Pimboo. Twinkle toes,* because I walked in a delicate fashion, almost on tip toes, and the sisters said it was like a ballet dancer. When I was embarrassed, I had a certain face, a sheepish look, and that was indeed a *bonnick face.* That was the mother's own insult for stupid people. *Empty pants,* because they said I was skinny. *I'm not skinny, I'm not just fat like you*, I protested. I especially didn't like *pimboo*, because it made me look silly and weak but, I didn't know what it referred to specifically or where it even came from. I thought *pim* was like a pin and *boo* was like a baby. They would just keep repeating *pimboo* whilst laughing until I almost laughed an unreal laugh into a sob. *Pimboo, pimboo, pimboo, what you going to do?* These thoughts made me even more determined not to surrender the stolen fiver. It was a trade. The fiver was payment for my suffering. They would pay for their cruelty. I felt it in its folded thickness in my pocket. I would soon unfold it and show it to a shopkeeper.

Mercer's sports shop was where we'd head for. Merciful Mercer's, we called it, because Mercer sometimes gave you too much change. In your hand sometimes was more than you paid. Out of his door, you went in a hurry and laughed all the way up the street. Laughing at an old man. An old fogie with a foggy mind. Not entirely right. The joviality was contaminated.

I felt that nothing was ever just right. There was always the fly boy in the ointment. At this instant it could not be established if I was happy or not. If I was sad or not. If I was anything in the feeling department. What time was it? What moment? What man was McKeown at that moment? What was he doing? I couldn't understand him and his actions.

*

Shite! That's when I smelled it. Coming from below. Clear as crap can be. Rising up rapidly into my clean nostrils. Shite from a shoe. McKeown's shoe. On his sole. A flat, worn sole. Treadless. Barely stuck. He had crossed his legs and laid bare his sole. A singular smell. Powerful in the dark. The smell from hell. It smelt. Like coke from the gasworks on the Ormeau Road. They can't contain it within the high walls. Bad eggs. Appearance conceived out of the imagination reservoir. Bourneville. Dark dark chocolate. Laxative quality. The soft shoe shuffle in the can. Can't get off the pot. He couldn't shift his arse. That old uncle. The moment he stood up straight was a moment of agony. Murderous muscular madness. The gravity of it. Gravy in the seat.

Clit, said McKeown. *That's the dirtiest word there is. Shite is not a dirty word. It's just shite. Dead stuff. A waste. Bastard is a word that is written in the Bible. That can't be bad. But clit is sacred. It's bad. It's a man's word. When you know the meaning of it you're a man. It's a man's thing to think. It's a whole world of a bad idea. It bewitches men and leads them to the road of destruction. The mighty clit poisons a man. Sends the fear of God into a meek mouth. It makes you a man and destroys the man it makes.*

McKeown didn't seem like a man. Like an old womany man, the mother would say about some men. Not like the father. What was he doing with us? The father would never do this. His mouth would never utter such things. His mind would never attach itself to such ideas. His will would never take him into such a world. Did the father know the clit and deny it?

What's the meaning of it, said Linus. McKeown stood up with a frightening force. With the straightening of his legs, the chair upon which he comforted his arse raced across the floor to the wall. He stood in all his enormity above us. An enormous man in every way. Enormous trousers flapped in the wake of his upright erection. Big gabardines. Stained and worn, but with a perfect razor-sharp crease. His mouth foamed. Gob stoppers of bulging eyes. The mass of bloody veins in the whites were like the tributaries of the Nile delta.

Like a curtain dropping at the unveiling of a heroic royal statue, McKeown's trousers dropped. A ritual, it had been done before. A smooth performance. Military precision. Religious fervour. Like a cricketer at his crease. The parts were like a singular event. Braces off at the shoulders, waist and fly buttons undone. Knickers released to less than half mast. Before we knew it we were staring his peeing horny mountjoy straight in the eye. The wrinkly balls hung ornamentally behind. It all demanded attention.

Linus gasped. Sufficient to leave him concave in the chest with the deflation. A Christian chorus raced into my head. *Jesus, Jesus, Jesus, sweetest name I know, it fills my every longing, keeps me singing as I go. What's my longing? Exactly.* The room seemed darker than ever, with all remaining light attached to McKeown. There was a dribble on his horny mountjoy. A clear dribble. A little leak from the eye. A teardrop. From way above us McKeown nodded his head. An affirmation of what? *There are no clits here, boys. There are no clits in this place. It's clitless. This before you is the holy cock that is ruled by the clit.* We had a look of empty headedness. Stupidity. Ignorance. Daftness of the dead head. The words were not living words. They were like the deadest shite.

Home! Sweet Home! The clit is a home. And without a home we are lost. The clit is a slit through which we pass into glory. The tantalising crack of Clytemnestra. Deprived of it, we pass into the hell of loneliness and deprivation. Just like you pass into your home through your front door, and into your home, and feel the satisfaction of its warmth and tight love, so too do you feel when you pass into the clit. This sorry little dribbler needs a home boys. Help this lonely creature boys. Have charity.

Can we move the furniture? pleaded Linus. All was as if nothing had happened. Indeed, all was about to commence. We were in the middle without having touched the edge. *Ten bob for moving the furniture,* Linus continued in the monotone. There was a desperate attempt to deny the undeniable. There was something of rage in McKeown's eyes. Then it mellowed completely to a meekness of the mad variety. How? I had seen similar expressions in the features on display at the mad hospital that the mother worked at. The gentle smile of a murderer.

Please boys. Please. Have clarity. Have charity. A fiver for your charity. I'll put the ten bob away, here's a fiver. I have no faith, no hope, so just give me some charity. McKeown was unfolding himself, his very finite self, before us, before our disbelieving eyes, but nothing of this revelation was understood to these absorbed observers. In ignorant bliss, but not quite bliss, we saw a madman. Though it was really ignorance. McKeown's was beyond our grasp as he delivered himself to us. Nevertheless what he said seemed to detain us. It compelled us to stay. There was fear of his madness, of his mad meaningless ramblings, but there was novelty. There was something to know, that needed to be known, the character of which was unfolding in a confusing manner. There was a necessity to follow its development. It was like a compelling drama, the final act that required our attention. Our intention to participate. And as a drama, it needed more than one actor. It needed us to be a part of it. Part of how it played.

Emanations boys! McKeown howled.

Linus's hand was again on my shoulder. Lightly, fidgety. Too light to be pleasant. His fingertips rubbing the material of my shirt on one spot, which was so annoying. He was reaching for me. Wanting my courage. McKeown shuffled to the door and stood against it. He tested it for its full-fitting flushness to the frame.

A secret boys. Do not, please for God's sake, do not tell on me. This is not bad if bad is what you smell. They'll all tell you it is bad, in the sad world, but it is harmless. It's not badness. It's a desire. It's a wish.

It's a pleasure. I'm lonely. In my loneliness, I'm empty. In this empty house. Save the shadows. Take my word. I give you my word. Everyone has a secret.

I felt the secret fiver in my pocket. I felt the thief in me. I saw the thief that I was. Nearly all of me was a thief. But was McKeown seeking to steal our minds from us?

If you are charitable to me you'll be giving me something of yourself. Something of your goodness. Divine pouting pair—enough to make a gentleman forget his inhibitions!

In this fiery furnace room, his words fired our feeble minds to fear. He had the proper babbling words alright. A barbarian, a babelite. A devil. Our little sporting hearts pounded. We could run and play all day, and our hearts would not pound like this. Our bodies would never tire. It was the pound of excitement and fear here. Stripping us of strength. Desire and fear. The fear of him and his insane words. We put a fear mask on him. What did we desire? The imagination makes desires unlimited. How our minds wandered in that limitless empire of imaginative desire. But what were we to McKeown really? What did he desire? It was too tiring to think.

There is the desire that has a definite object and the desire whose direction is indefinite. There with McKeown both were present. The money on offer was a large inducement to stay and do his bidding. But money for what? What was his bidding exactly? Would it be for old rope as the father would say? Was McKeown old rope? Or for the old dope?

The old dope before us dropped to his bare knees with a painful bone thud. His face screwed up with the agony. Crunching knee bone agony. There was nothing like it. I can testify to it, because I was kicked on the knee playing football. You lose all dignity in your writhing. The agony seems to go on endlessly. McKeown, in his private agony and higher state of want, put his hands together as if to pray. The rough hands bound together in a two-handed fist, which he placed to just below his rigid ventriloquist doll mouth. His whole demeanour reminded me of the beggars in the city, pouring themselves unreservedly into begging. All of himself was in it, as the full flower is in the seed.

Linus had by now moved his arm around my shoulder as he had done in the street a few moments earlier. The worldly weight of him had returned. The intense closeness of him. Like God's fearful gravity. His mutterings made no sense, as I had an ear open mainly for McKeown. And an eye kept glued to him. McKeown continued his malignant rant, his words a signalling device to an unknown empire of nonsense.

What sense is there to be had from this? The backslider seeks his own sense and does not call on God for it. It is always tempting to call on Jehovah Jireh to provide a lamb in the thicket, but I don't. In danger there is God, there is sleep, there is escape, there is standing, taking a stand. Part of standing is understanding.

McKeown was not playing any game. He was deadly in earnest. He looked like an Earnest. Earnest McKeown. It was a serious life. It was not a game when you were trouserless, begging on your buck bare knees in front of two boys. He had played his game of words with us, and it felt like a game to us, but the game suddenly stopped being a game. At what point I didn't know. It seemed pointless. Directionless. I felt directed to irritation. The ton-weight tentacle of Linus on me, the time spent in a pointless ignorance. A not-knowingness. A just-being thereness. A distance from life in the street. From home. From football. From messing and mooching on the home front. A distance from the familiar friendly language where the point of things was clear, where the game was intimate.

Life is knowing what game you're in and what the rules are.

Did McKeown want to look a fool? What person wants to look like a fool? The room was sealed with his antics. The doorway was right behind his big begging body. Closed off to us. I wanted an opening. Just to see an opening. A crack. A clit in the door. Who was Clytemnestra? To know there was an exit. An out. But we were in. In this world. A room of a world. With no room. Very little room for manoeuvre. No light. No air. A furnace. We could run for it. One on each side of the old fruitcake. He'd fall over in his downed and tangled trousers if he tried to catch us. Then we could kick him up the bare arse as we left. We'd lace his arse like a lacing of a leather football. Leave a footprint on each of his flabby buttocks. And we'd laugh all the way down the stairs and spill out into the entry unable to control our bodies with all the panic-inspired laughter. We'd have the grovelling McKeown in our minds forever more as a notion to laugh at when we needed a laugh. We'd impersonate him as a perfect manifestation of shame and humiliation.

But we didn't move. McKeown moved. He crawled. He unclasped his begging hands and placed them flat on his floor. He then shuffled himself in our direction. I felt the Linus arm grip me with greater force. He pulled me to him. I could even feel him breathing. His inside breathing. A sort of a wheeze. I could feel his body pulse on my side. The arm of his woollen pullover scratched my cheek. He had me almost in a headlock.

What am I to do boys, whispered McKeown. *Look at me. On all fours like an animal. Half naked like a wee baby without a nappy on. I'm crawling like a baby.* A shaking accompanied his words. A shaking of his foundations.

At this point I had an overwhelming attack of dizziness, and in that rarefied atmosphere of mind, my thoughts took a peculiar path. I feared some aspect of the McKeown pantomime, but I also longed for something of it. What is feared? What dreaded? What dared? Courage. What peril? What risk? What threat that we felt we had to run from? What is longed for? Some huge satisfaction. A freedom in a particular determination. McKeown made himself a child and an animal. He was defiant in his shame. Defiant of himself. He lost himself in another self.

Just look at me boys. Gaze upon me. Stand up and gaze down upon me. See me down below you. This animal, this child has the mastery of me. I surrender to it. It has tamed me. 'Suffer the little children to come unto me.' Jesus said it. Suffer. Children. The child learns to suffer. The child learns the rules of suffering. Suffering makes the best of us. Do not worry boys. I am no danger to you.

He was transformed into a meek one. A weak one. A dependent one. Here he depended on us. He needed our help. We stood up and looked down at him. His inheritance. The inheritance of his meekness.

I have offended you boys. I have insulted you. I have lied to you. So, what do you think you should do? Here, here, here! His hand was way back in his trouser pocket fumbling a search. *Here!* He produced the supplementary fiver. The excess. The crumpled note which he offered up to us. He lowered himself to the ground, but his hand reached up to us with the payment. The payment! *Here, please. Take it.* His voice was now like a woman's. High pitched and feminine. Linus removed his arm from around my neck and pulled the fiver from McKeown's fist.

We don't need to do anything, said Linus. *We'll just go. And that is it. Simple.*

No! roared the feminine McKeown. *That's not just it. You must settle the account. I have to pay.*

But you have paid, said Linus, showing McKeown his fiver.

Not enough, no not enough by a long chalk. I calculate not. The fiver is for you to stay to make appropriate amends. Ten bob for moving the chest, a fiver for moving me. He was intensely obstinate, determined that we played his game and make him pay. *Woe betide the person who ignores pity.* He was in Linus' face. He had slithered up his front like a slug. He left a silvery trail. They were eye to eye, Linus and McKeown. Linus swallowed. He blew air out of his nostrils. It was like a laugh.

What does woe betide mean? said Linus. He raised his eyebrows in expectation of an answer. *Is it the sea? The deep swallowing tide?*

I smell crook, I smell thief. I smell evil doing off you boys. Evil. No good. An evil purpose. I smelt in the entry when you came to me. I smell girls, not boys. I wanted to save you from your sin. Not the sin of the Devil, the sin of life.

He was a sinner. It was a sin to take your clothes off and be naked in front of other people. Especially your bum and your horny mountjoy. The sin of nakedness. Right there before me. A vile and vital nakedness. His horny mountjoy was sinfully energised. A full sin. A perfect sin. A prize. That's why it was necessary to have tight underpants. So tight they crawl up your buttock crack. So as to keep your unruly and sinful horny mountjoy in check. It was a powerful thing, almost a law unto itself. An active thing. Full of highly-charged wattage. Almost freely functioning. But not really, as it was mine. I was responsible for it. You knew that without ever being told. The tight underwear was like a gaol to it. Holding it in

check. Mine wasn't guilty of anything, merely under suspicion. I
had to take it in hand from time to time, to readjust it. The mother
caught me once or twice with my hand down there fiddling, and
I rapidly removed it in response to the disapproving eye. It was
wrong to fiddle with your body. Or to modify it temporarily in
terms of making it feel good.

The father asked me to tickle his feet sometimes. It was a private
thing. The mother disapproved. In the middle of watching *Match of
the Day* on a Saturday night, with the mother absent, he produced
a knitting needle from the mother's very own knitting basket and
presented his bare feet to me. I saw his pleasure as I got to know his
feet. I ran the needle point lightly over the sensitive areas of skin.
He sometimes positioned his foot to receive the needle at the most
pleasurable points. The instep was very sensitive, almost unbearable
for the first few strokes. In between the toes was different and had
an unusual effect. Virgin terrain, a tickle and not a tickle. Not
an ordinary tickle. I poked the needle slowly through the spaces
between his toes. The father's mouth lay open. His eyelids dipped.
Like McKeown's when he kneeled before us. His eyelids dipped in
that fashion. As if they were too heavy to hold up. And his lower
mouth below the bottom lip dragged. The father rarely relaxed so.
He was a man of edgy disposition. The mother did not contribute
to his ease. She increased his edginess so that he performed for her.
She applied pressure daily. I thought that this was what he needed.

He had hairless legs. But his big toes had one or two hairs
sprouting out of the skin creases. I often felt a strong urge to
yank them out while he had his eyelids dipped and his mouth
open. I imagine him spitting out his loose dentures. I foresaw
his displeasure at the indignity. The father was a proud man. Not
conceited or arrogant but respectful of the need to be appropriate.
Right and seemly. Yet the tickling and the pose that it required, if
the bodily pleasure was obeyed, were not so. But he was alone with
the son and that was somehow acceptable. If the mother saw it, she
would show her disgust. So the father, whilst in a state of relative
repose, was quick to stir at any disturbance that might indicate an
approaching judgement. In a panic, he would sit bolt upright and
reach for his socks.

One evening, when he thought he was safe, there was a rousing rap at the front door. As the door was being opened, there was a swift rearrangement of pose and apparel to restore respectability. The visitor was shown in. It was the Pastor of our church doing a round. The father's dignity was disturbed. In his loose vest and standing in sock soles he tried to carry on a normal conversation. He stuttered and stammered and never really recovered equilibrium. Never again was he the man he wanted to be in the Pastor's presence. He saw the Pastor seeing him in his relaxed and messy mode of dress. He saw the Pastor looking at him with his new idea of him whilst delivering his sermon. That was an uneasy thought to think.

*

McKeown looked like a Broderick to me. Broderick McKeown, that would have eminently suited him. I pictured him being christened. And the name Broderick passing through the minister's lips. A little fat Broderick. Gurgling white baby froth through his gums. We were back in the light of day having scrambled down the McKeown staircases and out into the entry outside McKeown's backyard door. Nothing seemed to have changed except that McKeown wasn't occupying space in it. No leaning, no leering. He was occupying some other space and, to a certain extent, he was occupying a big space in our heads. An idea space. He was a massive nodus mode of thought. A knot to be unravelled.

Do you know Broderick Crawford? I said to Linus.

No, he replied.

Highway Patrol, you know? The TV series.

Know? No. Not know. Me not know. Me Chinaman. Me no watch TV.

He's a fat policeman in an American TV series. But his real name is Broderick. His first name.

So?

Does the name sound fat to you? He is fat and he has a fat name.

How's it fat?

It's Broderick. Doesn't that sound fat to you? It would be the same if it was Broaderick. Broad Erick. An Erick that's broad. But he also looks like a Dan and Dan is another fat name. So I call him Broaderick Dan.

Like Les Buttocks, you mean?

Aye. Just so.

But I don't see how Dan is fat. Now, Marius, your name is marry us, said Linus.

And yours is Line us. That's funny. Line us up!

If you're getting married, you'll have to say to the clergyman, please marry us.

Yes, line us up and marry us, I shouted into his face.

Linus stopped laughing. He was stopped by a thought. A laughter numbing notion.

I'm off to the hospital on Monday, he said.

What's wrong with you? I enquired. *You're fit aren't you? Fit and strong.*

Yes, but not in the head.

Your head! Your head?

I have to see the friendly doctor.

At this moment, I haven't a clue what you are talking about Linus. Shed some light. Glow. Show the way. This is Marius, so marry us with your lightness. Lead me up the garden path to knowledge. The garden of Eden and its tree of knowledge…

I'm mental. How light is that? I'm light-headed. The doctor says he's my friend and he wants to help me.

Doctors cannot be your friend. They only say that. Doctoring is their business, not friendship. And friendship isn't a business. In fact, it's none of his business. Wait a minute, you're going to the mental hospital? I gasped. *That's where my ma works.*

I don't talk to my parents so they think I'm mental. They say they are trying to save me from myself. You need saved from yourself, they say. My mother says it and my da nods. I tried to work that out but that sounds completely mental. Saved from yourself. Mad! Utterly.

That sounds like old McKeown telling us we need saving from our sin. It sounds like the church. I said. *They say only Jesus saves. If that's the case, he should be on our football team. Fat Riley can't save a twatting thing. He doesn't dive across the goal. He bounces the fat good for nothing.*

Do you think I'm loony? said Linus.

You couldn't be loony, or else if you were, we couldn't even talk, and you have to have rules to talk. Loonies have no rules. That's why they are

loony. There's no em... There's no sort of em... but it was a right loony
thing you did with McKeown. But that was only a loony thing. One
thing. You can do loony things without actually being loony. In general.
  He was a loony. A true loony. If not a fully-fledged loony, then a
verging loony. That's why we didn't understand him. Maybe. His rules
are not our rules. He needed seeing to. Straightened out. He was a dirty
mind. A filthy fella that the world should be rid of. He called us dirty.
The cheek. I despise the smell of old filth. The filth of his body came
right through onto his clothes. And the other way round. The only good
thing about him was that he was begging to be punished. He was guilty
of something. The electric chair would sort him out.
  That stair rod was handy... and I'd appreciate it if you wouldn't
mention the death chair.
  It was perfect. Solid, cold brass. I felt the swing of it before I swung
it. I felt the air passing through it. I felt it natural for something
like that to be in my hand. It made me feel strong. In command.
Powerful. He stiffened his body and lifted his head towards the sky.
We moved along slowly away from McKeown's property. Further
down his entry. The Albert Clock's chimes in the distance entered
our heads on top of a heap of other active notions. Rhythmical
notions. Musical. Some they activated from passivity by pointing
us towards the ten o'clock hour. And left the passive ones for dead
and dead they should be, for if they get a hold of you, they'll sever
you from your nature for sure.

CHAPTER 20

I hummed a song I had in my head. Unearthed it somehow. The tune just came to me. Then the words came. A heavenly tune with heavenly words. It was a pleasant noise. And the words were oddly interesting. It was a church tune and I had it all there.

> *Will your anchor hold in the storms of life,*
> *When the clouds unfold their wings of strife?*
> *When the strong tides lift and the cables strain,*
> *Will your anchor drift, or firm remain?*

> *We have an anchor that keeps the soul*
> *Steadfast and sure while the billows roll*
> *Fastened to the Rock which cannot move*
> *Founded firm and deep in the Saviour's love.*

The words flowed out of me as smoothly as the tide out of a harbour. But like the tide, they didn't entirely leave. They washed in and out picking up on the debris of the mind on each return. Something new was added on each visit. Something really new. Like when the word *germ* entered the common vocabulary. Not the discovery of a new germ, but the idea of germ itself. It germinated. It grew into a mini-language. The language of germs. Mine were words from another realm. The idea *of being saved* and the colourful expression of it. I was told it wasn't about actual anchors and sea and storms but about the manner in which God keeps us safe and is true to us if we believe in Him. But I couldn't help seeing an actual anchor and the stormy sea. The stormy sea was one of the most frightening things I could think of. When you are there looking at the power of it. The swell, the depth, the noise. In the black night, among the merciless massive swell of waves, sucking you down to unbreathing death.

What's that you're singing? said Linus.

It's called Unbreathing Death. I caught Linus's unflinching look. A static expression of puzzlement. I didn't know whether to continue with the lie.

It doesn't make sense, said Linus, *death is a state of unbreathingness. There's no other type of death.* He didn't believe me about the song title, but he spoke as if he did, just to keep the idea alive.

What's a billow? I said.

A what?

A billow. A line in the song is, 'Steadfast and sure while the billows roll'.

No idea, said Linus flatly. *Sounds like a name. Big Billow. Big Billow McHallion. And his wee brother, wee Hallion McHallion. Favourite food, scallion.*

I wonder: Is Big Billow McKeown breathing? Is he still and stiff like a brass stair rod? I heard the thud. A body thud. Clean as a whistle. And there was a whistle, coming out of his cake hole as he hit the floor. Like the air out of a plastic baby doll, if you stand on it. And he rolled forward like a billow's roll. I felt the urge to rhyme *billow* with something but couldn't think of a thing. It felt good to rhyme something with an actual word. Not just a nonsense word. *Billow, millow, killow, drillow.* That was driving me mad. Was there not a real word that rhymed? I didn't mention it to Linus in case he had a rhyme. I just kept going in my own mind. *Marshmillow.* A posh form of marshmallow. *Ayll hev ay mershmillow playse. Window sillow. Amarillo! Is this the way to Amarillo? No but who cares. Is this billow on the way to Amarillo?* I said to Linus. *Amarillo is the only real word that rhymes with billow. I bet you can't think of another one.*

It doesn't count, said Linus, *it's Spanish. It means yellow. So billow doesn't rhyme with yellow. Mellow yellow. They call me mellow yellow.* He sang.

And what is mellow young fellow?
It means. A sort of yellow.
Can't you have a mellow green then.
Nope! It's only a sort of yellow.
Strange that they rhyme then.
The world is full to crapping with strange things like that.

*

A man was shovelling cement at the end of the entry. We passed him. We were talking of rhyming and passing. Passing things. Passing wind. Passing the ball. Make a pass. Passing the time of day. The Pastor of my church. Pastor whose Sunday message passeth all understanding. Passing him, the man, as he bent down to shovel. It was just a big pile of cement up against a wall he was shovelling. It had the same consistency as a pile of shite. It had slowly moving folds like loose shite. And when the pile got too high, the peak slid back down on the rest of it. But he kept piling it up. He shovelled and sweated. He rubbed the sweat with his forearm. He mixed the grey substance with his spade and then shovelled it from bottom to top. I said it was grey, but Linus said it wasn't, but he didn't know what colour it was. He said there wasn't a colour for it. I said there must be. Then he said there wasn't a word for it and that not everything had a word. That made me think fast but not fast enough. Linus thought he had won.

Well, tell me the thing that hasn't got a word? I leapt at him as the thought had leapt into my skull.

How can I, if it hasn't got a word? he shouted back.

Exactly, I said right up to his face. *Precisely. Elvis Precisely!*

What? We both smiled.

The shoveller paid little attention to our passing or our thinking and shouting, but Linus and I looked at his task, whilst we were thinking, with intent to understand it. We were hypnotised by the act in itself. The shovelling, as the spade passed between the cement and the ground, was a pleasant noise. A clean gravelly noise. Like the ball bearings in a spinning skate wheel. The layers of wet cement weaned us off our crazy course of thought. For a moment. The shovelling man looked back briefly as we passed. In his bent shovelling pose, he looked back at us. Almost under his working arm. He must have just seen our legs and feet.

What right does he have to look at us like that? said Linus.

He's just looking at us, I said.

There's no such thing as just looking. Linus was angry in that moment with that thought. *Just like my parents, the way they look. They never just look.*

Opening up at the end of the entry was the world of commerce. It was the crazy world of rushing customers. All crazy to spend and buy. Cars were queued up at traffic lights with desperate and excited people inside. They looked out of their misty compartments with their bright eyes. The pavements held the throngs of pulsating bodies. What an assemblage! Annoying marching out-of-step legs. Swinging hips. *Free Consultation* ! *Healthy Breen's Bile Beans* ! *Big Sale* ! *I Buy Anything* ! *Made to Measure* ! *What's in Store for You* ? *Browse at Your Leisure* ! It was all there for them. The slogans for slow minds. Slowgan. Slowgan, Slow-gan. Gan, gone. Disengaging. Their silly bodies reflected their silly minds. The selling society. Weaned from the fountain tit of wisdom.

We walked into the hullabaloo of the human traffic and away from the quiet entry and the concrete shoveller. *The city centre,* I said.

The shitty shentre, said Linus. *He's putting broken glass on the top of his wall. The shoveller is cementing bits of broken glass on his wall to stop burglars. I just realised. He had a cut on his finger. I just realised that too. It seemed deep. Dark blood was oozing out. He sucked it off after he wiped the sweat off his forehead with his sleeve. And there was a bucket of broken glass beside him. Didn't you see?*

CHAPTER 21

Wandering the busy city—looking at the Belfast people. Wondering in the spirit of discrimination and discernment. Not just looking but looking for. Looking for the source of a laugh. A cracking up laugh. A laugh to take you on to another one. *Look at him, he thinks he's a private eye, I murmured to Linus. In his dirty raincoat. His cigarette. Look how he holds it. Inwardly between forefinger and thumb. The smoke sailing up between his fingers. He wants to stub it out on somebody's face after a long drag. Like Bogart. He thinks he's Humphrey. More like Bumphrey. A free bum. Look at him, he thinks he's a tough guy. A Shankill tough guy. Look at his swagger. Low down, upper half swaying on his waist. Jutting head. Looking for trouble*. But not really. His eyes betrayed his cowardice.

And look at him, said Linus. *He thinks he's rich, standing upright, chest out, with his hand in his pocket rattling his change. Looking over the crowd. And look at her, the plain woman. She thinks she's lovely, all dolled up. Hey doll! Thinks she's a beauty. A film beauty*. She wanted us to see her beauty. But all we saw was her ordinariness. Everyone thought they were someone else.

We were looking at feet. Feet that rolled the dirt and stones under them, feet that scratched the earth. The impatient foot on one leg and the tired one on the other. Two feet on the same person doing different things, feeling the different moods of the owner.

We were heading for Mercer's sports store. That's where our minds were now. *Mercy me,* Linus kept saying. *Mercy. Lord be Mercerful to us as shopping sinners! Mercy me Lord.* In a southern US drawl. *Mercy.* Like Roy Orbison. *No one could look as good as you.* The idea of Mercer looking good was almost fatally amusing. It nearly drove our extended modal selves off the pavement into the traffic. We held on to one another. We held tight and swayed. We tripped over our own legs. People looked. They looked worried. Thought our laughter was madness. Thought our madness was a threat. Thought we were stupid, idiotic, thuggish. Thought it would turn on them in a form they feared. They feared our harmless madness more than the bombers. Thought we should be in a madhouse getting electric shocks to our heads. Then I thought of Linus going to the doctor of madness. If only the onlookers knew.

Commercer Mercer kept his store just off Royal Avenue. It wasn't big or commercially bold enough to be on the Avenue itself, a broad thoroughfare for thoroughbreds of the retail world. Mercer's was an old nag, with a well worn friendliness. A bit threadbare in fact. A deathly slow pace of selling for a business that was quickly expiring. It was messy. No neatness or subtlety of display. No attention to the intricacies of window dressing. Or personal dressing. Delivered stock lay about in brown boxes by the counters weeks after it had been received. Opened and unopened. Never taking stock of stock. Dust gathered on any glass or shiny surface, including Mercer's spectacle lenses. Long sighted lenses, massive bulbous lumps of glass. Frighteningly large eyes through which I believed he saw everything in huge detail. They weighed heavy upon his bulbous nose. A pitted snout, a grunt given for every purchase. A tune played from his sniffing organ in the busy period. A big pig of a nose organ. Upholstered with pinky pigskin, pitted with holes. Holes that something should have sprouted from.

Mercer knew us through his big lenses. Whatever existed for him, it did so through those magnifiers. We were right at the end of his nose. But he also sometimes couldn't identify us in that fusty old mind of his, so on those occasions it could be said he didn't know us. Or didn't appear to. However, we were frequent visitors. Lookers, just there to look at the sporting line-up. Both what was new and what was old. What was going cheap. What was soiled. Orange, bladdered footballs, pumped and unpumped. Laced and unlaced. Old bladders lying around. Mercer's old bladder creaking under the strain of pumping up a ball. Unsewn balls needing resewing. Mercer's lifeless old balls. Unfelt, empty, sagging sacks in loose, baggy gabardines. The archery section. The shooting section. Lethal looking metal-tipped arrows. Giant straw targets. Birch bows. Mercer's bow legs. Piles. Air guns and starting pistols. I desperately desired a starting pistol in my possession, in my hand, just to scare the shite out of people. Say, the cross-eyed park keeper came to chase us off his precious bowling green grass when we were playing football on it. I would produce the gun, aim it at him and reduce him to kneeling to pray for forgiveness. I was always wondering why kneeling was required for praying, but here it is: praying is really begging. Cross-eyed Dixon, the parky, would be begging. He'd be saying to himself inside his restricted, parky mind, *This is the moment you die.* Then I'd say, *Forget all your stupid park rules, cross-eyes.* Then I'd fire it and he'd think he was heading for dead land. His dreadland. Better to die in bed in old age, he would think. In a cowardly fashion. In that instant, he'd think everything there was in his skull. It would just spill over like a waterfall, but it couldn't be contained. He would mumble the things that he caught in the passing deluge of ideas. He would curse his mother for marrying a cross-eyed man.

I would just be grateful to see him on the wrong side of a telling off. I wouldn't kill him even if I could. I just wanted him to live with the fear he once had one day in his life. Instead of the false idea that he was a tough guy in a uniform.

We proceeded. The continuing selves. We continued, we moved our continuity. We felt our power to be continuous. Towards Mercer's we persevered, knowing that Mercer's would be there no matter what. The sun had gone. As usual by mid-morning. The sun continued somewhere else. But Mercer's continued. And we saw it. Off Royal Avenue. Mercer's Sports and Athletic Store. In green paint. Scuffed around foot level. An old woman with a mop washed it. It was dark green and unscuffed when wet and lighter and scuffed when it dried. There seemed no change for washing it.

It was like when you tried to polish your scuffed shoes with spit. They were OK until they dried. That's what you did when you went home in your good school shoes. Just to get past your ma. But she'd always find them when you took them off. She wasn't daft for that sort of thing, just daft if you wanted her to do your homework. Only your da could do that. The da had a mind for it or liked to think he did. My Uncle Robert said he was good at maths. He said, *Give it here son,* so I gave him my maths exercise book, and he took his pencil from behind his ear to check my sums. It wasn't two minutes before he gave it back and put his pencil back behind his ear. He was stumped, but he never said that. He just said that he had a headache. He wasn't stupid, just mathematically daft. The mother said he was a crafty git. And crafty meant clever. But he wasn't crafty enough for the maths as maths is not a craft at all. It's logic. Crafty was sneaky, but you couldn't say maths was sneaky.

Mercer had his football kits behind his counter. You couldn't say that you were just looking, for you couldn't see anything. So crafty Mercer had you there, as if taught by my Uncle Robert. But he didn't really have you. People just went elsewhere to look.

Fewer and fewer people were using his shop. He looked angrier and angrier on each of our new visits, the cheek of him. He grumbled inside. Lesser and lesser the man we knew. His magnified peepers were watery with sadness. Sadness straining out the eye juice. The ghosts of the non-being of his being were upon him. His status as shopkeeper was threatened, and so precious was it to him, that his status as a man was also in peril. With the weight of worry and sadness, he saw his toes more than usual. Bent more and more like a hairpin with everyday that came and went. The effort to stand erect required more effort the more bent he became. And his sparse head hair was greasy grey. In the absence of Brylcream, did he moisten it with the lard in his frying pan? Long strands of that wiry greyness fell forward, gravity urged, sinking into his eyes. Blinking strands! Blinking eyes! More water in the sockets by the minute.

I had the urge to take my forefinger and push the hair from his face, but the complex idea of dirt grease on hair quite rapidly nearly made me boke, boke from the depths of a stiffening stomach. I heaved with the idea of grease and hair mingling and having it in my mouth through the placement of some ridiculous bet or having it shoved there in some tasteless torture. How would Mercer stand up to torture, was a thought I had. There were people in the world who never ever foresaw themselves as victims of torture and to the outside eye would have been truly unlikely sufferers. What would a simple shopkeeper do in response? All he cared about was shopkeeping. Selling balls. I would have respected him more if I knew he had been tortured. Even if he had begged and cried to his torturer for release. Even if he had spilled all the secrets he had to spill. It occurred to me that everyone should have to suffer something terrible at least once. It would be something we could all share, something that would unite us in respect of one another. But here was Mercer, without respect from us, being what he was, just being an obnoxious shopkeeper. He could keep his shop. Keep it. Keep it 'til he died. His dreary shop was like a keep, his stronghold, a tower, a prison, a cell. He earned his keep in his keep. He was ageing and old without anything new to point at the world. He had nothing new in the merchandise of his character. It was all old stock. And he offered us nothing new of himself. Nor did he show himself anything new. He dismissed his own primitive order of being. He rejected himself. But what was so good about the new anyway?

He should have seen us as good customers, but he was impatient that we weren't there more often, less lookers and more buyers, or that there were not more like us in there, upholding his livelihood. He still behaved as though there was a shop full of people but there wasn't. He rushed each customer as if there was a line waiting. His head was stuffed full of confused ideas.

What was it that made me see him differently, with my mind's eye, on this visit? With my riches in my pocket, I saw his old being, I saw him in otherness. In bed otherness, sleeping otherness, dreaming otherness, rising with his old body to the day otherness. I saw him buck naked in the bath. Then drying himself. Except for his eyes which were always brimming with old man moisture. He dabbed himself here and there with a small towel, as if the wetness was in discrete patches and not all over. The whole process was oh so slow. But there was pleasure in it for him. The pleasure of slowness itself.

I don't like slow, through that inability to wait, and there seems always to be something waiting to be done, which cannot be done unless that which is more pressing is done first.

I walked in on him and he smiled. I dreaded his friendly smile. It was an invitation to an event I didn't know anything about.

Where are you boys going? said the sad and slow shopkeeper. Slowly, of course. He was afraid we were going to be bad to him and his enterprise, he wanted knowledge of our intended action.

Going? Going somewhere to buy something, my good man, said Linus with a snap of arrogance. *Our destination is a purchase. We chase an object of our desire.* Linus offered him something new. A new language. Not the language of the cheeky brat, for which he was prepared. We were standing still at the long glass-topped counter, which seemed to generate an atmosphere of fragility, but Linus was going somewhere in his head and taking Mercer for a bit of a ride with him. This was Linus territory. He had woken to a world and wanted to play with it. I took some credit for this awakening. It was Linus but also partly me. It was the emerging backslider in him.

We're looking for football attire for this young gent here, said Linus pointing to me. He had ditched his Belfast accent, substituting it with that of an upper class twit. I loved this codding on. He was suddenly in control of himself and the situation he desired to develop. It was an experiment, theatrical, but there were no rehearsals. Out of nowhere. It just came to him. Was this his madness that I hadn't seen? He seemed to be entirely the source of his own actions, and there was nothing in his mind but his own actions, his will to act, his idea to act. The world was now merely a field of play. His mind affirmed itself instant by instant. The essence of his character was his endeavour to create his own self over and over again in new expressions. He listened carefully to his own mind, and carried out its intentions. Even though I was in there also.

What football attire exactly? asked Mercer. *Is he an outfield player? Is he a keeper?*

Am I my brother's keeper? responded Linus. In deference to Mercer he turned his gently smiling gaze to me. He laid the flat of one hand on the plate glass counter top and the other on his hip. A commanding pose.

Then out of the shadows of shadows came a commanding vision.
Out of the dust of the air came woman. A woman of imperfect
splendour. An unalienated transmission of womanhood. Unfresh,
floating femininehood. A primitive encounter over a counter,
leaving us somewhat glassy-eyed. Naked. Naked womanhood, not
skin nakedness but nakedness of a woman. Womb-an! Womb-man.
The man with a womb. Was I misunderstanding something here?
Words of a sort, where in my mouth I knew not, were in my mouth,
but mouthed silently, lips slightly pouting. Was I understanding
a misunderstanding? Was this phenomenon on the other side of
Mercer's counter? Oh *his* side? On the other side. Not our side. Was
it us here and her there? Countering us. Demanding in her look
that we be counted.

I have it, Mrs McCullough, said Mercer with a slow opening and
closing of his old jaw. *Football kits. If you allow me, I'll deal with
it. Football is my department. The man's department.* He smiled a
respectful smile at her that claimed a certain understanding. He
smiled at Mrs McCullough a lot. When he took her into his gaze,
any gaze, a short swift gaze or a longer one, he smiled that smile.
But did it always mean the same thing?

I knew many McCulloughs, but she wasn't one of them. She lived
with a Mr McCullough presumably. The big hard C of McCullough
stuck in my throat. It co-habited in mind with recent residents
fuck and *cunt*. *Fuck!* Annoying. I opted for a soft *C* but when I said
McSullough, my mouth developed an unusual dryness. Like in the
instant she smiled straight at me.

*This young man would like football attire, but I would like some
cricket wear,* said Linus. He now had that heavy hand on my
shoulder. A pressured, directing hand that kind of pushed me in
the direction of Mercer whilst he looked at Mrs McCullough. She
offered something new to his curiosity.

The cricket section is also Mr Mercer's, said Mrs McC. *You'll
have to wait for your friend.* Her tone was not a representative of
friendliness. Rather, it was one that expressed, *no bullshit.* And
what followed between Linus and the saleswoman sounded to
me like Fred MacMurray talking to Barbara Stanwyk in *Double
Indemnity.*

Which section are you in? What is your section? said Linus to Mrs McC. *I'm interested in several things.*

What things would they be? demanded Mrs McC.

That depends, said Linus. *I'm open to suggestions. I'm open. Is there anything you'd recommend?* Linus opened his arms to the whole emporium.

That's a good question, said the redoubtable Mrs McC. *I could recommend something you haven't got, I am sure about that.*

And how would you know that?

I can read your mind. And she looked at him as though she indeed was.

Whilst Mercer was toiling in some distant drawer, I reawakened myself to Mrs McC. I was interested in the mind of Mrs McC reading the mind of Master L.

Any mind that can read my mind is worth paying heed to, declared Linus.

Pay heed then. Not half heed. Whole heed. With your whole head. She said head like a raw Scotsman. A Glaswegian. *Heed.* She huffed out the *h* and ended with a drilled *d.* She nodded her whole head in agreement with her own self. Her idea of what she said matched her idea of what she thought. She laughed at her own joke. She, the morning and the evening star of our lives in that moment.

What was she? Was she old Mercer's woman? How blind was I? Blind to the truth. To the fact. Deaf as a leaf. A corn sheaf ear. Old Mercer called her Mrs McC. Not Mrs McCullough. Did he? I couldn't remember correctly in the instant I needed to. I was in distress. Was she really Mrs McC? Did he not say she was? Saying is not always the truth. Saying can be a lie. She placed her hands fully flat on the glass counter. Fingers splayed, the considerable strain of an angled form, angled towards Linus. The hands were remarkable. Long and lean. Long, pointed painted nails. Strong like perspex. Our little bitten flaking nails were shite compared to them. And comparisons were always a major part of the mind's activity. Of this and that, the mind never stopped the job of matching one thing with another. *What do think is best?* was a common question amongst us.

Cascading, dripping off our weak little mindlings, with the whole *reading the mind* thing still ringing in our ears and her shocking scent burning our noses, were notions of dress. Words dressed up, clothes speaking. Is there a language of clothes? I dare say there is. I thought of Les Buttocks's pants and the message they conveyed.

What's that she had on? That she in fact put on? On her. On her mind. By her mind. Over her. A powerful dress. Formidable. Heavyweight wool, tweed, on the weighty hips. Broad-belted leathered waist buckled. A governing impenetrability. A governess. Destructive of weak pomposity. And on her material maternal knee I'd love to be. What's a dress? What's a skirt? What's the difference? The sisters explained it once to me. I couldn't ever remember what they'd said. Which was which?

Mrs McC's lips were lightly glued closed with pink lipstick and some locking jaw pressure to a potent pout. What a union! A union of plumpness. She gave Linus an eye. Again and again. First the wide open eye and then the squint. The narrowing of purpose. The narrowing down and the pouting up to meet one another. An eye that didn't tell a lie. Her eye to his I. His I was in her eye, his I totally hers. An eye to add to his thoughts. He thought to change her eye and its intent. Lucky she wasn't on this side of the counter, I thought. She had the hands that do buttons up in a trice. The long and the lean. The soft and the sure. I always had trouble doing and undoing buttons with my stubby mitts. If in a hurry to dress or undress, she was the one for buttons. No fumbling with those hands. Surety. Those hands. Merciless precision. Perfect for the laying on of hands for the sin sick soul. The mother couldn't do up buttons with her fat fingers. She spent an age with you on her knee when you were small, all the wriggling and wriggling and sliding down on her knee to get away as she fumbled the buttons. If I was on the Mrs McC's course woolly knee I would allow her to do my buttons. I would sit still knowing it would be quick. I would feel the pleasant nimbleness of her touch. The effortlessness that would quell my restless boyish intent. She would have my still buttocks on her firm knee.

I know minds like yours, you see, whispered Mrs McC, harshly through her pink pout. *I have had the pleasure of serving them. And when you serve someone whose mind you know, you know exactly what they seek. And I know exactly what you seek. I have just the thing.*

I felt sleepy. Like a child ready for bed after a long day. I just felt weak and heavy. My face was numb, my eyelids burdensome, my mind muddled and dreamy. Linus was silent. He was silent and smiling. It wasn't a smile of confusion, but it was a silence of not knowing what to say in an interesting way. His smile showed Mrs McC that he understood something. Something that he couldn't say. At least in the words that locked his mind. They understood each other in another way, not about this or that but probably about nothing, nothing that was sensible to say.

He understood her skirt, or dress, he understood her hands that were flat on the glass and the way she leaned towards him. They said something to him. The dress said something. The long fingers. He came back to them time and again. The closed and open lips. Her eyes. Especially the eyes. But not entirely on their own. And she understood him in his little corduroy shirt. The smart shirt said something. Something grown up but not. It was ironed and that said something. The fine vertical creases. His curious curiosity within that shirt. His empty curiosity. His dreamy emerging adulthood. His fanciful wet mind. A swamp. A damp birthplace of creativity. The obscure and oblique manner sprouting out of it. His head held back. His vagueness. His actually saying nothing. His empty look. Like Les Buttocks's pants. Empty but nevertheless saying something fully. Saying its piece. I could never have been in his place.

This way, she said, not indicating any way except the way she was walking. She walked along the back of the counter away from Mercer and me, sliding her forefinger behind her along the glass counter top. A finger trail which Linus followed. I saw only the magical trail of the finger after they left. The traces. Linus never looked back. Which meant I looked until he and her were no longer in sight, and all I saw was the back of his head in my head. I had expected a swift back glance and a smile of the intrepid explorer. And then old Mercer came back into view. My view. But I had in mind Linus and the powerful woman. Her finger beckoning Linus. Of Linus with his vision of her shapely back.

CHAPTER 22

What did she sell you? I asked. *What did you buy? What did she buy? Your bullshite?* We were out in the cold air once more. Shivering in our flimsy clothes with the air holes at the waist. In amongst the human traffic again, feeling the pressure of all their wanting bodies hurrying here and there and not minding if they stepped on your feet or shoved you into somebody else. Not a word of apology. Just the mad shopping minds madly wanting to get there first. Their first. Their grubby grabbing mitts on items of desire. They laughed amongst themselves, but the laughing was all fake and unfunny. Excess guffawing, excess excitement had to go somewhere. One had to be aware of the fakery. Of fakery itself. A wise boy knew fakery and laughed at it. *You oul fake!* he declared. I had my purchased package firmly in my grasp. Not unknown for a package to disappear from your possession in a crowd of fakes. I squeezed the top of the plastic bag so nothing would fall out. Nor would it be taken from me without a forceful pull. Mercer's name was all crumpled. Like Mercer himself. He sold me his crumpled self. What a self it was. A sterling silver self among all the fake farthing selves.

Hic puer est stultissimus omnium! said Latin Linus. He spoke Latin when he was disturbed. When he was angry, when he was disappointed with himself. *This boy is the stupidest of all! Cunnus!*

Stercorem pro cerebro habes! Stercorem pro cerebro habes!

What?

Shite for brains, that's what.

Why, what's the story?

The story's ending. A bad ending.

What happened?

What did not happen? What did not transpire, did not take place, or befall me? She cut me off. She withdrew herself. She read my mind as if it had the content of a baby's book.

With Drew? I thought she was with you? But you do suit the name Drew.

Funny! She offered… something. I asked her what was in my mind. An experience, she said. A happening. Something new. Something that would help me understand. Did I want it? Do you want it? she said. What is it? I said. That would be telling, she said. Well, I have to know, I said. But telling won't let you know, she said. What then? I said. Then she went behind me and I traced her as she went around me. In the room with all the balls. All the bails and wickets. All the bare bladders. And the flat lumpy outer cases. Pumps and all that as well. She was behind me saying nothing at all. I could just feel the breath of her. Coming off her. Closing in. The sweet smell of her circling my head overpowering the leather and the fustiness. The rustle of her crisp clothes and the jangle of her jewellery crowded my ears. What? I said. What? What is it? I stepped in her direction. So to speak. Then she took herself beyond reach. My reach. That's badness for you. Teasing you. Testing you. Treating you like an idiot. Like feeding a baby.

Sounds like she gave you something, I said. *She gave you something and then removed it. But not all of it. You have something of it. And you have something to understand. Something… oh shite! What in holy… I'm mystified with mystification. It's a mystery like religion is. One of those really annoying things they call a mystery. The miracles.*

Not just enough to make me want to have all of it. She said, do you want something or not? I said of course that is what I am here for. Well, there's no harm in wanting, she said. What's that supposed to mean? Where's the meaning in it?

Confusing terribly. I laughed and gave my head a scratch. The itch seemed to come precisely at the same time as the confusion. *The meaning of it is hilarious. Because it's mad completely. Mad meaning. You'd have to be mad to know it.*

What it is, what it really is, is a world that has come to be gone. Has come to be gone. Has come to be... and then is gone away. Passed away but is. A few minutes ago it was to come. What a being she is. Was. Is. I'll never forget. Then he whispered. *Coming off her.*

Never forget what you didn't even get. Or you'll fret. Let's have a bet.

Get the fuck! Where are we going? Have you got what you want? I was thinking of Smithfield for a bit of a laugh. It's only early days yet.

CHAPTER 23

Are you saved? bawled the Pastor from on high. *Are you saved, gentleman? Are you saved, lady?* he bawled even louder. *Are you saved father, are you saved mother? Say saved,* he instructed his audience. A few repeated his words in a bit of a mumble. His throat crackled with the raw power of the shout. He bawled to them, *Say it again, say saved!* He got a slightly louder mumble. Still unsatisfied, his vocal chords strained to snapping as they received all his internal gusto. *Are you ashamed of the Lord? Say it again!* It was frightening when he bawled. Simply an unpleasant noise. Deep into the psychic recesses. How was that voice possible? He made me jump every time he hit that pitch and transmitted that mangled rasp. I felt like taking a rasp to him, like the ones they had in woodwork classes. Rasping his mouth, his nose, his bounteous buttocks. So he'd scream for a reason that I knew.

I'll give you something to rasp for, I'd say like the mother says. I felt like hitting somebody when that pitch was hit and made me jump. It angered me. The unconscious anger. I felt my bottom teeth jut out in my jutting-out jaw. A raging jut. The battle of jaw jut. But I laughed when the others jumped. If one jumped, the whole row of seats quivered. I heard people squeak when they jumped. Such a total geg. I could hardly control myself in the holy midst when I saw the discomfort of the saints. But out loud, open-mouthed guffawing had to be suppressed.

Then the Pastor would suddenly shut down the shouting, whispering close to his microphone, *Are you saved?* It's holy hypnosis time. I thought it was whispered to me personally, one to one. The shouting was to instil a blanket of fear, the whisper to effect sleep. In that whispering time, he divined me as a sinner. I had the black water of sin in me. The bitter, black bile of the prince of darkness. Upon which his message shone brightly. I had that dark idea with me every day. The question to myself was always, *Are you saved?* I sometimes answered yes, but sometimes I said, *I don't know.* And when I sinned, I said I was not. Then I cried to God to forgive me and all was well. But then I sinned again and I cried in my sin after the sinful thing was done and its pleasure was over. In my solitude I realised the fault in me. Not in the world, where sin abounded. But I was in sin now. Sin row. The sin of stealing. Was there a stealing that wasn't sinful?

Steal away, steal away,
Steal away to Jesus.
Steal away, steal away, steal away home
I ain't got long to stay here.

My Lord, He calls me,
He calls me by the thunder;
The trumpet sounds within my soul,
I ain't got long to stay here.

Steal away... Steal away...

What sort of stealing was that? We sang that almost every Sunday night. People cried. People yelped like dogs and had fits like mad dogs with their mouths frothing. But no dog did that. That was the thing about the word. They shuddered as if freezing on account of the word. They collapsed on account of the word. People quaked in their seats, and waved and flapped their hands dangerously about in loose fashion without shame on account of the word. All when they said, *Steal away to Jesus.* Sung in a quiet reverence until the words *The trumpet sounds within my soul.* It was hilarious. The spirit of laughter was within me from all that was without. My sister without a brain, babbled in tongues in the middle of it all. Then she inspired more tongue wagging until the air was full of babbling and yelping and shuddering. Sisters and brothers in the Lord confronting Satan with their holy lunacy. Stealing to Jesus.

I asked the sister in the Lord, who was also my sister not in the Lord for most of the time, what *Steal away to Jesus* meant, and she didn't even know. It had a spiritual sound to it she said, and that is why it counted. But, I said, *steal away is hardly spiritual.* She mumbled something that I didn't care to hear. She was thick anyway, so I didn't know why I was asking her beyond exposing her daftness. She wasn't one for words. Just babbling. Flushed with stupidity. It was an embarrassment. A good old laugh, but only if you kept it within the confines of your own home and not let it out. You didn't want to be near them when that happened. It was stupidity sometimes you could throttle, a throttling accompanied by a mad joy as you were throttling stupidity. Her joy said, *how happy I am to be so stupid.* She sang it. She sang it about the house. With a skip in the step. Happy step up the steps, up the stairs to her room. That smile with the singing and stepping! I smacked it once in a rage when it smiled right at me. I did it seemingly without a thought to inspire it. My hand just rounded on her face with great precision. Instinctive. But I must have thought about it somewhere. Like my crime, I must have considered *not* doing it. Maybe a crime of passion. And then, when I did it, I ran for it. For she had a temper like the mother. An enormous reservoir for anger. A stored anger boiler. Not the boiler type with instant heat at every moment. It was there already but had to be lit. Somewhere. The inner potency to seething action. Seething and teething. The upper and lower teeth grinding like millstones.

*

What did the Pastor of the church know of the full ball sack? And the empty ball sack that's been emptied? How it all emptied out of me in my waywardness. You couldn't sit there listening without a worldly thought emptying out of your head. *Empitied,* said the mother. Not of the ball sack but of anything. *Is the bath empitied?* Like her mind had been empitied. But the Pastor had a full mind. A mind full of Holy Bible wisdom. He declared he knew the world as well as he knew the Bible, but the world held nothing for him. He said he knew all the bad words the Devil transmits to the sinner. Everybody listened as if he dispensed healthy words. Like they'd listen to a doctor. And his mind was a miracle, for he kept emptying it and it just remained full. Every week he came and emptied it on those empty heads all below him. And they were none the wiser. They just repeated amens and praise the Lords. But did they need wisdom? Was their experience the thing? The thing they knew most intimately. They just needed some additional words to fill in the gaps, an idea here and there that gave it all a sense. And they'd sense it. Like smelling home. But what was really going on? They were on the Pastor's mission, which they thought was God's mission. But the Pastor had the upper hand. He fed them his powerful medicine and got them to pay for it. Like medical prescriptions.

I sat with them, among them and looked up at the spiritual leader, thinking about his truth. The truth about him. Was he a liar? Was he even a backslider? He always mentioned the backslider. He wanted them to come forward and deny their fallen ways. *Is there a backslider,* he said in his sincerest voice, *is there someone who has gone astray, lost the friendship of Jesus? Are you denying him like Peter did and are continuing to deny him? Not just three times but thirty-three times. The number of years of Christ's life. You may turn away from him but he will always be faithful to you. You may think you are alive but you are dead. Dead spiritually. But nothing is impossible to God. He raises people from the dead, dead bodies like Lazarus, and he raises spiritually dead people from their spiritually dead lives all the time. Because that is what he wants. That is his work. His purpose. Uniting all souls together with himself. Just think of the parable of the prodigal son. The welcoming homecoming is what we will all receive in Heaven. But there are some who will never return. They will be lost forever. Their denial is so profound that they have nothing in them to inspire them to come back. They are doomed to eternal damnation. Don't squander your soul, sinner and backslider. You may have, like the prodigal son, squandered some spiritual power that you had, but it can be renewed at the fount of faith. At the rock that is Jesus. Come to your spiritual senses, sinner. Has sin made you mad? What are you rejecting? What are you accepting in its place? What do you now stand for? A night on the town? A drunken frenzy in a smoke filled bar? A lusty liaison with a harlot? What? What did he say, I hear you say? That will not only kill you dead and put you in the earth it will send you to spiritual hell, and spiritual death. There will be no reconciliation of your soul with all the pure souls in glory. You will be in spiritual torment, forever seeking to clamber out of the unscalable walls of hell but forever falling at the first step.* And on and on. I felt tired with it all, sleepy with the repetitive message. If I closed my eyes, I would sleep or wander into some dream. Right there amongst the faithful. Head bowed and brimming with the heathen thing. On a heath, playing, cavorting, writhing. The body uniting with earth.

With the glorifying hymn, *Just as I am without one plea,* softly landing on my numbed mind, I eased into a deeper dream. A dream of a lusty thing with a harlot. I'd be a whoremonger in my dream. But the word whoremonger was unreliable, as it would lead me to end up thinking of a fishmonger where I went to buy fish for the mother. Old Routledge's on the Avenue. The smell. Not of a whore. A dead fish. The best situation would be to have the lusty thing and then come back to Jesus after it has been enjoyed. This was the essence of the backslider, says the man on the pulpit. What then if you had a heart attack in your lust? Right in the middle of it. Right at the moment of maximum lustiness with your eyes all lusty and your body responsive only to the call of the Devil. I knew the lusty eye and had to hide it. It was a dead give-away. But I could never think lustily exclusively, so there was never a real maximum that would be easily detected. But, I always had Jesus there beside me. The holy gatecrasher. Lust, Jesus, lust, Jesus, lust, Jesus. Jesus was always last, after the lust, but only up to now. I worried about the not now, a future that would be absent and also an absent Jesus. Only lust there, with nothing to remove it.

There was always a backslider coming forth in the froth of spiritual excess, because the message of eternal doom frightened the sinful shite out of them. Furthermore, the preacher told them that deathbed confessions were worthless words and thoughts. They would fall on emptiness. The emptiness of deserted holiness. A endless desert of sin. *I have no time for it,* he shouts. *When the Lord tells me, No more! There will be no more. No more pleading. The soul will be stillborn. It's too late on the deathbed. They've flirted too long with the worldly things, playing brinkmanship with God Almighty, and so God does not attend their desperate, begging declaration of repentance. I am sorry, believer, if that sounds harsh. But I believe it. You cannot play brinkmanship with God Almighty.*

The preacher said he would never credit such a declaration, for God himself would be absent. What a way to die, alone in the universe. God departed. Spiritless oblivion. Every positive presence withdrawing. No one to call upon. Just pain, empty, neglected words shouted into the void, then the abyss itself. I saw the scene clearly. I cursed my sliding back into worldly ways, my harlot dreams and my unhealthy jaunts in heathendom. On the heath rolling and writhing about. I denounced it all with all my might. I intended it to be true, because if I did not, it would just be another example of my failing the Saviour. I distilled the idea of the gaping abyss and the empty words that were spoken into it. I closed my eyes and stiffened my body to sustain the firm form of my thoughts, to help purge them of the crippling infectious doubt. And I asked myself at the very same time, *What sort of game is this?*

*

I always sat in the same row. In the same seat. On the left side as you enter the church hall. Towards the front, but never the front seats as that was too exposed to elderly looks. We always arrived early to get our places. We felt the church fill up on all sides. A friendly filling up. The brethren breathing contentedly in unison. The murmur and mutter of the matter of spirit. The form that matters. Good form in the form of good godly cheer. The cheer was all around our ears. *By God, it does you good brother. Bless the Lord, brother, bless the Lord, sister,* said the meek elder at the door as the brothers and sisters flocked in. The flock that flock. The throng that couldn't be wrong. All around us was the building reverence in the Lord's house. Until all the reverent were all around us, behind us, beside us, hemming us in. I wouldn't like to try to get out. All eyes would be on me. They said Jesus was here as well. And the Holy Spirit. Their joint presence was here. Was that the same thing? The Lord and his Spirit? There was the schism of *Oneness* about the place. A troubling undercurrent. Identities unknown. Some said he is *Oneness*, some say she is. And point the finger. Nobody knows for sure. But the preacher made his *threeness* position clear. *The Holy Trinity or nothing*, he proclaimed, and the *Oneness* believers remained in hiding.

Oneness was on my mind but not the oneness of God. It was the oneness of a girl. My gaze suddenly moved across the church aisle. The aisle of dreams. It was a realisation how little individuality I had, though not at all conscious then. It was the beginning. I looked around and saw the people who took my life from me. That is what is to be. And there, over there, was a girl and her presence. Her particular oneness. Always this girl in the row across the aisle to my right. The same girl in the same seat. The same pleasurable waft of presence. Not just her in the row: she was flanked by the blessed ones, but she was all I really saw. What a blessing what a joy divine. I'd love to be leaning on her everlasting arms.

My attention oscillated between her and the mighty Pastor. An attention divided between the exhorting, threatening, inspiring, commanding words of the shepherd and the so sweet, silent, feminine message floating from the girl in the row to my right. When we were supposed to be closed-eyes praying, we squinted across at one other. I liked her white, knee-length boots that were part high-heel shoe, part supple clinging soft skin. I could see them only partially from my seat, but I could see them all in my inventive mind, caressing her legs right up to, and just over, the knee. Her fifteen denier knees. Like a light suntan. The mother always asked me to get her fifteen denier stockings in the chemist shop at the bottom of the street, on the corner with busy Botanic Avenue. I hated going to buy stockings. Asking for them off a woman in a clean white coat behind a counter. How tidy she was. Messiness was banished in chemist shops. Sometimes she was not behind the counter but floating about filling up racks and shelves. If they didn't have fifteen denier I wasn't to get anything else, I was told.

I didn't like saying the word *denier*. It wasn't at all familiar to the mind or the mouth. I found it difficult to say other than with a French accent. *Dawn-ee-ay*. Because it looked French. I asked the mother over and over again how you really said it, but she said she didn't know what I was talking about. I said that I had to stand there in the chemist and ask for it. I needed to know. I tried so hard not to say my French version. I thought how the mother said it and that sounded nothing like French. And then, with the feather light fifteen denier hose in a flimsy chemist's bag, I had to run home in case I was stopped by someone I knew who would most certainly ask what it was I had there in my hand. I ran until I got a stitch in my side but kept on running.

I always went to the chemist for something in the afternoon after school. Just when I wanted to play. The same with church, it was playing time wasted, so it had to be made into time not wasted. Pay attention. Understand something and make it interesting. Experience it. Make it pleasurable. But just sitting there for two hours was hopeless and painful. On those wooden seats. Fifteen denier coloured seats. The arse ached deep inside. Leaning forward to pray was a relief on the buttocks. Mildly more painful to start with as you eased them off. Worse if you'd been kicking a ball all day. Cramp in the back of the thigh, in the hamstring. The charley horse cramp. Murder most foul for the legs! Like the leg was dying. The leg required straightening in a small confine. *Aye, aye, aye!* The sheer ache of it inspired new linguistic forms. The contracting muscle. With a will all of its own. I once had to stand bolt upright in the beseated church when a charley horse seized my right leg. I kicked out with it but there was no room to stretch. The pew in front was practically backed on to my knees. I pushed myself up to full erectness and with agony on my face and with watery eye, I saw across the human summits. Heads with and without hair. Snowy peaks. Egg heads. A new aspect of the blessed was mine, and I was theirs, as they interpreted the thrust upwards and the attendant grimaces and gasps as a holy fit.

*

Sacred Darkness! The insurrection of my being against holiness. Or was it a resurrection? The unlit appropriation of me. It was a black, black canvas with your eyes closed in church, but with some staunch soul always droning on about some pious thing or other whilst you press your eyelids tightly shut, lots of things came to pass in your mind's eye that could be seen only on black. It was a step back so to speak, indeed a step black. And you could see the things that came to pass so clearly. Almost made you not want to open your eyes. If I held my breath there appeared to be an even greater clarity. In this shadowy world, I asserted myself against what was happening in the world I saw when I opened my eyes to the bright light. I saw in the darkness the areas of life that I was not supposed to see. It was resistance and the assertion of my absurd imagination. Some of it had to do with the droning soul and some not. And some just inspired by the droner.

There was no bulb in the landing up the final flight of stairs to my bedroom. At night, I leapt up past the darkness as fast as I could leap. Two steps, or three at a time. Two and three, three and two. Until I reached the light switch in my room, and closed the door, but not before looking back at the darkness one more time through a small crack and then I shut it out. But it was there, and I was aware it was there even in my light. Sometimes I could forget it, sometimes it lingered. If there was something in it, I would never be able to get help. Not even from the Holy Ghost.

There was once a man called Hugo Boxel who wrote about ghosts hundreds of years ago. I opened an old book in a moment of boredom, in the light beyond the darkness, and there was his name. I loved his name as a comic name. There was a man I saw who looked like a Hugo Boxel. He passed our door every morning and marched on like a sergeant major to wherever he was going. *There goes Hugo Boxel,* I said, and if someone was with me they always asked who the hell Hugo Boxel was. *That's Hugo Boxel,* I'd say. *The very man. But who is he?* they'd say. *He's the man who believes in ghosts, apparitions and spectres,* I'd say. *His mind is in a box. A wee box. A box of tricks, a box of superstitions.* Baruch the blessed boxed his ears and told him to wise up. Boxel went off with a flea in his ear, none the wiser to think more about ghosts. *You're mad,* they'd say. *Who the fuck is Baruch the blessed?* And I'd laugh and say, *Don't you like the name?*

Names are hugely important. Modest Mussorgsky was an important name. Linus spotted it on an LP in Harry Hall's second-hand music store in Smithfield Market. William Makepeace Thackery. Makepeace! The name not only amused, it identified a thing, it maintained a distinction, erected a singular connection. Makepeace in one man is not the same Makepeace in another. They are different Makepeaces. Makepeace this man, Makepeace that man. Names carry with them a sense that defines a nature and a connected nature. Linus was the Linus of this and that. Linus meant this and that that was Linus himself. When I thought *Linus*, I thought the things that were proper to Linus. It had a unique reference even though there were thousands of Linuses. So we wanted to know who was the *Makepeace* of Thackery and the *Modest* of Mussorgsky. That was education.

Talk of names was magical when we were young. Powerful communicators of our natures and the nature of things. Think of a world without names. The man with no name. All men with no names. In gulags and concentration camps. My name is nobody, but that is a name. How different it would be. Marius, that's me! Here comes Marius, they say, the same old Marius. The same old me. Me! Marius me is not all the other Mariuses. It's me. When I come around the corner tomorrow and they see me, they will all know me as Marius and Marius as me. The same old me. The parents called me Marius when I was born, but that was inclined to meaninglessness until they kept using my name for me. Then I became the real Marius. The very same. Someone will fall in love with me, Marius, because they know this Marius and how he acts. I wanted to call Linus, Makepeace, Makepeace to replace Linus. Sometimes I did for a laugh. He called me Modest. Modest Moonston. It was Makepeace and Modest together.

From the anonymity of my high in the sky attic room, I shouted down to the street far below, *Hugo Boxel!* as the passer-by Hugo Boxel passed by our front door. He looked around, mystified by the voice, for he was the only soul in the street. Sometimes I took a risk and shouted it again. I withdrew my eyes to the very edge of the guttering. That was a real inside laugh. I told someone at school what I did, but all he said was, *What's funny about that?* Then he laughed at what *he* said. He thought he was being smart, and he said it for others to hear. I thought to myself, what *is* funny about that? But I didn't say it to him. That was polite. What's funny anyway is hard to answer. It's just funny. But what about things that people think are funny but you think are not? What is not funny about them? It was all about theft, stealing something, gaining an advantage at someone's expense. An expense account for those disposed to the joke, taking the mick. An affirmation and a denial.

I stole five pounds and stole away with it, not to Jesus, but to town, and with all my stealing away, I felt riven with guilt but never felt an ounce of guilt when I stole something of someone's self-esteem. Steaming, powering ahead with new self-esteem. The pinpoint essence of us. To persevere.

Nature at war with itself. How can that be? Everything seeking an edge, said the old Cherokee Indian. Imagine hearing that in an old film and remembering it. An edge, an advantage. Dominance, governance, supremacy. A struggle at every turn, but we don't often recognise it as such, in fact we rarely do, and we even see it as a harmonious playground.

Some gargantuan Protestant brute sent me spinning off the witch's hat once in Daddy Winker's Lane playground in the Loyalist east of the city. He shoved me in the back, and I lost my breath as I was suddenly thrust forward from my pleasurable relaxed perch. I heard his massive reservoir of laughter squeeze out as I gasped for breath. He was a fat gasper for breath, and I was a lean gasper, but his gasping was of pleasure and mine of painful fright. He was above me on the swaying witch's hat laughing at me on the ground. He thought he had an edge. But he was just an idiot, too thick to have an edge. A more sophisticated awareness is required to persevere. It's not just brutes against brutes, not even survival of the fittest. It requires an affirmation, a stand. An unselfish self

*

Smithfield Market in the City, was a name that took a stand and a veritable paradise for queer and unique looking names. Before it was converted into a pile of cinders by an arse. A name that attracted. Blokes and dolls stood in doorways or slunk and slouched in or around the seedy shops and stalls all day long. All interesting second-hand stuff that smelled. No waste there. Addictions abounded in the bookies and pubs. And there was always a buyer for the seller. Always a demand. The demand for goods that demanded your attention. And the seller who knew the demand would sell his good self in his talk, his friendly idle talk. If you knew the good self that sold, you were sold something. As did the buyers sell themselves, in their idle walk and talk. The walk and talk of want. They'd saunter about and spit out their intimate lives to the shopkeepers, of their deepest worries and fears and the great, courageous exploits in the very ordinary world they existed in. The shopkeepers listened because there was money in listening. Customers would stay longer than necessary for a purchase, because they're looking for company, looking for a place to be known. You just had to watch them to know. And we watched them in their gatherings. In a daydream.

Have you no work to go to? That's what we said about them when we woke up from our staring somnabulance. As a joke. It was a place of dreams and illusions as much as it was a place of pubs, gambling, and fighting. The dreams often came from the drink and the tiredness of drinking. Smithfield Market had ghosts, they said in their wretched weakness. Out of their disabled minds, to establish itself with greatest notoriety, was the case of old albino eyes, Bridie O'Keefe, who rose up as a spectre from her deadness every Loaf-mass Day to walk the entries, seeking vengeance on the lynch mob who burnt out her demonic eyes, cut out her tongue, and hanged her high by the scrawny neck. All to silence her hymns in praise of heathen passion. That called forth an upright man's flimsily harnessed lust.

Was she, that blind biddy, silently shifting about seeing in the dark landing outside my room when I shut the door on the darkness? Old people ghosts gave me the most hideous nightmares. Wrinkly old cods. When the light went out in my room, the dark was black and thick as the dying granny's cancerous crap. Here Hugo Boxel's world came to life. Intimate terrors abounded. I heard something in the blackness, heard it as a small sound, then as a creeping sound, getting louder and closer, until it was there before me but still unseen. And then a white old face with jelly-like blind eyes would shove itself through that blackness at me in my bed. Oldness unto almost death and blackness of night. Such was the fear that I saw myself as a dead person. I saw my whitened, stiff dead face in the place of the old face that faced me. Death receiving death-like life.

Like my Uncle Hughie, and he wasn't even a ghost. Not quite dead yet. He, the lodging lout in the attic next door, crept about our house like an animated corpse, given breath by the Devil. A ghost in fact. His hands were all slimy and shaking, his skin all loose. Not just the look, of course, but what he did with those hands. When he touched you. When you saw him grasping a door knob and turning it slowly. His mouth also, full of muttering and bad breath, I couldn't entertain the idea of it in my dark house without being scared to sickness. He answered questions when no questions were asked. Was he speaking to some other spirit? Up the stairs on my own, in an empty house, old ghostly Biddy was often in my head, getting into my bed, and I couldn't get her out of it. Chasing me in creaking darkness behind.

The real, ghost-obsessed Hugo Boxel said that, *The measureless space between us and the stars is not empty but thronging with spiritual inhabitants.* In the lowest region, closest to us, *They are creatures of very thin and subtle substance, and also invisible.* But strangely, *They are only of the male sex.* He wrote to Baruch the blessed under a thin guise of friendship, asking his opinion on this, but really he was being somewhat foxy. Or boxy. Hugo Foxy Boxy wanted to put Baruch in a box, trick him into admitting he didn't believe in ghosts, and thus be branded an atheist in a place where atheists were condemned to death.

Ghosts abound in Ulster, of all sexes and ages, ghosts that are fools and madmen and even children. They are preached from the pulpits and you have to say amen. *You cannot think them away,* bawled the Pastor, *because God created them like himself in the perfect creation.* But four hundred years ago, Baruch thought them out of existence.

I wished I had the mind of Baruch to dismiss ghosts as he does. What was it about my mind that admitted them? Or any mind that admits them? They are no minds at all because they do not use the mind as it should be used. Ghosts are the product of the imagination where the mind is not in control of its own thoughts. Imagination is the source of error. We then confuse the language of the imagination with the language of the intellect.

It's like the amazing stories in the Bible, there to inspire obedience of the feebleminded. We are all feebleminded at times and some times more than others. We allow ourselves to be stupid.

I was being stupid in my bedroom thinking about the ghosts in the darkness outside. I read Baruch's letters by dim lamplight and sought his iron reason to make them flee. But it seemed I would rather have lived with my stupidity because when I shut the book I closed my mind, and I opened it again to a world of confusion.

Ulster. It was a society saturated with stupidity and confusion. The unique Ulster brand of stupidity. Branded on their brains from birth. The parents were as stupid as the shite of fools, fool's shite like fool's gold, and were part of the whole province of stupidity. They were, in their selfishness, part children, in part mad and in part fools, but as the whole society was like that, they were as sane as could be. It wasn't a kindom or a kingdom, but a fooldom.

CHAPTER 24

So, where were we? That was always the question. The question about where we were in our minds and where our minds were in our bodies and, in which particular geographical location were we, minds and bodies, in or heading for? There was us, me and Linus, Linus and the I that had a mind for Linus, and in our minds there were others in their place. But we were never entirely alone with ourselves and on this particular occasion as we wandered further from old Mercer's sports store, I had the parents with me as much as I had my ill-gotten gains in a plastic bag held tightly in my right hand. The parents bouncing about in some shop in town. Bouncing with excitement. Jouncing. Linus came up with that word. New to me, and I said it wasn't a real word. But he assured me it was real because he'd heard it used by his father and the people he said it to understood it. *That doesn't make it a word* I said. *What does it make it*, he said. I said that I didn't know at all but surely it couldn't. And we left it at that. But I thought about it by myself from time to time and I repeated the word *jounce* until it became a controlling presence in my mind. Every thought had *jounce* attached to it. I thought up names with *jounce*, a Christian name or a surname. Ted Jounce. Jounce McHalligan. The nickname Jouncy sounded good.

The parent's sort of excitement in the supermarket wasn't at all jouncing joyous. Excitement born of frustration. Getting the weekly necessaries in the cramped aisles. The supermarket in Union hijacked Protestant Sandy Row was the location where most of the bouncing and buying was done. People all crushed together grabbing their weekly food items. Bouncing off one another up the aisles. Not like church aisles, not the aisles of dreams. Decay at work and in progress. Into the mouth of decline. The National Health Service under siege by disease. Here were the examples of human limitation. Born deficient. Born randomly. Sired in some sinful act. *I'm browned off*, the fed up said in a declaration of depression. Fed up! How true. They filled up their guts to forget their neglect. They fed themselves on the morsels of what they fancied. Washed down with endless drams of the prescribed potions. Up to the last. Then up to the gills with the booze before bed. They knew what was good for them. They knew! It was in them to know. Not *them*, them that scoff. They foresaw their pleasure, their mouths watered at the flushy flesh of the pig. A big meaty joint for the disjointed. Or a sliver of pink flesh slipped into the sizzling grease. Singed appetisingly brown and then slid onto a platter and unceremoniously sucked in and scoffed. Oh, the pleasure in their beady eyes on each chew, on each swallow. Their greasy mouths bore witness to undignified gluttony. Etiquetteless.

There is a rhyme and a rhythm and a reason for eating etiquette. It is to stem the guilt entertained if the impatient craving of hunger leads us humans to the excited, unceremonious attack on the food. We do not want to appear as animals feasting on our prey. Etiquette draws the attention to the manner of the activity of eating, almost as if it is something else entirely, and thereby introduces a new pleasure. It's like sport, a civilised substitution of a primitive act, but not quite substitution enough, for we can substitute killing, but not eating. So it seeks to uplift the act to within the rule of rules. But there was no uplifting the acts of the Saturday Sandy Row shoppers. They were what they were, or a thing is what it is.

And bodies are what they are. It occurred to me then that people are not too much appreciative of the body in the way a mind should be. Somebody said that body awareness is the gateway to eternity and even the Christians say the body is the temple of God, which means to me that the human body and all bodies are parts of God in the way that all temples make up the whole church.

Utter rubbish, said the Pastor of the church. But the bodies of the people I saw were not fit for a human mind. Nor as a mode of God. Rather their minds and bodies coincided at a sub-level of humanity, in the basement of embarrassments. I always felt my body fit for my mind. It was fit and light and quick. I always felt I knew it was operating at peak levels. I had the idea of it, so much so that I almost felt that the idea and the body were one and the same thing. They had their sameness but in an inadequate way, as I was an inadequate being.

But inadequate thoughts in inadequate bodies ultimately signal the lack of power, therefore the lack of reality, and the awareness of decline, when it comes is harder to see. We simply slip into a thick soup of sameness, or into a supermarket of simple foodstuffs that are not the food for thought.

If the greatest reality is to know everything then that would mean that we have bodies that can do everything. Isn't that what God is? *Utter rubbish,* said the pastor of the church. *God is immaterial, just as what you say is immaterial.* He was a clever man in his way. He knew that shouting *utter rubbish* and the like into an ignorant face would make people believe him. And obey him. Not just because he frightened the holy shite back into them, but because, they reasoned with limited reason.

Where was I? There! That's where I was at a moment in time as we stepped towards Smithfield. Here and there. In the church with the shouting Pastor. And there with them in the supermarket. And they stirred me up to anger the whole lot of them in their frenzied feasting and shopping. Feasting their eyes. And their greasy, nose-picking, arse-scratching, itchy fingers. Tormenting themselves and me. The shopping is the primitive hunt. I sizzled like their bacon in the fat pan with the very idea of them. They browned me off. Just the fact that they had to be thought about and catered for in my estimation of things. Their lives are lived in me because I am partly them.

So, the parents did their utmost to come back home in a foul mood with their best buys and the buys that escaped them. Every Saturday they listed to us what they didn't buy. Something would always be to their dissatisfaction. And then they would start on about the missing fiver. If I thought about that, it would deliver

me into the arms of guilt and despair just when I had to be free
and happy. Happy with my plastic bag of goods. Their dismal data
of thought that dragged you down, down, down to the treadmill
of their tiresome existences. This was all so dirty and demeaning. I
needed something uplifting.

I needed to fight. A clean fight, a cleansing fight. The good
fight. I needed to find a foe for fisticuffs. Fight free of falls and
submissions and the like. Bound only by power. Why the good
fight? It tells you what you can do. What capacity for giving
and receiving. Especially in a time when the world frowns upon
fighting, and approves only affective apartness. A mere touch is
unwanted aggression.

When I faced someone in a fight, I liked to get the better of
them in the mind before any physical contact took place. Most had
a limited notion of a fight. The safety net notion. It was in earnest
but not really. No one really got hurt and so a fight was something
they could enter into lightly. I started by warning them against this
casual attitude. I told them that when I fought, I would not stop
for anything, I never used half measures. I took it utterly seriously,
in absolute earnest, and there was no messing about. I would break
arms and legs and ribs and wouldn't stop for anything except when
I thought I was finished. No words of submission were acceptable
to me. I would decide. I reminded them of this when they were on
the ground begging me to stop. But, I would not stop. I then saw
them swiftly reassessing the situation. I saw their eyes darting from
side to side in a manifestation of self reflection, self assessment. I
saw them frantically asking themselves, *Is this worth it?* I would
kick them and punch them until they were unconscious if need be.
I smiled as if all of this didn't cost me a second thought. My eyes
were constant. They looked straight into those frightened eyes. My
jaw was firm. My body relaxed. I cracked my fingers. It was good
for those who thought they were tough.

Linus said that fighting wasn't in him. In fact he said, it was not
him. *What is in you?* I asked. His mother and father were in him
and they must have been the source of the fear of fighting. They
said to him, *Fighting is for barbarians.* I saw a timid little couple
hiding away from the world. I looked at him and wondered about

them, them that I never saw but who were there, just there as a cause of him. An explanation of him. *It's not my nature*, he said. And he wanted to behave accordingly. But what was he? I asked myself. And what ought he to be? It was not at all natural not to want to be powerful, and to actually let some other being be more powerful than you. It scared the crap out of him, the idea of being embroiled in a brawl. He hated to be hurt or the idea of suffering an embarrassing injury, like getting his front teeth knocked out or his eyes gouged by a vicious dirty fighter. *Some people don't fight fair*, were his very words. *They are brutes, they just want to be... to be there above you just being harder or something. What does it all prove?*

I could quite see how he was extremely worried about being wrapped up by someone, so he couldn't move or being punched in the solar plexus, so there wouldn't be a breath to breathe. He visibly shook with fear at the least threat of a physical attack. It was common to encounter lads on the streets, out to give anybody in their line of vision a tough time, and Linus would whisper his cowardly advice in my ear that we should run for it. He repeated it in my ear with increasing worry, penetrating his tone until his voice quivered like a sissy. I was never in favour of any running away or retreat, a denial of one's status. I would rather have had the breath beaten out of me, or have my body dumped in a ditch for dead, than ask my legs to carry me out of their reach. Linus could run like anything. He said it would show them how fast we could run. I said, if they caught you running, it would be ten times worse. *Just say they're just as fast? Then they'd have no respect for you. They'd just beat you up and for good measure give you an extra thumping just for being a coward.* It was no excuse to say that such and such was your nature and that was it. It was OK if your nature was perfect for every circumstance and then you could say it, but there were areas for improvement in all of us. It occurred to me that he had it in him to be forceful and forcefully creative, like the way he had been in Mercer's with the beautiful Mrs McC. He could recognise his weaknesses, know properly what they truly were and then they would not trouble him. He could then stand up with me against the enemy. *I know that* he said. *Affectus qui passio est, desinit esse passio, simulatque eius claram et distinctam formamus ideam.* He smiled and looked fearless.

CHAPTER 25

Smithfield was within smelling distance. The second-hand world was right there before us in its worldly waft, just around a corner or two.

Can you smell that stink? said Linus. *Beer and pish. Peer and bish. Old men's stink.*

And the reek of shite stink, I said. *Don't forget the shite from all the caged pets and the uncaged, windy wankers who slink around the wet streets. And the spit and sweat coming off the unwashed old gits into your flaring nostrils.* What was Smithfield but a wonderland of human misery? All the modifications of misery in the body and the mind, and the body is the mind as the mind is the body, the perfect idea of it. As modes, they were states of being and what a state they were in. There was the Free State down south over the border. This was the state of the unfree.

Their minds could be said to reflect the order and disorder of their natures in a physical and mental sense. Misery was the degree of disorder in their natures and what miserable natures they were. Not natures conceived by any God, nor were they as inconceivable by the Deity able to conceive of a God or a divine nature that expressed perfection. But it was misery from the perspective of the detached critical spirit, for they themselves would surely not have conceived themselves as miserable, at least some of the time, as they had a limited notion of perfection and therefore misery. Nor would they see themselves as in bondage, as unfree.

The human impetus to trade was set forth here and how miserable trade can be. It was the way of life, and ultimately life itself was traded. It just was precisely that. Trading in all its myriad manners. Trading in their individual variations and differentiations, in the knowledge of distinction, in valuation, in everything that hard earned money could buy and all that could be passed from hand to hand, body to body for a promise or a deal. Even the emphatic spit in the mouth was traded for something. Said with a spit it meant more. It got a response. It got a laugh. It got a compliment. One idea taken in and another given out another. Trade! Build up your reputation no matter how small it really was. Look tough. Look knowledgeable. Say a wise word. A word to the wise. A wise word to the fool. Old fellas spat out their dentures with a coughing or a laughing fit. All part and parcel of the human worldly weave. Old hags bartered with the collateral of their dirty stories, seeking friends of shite sacks that were hanging around them in wait and who waited for their moment to give their fast false friendship. They lined themselves outside the bookies and pubs. Pubs at every other door. Drinking dens. No lions, just The Red Lion with a Daniel or two wrestling with their drunken lives.

On the pavements, with their hands in their deep empty pockets. They rattled their dirty copper change looking for someone friendly to top it up, to make up the price of a drink. They showed us their teeth or the crumbled remains of them, and the shrunken mouths that had no teeth to display were displayed. What a grim sight. No wonder people believed in the other world, Heaven. *Is this all of it?* preached a solitary spiritual soul on a Smithfield corner. *No! My home is over there in Campground Jordan. Sunny Jordan. What we have here is purest shite. The waste of creation. Struggle and pain, torture, the failure. Death and disease and loss. Suffering. If there is any good, it is only the brief absence of pain and it is soon lost. Lost, lost, lost. Indeed, stolen from us. And the people who say there is no Heaven have to tell us that this world is a wonderment and this is it, this is it. This is the only reality there is, they say. No! We go to church to find the answers to the filth and the struggle in the filth and we need to see the promise of a bright new world. Church might not always have the answers that satisfy the truth of things, but we need the answers in any form so that we can approach understanding, even if it a small step at a time.* Nobody paid heed.

Linus kept saying his parents were atheists and didn't go to church. *They have all the answers,* he said. His parents said to him that God was dead. His father taught that stuff at the University, and he got paid for it. He woke up, had breakfast, went to the university and taught that God was dead in a country where everyone believed that we were dead without Him. The father told me that without God there was no living. And the Pastor in the church reared up at the doubters and simply demanded their belief in the Almighty. So no one believed Linus's father at the University because I had never met a single person who thought that God was dead. I came out one day with a brainwave and told Linus that God couldn't be dead because he doesn't die like the rest of us. That that is what God is, pure life, not like us who are part life and part death. That death is not in the nature of God only in the nature of men. Then one day Linus came out and told me that his father meant that God was never ever alive in the first place. *He's a monkey's uncle your da,* I said not knowing exactly what I was saying. It just shot out. The senselessness of it made us both laugh in a big double-barrelled burst. *My father's not a monkey's uncle,* said Linus, barely containing his laughter. Then we clapped eyes on Meekin. In the midst of sin, we saw salvation. Meekin the saviour. And the laughing halted.

Old slinkin' Meekin slumped against a lamp post near the entrance to the inner Smithfield. The inner sanctum of selling second hand goods. Like a St Peter to the gates of Heaven. Genial James Meekin, Meekin Mild was our name for him. *The Meekin shall inherit the earth,* I said to Linus. *Inherit the wind more like,* he laughed back. Meekin had the big shiny over-ironed trousers that sagged in the traditional manner into massive material rolls on his shoes. Plenty of room for the wind, and the wind was a free flower from the Meekin manly arse. There was no fear of his particular fart. In fact, a celebration broke out to greet its every expression. Like the launching of a ship.

Would you credit that? I said to Linus knowing he knew. *The launching of a shit.*

No! Credit is where credit is due. I believe not here. Laus donanda ubicumque merita.

Meekin, however, gave himself sufficient credit where it wasn't due as did his admirers. Undeserved credit is a dangerous thing. He was a man of measure in the place where his measure mattered. In physical features, he was a man of generous proportions, using up the bulk of a tape measure in chest and gut areas. A possible sign of present or previous toughness. He had the big, bald, roundhead skull of an idiot, with the glow of an ivory snooker ball. Such heads were groomed to a marble hardness for the first use in a fight and put the fear of Satan in people who were unaccustomed to such.

That's a fearful weapon, that skull, said Linus.

It's what inside the skull that counts, I said. *He's an old empty skite.*

The Meekin mouth was a mouth of the massive moron variety. In its full opening, it resembled the irregular shape of Lough Neagh. If Ulster was his face, Lough Neagh was his mouth. And out of it came the fly boy and the lies of a fly boy. He smoked a pipe clasped into that grand, gaping, receiving cavity, and talked to every passer by out of the side not occupied by the clay Meerschaum. Smoke swirled out of the darkness of his open oral estuary and then around his skull with intermittent exhalations. I imagined porridge ebbing in and out with the smoke at his breakfast table then the pig snout finding comfort and sinking into the floating-on-grease fry. The breath from him that preceded his high-pitched words sent the grey haze into a frenzied upward whirl. He would present to us a smile through the smokescreen and asked us on a regular basis if we wanted to have a puff on his pipe. Then he laughed in a strange way when our sheepish silence informed him that we declined the offer. The two of us just looked. There was something of the woman about him, I thought, like a lot of fat men. Something on the periphery. And on the periphery of our awareness. A womanly way. In his voice. In his sibilants. In the manner his discourse. There was something frightening about it. Something to fear. Something queer. He could be nice and not nice.

On occasions that he partook of the company of mates around the corner lamppost, they all laughed in their strange ways to the pipe question that was addressed to us. *Have a blow, son,* they'd say in raucous fashion. A bunch of crude laughing boys, but they were ignorant of the truth about us, for we took delight in making them the objects of our own ridicule. Beyond their minds and their minds' eyes, they were treated with comic contempt. They were mere mutants in their mind-body imperfections, to be studied for the sake of laughter. The word *stupid* fitted them to perfection, and if the perfection of God's creation required stupidity, they were the divine manifestation. The stooping stupid. Stooping in the wind and cold. Stamping stupid feet.

If I could think of a road to happiness, it would have been in the pursuit of the funny at the expense of the ignorant. The spiritual gift of laughter. Why was that not in the Bible? I would write the book of laughter, my very own book. It was in us, me and Linus, so it must be in us all. Inside us, pointing out, and it returned to the inside in spades. It was a case of *being just there, there inside.*

Ignorant bliss in their pish-stained pants. Satinised by the stains and the amatuerish attempts to remove them. Unsanitised. But what difference did it make that they didn't know? Meekin's reality was what was known to him whether he knew the truth or not. *What* he knew. And he knew nothing of us laughing at him and his ways. If he was suddenly told the truth what would happen? Would his whole world change? He would know more of the world around him as it really was. Or would he? What difference would it make? I was unhappy not knowing as much as I could. Knowing my situation in its most comprehensive form. But Meekin was happy in his ignorance, was he not? He saw what he believed. I heard some folk talk behind his back, make nasty remarks about him. The ones, indeed, that laughed with him as he farted and befriended him in pretence. They cursed him and his ways out of his knowing. They called him a faggotty-arsed bastard and a queer fucker. *Why doesn't he smoke a fag instead of sucking on a pipe?* they said. *Because he likes his fags up his wide farty arse,* they guffawed. Good joke for them. He only saw the smiles.

*

We entered the enclosed inner sanctum of Smithfield, leaving
Meekin Mild to his pipe sucking and his world that sucked at
him. We entered into a fusty realm of old possessions. There were
inside streets, slab pavements and kerbs and cobblestones just like
the outside, but it was all enclosed with glass panes high above. A
plantless greenhouse, a greenhouse that would indeed have crushed
the existence of any plant placed in its midst. The air was stale
and still and soiled. No frilly flowers there. No frills, all spills. No
silk, just soil and shite. The damp air swept through at times but it
didn't leave, it was just sucked up by the occupants, both animate
and inanimate. Dampness was in everything you felt. When you
left, your clothes were smelly and damp. The mother sniffed me
as I entered her spic and span hermetic house, bringing in my
Smithfield smell. Her head shot back from my clothes just after the
first sniff of her super-sensitive smell sense.

What did we want there in Smithfield? The de-filed field.
Field filed. Filed under S for *smell*. Cross-referenced under W for
wankers. Or maybe under US for *unique smell*. What stimulated
the interest? The risk. The vast variety of things and the worlds
that they advertised. Hanging from the rafters was a giant key.
A key to unlock your attention. Always the key in your view at
the entrance. You looked up at it. And other giant hanging signs
beyond and about it in high rows that pointed with red and black
painted arrows the way to a bargain down below. To the left or
to the right, or just right where you were. The steadfast Belfast
people moseyed with their relaxed weekend bodies slowly along
the thoroughfares, thoroughly cramped, waiting for retail arousal.
Something that established a want. Your head could spin out of
control with all there was to see. All that you wanted to be in your
possession. There were the wants of necessities and the wants of
just wanting. Like the endless wants of children. Wives with their
men sauntered in their weekend casual wear. Cardigans and ties
for the men, and sharply-creased slacks, or a silly, shapeless jerkin.
Plain mini dresses for the women that showed off their titanic tree
trunk legs. They wobbled on high heels and held their cheap plastic

handbags tight on their wrists whilst their men clasped their hands behind their backs far from their wallets. This was slink shopping. Slugging it out. Bodies found pleasant resistance in the confines of this mausoleum of past and present enterprise.

And then there was the hindering presence of the proprietors. They lurked in and around the goods and the shadows of their goods. They smiled that smile of sleazy salesman seduction. They sought your attention with the greasy grin and used their special gifts to divine those who would easily part with their money. Easy money. The timid shoppers. It was all in their eyes and their apologetic slouched demeanour. The poise that seeks anonymity. The proprietors sought them out, and no sooner were they out than they were in the shop, where they'd rather buy unwanted goods than suffer the displeasure of the seller.

The sellers were strange creatures, all breath and no soul, like the Homeric psyche. The totality of their concern was selling. Their ultimate concern. The selling breath was all embracing like a bracing wind. And in the wind was a spit, a phlegm, that wet the hand that did the deal. The phlegm coughed up out of the unphlegmatic character, the character that, in good Belfast idiom, fancied itself. And indeed had, as the ancients said, a good opinion of themselves. Pure assumption. Pure presumption. Nothing that could be proved and remained on the border with that country that was called the free state of false estimation.

That was the essence of their very nature. What was such a nature? What was the state of their nature? Their occupation was a preoccupation. The sale, the deal was everything. The productive thought was to sell, but not to sell out. The cowardly shoppers sold out, they betrayed their better judgements. Me and Linus sought to avoid them and not to sell out. Like bluebottles that buzzed around your hair in search of decaying bits of your body. Not that they would get us and our money, but they were not worth any of our time spent in their weasel presence with their weasel words. Rat arses, we called them. Wee rat arses. Rat crap. Crap human beings. We gave them a wide berth. Not a single buying idea would be born in us. But we knew them to laugh at. From a distance. We observed them, and we knew intimately their peculiar mannerisms.

The slinky rhythm of their movement. They slipped themselves into slinky slim suits in the mornings and felt their essential slinkiness in all its sameness. You could do your morning fry in the glutinous grease of their hair. Pressed flat, stretched, shiny. They deserved nothing of our respect. Not even the slenderest slice of respect, as finely cut as the finest sliver from the bacon slicer in McClure's butcher's shop on Botanic. They snarled *clear off* if you went anywhere near their inferior cut-price commodities, if they saw you were there for a laugh.

Silently on show! Their greasy old cookers, bits of smelly carpet, teetering piles of dusty books, tarnished medals, shapeless military uniforms, boxes of old squashed well-worn shoes, piled up settees, uprightly stacked pish-stained mattresses, iron bedsteads laid flat out. Who had been laid flat out last on one of those rusty frames? Did someone die on one of those old mattresses and settle their last moving bowel waste in the stuffing and springs? Everything had a merit in the mind and vocabulary of the seller. *All solid pieces of merchandise. Craftsmanship. Just a wee bit of dust and dirt that'll soon clean off. Dust and dirt never had the beating of quality.* A bit of spit on the finger to demonstrate. The forefinger wiped the spot clean with a flourish, a demonstration of supreme confidence in the product, as if the dust was merely a protective coating. It was a confidence trick, a confident conjurer at work, diverting the attention away from the reality towards the illusion.

You won't get anything like this in the shops these days Missus. Not on your nelly. Not on your life. This is craftsmanship. A product made by people who cared about their reputation. Crafty craftsmanship, more like. And they, the sellers, were the people of craft, crafty swines with the gift of the gab. Means to an end was their gab. Crafty from the day they were born. If we had the chance we'd kick their commodities all to hell. Put a boot in them and run like a fucking greyhound. Linus, who liked to run was all for it, kick and run like hell. And laugh all the way to safety out of sight from the shysters and skitters. The unshy shyster couldn't leave his shyster shop. *Bring your bakes back here yous wee shites and I'll kick your fucks in! Yous little hallions yous!* The shyster shouted his threats into the echoing rafters. As I ran I saw them all, all the shysters in and out of there in my mind. What a bunch of criminals. A bunch of skivers. The thought was precisely that. A bunch with no idea what a proper life entailed. Only retailed. Not interested in what was true, even about themselves, their insignificant selves. *Omnis determinatio est negatio!* They renounced themselves, but in their renunciation was the affirmation of their individuality. As I had affirmed and denied myself with my crime. I had taken a fiver that was not mine, the only crime I had ever committed in the world of crimes as what counts as crime, or wanted to commit. Yes, the fiver! And that was it, my life of crime. My bad act. I didn't live as if every act was a denial of the good. Like them. That was the state of them. Their language, their world was the language and the world of the Devil himself. The life of mischief.

But there were things we wanted to see, to get our beady eyes on and think about having in our possession.

CHAPTER 26

Linus said he felt like going home. He said he was too far from home. He wanted to leave. To leave me in the far off land. Not so much in the measurable distance from his house and his parents, but the fact that he had travelled too far from his own zone of self. And that he had given too much time to being bad. In short, he was not being himself for too long. He had laughed as much as he had ever laughed, he said, and had been the originator of a way of being funny with that Mrs McCullough woman in old Mercer's shop. He had also put his boot into an old cooker of one of the marketeer shysters and laughed at the boyos standing around the lamp post with Meekin Mild, who thought they were just the pure essence of all things masculine. *Pure essence of crap and human idiocy!* But Linus felt he needed to return to something familiar and comfortable. He was at the very edge of his experimentation, the very edge of what his nature said he should not be. He was feeling the effect of the edge. *I feel like going home.* His words, assisted by the expression on his face, meant. I, on the other hand, did not want to return home. I knew I would have to face the music, a chorus of accusations. A forum of judgement awaited.

I'm just tired of it all now, was Linus's unkind remark. *It all makes me feel dirt tired.* He seemed to be casting an aspersion. That phrase, *casting aspersions,* came to be for me from the mouth of my auntie Josephine who made a habit of using the term. *Are you casting aspersions?* she'd say, with the aggressive manner of a big, fat powerful woman. And it lodged in my mind and came to the fore on this occasion. It was demoralising. It was Saturday, my favourite day of the week. It was early. There was no need to go home. I appealed to him. *We'll just have look at the shop with the knives and the pet shops on Gresham Street. The man with the monkey. What about the man with the monkey? I'm going to buy a Mexican jumping bean,* I said. *I want to cut it open and see what's inside. What makes it jump.* There was a look in Linus's eye that captured perfectly the idea of protest. I returned the expression that I thought captured the idea that it was all a joke.

Saturday was only enjoyable if you could put it out of your mind that there was a God-awful church service to go to in the evening. But that effort of ignoring meant denying God himself too. Putting him right out of your mind. Out of the picture. Seeing only the world of imperfection. Deny him like Saint Peter did. How did he get a sainthood on the back of that? Church on Saturday was an event that preyed on the praying mind if the mind allowed it. I prayed that it wouldn't come. Imagine that, praying to God not to think of God. It always came but you could think that it never would. The guilty man's endless expectation of a reprieve from execution. Time would be conceived to go so slow that it would almost stop. You could seek to enjoy the enjoyable things with the thought-paralysing paradoxes of Zeno being truly believed.

It played on my nerves and made me fume a bit when I realised that a lot of time had gone by without me being aware of it, on a day when I wanted time to go as slowly as it could go. When I was ranting on to Linus about not going home and the Mexican jumping bean and the pet shops and the monkey, all of a sudden almost an hour had gone by. How? A whole hour closer to going home and facing the music and going to church. I harboured a small hatred for Linus just for that. He was being cowardly. As cowardly as a stone, or at least a Mexican jumping bean. He sometimes seemed to me to be a powerless creature. He was scared, scared to be himself. To even be beyond himself as himself. To stretch within. To reach within. To encompass without within. I think he saw how life was diminished, how life was miserable and weak in so many places and from that he sort of concluded that there was nothing truly excellent to be had. And yet I saw something of the spirit of excellence in him and I felt excellence by the fact that I could see it. The potential of greatness in our small world. And that was the only world that counted. It was only a short way from cowardice to courage. It was the shortness of an idea. It was in the denial of the mediocrity of life. How mediocrity and suffering clung to life prolonging mediocrity and suffering but suspending life.

The mediocre life loves life in its quantity. The lover of life as a quantity cannot be courageous because courage belongs to the person who is willing to accept death as part of his act to live. Life speaks nothing of itself to the weak because they will not know themselves truly; they will only know their weak selves, their sad and fearful selves.

Linus denied his good self when he needed to. He didn't know how to enjoy it by obeying it. He obeyed something in the distance. What was within and close commanded him and he failed to obey it. But he mostly obeyed the life from outside, so not himself, and felt safer in his submission to it. I knew when he was being obedient and when he was being submissive, for the first I felt joy and for the second hatred.

He failed to be obedient to his will to power when he encountered the woman in Mercer's shop. He had the idea, but the will deserted him, to obey his own command to make that appointment with a female body. To triumph in his bodily form. What prevented him? What stood over him? I felt detached from him. I looked at him and saw him but saw him not. I felt a cold that was not the cold of the wind. The sobering cold of my singularity. Which in some way I wanted to be sovereign. He departed and I felt my lone self. He withdrew his commitment and I felt the draught. But it soon passed. I wished him to go, wished his absence. I felt like saying *fuck off*, and felt bad that I couldn't bring myself to actually say it. I didn't want him but I didn't want to say I didn't want him. That felt like failure, it felt as though I was occupying the two opposing worlds. I disliked him for his desire to depart and leave me. For the choice he was making. But there was something of it that seemed necessary.

CHAPTER 27

Rehearsal time. *So you say I stole the fiver! Looking at me with that face, the look of you as if nothing you do is ever wrong. I can't take your look. The look of something superior. But you steal all the time. You steal away and you think it's OK. Not even stealing at all. Life. You take my life with all your stupidity. And you obey some lifeless rules of goodness. What is wrong with your wrong? It's all wrong, that's it. Yes, I took the fiver, because I was told to by myself. I was obedient to myself. You cannot convict me for being myself.* No I could never tell them I took the fiver. I would not admit a thing. I had to lie. I had to make them believe that I was not a liar. I had to lie until they believed me. I had to hold out, for my truth of lies was more important than theirs. What I did was more important.

There was waiting going on, just for me. Lots of waiting. I could feel it and I was warming with it and yet nowhere near it. A cold sweat was coming upon me. But it's a powerful thing, waiting. The waiter's attention had distilled out of the initial unfocused frenzy and the focus was fully on me. The absent me, whose absent mind familiarised itself with the events to come. Home was not where I wanted to take myself. The self that was in the midst of freely enjoying itself. I didn't want to relieve their angry waiting and I didn't want to enter, to enter their world, their attention, simply to enter and have them see me with their made-up red hot minds ready to grill the fucking life out of me. They always left their burn mark. Their branding. The high heat of accusation. I knew their minds' ways. Like bull terriers with their jaws on something. They became massive in their rage. *I'm raging,* said the mother in close up. The body expanded in preparation.

The interrogation would involve mostly threats and shouting and trying to show me up. Show me up as some very bad egg. Humiliate me. They would keep going until I cracked into tears. They would have me paying attention to myself so much that I would condemn myself. The mother was mad. She had a mad streak. What was it to be mad? Are we not all a bit mad? Not as mad as her! Like she loathed the world. We were all in her bad dream making her angry at every turn. Freud would have had a field day except maybe that Freud would not have been interested in a peasant's mad state of mind. There would be no intellectual joy in it. What ideas did she have to share, she who had a fullness to overflowing of inadequate notions? A wild ocean of such notions. Wave after wave of foaming tidal stupidity. Nothing had entered it, as there was nothing to receive it and shape it in any cultivated way.

Yet, here was a mystery in the shape of a squat female, her anger and hatred directed at the world at large, the source of which was hidden, derived from a more general human disease of the mind. Deep, deep, deep, driven back to inaccessibility by some devil of a deity. God and the Devil, one and the same. A demonic driver of our lives, a detester of the life that it controls and hell bent on the destruction of the self that it so comfortably inhabits. Hell was her destination, though she was not aware of it. Her deceiving mind thought that heaven was waiting just around the corner. This was her imaginary world. Her saving grace. A mess of a world, entertaining a host of ghosts seeking to dominate the centre stage of her personality. She was simply one massive, unresolved internal conflict living in midship, drifting amongst the directionless, heaving, external mess that is daft humanity in general. And this entity of internal chaos was a mother, the being I was to face with my crime in the sickly place that was home. Sick with the normality of mind. She would go to work on me to clean me up just like she cleaned other people's houses, or the mess of other minds in mental institutions. I was indignant that such a mind would stand in accusation.

I had in me a thought, several thoughts, slow and fast thoughts, and even a train of thought, locomotion driving to destruction these hindrances to life. Me, sitting, tied into a baby high chair. The mother, sitting before me, tortured me. A bowl on the tiny chair table containing a steaming mix. She force-fed me tinned creamed rice with a fried egg in the middle of it, but before she put it in my mouth she put it in hers to cool it. She pulled the spoon slowly out of her mouth, through her tight resistant lips that flattened the food on the spoon, and then forced the germ-laden mixture through my own tight lips and into me. Her hair was stiff and gingery. Her face was stiffly stern with the serious task of feeding. The spoon was kept in my poor sad mouth until most of the lumpy food was sucked from it and swallowed, and it was then tilted up and withdrawn tightly against my upper lip in order to remove any lingering morsel from the plastic. Rice and egg and plastic. When it was all gone she wiped my mouth firmly with a smelly dish cloth, pulling it across my lips with considerable painful pressure, from one corner to the other. I withdrew my head as far as it would go in a miserably pitiful resistance.

She threatened to put the dress on me if I didn't eat properly. Cabbage made me sick, but I was frightened of the dress thing. Cabbage was fat granny's house. The very idea of it made me almost croak. Preceding even one spoonful, from the deepest recesses of my gut, I would lurch forward in my chair, retching only air. The mother hastened her lower jaw to a protruding outcrop of her face. Her lower set of teeth visible in the angry expression. The others around the table howled with gaiety. The brother was in spasms. The sisters beamed with pleasure. *What dress?* they asked. *A nice wee frilly one,* said the mother with a wink to the others and a half-smile to herself. The thought was unbearable. Humiliation was her game, the disobedient will to contain. Amusement a hidden refrain.

You're just going to get me mocked, I sobbed.

Never mind mocking, she said, *Jesus was mocked and he never minded. He just smiled.*

I wasn't impressed with the idea of Jesus as a situation smiler.

A passive responder to active intimidation. He showed strength to resist the Devil but weakness with people. I wanted someone to save me to a substantial strength.

A new being, yes, but a Being, being absolutely me, not merely being a member of the church of the meek. A gathering of sissified souls, crouching in terror at the altar. Speaking big in the absence of threat but really the smiley meek who are laughed at and corralled like livestock.

And yet, as it turns out, the meek do inherit the earth, and the longer the earth exists, the meeker it becomes. Both the strong and the weak meek. The dictatorship of the meek in place with meek lynch mobs at every turn. And they make Jesus in their image. The meek rule the roost and deliver to us a meek saviour. But it is a phenomenon of manic meekness. It can turn nasty. Having the mad eyes of meekness boring into you, searching out your soul is a thing you want to avoid. All your sins will spill out, right before your very own attention.

The father was a mild man of a rather nervous disposition. I thought he could have been Jesus, as he was strong and weak at the same time. Not the sort who cannot watch very bad things, horror, cruelty and the like, but the sort who experiences premonitions of pressure. The two, mildness and nervousness, usually go together. And not surprisingly, considering the nature of the mother. He was no interrogator like her, and I felt him to be more friend than foe. But he had his limits, and there was indeed a point where his temper snapped, and when it snapped so apparently, did his body manageability. He twitched and grimaced and all of his intended-never-to-be-spoken thoughts were on his lips, being expressed in a minimal mouth movement. All present there for any half-decent lip reader. In any form and degree of temper he would speak the words intended to be spoken but after the exit of the intended words, his mouth continued to move with silent words that declared the persisting internal turmoil of reflection.

Once upon a time, he leaped silently up the stairs, shot into my bedroom, the door almost leaving the hinges, and tore the bed clothes from my inadequate grip, then set about skelping my bare legs unmercifully with his strong stubby workman's hands. My brother

Rob had caused this violent intrusion. He kept shouting downstairs that I was annoying him, and whatever it was the father was doing downstairs, the idea of me being the cause of its interruption, sent him into an almighty wrath. In my post-skelped bawling and blubbering plight, I saw him leave with that silent-moving mouth of wrath, words on lips that were meant for him alone but that almost found an outward manifestation in the world. And to my brother Rob, wrapped in cosy self satisfaction, I croaked and spat out the declaration through all the saturated slimy obstruction that I hated his stinking guts. In a very specialised needling manner, he threatened to call the father again. I swore I would one day kill him. Tired with the struggle to avoid the beating, the kicking and wriggling, and the bawling and blubbering, I finally fell into sleep. But I woke again with the hatred of the brother still intact.

*

And so, as I stood there in the open and cold Belfast City centre, still, a mad plan was even hatching within me, running alongside hopeful ideas of a miracle in the Markets. Could I hope that something would happen in my absence? A reprieve, perhaps in a gas explosion? The father did all his own gas work to uncertain excellence. Or maybe a mass murderer would break into the house and dispose of my problem. A car crash on the way to or from shopping. A bomb could go off in the supermarket, blowing them all to holy kingdom come. The big buy, where they all bought it!

I met Impy outside the Milo Betsy's Fenian bookies just off the city hall. Impy Godthorpe. His face buried in *The Starting Post* horse racing paper. The newspaper without news, the only news Impy ever needed to navigate his life. I couldn't make head nor tail of it. It was used for lining the bin in our back yard. Gambling addicted, old lodger Hughie brought it into the house. The mother cursed him to Hell for it. The racing paper had the names of places where horse races were held. In small print, in endless columns and rows, were the names of the horses running, with all those confusing statistics and betting numbers all over the place on the pages. It was just a mass of print that had no attraction for me at all, but for Impy Godthorpe it was the true book of revelation.

Linus had sickened me by taking off to his home. I couldn't convince him to stay. He walked off at a brisk pace as if his life depended on it. Before he took off I asked him if it was OK, if he could confirm that he was with me this morning if anybody asked.

If anybody asks? he gasped.

Just anybody. Just in case. And then I thought that I shouldn't have said a thing. If I used him as an alibi in the parental interrogation about the stolen fiver and they asked him, then he would smell a rat. Would realise that he hadn't actually seen me pick up the fiver. I just produced it after having declared its existence from a distance and then running towards it. *Did you see the fiver on the ground?* the mother would ask him. *Did you see him actually pick it up?* She was daft, but crafty daft.

Got any fuckin' dough, said Impy. *I've a shitting cert horse here. In the 12.45 at Kempton. You'll get your money back and more. I swear.* He axed my train of thought. I didn't know him at all well, even though he was in my class at school, and I had bunked off with him on a couple of occasions. Lousy boring days messing about. Slinking and dodging here and there, usually in the rain and cold.

Kempton? What's that? I inquired.

It's a fucking horse race at Kempton. In England, but it doesn't matter a fucking, fucking fuck where it is—it's at fucking 12.45 and I need some fucking dough to back it. It's a 10 to 1 shot, and it's a dead fucking cert. I immediately felt the weight of money in my pocket. Change of various denominations, all in one trouser pocket.

Backing is a sin, I said in haste.

What the fuck! roared Impy. His attention came out of the paper fully for the first time. *What's sinful about it?*

My Uncle Hughie is addicted to it, and he hasn't any money anymore because of it. He's no family anymore, because they threw him out of the house because of backing. Backing and drinking. And on his back drinking. If he won something he would drink it all away. And then he'd spend days on his back in bed. And he always asks my da for money, out of the hearing of the mother, either to drink or back. And he lives with us because he cannot afford anywhere of his own. And the Bible says it's a sin.

So what's a sin about it? All you've said is that your old shite uncle is a lousy backer. Sin's a total load of shite anyway. I wouldn't bet on it being anything else than a sham. A non-runner. Like Jesus. A born loser. Now the Devil, I'd back him any day. Impy was clever. He made swearing sound clever and curse-intensive speech led you to consider what he had to say in a new light. He appeared tough and courageous, living part of his life in the adult world of gambling men. And he understood all about backing, all the odds and things. All the form. All those pages of lines and lists in the newspapers that we used to wipe our arses in the toilet. When I sat on the bog having a crap, my mind was drawn to them, and I just followed the lines and lists without understanding them. It was impressive that Impy understood it all.

In any case, you don't have to do the backing, Moonston. I'll do the deed. All your deed is to loan me some money, and your deed is then done with. I go away, and as much as you know I could be going anywhere, and then I come back and return your money and give you a gift of some more money. Call it a Christmas present.

But I know exactly what you are doing, and so I may as well be doing the backing. I know what you are doing and I know what I am doing. In fact, by lending you the money, I am allowing you to do it. Accessory to the fact of a sin, I'd be.

Accessory to the fact of sin? Are you fucking kidding? he announced. *Haven't you fucking ever heard of pretending, fooling your fucking own self? Pretending is like fucking acting. Fucking actors believe what they are doing when they act. They believe they are somebody else. Fuck! All you have to do is pretend you are someone else. For fuck's sake.*

That does not make sense at all. I am me. Me, me, me! Even if I pretend not to be, I am, and I know I am. I laughed. Godthorpe looked irritated.

Well, does fucking you want to lend fucking me some fucking money or fucking not? Just fucking tell me. Fuck me! You'll be investing your money like in a fucking bank. Same fucking risk. Same fucking type. It's a fucking gamble. Fuck! I need it right now, if you want to. In fucking fact, I've just thought, if I give you your fucking money back and nothing else, you would not have done a fucking thing. Fuck! It would be just right back where you fucking started, as if you'd never fucking met me.

That's all wrong. I am not at all sure. But my hand had already been in my pocket for several minutes with part of me, in my right mind, considering doing the wrong thing. I was feeling the change from the spent fiver between the tip of my forefinger and thumb. The change in my hand and the change in my mind. On the verge of handing it over. The money wasn't really mine anyway. I could have spent the whole fiver by now already. Say I had. What then? I wouldn't after all be giving my sister the change. And I was telling Impy that backing was a sin when I had stolen the money. Why didn't I just say I hadn't any money? But if he won the bet I might get the fiver back that I stole and I could just put it somewhere in my sister's room and that would be it. It just occurred to me then that Linus had walked off with the gains he had made from old McKeown. My mad calculating grimace was a momentary mystery to Impy, but all he was interested in was racing, so he didn't ask what that was all about.

Impy looked like a dormouse to me. Impy the dormouse. The Impy name was probably because he was unusually small. His mother was a wee, brown, Maltese, dormouse woman. A nasty, wee, swarthy woman with a foul mouth. His father was a big, Belfast, bus driver. Or a milkman. Or both. I could never remember which. Maybe he moonlighted with the milk. But Impy took after his mother. A wee darkie. And swore like her. I always wondered where his father found her. In a woodpile? They had a black Austin 8 car with doors opening out backwards. That was a laugh. Low, low leather seats. So low the wee Maltese woman could barely see out of the windows. From the outside, all that could be seen was from her glasses upwards to her stiff, black curly hair.

To me, Impy was not a Maltese. He was always a dark dormouse. From the moment I met him that was what he was. With black pupils that seemed to fill his entire eye sockets. His ears were high up on his skull, giving the impression of an unusually small forehead, and were so thin you could almost see through them. Like bat's wings. Or tracing paper. And his face was elongated from the chin and forehead out to his nose. From the side, truly like a

rodent. His habits were of a dormouse. He repetitively wiped his
nose with the back of his hand. He sometimes took a dirty hanky
out and, with both hands, frantically rubbed away any excess. And
sniffed like he had a permanent cold. He sniffed the air, and as
he sniffed, so his lips pouted kiss-like and his eyes squinted into
slits. In conversations I was often not acquainted with what he was
saying, so interested was I in his features and habits.

Don't fucking stand around here, he said as I dropped two quid
in change into his paw, *the fuckin' peelers'll have ye for underage
backing.* I slowly sauntered off to the next block, back to where
Meekin stood, as Impy scurried through the legs and lower bodies
of an assemblage of smoking bookie lice, eventually disappearing
through the swinging bookie doors with his racing pages securely
under his arm. He would grow up as a bookie louse would Impy.
He was a lad with a mind set on a life on the streets. On a corner
with Meekin maybe. A strayer mind never satisfied with normal
restrictions. On the edge. On the surface. Like a fly epicycling.
Never in the stronger and more settled middle.

In cricket, hitting the ball with the middle of the bat is sound
and safer, but the edge can have unexpected results even though it
is risky, often unintentional. The edge is always thinking with a
view to action. The fly boys are not those who contemplate. They
move swiftly on an airy thought. *Shall I do this? Or shall I do that?
Or neither. Is there something else?* Action over truth.

What was truth to Impy? Nothing but the pursuit of pleasurable
action; that was his truth. It was information that made him tick.
He gathered it like a dormouse gathers its nourishment. Using it to
be a wee wise arse amongst all the wise arses. To be a respected wise
arse. To pinpoint areas of experience that could give him an edge.
Like the old Indian said. Part of that was to have the vocabulary
of life that was on the edge, always looking for a skive, an angle to
beat the system. And it all started early in life. The earliest. As a
disposition. As an essence. Education meant little. He had his life
sorted out as far as his mousy eyes could see.

I was well out of the way of the bookies, as Impy had advised,
when there was a big thud, a warm wind, a shaking of foundations,
and a beautifully formed puff of grey smoke. Like an Indian

smoke signal. A sign above and beyond the place of signs. A big singular signal, one big cloud, with a singular message for me: *Impy Godthorpe, dead as a dodo.* There was a distant clatter and lot of human noises to be heard. Of the shouting and screaming variety.

Impy didn't re-emerge from the Fenian bookies, and I wandered off after a time. I was resigned to the knowledge that he had got the edge on me. He had rimmed me good and proper. He was a *Jimmy Rimmer.* Took my money, fooled me with his talk, and backed the wrong horse. He didn't want to see me. So he'd wait it out inside. In the smoky Fenian bookies with all the smelly backers around him. On this occasion, he did back the wrong horse in a big way, by entering that swinging door at the wrong moment.

I made it out of Gresham Street with pandemonium all around, not knowing in which direction I was heading. It was just a minimum movement away from one place to another. I hadn't made my mind up. Neither had a host of fearing fleeing people. They were on a trip to destinations not of their choosing. One instant, my head was full of heading home, and the next I was keen to stay in town and wander some more. The definite versus the indefinite. The articles of faith. The thud had entered my ear a wee while ago, as did the hiss of horror, and was slowly agitated in the mind as an idea of an incendiary. *A bombaleerybizz!* The mother's dreamy nonsense words to a baby on the verge of sleep. The language did its job. A sleeping bomb. The bookie *bomaleerybizz* sent the backing babes back to sleep. When I turned, I saw the cloud still rising, not too far in the distance. A not unattractive thing, I thought. I thought of Red Indians. Smoke signals and Chief Grey Cloud.

The infantile impressions commenced in the cloud of confusion. Rather like the prompt that was the valley of decision, in which sinners wandered in a limbo world of spiritual inadequacy. Thoughts, nevertheless. What is the idea at work, when its own body is struck down by such a thing as a bomb? What is the thought at the moment of impact? The thought that is yours and yours alone in an expanded millisecond. A lonely notion enduring as you stop all notioning.

What did Impy think last? Was there a moment out of time when he knew it all, when all became clear? Here maybe is the realisation that all thoughts are thought at once without obstruction, with a velocity previously unknown. A composition of all thoughts possible for that life.

In it all, did he think at all of me and my money? The poor little imp. Just maybe he was heading out with my money in his mitt when the combustion shattered his little being. I bet to myself—in a small tribute to Impy—that unbeing was never a thought in his wee dormouse mind. It was always in a perpetual state of affirmative perseverance, striving and striving to be the wise guy in that world but never ever conceiving the precarious edge of being in existence. He lived the edge, but never had a notion of edging into oblivion. Yet, there he was, and then there he wasn't. Can't put those pieces together again. No more Impy. Limpy Impy he'd have been if he'd have survived. And would he have been the same Impy? As Limpy Impy. But it'd have been a right old laugh to those mockers who seized upon weakness in a flash. Indeed it would. It would have been right enough. The mother's tongue came into my head. The forked tongue for her persistent ambiguity of thought. The shopping folks all around looked around. Unconcerned unless it was blowing up their shops. A Fenian bookies, Fenian backers out of sight didn't matter a jot to a Protestant bigot.

An old, toothless, musical beggar played on in his element, holding on to life by a tune. Unmoved by the blast. Holding on to it in desperate weakness, by a string. A chord. A slow tempo. One day I would pass that spot and realise that the string to his existence had snapped. An elementary talent for music and living was to play no more. I wanted to whisper sour somethings into his ear. Why wasn't he the one that was blown up? He and his instrument and his tunes and his bad begging. It would have been more lucrative if he had sat outside the bookies and cadged off the lousy betting louts. I heard his crap contribution to music and saw his limp grasp on existence. His head limply bowed over his instrument, unable or unwilling to look at his unlistening public. It did appear that he had a will, but not much of an edge. Was his music more useful than Impy's edgy activities? Was his abject and impoverished being deserving of any existence? The beggar was there, but just there, just about there and he attached his thereness to all else with the tune he played. The tune preserved a modicum of harmony for him. But it was a weak tune, as he was a weak player. What did he say with his music? He said, *I am overcome, please assist me.* His presence was an insult to what presence should be. When the tune died, he would be dead and gone. Just not there. Impy wasn't just there when he was here, he was really there, willing, strongly therein. He said with his ways, *I need no assistance.* He didn't even need my money for the bet. He would simply have leapt into another one of his dispositions or turned another corner and became something else to someone else, whilst remaining himself. He had many a tune in his modal makeup and his tunes were powerful. He once said to me that he knew how to do magic, to cast spells. His Maltese mother had taught him. But strong or weak or with the gift of spells, a decent enough bomb saw the end of them. What's the meaning of that? The Impy spell had died with him. But spells? They weren't magic at all. Just another illusion. A misunderstanding.

CHAPTER 28

Where's the nigger in the woodpile? That was my old history teacher, Mr Peahead Purvell, talking. What the boys in my class thought was pure hilarious shite. Any of his utterances, in fact. *History is shite*, they shouted. But the new image of the nigger in the woodpile was consumed unadulterated as a piece of humour, and all us boys cracked up in laughter. The issuer of the words said in a very emphatic way that it wasn't in the least funny. I sat at the front as always, my desk adjoining his, his a little higher, and from behind it, he always seemed to give me priority with his arrogant enquiring gaze. *What's amusing you Moonston?* I enquired precisely the same thing of myself, but I settled on the fact that I was laughing as a result of the general outpouring of laughter. Laughter begetting laughter. And then quizzing myself in a half-daydream about the funniness of it, and the funniness of anything, for that matter. Somebody with half a brain said that what made something funny was that it made no sense. But that made no sense, as not all things that made no sense were funny. But then they said that somebody might find it funny.

I regressed in a way that makes you sleepy, the mind fondling itself with pleasantries of its own past. History within history. In a class of its own. When my response to the teacher came, it was about to be the usual retort for ignorance that is despised in the teaching profession: *Don't know, sir.* It indicated lack of effort or interest. It meant you didn't *care* to know. But Impy Godthorpe piped up in the nick of time from the back, where he lazed in alternative education, and said, *Sir, it's funny because niggers don't normally reside in woodpiles but would be content to do so if encountering one. When you picture a nigger in your mind just lying in a woodpile, just lazing there comfortably, well that is enough to make you laugh. But that's not all...*

Godthorpe! bellowed Mr Purvell, instantly dispelling Godthorpe's belief that an answer from him was actually required. *You're an ideal case of ignorance and your idiocy is an education to us all. What would you know? You little savage. Your tendency with everything is to make a joke out of it. Usually at someone's expense. You're a little darkie with a bigger than usual dark space of a brain, where no light can enter.* Laughter broke out. Impy himself was smiling.

But jokes are funny, sir, said Impy with cheek. And then something threw Purvell into a coughing fit, something internal and immaterial, an idea that arose sharply to choke him. We all sat in silence thinking beyond the nigger trapped in his woodpile, way beyond that to whether our educator was going to expire in our presence and slump over his desk to death. Impy was taking bets in his dark and feeble Maltese mind. Catching his dark desiring face, I thought for a moment that Impy had cast a spell on Purvell, one of his mother's Maltese spells that he told us about.

...and out of that savage ignorance of yours you will end up in ruin, Purvell gasped out of his fit. The troubling, asphyxiating spasm had not sufficiently abated to reduce the reddening and swelling of the face and to suggest to the observing class that collapse and death were not imminent. And death is something we all wanted to see. Desperately, as it would be an event, and could even mean a timely cancellation of the class.

Death was all over the place in history and if anything was interesting to boys in history it was death. History was shite except for death. That was indeed a lot of history, as the occupants of it were in the main dead. *And if history teaches us anything, Godthorpe,* Purvell spluttered, whilst holding his throat for constancy of tone, *it is that short, dark, smart-alecks like you do not live long enough to tell their own tale. History is full of little dark people like you who are nothing but skivers and who skive themselves into an early grave, having given nothing to humanity but the notion of uselessness. You yourself are a little nigger in the woodpile, there to skive. Unfortunately it is a task we have been given to find you and drive some light into your skulls.* That constituted sufficient reason for more laughter. *Tell your da, Impy,* someone shouted, in a loud muffle with the limited voice-throwing talent of a phoney ventriloquist. Teacher Purvell frantically looked around for the mystery adviser amidst the guffawing mayhem. This was all good learning that had nothing to do with the lesson we were there for.

It was put about by a mischievous immature mind that Purvell was married to a wee Asian woman with an ample limp. Someone had spied them together in town and started spouting about Purvell and the *wee chinky cripple.* There was a general attitude of condescension towards anything Asian, and upon that spurious arrogance and those meagre observed facts, implications and assertions abounded. That's what made him nasty and bitter; it also explained to weak minds his dislike of smallness of stature, swarthiness of skin and limitations of mobility. Awkwardness, uncoordination, was a particular hobby horse of his. He showed no patience for it. He flew into a temper if someone displayed slowness of mind or body due to such deficiencies. Purvell unashamedly inserted in his lessons disparaging remarks about one or the other of his dislikes, sometimes disguised as points of historical interest. Sometimes he sought to deliver them with a flourish, aiming a sly glance or a pointed finger at the parties he sought to injure. Impy always said that he'd never be a teacher, that it was a game for losers, and that there were no winners in it ever.

They fucking think they're great fucking shakes, but they soon find out how fucking small they really are after a while. Fucking second fucking raters, said Impy Godthorpe in the playground. Something in it made you the object of hatred and derision and that continuous unceasing assault led you to bitterness. *Just look at pervert Purvell. He's a fuckin' mental wreck. Already the fucking cemetery's calling him. See his eyes? You can see it in his eyes. My fucking granny had eyes like that just before she packed in. Watery and red and bulging with disease. And everybody'll say, Remember old Purvell? What a bad fucking egg he was. What a swine. And when he's fucking buried I'll go up to the city fucking cemetery and sit on him and have the last fucking laugh.*

I thought there was something wrong with that when he said it. It was not all about having a laugh. Maybe the last laugh. But I just looked at him in a neutral way, neither affirming or denying his utterance. Actually I looked at him and thought that I didn't really like him. That was an addition. There's a point when you do that with everyone. A point of hate. A point of conversion to an opinion. Just something. But with Impy the point turned into a line of dislike along which I walked even when I walked with him in his direction.

You could see how Purvell hated us all and sometimes you could see when it was that he reached the point of hate and really hated you, but at least he didn't suck up to us in an attempt to make us his friend. That would have been tiresome and a source of another form of contempt that pupils had for teachers. Impy was right. Teachers were losers no matter which way you looked at it. There was contempt thrust upon them at every turn, the ridicule for the suckers and that for the sticklers for upholding of their integrity. Purvell sought to hold out against overwhelming odds like the soldiers at Rorke's Drift against the Zulus that he so much liked to mention, with us savages perpetually pounding his defences with ignorant noises He resolutely defended his existence, not merely as a teacher, but as a moral being and a being. He believed in it and was committed to it. So much so he wanted us to be like him. He occupied a space and strived to keep it pure and untouched. His desk was not to be touched and the area around it he guarded like a sentry. He would sometimes leave his imaginary stockade and march upon the person who trespassed to ward them off with a large wooden blackboard ruler, his rod of strength, and a defiant declaration of intent to defend his realm.

The Zulu hordes, the niggers out of the woodpile, will never triumph, he said. It was a lonely declaration. He seemed in total isolation and on the edge of tears as he voiced it. But we were his enemies and he tried, in the Biblical tradition, to make us, his enemies, his footstool. Rather our ignorance was his avowed enemy and he was haughty in his distaste for its presence. *Haughty* was a word he taught us. There it was on the blackboard. *Haughty*. Underlined as he slowly said it. It meant arrogant and arrogant was also written there and it meant a boastful person. And so we all went about saying *haughty* for this and that which had no relation to haughtiness. It just didn't sound as if it meant what it did. But someone made up the name, *Charles Haughty* to call someone that when they were being big headed. *Hey, look at Charles Haughty.*

In the presence of ignorance, Purvell held his head back as if he were about to taste deadly poison. Or lurch forward and spit out the venom. But our ignorance was more arrogant than his knowledge and we were determined to make his history our footstool and make him history as far as our lives were concerned. Did our ignorance prevail? Did we persist in it? Hardly, the defence of it required something of the critical spirit, some primitive knowledge, but some benefited more than others and those who did soon found, through reflection, that the world and our place in it was not all about action and even the will. Impy Godthorpe was not one of them.

We hated being in school because it restricted action in favour of thought. What came from him and his history lessons in particular? Something or nothing? Nothing directly but something dispersed itself like a mind mist and filtered into my restless receptacle that was the place for a form of reason.

Where is the nigger in the woodpile? I kept saying to myself, and nothing came from it, until one day something did. It meant hidden facts. What were these facts? Purvell taught the dogma of facts and that's why history was shite. Facts made no sense. But all you ever heard when something required to be proved was, *is that a fact?* History itself was then a nigger in the woodpile.

Facts. Ulster was a fact factory. A veritable mine, where all were digging frantically for the best facts. Disparate minds desperate for expression. Desperate for allies. Attention was their aim. *Pay attention to me,* was their declaration. Noticeable that they thought and spoke exceedingly slowly. I was always wary of this. A fact is a slow thing.

Would you kill him? I asked Impy, while standing in the war zone that was meant to be an orderly queue in the corridor for the next class. *Actually kill Purvell? Make his body history. Make him a dead fact.* Impy kept saying how much he hated him, and that Purvell had no call to call him by those names. As we were being pushed and jostled from all sides by unruly idiots, we placed ourselves in the shoes of two accomplices to the murder of Purvell the history teacher. We became angry with the pushing idiots and that seemed to inspire a particularly fierce effort in the imaginative means to murder.

You mean murder him? said Impy. *Not just kill him. Like you kill an enemy. But he is my enemy. So it would not be murder. He calls me a nigger. A wee darkie.*

In fact, there was no need for Impy to do the deed. Mr Purvell did it for him. Or, to be exact, for himself, as he probably didn't know that others wanted to do it. He murdered himself. When I thought of his life, I thought he had made the right choice, even though I had a very flimsy foundation of knowledge to judge him by. I saw a life with a limpy Asian wife and the job of teaching the likes of us, sufficient, I thought, to take anyone to the emotional horizon, beyond which was only the abyss. Had that sad life conquered him? Not a decent Stoic response, if it had. For he had lost his endeavour to be, to strive. Was it a cowardly soul that he had? Did he bully us and demand of us to be what he thought we should be, but could not stand up for his own self in the courageous manner?

*

James Meekin, Meekin Mild James Meekin, jumped back into the mental frame from somewhere. The meek shall inherit the earth came with it. Maybe it meant the earth, as a big lump of worthless shite. Meek, as cowardice. The cowardly shall inherit the earth. Those with spirit, the courageous will have no inheritance. They will make their own world.

Suicide! That was the connection. When to live and when to die. Purvell, Christ and Socrates. Where did I hear of the man Socrates? He came upon me like the Indian sneaking up, seeking an edge out of history. A man hidden by Jesus. Socrates went down the suicide road. Like Christ went willingly to the cross, but we only ever heard of Jesus. As a backslider, I took to Socrates. In the year 399 B.C., Socrates was put to death for impiety. In the year A.D. 1972, Mr Purvell condemned himself to death. He held a small private tribunal with no witnesses. In a weakened form of will, all the world cascaded in on top of him and dragged him to his demise. But Purvell was an accident ready to happen, whereas Socrates was the essential man *who happened*. He was no accident. Like Jesus, he had the will to die. He persevered in death as he did in life. Purvell suffered the *libido moriendi*, the disgust and despair he felt of himself and the world would lead him by his snout to it. Lynch-like. For all his emphasis on knowledge, he was, himself, ill equipped to rest peacefully in the world. He died a frightening death. He placed a frightening mask on it as he had with us in his classroom. There was nothing really to fear from us but the fear that was inside him already. There was nothing terrible in us but he made us terrible to trembling at times. The trembling you get at the unpredictable antics of a madman. Just as I made the home terrible. I placed a mask on the home; it covered the windows and doors. On the brickwork. Hideous gargoyles of old men like malignant abscesses on the plinths under the windows. I feared it. I felt the beginning of it as time pressed on and the moment of moments was approaching.

But what was there to fear? The mother's terrifying shouting. Her vicious screwed-up face. Her motherhood? The anger and disappointment of the father? His sad shaking head? His bowing head? Disgraced. Enclosed in the shambolic shame? Being sent to my room to think in absence of the malice raging against me elsewhere. From there I would hear the muffled sounds of normality. The lingering attitude of contempt. The withdrawal of love. The withdrawal of the TV as punishment. *Hollywood in the Sixties*. Silent Universal world in colour. The *Midnight Movie* on a Saturday night. RKO shadowy black and white excitement. Thunderous Warner Bros intro. The rough monochrome hessian backing to the titles. A big book slowly leafed through. Unlikely actor heroes. Fat Paul Douglas. Wilde Cornel. *The Big Combo*. What the hell is

a combo? Cornel, what a name! Like Colonel. A man in charge.
Rugged Rory Calhoun with the greasy hair. *Johnny Guitar*. I didn't
like the singing. Sterling Haden, *the most beautiful man in films*.
A hard man in *The Asphalt Jungle*. The sly Dan Duryea. I wanted
to change my name to Audie. That's a name and a half. Made the
no-good name Murphy almost respectable. Couldn't imagine my
own name in films. Audie Moonston. It had a ring of absurdity.
But Audie Murphy already had the name. Film people realised the
importance of names. Like in Ulster. Rory Calhoun's real name was
Francis McCowan. That's no name for the big screen. He could've
been from Sandy Row with a name like that. In westerns you had
really strange men's names. Lin McAdams. Lin, what's that short
for? Lindsay? Couldn't be. Surely! You'd never survive, unmolested
in school, with a name like Lin, but in a western, it was the name
of the tough guy hero who probably never went to school anyway.
Diminutive names. Steve. Frank. Clint. Joe, Chris, Matt, Walt, Gil.
Gil Favor. *Rawhide*. There was an argument at school: who was
better in *Rawhide*, Gil Favor or Rowdy Yeats? Gil Favor was my
choice. But I was always *Steve* when we were cowboys. Everyone
else wanted it but I had it every time. Those who wanted it but
didn't get it went into a short huff, until the action began.

From the punishment bedroom, and amidships in such
diversionary thoughts, I'd be able to hear the playing outside.
Somebody else was Steve. Not me. Not me. That form of playing
was losing its appeal. But not the desire to be someone else.

I'd have to go to church later in a state of disgrace. After the
interrogation, I'd be the fallen one from grace, made to feel
the sinner in the midst of saints. Even though grace was never
entirely clear to me. Saturday night church was intended to be
saints only, the gathering of the saved to have a purely saintly
time in the presence of the Lord. A spirit-strengthening service.
A bit of intense prayer, a bit of Bible study, a bit of spontaneous
worship. The Lord would be there as they said he always was,
and not in any particular place, spread out like a gas in an empty
chamber, and I would be in a mode of self examination the whole
time, through the prayer, through the Bible study, through the
spontaneous worship.

The holy person of the Pastor could scan you for sin like an ultrasound for big malignant lumps of it. I couldn't see any sin in him but I never really tried to see. I think I thought that was impossible. He simply could not sin. He was a sinless being unable and unwilling to sin again. He had the strongest will. He said that he was saved from sin when he was seven years old by the saving power of the blood of Jesus. If he could know Jesus at seven years old, I thought I could know Socrates at sixteen. What could I do to appear before him as a sinless person just like him? He was intoxicated with his own purity. His every expression was as a pure being. He lived every single moment in the shadow of the Lord. He could identify anyone who was not living in that shadow of the Lord. Maybe because there was no shadow. And of course he had the Lord's omniscience to advise him. He would say from the high platform, in the spontaneous worship part of the service, that he—with eyes closed—could see someone there in the midst who was not following the way of the Lord in the way they should be. He *saw* them! The Lord, he would tell us, was telling him this. Telling him who it was. He never named names, he just said that it was such and such a person with such and such a sinful problem, and they are striving with the Devil. I felt his mighty power when he looked upon me and I felt unable to wriggle free of it whilst in this sanctuary. I couldn't hide the fact that I envied him. I resented him too. Which was first? Resentment perhaps. Because I thought I could never be like him. Envy because in one way or another, I wanted to be like him. In his element. With his certainty. With his power. With his singular unwavering direction of mind. I soon realised it was simply not for me to be like him. He was chosen. There were not many like him. Like being Moses or Elijah.

But who was I when all was said and done? And what ought I to be if I was nothing? I felt like nothing in the shadow of the Pastor. Out of this dark nothing what could I be or become? I felt the striving force out of this nothing to be something. How did I get to this point of nothingness? In the church? At home? In the street? Anywhere. What particular avenue of ideas had led me there? My mind was a bumpy ride for any ideas that tried to settle in it. They entered and bounced here, there and everywhere like the bouncing bomb. Everything wavered as soon as it hit my Marius mind. Certainly an infertile ground for the whole absurd system of evangelical ideas or any other system. The evangelical spores that were in the air at all times had rooted on occasion, but never bloomed in me like they had in the brother Rob or the sisters. Why the fuck not? Why didn't they bloom? Why didn't I bloom? I could still say or think the word *fuck* and that was fucking annoying. But it was an indication of an essential unwillingness to conformity.

I escaped from the evangelical madhouse over and over again but without ever succeeding in a total freedom, because even though I felt something of the escape, I knew not to where or to what I would escape. I was, however, recaptured and pulled back into the encampment, where I started behaving just like them again. Not as a pretender, but as a real believer. Fooling myself. Yet not any believer, my belief was constantly the subject of auto-testing and if found wanting, to a personal *auto-da-fé*.

What is becoming of me?

CHAPTER 29

Unlimited desire has a tendency toward death. Joyless wanderings. I lost myself in them. I needed wanderings that were joyful, full of wonder.

Charlotte the charlatan knew me for what I was. So she said. She'd seen me with my trousers down, so to speak, and that was the very nature of her speak. Undressing you. As was her habit, she wanted to tease and through it generate something of a scenario of intimacy. Me with trousers down, her doing the pulling down of them. To revelation. Charlotte came into my head as I hit the road for home. Like finding the nigger in the woodpile. I had wandered enough. Definite direction was required. There was never anything more important in life than football and films and the occasional fight, but her presence in my mind at that moment wiped all else out and was an introduction to the inspiring ineffable. Something life giving. She was like an objectless object. Not like in a sentence in a school grammar lesson. In fact not an object at all but a subject. Neither a subject like at school, like maths, but a person. She subjected me to her presence. I couldn't place my desire for her presence in any normal circumstance.

She was more this and more that. She was neither this nor that. She was what she was but I didn't know what that was. I called her a charlatan because it fitted her name—out of the blue

I just began calling her that and she didn't object—but there was something of the real impostor in her. A posing impostor. Oh her posing! She cheated the normal intuition of integrity and made that incompleteness a virtue. Her hiddenness was attractive, for there was always something new revealed on every encounter and more was always expected. She created more questions than answers on every revelation. The uncertainty was disturbing in a pleasant sense. But the senses were disturbed unusually by the pleasure. Oh for everyone to be like this, not to have the tyranny of their own professed honesty up in lights. How clumsy seemed that honesty. The sort of honesty that I was going home to meet. What honesty was it of theirs that they became overnight turncoats to the tradition of their birth? That they held to be preciously true since thought became the mainspring of both their individuality and belonging? Their action was rooted in an unhealthy self interest. A selfishness. They became evangelicals in order to advance their claim to the truth of their salvation. There was more certainty of that in the narrow and focused idea of justification by faith than in the unwieldy realm of ritual. A personal moment of salvation counted for more, and the necessity to perpetually testify added to the importance of the individual.

How light footed that dishonesty of Charlatan Charlotte. Couldn't God or Nature deliver me into the hands of Charlotte right now on this road? Into her true will to deception on the Dublin Road? She who woke me, she who woke me and all the joy that filled my soul. But the encounter with the lords of dogmatic honesty was close at hand. On the threshold. They would be willing me to truth. What questionable questions would they ask in their quest? If I had have thought with greater anticipation, I could have had Charlotte teach me her own laws of deception. But she would tell me for sure that I had to have my own. They had to come from within me. I now doubted my deceptive qualities. To be me and not be me. And her voice, when it came, was like the softest soprano sent forth from a large humming chaotic chorus. The vehicle of voices that always interrupted the silence. The singular standing voice. A celestial vibration out of the midst of the worldly din. And it was my name that I heard from afar.

If I had met Charlotte, I'd have taken her home with me, and she'd have made a meal of the parent's honesty. She wouldn't take the sort of shite they liked to shovel fully into your face when you fell from grace. She would deny them their moral superiority. She would rebel against their power to denounce me as disobedient. She'd tell them that I was obedient in the only way it mattered, obedient to my self. She told me that she had never met anyone nicer and that I must not change for anyone. That was sinful Charlotte.

I encountered her for the first time one morning on the way to school. Hardly out of the door when she boldly slid up beside me and walked at my lazy pace. After a brief period of purely body articulation, me looking the portrait of puzzlement and sheepishness, she showing me her most convincing confounding expressions, she said that she lived around about the area and knew exactly who I was, but wasn't precise either with where she lived or how she knew me. *I am unconnected,* she said and immediately I felt a connection. I didn't really care a jot or a tittle, those words of familiarity simply slipped by the way as her hypnotic forms of expression lynched my need for novelty.

Short, short skirt, green Fenian tartan, short, sharp wit. Sharp pleats. A pin brooch near the hem that was not to be touched. This garment hem attracted me more than Christ's. Daintiness in diversity. The face of a question that had just been asked and was now waiting for my answer. Unsettling. I stuttered in attempts to settle. She was a much-desired dose of daintiness. What I desired without even being aware. Another thing that sneaks up on you. All of her over me like a refreshing mist. The breath of her swift movements and the perfume. Oh, that pretty oval face and tiny body. Almond-shaped eyes converted me to joy, to sincerity, to sadness, to curiosity, to the mischievous in an instant as they looked into me. But, insofar as these affects were not contained within me, they reigned over me from beyond, and there was a sense of weakness. They at once excited me and acted as a sedative. When I felt them I found peace. A look up or down or sideways with these eyes would hinder my obedience to any other form of command. She had my attention. Short sleek straight dark hair I was desperate to touch. It was the source of my satin fetish. Weak wrists. Long thin fingers on hands that dangled dearly from the wrists that seemed incapable of holding them up. Dear dear, dear, from the first words she uttered, *Mr Marius man, I know you,* I was a slave to her. Not a submissive but an obedient servant. I commanded myself to obey my idea of her. I affirmed myself to deny myself. *Mr Marius man!* That was uplifting. Intimate Charlotteness. An essence, not an accident. Perfectly peculiar. She spied me with it. And to think that the sense of my own peculiarity I thought was mine and mine only. It was a result of my own persistent self analysis. So what of this outsider's professed knowledge of me that I took and accepted at face value? I took it because she looked as though she knew me in a way that I knew myself. On our way she said that she was just killing time until the world comes to an end—and then she laughed. Just gently and it made me rumble inside with a small stupid internal chuckle.

When do you know it's coming to an end? I said.

When people are incapable of saying anything more about it, she said. Crazy girl. But I sort of felt that my world was coming to an end, because I was finding it harder and harder to talk about anything. Silence was the thing. In some way, I had a strange foreknowledge of my death. My inability to think of anything more to say. Yet, things simply had to be said.

Oh, and if people just talk science, that's the other thing. That really is the end. Why do you talk to yourself? she said, almost without an intervening breath. *Oh, don't worry, I like it.* So, I had indeed been spied by her as I walked alone conversing with myself. Like I saw the father sometimes. A sense of embarrassment would have been normal with this revelation, but I simply smiled a smile of satisfaction back at her, knowing that all was well with this little act of madness.

Charlotte was nothing like Eva, the beauty I admired in the church. That recognition was an effort to affirm my status as the backslider. I had also taken the name Eva as a sign. Evangelical had the name Eva in it. But then I thought, so do lots of words. Medieval, devastate, evade. That was the way evangelicals thought. Then I thought that the word evangelical was a sign, a sign of Eva Angel. The name Charlotte, however, stood on its own.

*

The road that I was now taking towards home, by name, the Dublin Road, ran parallel to Great Victoria Street, the route Linus and I had taken to town together that morning. Going in the opposite direction, I thought about the way streets became what they were. The place we simply found ourselves in. Two entirely different thoroughfares, yet both springing or sprouting out of the same great hub that was Shaftesbury Square. Great Victoria Street was rich with speedy movement and life, the commercial and entrepreneurial spirit, the dynamic soul to this kinetic composition. Shops and businesses, pubs and hotels indispensable to the life of the people increasingly became locations of death and destruction indispensable to the life of the madman. Indecent men with heavy loads to bear sought to end the movement of this spirit. And so, people shifted uneasily about, here and there, in the spirit of equal ignorance, content to be here and there on this street. In their place. *The* place. Their first love of life, what drove them, and they even laughed in the midst of danger to their natural movement.

The Dublin Road was slower. It didn't exactly lead to Dublin. If that's where you were expecting it to lead, you were well astray. It was wholly lacking in movement, a dead street, lacking the spirit of motion. Its soul was at rest, with few businesses or places of communal contact. People who used it walked a less accelerated pace, thought in a less active manner, to their destinations, as if they had no desired destination at all. I felt an acute sense of that as I moved on, as if I was not moving at all. Not a lot happening you would think. Modifications were few. There was an antique shop as you left Shaftesbury Square going into town, like a stray commercial entity trying to break free. But it didn't really seem to count as a shop as no one ever seemed to make the journey from one side of the entrance door to the other, and the merchandise was not generally agreed upon to be of commercial interest. I could have stood there all day and not have seen such a person go past me into its dark innards.

It was always like an early Sunday morning on the Dublin Road. There were a few side streets that led to nowhere. Some of them cul-de-sacs. Empty entries. A perfect place to see to someone if you had someone to see to, to commit a crime, to dump an unmoving body. A dead end. Were there any bodies there now? In one of those dark nooks beyond the vision of bins and skips, rubbish and rubble. A lifeless body slumped. I thought I saw one. Did I see one? Or did I make a mistake? Did I see something that merely resembled a body? Something black. Lying there, gathering dirt, and soaking up the damp. Smelling. An old carpet. A tarpaulin. Would I put my hand in the pocket of that dead man? In his dirty wet pouch? Popular gabardines perhaps, of the dark grey hue, possibly black with a white crumpled lining in the pockets. Tight and wet. Nothing worse than wet pockets to get your hand into. And out of. You knew it when you got a good drenching on a freezing day. You wanted to get your hands in there, and if your insertion was too clumsy and you simply kept pushing, you'd pull your zip open and chances were you'd not notice until the cold draught told you. In my experience, gabardines of the day usually had weak zips

All this nonsense in mind as I walked by, together with the gathering thoughts of what lay ahead of me. Thoughts that did not even yet exist in the open mind drew me. I was going back home. Back. Going forward to go back. The thoughts were ahead but they were also behind. And to the side there were other thoughts. To each side. The black slumped body on the heap of rubble. I saw a body and would say I had seen a body. If I went to the side, that side, I wouldn't go home. Home was always straight ahead. It was a principle. A principle of mind movement. We didn't point north, we pointed home. It was the safest place to go. Off Dublin Road, through Shaftesbury Square and on to Botanic.

CHAPTER 30

A rrival! Departure from pleasure. Incoming impressions of hostility. The front door was left open for me to march through. From a distance I could see the deep darkness that replaced the green paint. I left it open to preserve some silence and slipped down the hallway, but the more general the silence, the more my presence was felt.

Skitter! You skittery git! Get in here you looksee! You skitter ye! See what you've done, ya wee skitter. Behold the menacing mother! The guilt was already established. Right there in the pre-established inharmonious ignorant mind. Whatever happened to presumption of innocence? Good enough for the nation, but not in this godly house, where God's summary justice was held in highest regard. Worshipped indeed. That notion of original sin and original guilt. Barely through the front door and the arrest was swift and without ceremony. Taken by the armpit and raised half off the ground until I was practically hopping along on one leg. The underarm skin painfully nipped by stubby powerful fingers that more than indicated business. Then rushed into the interrogation room with a ready audience there to witness the spectacle. Part jury to pass judgement, part congregation to represent God, part cheering crowd to see the sport, part cynical sniggerers there for the mischief.

Impy Godthorpe got blown up today. Got killed in a booby trap. He got the booby prize. Startled looks all around. Even the mother took the bait for a split second. But then she put her hand out, her palm up. Godthorpe was already history in her head.

The truth, said she.

It's true, I said, trying to revive the dead Godthorpe story from its grave. Her eyes and ears were closed to that. She wanted the truth in the open flat palm of her hand. In this little kitchen, I sat on a cheap little chair and saw all around me what they lived for. Not the truth. What did her notion of truth correspond to? What did it represent? She wanted the fiver and the confession. The object and the words. And the power that this possession would endow. That was her need. Her real need. What did she think when the discovery of the missing fiver was made? She thought that she would discover in herself a power to be the discoverer of the perpetrator. She was about to be in her element. Uplifted by an urge to power. The truth depended on her, and her nature. Not *the* truth but the truth that would be her concealed and devious way of affirming her wily and wilful nature. Her truth depended on who she was in life. Just as her idea of God depended so much on what sort of person she was. Her God was wonderfully mean, just like her. He was bitter and resentful. He was the God who chastised. The God who raised creation with a thought that was also an act of will. The God who damned it with another thought that was also an act of will. What an idea, what a will! In the name of God, what a God!

And so she, with her own idea and her own will, raised me. She raised me as an object for herself as her God had raised men as objects for His own pleasure. She wanted to be worshipped, as He did. What a funny thing that worshipping was. *Aren't you grateful?* she would say. *They are never grateful,* she would say, answering her own question. Just as in church we were instructed always to be grateful to God for all things, good and bad. For existence itself. And we got down on our bended knees and worshipped the Deity for His goodness and asked for His unfailing forgiveness. If we were ill and suffering, we were so due to our own unfailing failings. If it was apparent that a few had acted impeccably and were still ill and suffering unbearable pain, it was a mystery, the unveiling of which was never going to happen. At least not until that day of days when all would be revealed.

The father was no longer *grateful,* no longer an object for her to feel good about. No longer a pleasant object for her nor she a pleasant object for him. Only of hate and loathing. He no longer worshipped her as he once did. So she scoured the earth for people who did, as ruthlessly as she scoured pots and pans of the dirt to find cleanliness. And as there seemed to be no ready worshippers, she sought to punish the whole human race with her wrath.

In the name of the holy Lord, I 'll skelp the truth out of you! Things were unfolding. Becoming what? Being was coming. She was certainly not becoming, especially in this mood. In this mode. But there was a situation that was most becoming, in the frightening way. Beautifully frightening. So beautifully frightening I felt a bodily response to both the beauty of it and the fear of it. Bracketing everything whilst I sat in the midst of it alone. I felt my lips twitch, and then I was in the land of the lips. My unclean lying lips amidst the people with clean and pure and holy lips. And I was in the land of watery eyes. Unholy water that would sanctify my lying lips and the eyes for seeing holy things. When she invoked the holy, I faltered in my resolve to be me alone. I was alone but not entirely me. I wanted to call, just to call on someone, to help me in my deception. But where to find such a help?

Holy Jesus! Tell me the truth? Hell roast your dirty lying lips. I wasn't lying yet, as I hadn't said anything. She hissed like the wild breaking surf. She wanted the notion of *holy* to rip me asunder like a tidal wave of holy water extinguishing the fires of Hell. To open me up in spiritual surgery and have all my iniquities pour out. She bent down slightly, placed one hand on top of one bent knee, and raised another to the heavens with the forefinger thrusting and poking holes in the air. *The Lord in his perfect holiness does not like a liar and a cheat.* She thought she had the holy seed growing within and the holy see looking out from within her. From without you couldn't see it. She thought herself pure of human impurity. Her holy ravings tried to rat me out. What was holy to her? In her ugly vesture of decay. How could it be holy? She shook my foundations but not with holiness. If she had holiness, it was the holiness of the witch. She had the majesty of wicked holiness. With her lips, she preached the gospel of wickedness, the wickedness that had its source in the belief in holy purity. She claimed to be of God and purified by God and this lifted her high in her own estimation and the estimation of all the followers who wanted always to be flattered and who believed that everything was spiritually settled for them. Being continually praised for their virtue was oh so much better than being virtuous. They needed a hot coal placed upon their arrogant lips. To shut their mutual praise up. I would volunteer to be the doer of that deed.

I wanted to make my ears heavy so they would close. I didn't want to see. I wanted no more of this assault of devoted ignorance. My lies were holier than her words that claimed to be seeking the truth. It was not that she was just daft, it was that she never really communicated with holiness and she believed she did. Her unholiness simply stood out. As she accused me of unholiness, I encountered her unholiness, but in a way that was not in any way reflected upon. The implicit not yet made explicit. I saw the whole majesty of it. A majesty that had a power over me. So it was her unholiness that was the power, though I recognised it not as unholiness. It resembled holiness. But not just resembled, you don't mistake something for something else merely because it resembles it. If my mother came into the bedroom one morning, as I just woke up, I would not think that the mother was actually me because she resembled me. People always said I was the spit of the mother, but they never confused us. I mistook holiness because I misunderstood holiness, so if I saw unholiness I would mistake it for the holiness. Just like I mistake one person for another if that person is disguised in some way. But how did it appear? It appeared as one thing *and* the other. Therefore it was deceitful.

So, here, the deceitful mother sought to reveal the deceitful son and, with her holy face on, free of any cosmetic corruption, she placed the son under her dominion. That brand of holiness is a power for evil, if it is seen as a power for good. Whose deceitfulness would win the day? The whole kitchen was her domain and the people in it were swayed by it. The brother and the two sisters were

there as witnesses to the power she wielded. It was a heavy power.
A weight that I felt hard to endure.

Blessed are the persecuted. Aha! So, where is my blessedness, God
of blessedness? But there was something of the persecution that was
a friendly weight. It was the weight that belonged in this precise
situation. If I didn't not want the weight, I would have to give up
the whole way of life, the family life, and maybe even the context
in which the life of the family was given significance. I could shout,
I'm not going to be possessed, to have this thrust upon me. I'm leaving!
But where to? And to what? Back to nature? Well, where exactly
is that? So, I couldn't leave for fear of the emptiness. The silence.
The torture of the ever demanding law is always preferable to the
wilderness of seemingly purposeless scepticism.

I encountered the desperate vision of entrapment. In a perfectly
parallel bodily manifestation of affected thought, I gasped, gulped,
and twitched. I held my breath in order to stiffen the body and
prevent any outward display of discomfort.

I felt the guilt press upon me. It tugged and gnawed, and it was
all mine. *The worm of conscience never dieth,* said old hobbledy hoy
Hobbes. *We trusted you! We educated you in honesty! You learned from
us the nature of truth and how to be true! Just look at you!* It was the
application of the law of conscience. They wanted me to look into
myself, to condemn myself and even pronounce the punishment.
They accused me in order for me to accuse myself. These laws of
conscience. The laws of the tribe. The laws that give life to sin, said
St Paul, that make us labour and toil in the whole of life with the
promise to lift us out of savagery. And we promised we wouldn't
depart from them.

The little Leviathan mother would certainly not depart from
them. She had promised herself to abide by them and in her
scrupulous observance of endless commandments she risked the
most important thing, love.

I looked to the father who stood behind her. Slightly to the
side of her, siding reluctantly with her. In nervous perpetuity, like
he'd been shunted up a bleak siding that had no point of return.
Perpetuating in his supportive stance the mother's idea of holiness.
I saw his holiness too. It was kinder. He was kind. He lacked any

natural direction to madness. His face pointed that way at times but mostly it pointed to sense. He acted as her accomplice to keep her happy, but she was never happy, only less unhappy at times. That inspired him to incredible nervousness and several behavioural oddities indicated that state of being. He had the tie that he twisted to strangulation, the habit connected somewhere in his mind to a certain mysterious frustration. He twisted it in conformity with inner and outer events. Slowly and then quickly. Loosely and weakly, then tightly and forcefully between finger and thumb. It was a Saturday so his shirt sleeves were rolled up to the elbow as a concession to the casual. He wore a watch that had a silver expanding bracelet tightly clasped around his strong, pulsating wrist. The watch had a clear plain face, and an incredibly loud tick that often received comment in moments of desired silence. It was purchased, proudly as a bargain, from the pawnbrokers in Donegal Pass, not far from the house. Down near the Constabulary fortress. *A bargain is a bargain*, he'd say, and apparently this timepiece was a bargain, haggled down from thirty-nine and eleven to thirty bob. That put a skip in his step, as he took his purchase and marched up home from Donegal Pass to Botanic. And it passed the test of time as it kept good time. Nobody's watch kept time. The father was impressed by watches that kept time. *The time is in the movement*, he said.

Seventeen jewel movement, he announced. And a gem of a movement of the minimum kind was accurately descriptive of his lips in this declaration. Then the lips pouted to safeguard the idea in the significant silence. *Incabloc shock protection*. A respectfully large intake of breath always accompanied this comment. He liked the word *Incabloc* and his respect was for the word rather than the nature of the shock protection it named. The word appeared to have a power to please all of its own. I thought of the Incas of Peru and a block of something like concrete. A high and hardened culture. The father's thoughts were locked for a time on *Incabloc* when he thought it.

The watch showed off his wrist as manly, thick and powerful. Especially after some act of labour when it swelled up. And due to the tightness of the bracelet itself. Several of his wrist hairs were usually trapped between the links. From time to time that captured my attention. I wanted thick, hairy wrists. A manifestation of manliness. He only ever took the watch off to wind it. When he did the bracelet imprint was there in great detail on his skin. He wound the watch slowly and gently in order not to over-wind it.

You'll snap the main spring, he declared. I had a picture in my head of a tiny settee-type spring. Other terms he mentioned - escapement, coils, other springs, wheels—fascinated me. A wheel so fine they call it a fly wheel. A crafty little wheel worn by a fly boy. All dependent and working together. I saw the inside of a watch. In the very same pawnbroker's window, there was a large watch movement the size of a wall clock. Working away, everyday. There was, beside it, a chart to describe every part and explain its use. I paid no attention to the explanation of the workings, the whole mechanism just borrowed my mind for several minutes. The full working thing. The reduction of the whole to its parts didn't seem to hold any interest for me. Was this a weakness of mind? An unwillingness to know in detail? I was too easily distracted, mesmerised by the beauty of the whole.

The father struggled to place his thick strong fingers around the tiny winder, to feel the notches of the metal with his dry, cracking fingertips. He lacked delicacy to an annoying degree. If you watched his antics with the small operations of small things, it placed great strain on your patience. *Fiddly thing,* he said, with a little bit of anger. The mother could barely contain herself. New forms and sizes of sighs came forth. When he eventually did get a grip, he forcefully wound it in short fast twists between the tips of his forefinger and thumb. He wound the spring until it was almost tight, just a slower single turn before the winding button didn't turn any more. There were occasions when he couldn't wind it because his fingers were slippery from his greasy fried meal. The slivery fingertips just slid over the metal button. But he persisted. Slowly he got a grip. Sufficient to do the job. If only he would get a grip on the mother, the wife, the woman, and take her in hand. To unwind her. To remove her automatic mechanism. To unravel her tight springs that stored her insane energy. Remove that mad strain in her. She needed a flywheel in her brain to regulate her moods. A balance wheel to regulate her instability. We all had our flywheels and balance wheels, except her. But the mother, in her constant capriciousness, had the upper hand. Her madness ran both fast and slow and carried us all in her direction. We were her little springs and she wound us up, sometimes to the point of being over wound.

An over wound person, just like an over wound watch cannot do its job. It becomes unregulated. It's not that it does not work, but it never tells the right time. The others, however, were now in her time, following her movement. I was alone, unsynchronised with the general set of relations.

The brother and two sisters watched what was before them. They liked the spectacle. The brother was the loved one that they say they love. He's older and smarter and his smartness was always the loved thing. The smartness was rewarded with greater love. His nastiness was really smartness, his sarcasm and arrogance also only smartness. He was sent on the school trip to the Mediterranean because he was smart. They said he deserved it. There was no sunny trip for me, nothing of a reward for my ignorance. But I imagined it, then desired it. The welcoming warmth and blue brightness of sky and sea.

They sent me to the shop for messages instead of him who was never sent. His smartness carried with it a dignity that would suffer if he had to be a message boy. He laughed at me running here there and everywhere. *Running messages are only for the stupid,* he said. They told people about how smart the brother was. When will this show end? I thought. Like *Sunday Night at the London Palladium.* Endless tedium. The Tedium Palladium. Act after act of him, alone, performing his three ring circus of showing off. All night and day long every day. Praise, praise, praise. The little Lord of the house.

This interrogation, I could see it continuing beyond the football results. Four forty-five p.m., the matches were finishing. I wouldn't see the ticking teleprinter with the results as they happened. Scores as they came through, a Saturday ritual. I would give them my story and see how it settled. The bag from Mercer's was on the kitchen table. Was there before me, before them. And before me the questions. Where did I get this? Where did the money come from to get such a thing? What a coincidence! I found it! I had a witness.

Linus Larkin was with me—he would freely vouch for me. He was my free voucher for truth. The parents were mad for vouchers for all else. They scoured the newspapers for them every week. *Linus almost got it himself,* I declared. *Ask him. Go and ask him.* Their disbelief receded no further. They weren't going to say they were calling the peelers, were they? That old trick. The peelers wouldn't be havin' it with all that shooting and bombing about. People disappearing in the Dublin Road cul-de-sacs, up entries, inside rolls of carpet and lino with no brains left in their skulls. Bodies splattered over streets and being shovelled up into plastic bags. Peelers themselves living in fear for the lives. And they wanted to know if their son nicked a fiver! They wouldn't have it.

*

The knock on the door came as a welcome distraction. A nimble little knock. Not one that anyone immediately recognised. If it was fat Uncle Johnny Ratchitt, the knock practically took the door off the hinges and the brass off the knocker. The mother gritted her teeth at the Ratchitt knock. That was enough to prompt her to tell the father that he should transmit to Uncle Johnny the idea of moderation in his knocking. Neither was it the constabulary men and their fierce knocking.

You haven't the guts to tell him, she said to the father about the Ratchitt knock. She always questioned his guts. No one liked to go to the door if they didn't know who it was. An argument always erupted. It was the general dread of the door to door seller or the rag and bone man. The fish man smelled powerfully of fish and it wafted up the hall if you opened the door to him. He wouldn't go away until he'd said all he had to say which was how good his fish was. Or the Mormons selling their fishy beliefs. Sometimes welcome but not always. The Jehovah's Witnesses were not the witnesses to anything anyone wanted to know about. The persistent selling buggers that smelt weakness. Johnny Ratchitt was also persistent, he wanted in the for the food and mechanical conversation, but it wasn't him. Or maybe now, hooded men looking for turncoats.

Linus stood close to the other side of the door so that he could hear if his knock had any effect when it was opened by the older sister. He practically fell into her bosom when she did. The booby prize. From the kitchen, we heard the squeak of his voice but not enough to stimulate recognition.

It's that boy you play with, said the older sister in a sort of whisper. *He says he wants you. The funny one.* They were the dismissive words that were added to the general dismissiveness of body language. *He's wearing funny trousers,* was the whisper. *I heard that!* It was whispered to the other sister. How on earth did she spot that in five seconds flat? It took me ages to see it. That was a girl thing. Everyone they encountered was eyed up from head to toe for a full critique of their appearance. *There's something wrong with his trousers. Are they homemade?* The whispering and the subsequent sniggering between the sisters went on. I wanted to say that their friends were just as funny but didn't feel the time was right. But my mind was full to brimming with ideas. *Pimple pus face. Fatty. All the fatties you hang around with. A menagerie of uglies. Ugly and fat. Your pimples are bigger than your tits. Faces like batch loaves. Like an old wrinkly haggis.* I called one *Henny* for her skinniness and the other *Katie Pimple* for her mountainous acne and as an allusion to the TV personality Katie Boyle, who advertised soap for keeping the skin pure as silk.

Linus appeared. There he was in his glory. Just as I got into the swing of cataloguing all the insults. It was a useful distraction from the interrogation. But things had sort of stalled with the Linus nimble knock. He shuffled into vision and just stood there. In his pocketless trousers, he pockets all the stares. His hands were awkwardly, publicly presented outside the pockets that would conceal them, if they were there. Why should hands be so conspicuous in their conveyance of a general state of unease?

The key. I'm locked out, he said out of the mountainous silence and the menacing mood. No key to unlock this situation. There was a moment when those words of Linus's floated meaninglessly in the air. His face, sheepish and becoming increasingly red, looked at me, surrounded in my seated solitude. Unaccountably, I felt the bubbling of inner laughter. The trouser thing was a sudden glorious idea. And if I was not mistaken, it was a shared idea of all those in

the room with the exception of the trouser wearer Linus himself.
Shared for an instant. It was a shared conception that was both
revealed and concealed. But just as the glorious idea was about to
take flight as an outward-bound expression, bound for glory, the
mother invoked her powerful power of veto over any manifestation
of the glorious.

You've got it coming to you, she said to me. Almost privately,
as all declaration of intent was issuing from one side of her face.
Closing in on me, the words came out of the side of her mouth
like a pipeless Popeye, like old Meekin, and the telling glance was
sideward and angled towards me, all of which revealed that she
sought to conceal the exact content from Linus but, at the very
same time, reveal to him the existence of a grave matter. Graver
than his search for a key. It sought also to rupture the Linus
connection that complicated my version of events in her mind.
The drama she sought to sustain without the Linus contribution.
To steal the scene was what she wanted in her acting capacity. She
wanted to see the absence of Linus and the presence of her own
possession of events in a simple procession, in her simple mind.
Her life at this point was one of captivation and control. Her
present power. The establishment of blame was paramount to her
especially if she established it. In fact, *only* if she established it.
And only if *she* established it.

I retrieved the key from my pocket in my pocket-possessing jeans
and handed the item to Linus who barely moved from his spot at
the door. I leaned slightly off my interrogation perch and stretched
past the mother to Linus's own outstretched hand. When he took
possession of the key, his face was a powerful red, as he had at the
very same time taken possession of everyone's attention, something
about which he was clearly uncomfortable.

I had a thought before—a fragment of a thought I had earlier,
an essential attachment to the thinker of the thought, but it
came back to me then in the appropriate circumstance—that I
did not want to be judged for my actions by any outside agency,
like the mother, especially the mother. I wanted to be judged
by myself. If I had a burden it was my burden. It was my guilt.
I would determine the offence and decide on the punishment.

I could not think of any complication to this. I focused on its rightness. I could settle with it inside me but I could not take it from somewhere else. It could gnaw and nibble and bite and chew at me until madness, but at least it would be a self-induced madness. A madness of the self, caused by the self. The madness of the self commanding self.

The universe which consists of only a single hand. The hand of God. So which hand is it? Left or right? Dear Kant! You complicated cunt! How do we know which side to sit on when we are directed to the right hand of God? The Lord says let your left hand will not know what your right hand is doing. That's hilarious! The Word of God is a shameless exhibition of entertainment. It indulges the merry mind if you let it. If you will it assertively. With optimism.

But they had their sin and all of that. I was a sinner to them. Their sinner. As much a sinner as a shinner, was what I thought. They wanted me to play their sinner game and say I was a sinner, to say it their way, that I had sinned and that I had shamed the whole family in front of God. I had come up short of the glory of God. That was what this was all about. The evangelical *auto-da-fé* and did I not say that I had already performed my own *auto-da-fé*? The only question that remained there was, how did I know the judgement was the correct one?

Public evangelical denunciation was their aim. *Evangelastic* denunciation, as the mother would say, in her uninhibited dyslexic ignorance. That's why they all stood around looking all that was holy, waiting for that moment. The defining moment, that would limit me and leave me weak and vulnerable.

All definition is limitation.

Lowered to the position of sinner. I wanted nothing of their defining sin. Their evangelical sin. Their infinite all-conquering sin. Their stain. Their great smiting weapon of judgement. I would smite them with my great smiting resolution to deny them their victory. I would make a set of commandments that I could apply to myself to circumvent their denunciation. They would not condemn me. I would do that and damn myself if I had to. Was this the moment, was this the point at which I fell from grace? Where I no longer understood it the way they did? I took my freedom and escaped from the law of grace. Grace being a burden that crushed from beyond. An unreasonable burden.

Grace and sin. The twin holy offspring of God conceived in and of Him. In His mind as all things are in His mind. How would I declare myself to bear any fault under it? And what of evil? What of the Devil? The Devil is within me. The Devil rides in. So who the devil am I? I am he who acts as he does. I am what I am. He is what he is and takes the blame. But not the blame of sin. I didn't agree to any of that. It is my own blame. Yes, I took the fiver, I could think of that right in front of them, and they were so close to it, but, as I said, I could also have decided in that defining moment not to have taken the fiver. All that thought right before them, and they knew none of it not. It was within me.

Me, me, me. When did this *me* arrive? For arrive it did. An idea sixteen years in the making. As I did the act, so did I arrive. As I stole the money, so did I declare my being, for I saw the weight of the before and the after of it, and the weight was not just on me but in me.

Where had the time gone? What had I done on the Dublin Road? All external existence had apparently ceased. All erased by the mother's rage. All that was in being was a kitchen room and six people. The presence of Linus had no real force in this respect. The mother looked as if she was about to force march me in the direction of an alternative measure. Her measuring mind was fixed and ready. She shook. There was redness in the shaking. It was foundational. Corsetry under pressure. Dynamic. Swift shaking. Swaying and trembling like Jeremiah's mountains. The swaying and trembling that would leave a desert in its wake, free from diversions to other domains and to the ease. There was a grinding from somewhere within her. There was gargling as though she was gargling pebbles. Hissing like the dead, retreating Atlantic surf in Ballycastle. Low humming, also present, was in contention for prominence. The father's ticking watch. His fingers sliding on his satin tie. The body of the little empress was bulging with messages. It was especially good at spelling, for it spelled out clearly that her patience was wearing thin. I myself was feeling thin. Unfed and weak. And my thinness of mind was becoming strained. I thought of the pinnacle of thin thoughts, the concentration camps and all the thin and weak thoughts that abounded there. Resistance was low. I saw myself in my own stripy pyjamas, the nearest garments I could equate with the holocaust victims. Buttoned right up to the neck and speaking severity and coldness. What must I do now? What could I do? Could I do what I must? I didn't want to look back and say to myself that I did not do what I should have done. That I failed to live up to what I am.

Do you think you are a law unto yourself? spouted the mother. Spouted with spit. Oh I liked it. *A law unto myself, a law unto myself...* At first I liked it then, in repetition, it didn't seem to make sense. The moment had come where a confession was becoming surplus to requirements. The imposition of guilt was about to be finalised. I would be branded a liar and a thief. What Billy MacCauley from the council flats calls a *fieth,* which sounds altogether and entirely more biblical. *The Devil will come like a fieth in the night,* he said at Sunday school when repetition of it was required. The mother would, for the benefit of all convened, declare that everyone knew the truth. Linus, in all his glorious pocketless trousers, was still present though absent too, in terms of the interrogation, and he would hear the declaration but in the abstract, for no mention was made in his presence of the particular nature of the crime. Was it any use to call Linus to the witness stand? He was standing but not witnessing. Was I to be stronger or weaker in my perceived guilt and lack of confession or in a refutation of the condemnation, even though it would probably have only remained a troublesome doubt in the accusers' minds? They would scratch their heads. It would remain an obstacle to their certainty and I would be happy with that.

You are evil! said the mother, to stun the son, and the son was stunned. Linus winced in his witness of those words. There was a dirty spoon on the kitchen table, so she must have been serious. Also some crumbs. Breadcrumbs. The body of Christ, I thought. The imputation of evil was stunning. She came out with it just as I was thinking it. The two together compounded it. But I thought a different evil than she. Hers was of the Devil, out there and spread about and lurking, as a wolf lurks. Mine was within and dependent on the will that chose for or against the right way.

Sitting there... my sitting now became an irritation to her. *Sitting there,* she repeated with a heavier hiss than the first one. Sitting in simplicity. An impossible idea for her to stomach. I was too comfortable. And my strategic position was equally annoying. Centrally situated, which at first was meant to dispense discomfort, seemed now to place me powerfully still and unperturbed at the centre of this small universe of orbiting frustration.

You're nothing but a backslider. There it was. Its eventual arrival. *You know what the Pastor says about backsliders?* There he was as well. The holy man. That was when she turned her back on me. The first time in this whole charade. She was now facing the lonely front of Linus but not to effect a communication in his direction. The expression was all for me. Her back. She disowned me. But she was pretending. Pretending to disown me. It was a sort of game. And I had to play my part which meant not encouraging her action. Not pursuing a line that would involve confession. And as it was a game it would all come to an end, the next day, the day after. Like nothing had happened. She would cover it up in her mind. Especially if it involved the idea of loss. Life would go on and the idea of me as a major disappointment would not persist. I was the highest ranking disappointment to her. Major Disappointment she called me. But she needed me. Her need would persist as long as she did. She would never actually disown me. What if she did? Where would I be? What if this moment was the moment of true disownment? I thought.

Somewhere deep within me I felt for her more than I felt for me. With her back turned, she suffered. Was suffering. I saw the suffering. Oh how she strived to suffer. And to find a place in suffering. Her requirement was to suffer and to find a place and to know that someone cared for it. She always said that she was heading for an early grave.

Would a confession suffice? What I needed to do now was kick a ball. Score a goal. Have the ball at my feet, in control. In my new kit. Close control. Beat a few players. See them gasp in my wake. What skill. Or save a penalty. I liked the role of goalkeeper. Predicting the direction of the ball. Outwitting the kicker.

What are the signs? His eyes. His body shape. His temperament.

Does he look nervous? Or confident? He has the upper hand, he has the ball, he has the first move, and I cannot move until he moves, but there are ways to enter into the future. Leap into it! Beat him there. Dive full stretch. Not just keep it out of the goal but grasp it into my possession. Hold it. Tightly. Keep it from the opposition. What it is to have people in awe of an act of skill. What is it?

How do you do that? a lad once asked me as I kept a ball up off the ground in regular upward strikes with the foot and the head and the knee. Both left and right feet. Then I'd cushion the ball between upper foot and shin as it dropped out of the sky and hold it there. I'd loft it back into the air and catch it behind my neck. From there it would be rolled down my back, and with a flick of the heel, it would be up in the air again. When it returned to within my control, I'd strike it with all my power. Put my boot right through it so my very own power was in it in its flight to its destination, to its target. *You're a juggler,* they'd say. *You should join a circus.*

The mother had no such skill in any area with which to express herself, with which to reach out and impress. No one asked her how she did something. Expression is aimed outwards and takes up residence in relationships, but her expressions were always uncomfortably housed. And her relationships were never harmonious. No one was ever in awe of her. The father must have been in awe of her beauty at one time but beauty itself is not a true expression. As the will is. It does nothing to recommend the person. Beauty can be cruel. To be beautiful and have nothing significant to express is almost worthless. Empty. Mere proportion. Powerless proportion. You can be fooled into thinking beauty has something it hasn't. And now she no longer had beauty. What she had was her beautiless back to me.

The waiting game. I waited. Like Jesus waiting for us to come to him. He'll not always wait. That's the message. He'll turn his back for good. Jesus again. Omnipresent nuisance. Jesus was pissing me off. Coming in at every opportunity. Nearer my God to thee, but how near does he want to be without taking over the whole show? He's like the friend who calls for you when you don't want to play with him. Only there's no pretending you're not in with Jesus. He doesn't even knock. Yet he says knock and it shall be answered unto you. No common decency with him. There's no warning. Like the worst friends. Even with good friends, there are times when you don't want to see them. He should only make his presence felt in times when we have nothing to say, and do not know what to do.

Get out of my sight! she said with her back to me. I was in point of fact already out of her sight. She repeated it, only this time with her arms accompanying it in a mad flailing manner, a manner of dismissal. Like an unhinged windmill. Detached sails. Heavy grinding. Nose to the grindstone. Nose out of joint. It was a moment of decision. There was concentrated gaze upon me. Concentrated judgement. In the name of Jesus and the holy world order. The moral order of things there to crush my small resistance. Me against the world of goodness. For goodness sake! For goodness's sake. To establish my badness, my guilt. It was all there to crucify me. To bear down upon me. The great weight. And they wanted their Saturday tea. Their pig's feet and pineapple chunks that they would chomp on before church.

I sensed the Linus discomfort, still standing there in his pocketless pants. The fear of Linus following from his just being there. Out of context. Hanging there. Loosely. A loose end. No beginning, no end for him, for he could make no sense of it beyond the fact that I was in trouble of some sort. He was quite literally senseless, as nothing he was experiencing made any real sense. It was foreign to him. The mother's back meant something, I suspect, but not in the way that we knew it. Her flailing arms. Her use of the words *evil, backslider, sitting there, skitter,* all of that shite and more were the things we understood within *the form of life.* Her with the father was another thing. The sister used to say, *They're at it again, the same old thing.* But she didn't understand, none of us did. She just didn't quite understand *the same old thing* in the same way they did. Then there was the world with the mother and us boys. And another with the mother and the sisters. That was special in a crazy way. They appeared crazy to the brother and me. My context, however, was all too familiar to me, because it belonged to me, and I belonged to it, and I to a large extent made it. It all belonged to my peculiar understanding. The ideas and the relations all one thing. Coherence.

*

The form of life that was this whole family was really only meaningful to the family alone. To understand it was impossible without becoming a member of the Moonston club. There was society at large, but this was *society at small*, with its very own rules. There was confusion in the psychiatric profession when the mother entered within their walls and encountered their frame of reference. The head doctors scratching their doctoring heads because they failed to find Mother Moonston with their big ideas. So instead they stopped scratching around, and they found a place to put their pills, to bring her up to seeing size. Impossible. Unless the doctors were mad as well. The mother was not mad in their way. She understood exactly what she was doing until her understanding failed. And the Larkin family form of life was elsewhere. I didn't understand that. But Linus and I had our form of life which I did understand.

The form of my actions was now paramount. Actions that were part and parcel of the family form of life here, statements of significance, modes of meaning. And particularly now. My progress out of the mother's sight would be crucial to my own self-esteem and hers. Just as Linus stood awkwardly without refuge for his hands, thus defining his weak state of mind, so I would have to make my escape in such a way that would avoid any conclusions about my guilt and my form of guilt. Should it be slow or swift? Head down or head up? Back bent low or fully erect. Look straight ahead or take in the eyes of all who were there. Out with a sheepish shameful smile or a victorious smirk. Be body or mind aware. Be both?

But the thing was, I wanted to jump, leap, a geometrical leap, skipping over everything connected to what was now, to then, there, on to there, beyond, to possible things, to meet that which was coming, to the whole bloody business of life. To approach the never-ending horizon. Marius's horizon. Out of the mothers poor sight and the mother's clumsy touch and the mother's sensitive smell. Away from the shaking and swaying, the grinding, the flailing. Out of the family sight, the ticking watch on the thick hairy wrist, the silky shapeless tie, the sibling sniggers. To the horizon that opens up so much that it closes entirely what is behind the viewer. All is horizon. Nothing that is past or present belongs to it. The Biblical salvation was an idea I liked: the idea the new person. *Old things pass away and all things become new.* A new creation. A bloody good idea that. A good Christian idea.

What am I to make of you? she said. That was a funny thing to say, I was thinking. I didn't want her to make anything of me. Just as I didn't want to be made something by God. I wanted to make myself. But what was the idea of a new person? It could not be the same person in the same social circumstances? I wanted to be wise unto salvation, that is, to know a new way. I didn't want Jesus to be the author of it. *I* wanted to be the author of it. I didn't want to die unto the self. I needed to work out my own salvation without fear and trembling, without a murmur or dispute. Commandingly. For a time I thought it was available in the church, with all their ranting about newness in Christ. Christ, that wasn't newness. They all remained precisely the same people. Authors of their own insignificance. A fool's parade. Full of idiocy.

I was bound in my acts and ideas to here, so what of it? So, so so. The brother liked to say, *so,* just to be clever. *So what?* If you said something, he'd say that *so,* so that you had to explain. And if the explanation was wanting he'd laugh or just terminate the communication with an arrogant terminating noise like *agh,* or a dismissive look, the eyes rolling, or a clever smirk. If words were used he'd say, *What are you talking about?* And laugh the dismissive laugh. That was the most annoying thing he said in that context. It dismissed everything I had said and set him up as the arbiter of all sense and reason. I often felt like performing the act of choking him to death. Choking the *so* out of him when he uttered it. So he'd be choking and thinking the word *so* as the cause of the choking. That made sense to me. Choking the arrogant life out of him. *So, so, so, so, so what do you say now clever boy? Am I making sense now? Say so now if you can.* I'd be saying this as his bulging eyes watched my furious revenge.

What makes you think you like someone if there is a constant stream of destructive ideas heading from them in your direction? What makes you persist to remain respectful of that someone?

People speak highly of them, they are liked by others. So, it's you that's the problem. You are not up to the mark. It's a mistake pure and simple. The destructive ideas are not really destructive or you are unable to destroy their destructiveness. You simply make them so because you are really weak.

So, I sought new ideas. A new creation. And I would start with the manner in which I would take my leave. I'd create a new set of rules to live by and I would carry on in the same way without deviating. And the ideas would necessitate the appropriate action, or the actions would perfectly embody the ideas. The old idea of me that others had would be there, but they would be saying, *What's happened to Marius? He's changed. He doesn't seem like the same person.* I would look at them with new eyes and scare the shite out of them.

I lifted myself off the chair, exited the kitchen as though I no longer inhabited my body. I didn't see their destructive looks. I felt light and unburdened and the master of what lay immediately ahead. But there was a doubt.

CHAPTER 31

I crouched and stiffened and fired out a tight flurry of powerful punches as if I was shadow-boxing, facing all my enemies at the same time in one spot. Jab, uppercut, haymaker, hook, line and sinker. Yes! I felt a good connection. Then I limbered to looseness and laughter. I was panting and out of sight. Out of sight and in my mind which seemed to be working as it should. In my attic outpost. Exiled. I could see the horizon from there. Relieved. Re-situated. Sitting a moment ago under the wonder working power of the blood. Family blood. Now sitting apart. Sitting above. Sitting high. Sitting beyond. There to work on my guilt and remorse and repentance. Meanwhile below, they thought with their thoughts secured by the anchor that kept the soul, *steadfast and sure whilst the billows roll.* The disposition of the bilious, yellowy, cowardly thoughts. They thought their thoughts had the full-bloodedness of truth and the truth in the blood, but they were lily-livered in their thinking.

But I was to be the first member of the church of unholy backsliders. What was the idea of the unholy? The withering of the holy. Like the holy it's ineffable, but unlike the holy it was wholly effable in the sense that the use of the *eff* word was a much desired form of expression. I would say fuck to God. First a single emphatic, *Fuck!* The freedom of the fuck. Then *fuck off God. Fuck your Kingdom. Fuck your Grace. The grace is in the fuck. Fuck your son and his cross and*

*his message of hope. Fuck the resurrection. To fuck with holy salvation.
And fuck prayer. Fuck sub contrario. Fuck transubstantiation and
consubstantiation.* I felt the substance of solid sin when I said it. To
say fuck to the Lord was the *sine qua non* of sin. Blasphemy. So the
new life of mine began by becoming acquainted with the sinful idea,
and therefore my new being was not to be equated merely with being
bad. That would be bad as an idea.

There is a confusion of the bad and the sinful as there is with
the good with the holy. The good and bad refer to the will in its
obedience to the inner command. This evangelical province is the
province of the saved from sin and the sinfully unsaved. Morality is
frowned upon by the evangelical. Morality is even conceived as the
mask of the sinner, the guise unto respectability. So, respectability
is despised. So, the preacher screwed up his face and gritted his
teeth at the mention of those who court respectability in place of
holiness. He embarrassed the respectable.

You think you are so good, he roared, *but you are nothing!*
The morality of the good was despised and denounced at every
opportunity as much as sin, for it sought to replace holiness
altogether with its earthly inadequacy of goodness. *It is idolatry!
The idol art. Artifice.* Man lost touch with the holy through his
obsession with goodness. So the evangelical despised the Catholic
religious experience as it has replaced the holy life with the moral
life. A bad substitution was the substitution with badness. *The
holy rises high above the good* said the evangelical. It is significantly
different. I see it. Oh how I see it. I see the holy but I do not want
it. Not for the sake of morality or immorality, or immortality, but
for unholiness. Not merely the opposite of holiness. My separation.

So I had to be so much more than the bad in my unholiness
in the very same way I had to be more than the good in desiring
holiness. I didn't want to be bad at all but I wanted to be true
to the unholy. What the assassin did on the streets of Belfast was
not sinful. Not unholy. It might have been bad. But maybe not
even bad, if only we knew the true causes of things. Nevertheless,
I didn't' want to be just bad, I wanted to be sinful. I wanted to
be rapt in sin, and wrapped in sin, with the worship of sin as
my direction. It's a state of the soul. Initially a contemplative

state, a gradual awareness of the evil within and the power and freedom one has to express it. God! It is before God that one places this freedom. Against *him*. So, what I had to do was that which I would not to do for God. In front of God I had to deny his promise of the kingdom of God that Jesus said was at hand. I would refuse to live under that promise and be master of my own life.

It had barely been a few minutes since I left the blood downstairs when I thought of them preparing to chomp. Their jaws limbering up. No jawing up here, just chewing the tasty excess fat of resistance, manifesting in no remorse, no guilt, yet. No future, no repentance. But, this was a most difficult period. I was meant to think and then make overtures to them, begging to be let back into their holy bosom. To chomp and chew with them and cherish them. The very idea nearly made me sick.

Usually, the next step for me would be to drift back, almost imperceptibly into their midst without invitation. There seemed to be no particular point of acceptance where the whole matter that incited the punishment was resolved. I did not say sorry. I was not made to grovel at a particular moment in time before the continuance of normal life. Things would just normalise gradually. But if I was seen, I would be seen to be wallowing under the weight of my realisation of wrongness, until I prayed for forgiveness. Then my burden would be lifted.

The room enclosed an imperfect silence for contemplation. The inevitable noise came in but not sufficiently to make me feel part of it. For a moment I stalled, not knowing what to think of myself. Like the horse in the stall, pinned in, facing straight ahead, blinkered, unable to turn, to slide back, or sideways. I knew not whether to sit or stand. Or lie on the bed. If I lay I'd think differently. It was more conducive to the dreamlike state. Bodiless. With just the eyes, I would follow the sloped ceilings to the walls. And think lazily.

*

I lay on the lazy bed. The mother called it that. *Get up out of your lazy bed,* she would shout when I would lie in. Looking up and around. A tiny unpainted patch on the ceiling—the father's laziness the mother called it, when she found an incompleteness of a task—carried the full weight of my gaze and I felt sleepy with it, so I rose and stood at the window.

Just looking was tiring. It was weighty watching. Purposeless looking. How free was I to be master of my life if I got so easily lost in purposeless staring? I felt infinitely removed from being my own master as I so often seemed intentionless. Directionless. A part of apartness. How could I be more than I was, what did it take? *I am what I am but I want to be more than I am*, I whispered. The self that I was looked for more selfness. I didn't want to be replaced by another; I wanted to be more of me. I didn't want Jesus inside me. *It is no longer I that live but Christ that lives in me.* Not in me, he didn't. *I* wanted to persist. To persist in a more masterly mode. What was it then? What did it take? More power? What sort of power precisely? Inner power. Inner knowing of myself. To self determine. Outer expression? Fighting? Killing? To know a cause? How was it possible?

I pressed my face on the window and wondered, if the window pane was not there would I continue to lean more and more until I tumbled off the roof and landed on the pavement dead? Was that a determination that would resemble a mastery of myself? My will be done. Not *Thy* will.

Is the will to death then an act of self mastery. The Christians don't like the idea of self-destruction, the idea of the will destroying what God has given.

I pretended that the glass was not there to touch my face. I leaned and leaned and felt I would go over the edge. I thought of what there was and what there will be. Affirming my demise was what sort of affirmation?

If I acted to kill myself it would be said that I did so as an act of escape, mistakenly thinking it was a flight from the condemnation of my deed, an act of an overly assertive will, a sign that it was an expression of evil. It might even be said that it was an act of admission, that I could no longer live with myself. My act would measure up nicely with their way of thinking. It would be death and dishonour and disobedience. Nothing in it was worthy.

The flight I needed was from them. To cut them off was what I needed. To deliver them into the abyss of my own self. To a place where they would be unable to see me anymore. If they did not want to know me as the backslider, they would not know me, and, in their not knowing me, they would not know themselves.

Life! What is it that makes us ever and always devoted to you? I cannot yet choose freely between life and death. That's to come. That thinking nature that is required will come. As nature itself will come. That's a hell of a nature that nature. It's why we exist. *Natura Narturans.* The eternal creative nature. But I don't want to be resigned to be one of nature's minuscule modes. I want to be more than that. I will even suffer for it. I would suffer like Christ. Christ is said to have suffered for us but I will suffer for myself.

I thought that nobody would come to my room until the next day. They would leave me to stew even longer than usual. But the room was mine. The space was mine. I appropriated the room. It was so much my room. Everything in it was intimately mine. So there I was. Just there. But there in a state of thereness.

CHAPTER 32

Theist, deist, pan-theist, a-theist, me-ist. Me in His midst. I and He must find an accommodation. Eyeball to eyeball, it was hard to escape the spiritual stare. My room was my place of escape from God. In an appropriate fashion I wanted to get in some practice in escaping. Practice dying was a little too soon for consideration. The essence of escaping was not to deny Him. Not to seek a refutation. That would have been fruitless and futile; a denial is in essence an affirmation, and I felt his presence so acutely.

There is indeed no *real* escape from Him. It's been the problem of men since Adam. It results in either absolute faith or disobedience to death. Finding a hiding place is an alternative but is notoriously difficult. The prophets of old asked the question: *Where could I go from thy spirit and to where shall I flee from thy face? If I ascend into Heaven thou art there, if I make my bed in Hell thou art there also. Even in the uttermost parts of the sea, the darkest darkness shall never cover me.* No hiding place, even in bed with the Devil. So what? No escape, no hiding place.

My task was to confront the holy Him and to declare my own unholiness. To take my stand. To say, *this is me. The essence of Mooston. De-deified in the appropriated room.* And then elsewhere as I spread out, I would preach my word of reprobation. The table in the middle of the room where we play our board games was my pulpit. I always wanted to be a livewire preacher, plugged in, lit up and lifting, with grand gestures, the spirits of the sheep with the idea of the profane, the regenerated unregenerate.

Fuck the Lord O my soul and all that is within me. Fuck His holy name! Brethren backsliders, we are gathered here to practice the unholy life. As we have all known the holy we know something of the nature of the unholy and choose the latter as our way of being. To sin like good sinners, to turn our backs on the holy realm, to think and act in supremely ungodly fashion. We are not here to deny God his existence. On the contrary, we affirm it, but in that affirmation we raise it up to stand against it, firm in spirit and firm in body, erect in mind. The holy erection. His creation in an unholy rebellion. His aim, His plan, is that we seek to re-unite ourselves, to participate in His being after He cast us all out into the state of half being. A simple plan. His threat is that we face non-being, annihilation. We are nothing by ourselves. He has told us that some of us will already be damned. His reprobates. Oh that sovereign fucker! Election to damnation is an expression of his majestic sovereignty.

Today brethren the mother turned her back on me. She shunned me. In the name of her God she disowned me. An act of disavowal. In her ignorance she branded me a backslider and a sinner. She called me evil, and the Devil's disciple. I shall not disappoint the mother. I shall give to her, offer up to her the backslider she thinks me to be. The sinner she thinks me to be. A bigger backslider than she ever thought possible.

We are not gathered here to uplift the senses nor to practice the praise of science and its motley mob of atheist offspring. The uncouth and uncalled for. Neither are we gathered here to enforce the pleasurable way we like it, for the pleasure, the way that is comfortable, to our minds and to our bodies. We are gathered here because we see something. A light that brightens our darkness. But not with light, with darkness itself. This is the province of darkness. Wherever you look, and it is hard to look when all you have is blackness to look into. There is the evangelical darkness, the witless, the unrefined preachers of repentance where the more you seek to know the less you are repentance material. Stop! they shout. How dare you ask questions! Here is the truth! In my shout. The shout of truth. In the simple fact that I shout, it is the truth. I say in a loud voice to you, Jesus is the way the truth and the life. What more do you need? they ask. Nothing! Nothing? they answer. We are fallen creatures, fallen so low we cannot see for ourselves. We are blind like Bartimaeus. Our reason is pitiable. Inept. Clumsy. God has created us so. We are to oscillate between hope and fear. The hope of the kingdom, the fear of the Devil. That is our fate. Accept it or else. Why would God dispose us to reason and yet have us determine the truth in the occult? The throwing of bones or in miracles or whatever else that the mind can imagine apart from reason? So the likes of the mother will be favoured in her preferred ignorance, in her wild superstition, in her nastiness, in her prejudice, for salvation? A determination of the understanding is not a requirement. The use of one's reason is not a requirement. All that is fucking necessary for eternal rapture is to ascend to a particular highly vague imagining, and to assent to the call of particular image. Ignorance is so seductive. What does one do to make truth palatable to the masses? Transform it into a religion. Plato becomes Christ. Aristotle becomes Muhammad. Then what do we have? Murder, bloody murder. The will to ignorance is at hand and the hand will smack the face that denies it.

Let's go back and sing together that wonderful hymn to sin, Fuck the Lord O my soul and all that is within me fuck His holy name... And sing with gusto brethren. Sing it like you mean it.

The room echoed with my defiling word. I was exhausted. I felt the word turning into flesh. My liberated tongue felt ready for swift and wild lalalaing. And I could hardly stop myself laughing at the nonsense I was spouting. But I wanted the unhallowed word on the street to know what the earthly ear would make of the mumbo jumbo of mammonizing. A gospel of nonsense that inspired unceasing laughter. Not applause. What would the tough guys in the Shankill and the Markets and Sandy Row and the Falls think? They were coming out, these boys, with a message of their own that had no laughter attached, and that would shake the foundations.

Eva... no, Charlotte was far down below when I stuck my head out of the window for the horizons of air to fill my lungs. *Is Christ still the king in there?* she said with a laugh. I could barely hear her but the thrust of it managed to get through. *Your Lord Snooty brother just went out the front door.*

Fancy a dander to a place? I asked.

What place?

To backwards. She sneezed a laugh.

That's no place at all.

In this place it is. I'm stuck here. In solitary. The only place is backwards.

Or downwards. Launch yourself and fall into my arms.

Across the street a front door opened and out came the trouserless toddler, Teddy Northbee, with his plastic spoon in hand to scoop up dog shite. His mother would soon follow in a blind panic, fouling the air with the skitter's name and other obscenities and revving herself up to lovingly skelp the bare legs off him.

I have to go forwards to church in a bit.

You're wasting your time. Come and worship me.

In good time Miss, in good time. That I will wait for. That notion was almost unbearable to spend a thought on.

I'll teach you the bad times. Can I come up there?

No, the time is bad.

Charlotte smiled, waved with her limp hand and walked off. Teddy Northbee was lifted off his backside before he got his wee plastic spoon into the dog shite. Swooped and spanked in a single movement.

*

I needed to move. I couldn't rest. Charlotte's departure made me restless. The body demanded movement. Movement to disobedience. Taking a stand against movement elsewhere. This was where life elsewhere was to be found. The transforming disobedient – the virtuously disobedient – towards tough guys with their movement in swaggers. Their disobedience was not mine but they would eventually meet. They ruled their roosts with their struts, struts upon which their lives stood. The South Belfast Sandy Row strut was the low-down upper body, the swivel from the hip. The Shankill Road demeanour was the stout, puffed out chest with hands resting, dipped into the front pockets. Elbows bent bow-like, like the best bamboo. The vicious Markets men would kill you for a sweetie wrapper. They could hear the faintest wrapper rustle and needed to have their simple satisfaction. To put you into your place. To take what was not theirs was what satisfied them the most. The males from the Falls were a foul breed. Having fallen foul of breeding. They smelled of hardened bad eggs. They were all the kin and culture of badness. A tearaway tribe related in their fitness for the diabolical deed. Their design was to deal justice. They ruled their rickety realms. And the rule was to obey their capricious natures, which was the hardest rule to follow. They were what they were one day and they were not what they were the previous day the next. They were something else. They required something else. So if you met them they would instil the fear of surprise. It would appear that there was an intention to have a laugh but not so. Laughter would indeed be present, but an obvious joke was not at hand. What was at hand was an intention to destruction.

*

Do you want that button? he said pointing at a particular button on a meek weakling's jacket. Warren is the meekling by name. It was the school playground, enclosed by bars like a gaol. The first day of the new term and the new meekling had entered the realm of the uncertain. Sent out by proud parents to learn. The approach was not long in coming. As was learning. His jacket button on his new blazer hardly seemed a proper point of interest. *Do you want that button?* repeated the impatient nature at closer quarters. The weakling spirit was disturbed but he must answer. He knew he must.

Yes, you can have it, spluttered Warren the weakling. *Have it please.*

I don't fucking want it, bawled his tormentor. *I fucking want to know if you want it. Do you want that button? Answer my question.*

Yes, yes! I want it. There was then an immediate intuition in the meekling, who felt weaker by the instant, that this represented the wrong answer. The expression on the face before him told him that.

So, you want it? continued the questioner.

Yes.

The questioner looked around with a menacing grin. The button was taken in his firm-fingered grasp and tugged right away from its thready connection. *Hold out your hand. Here's your button! The one you want.* The button, in splendid isolation from the blazer was placed in the weakling's hand. That was badness. But not sinfulness. Not unholiness.

The bad boys of the city shite-heaps hitched up their badness britches a few significant notches with the coming of the big cause. They answered the question posed to them in the affirmative and then were sent out to ask the questions. Their questions would come to you at some point in time. They would blow your brains out if the right answers weren't forthcoming. Hooded and bound, you would be in a game of deadly blind man's bluff , shouting any answer under the sun. Up an entry you would end up. A heap. A sad end. In a sack. A sad sack. It was badness and it was always circumstantial.

Sin is never circumstantial. It simply is! Always. It covers everything. Like the Atonement of Christ. Christ just about covered it all by dying on the cross. At one-ment. Clever John Tyndale. Transforming a word. A concept… a world.

The one thing the bad guys would not do was tell you a word of a lie because there was no truth in their world. They didn't need to lie. They would elucidate the nature of their world and their part in it and be happy to do it. They would gladly wise you up to it. They desperately wanted you to see their world. They wanted to share it with you, perhaps before they ended it all for you. But your end would be with the idea of them and their idea in your mind. If you ever had the pleasure of their company. The only thing that they would need to know, that they did not already possess as wisdom, was that they were sinners and the nature of the sin that covered them, and that it was their birthright. So I would not wait for them to come to me with their question. I would go to them. Would I be brave enough to bear witness to them this idea? To show them sin in their own back yards. And their error? Would they *see* the difference? Will I be able to deceive them?

CHAPTER 33

My being is just there to make up the numbers. Just being there. Is this the fate of the unelect?

There is the *there*
the *just there*
And, there is the *there as*
The *there as something*

To be *just there*
Bare of outward impact
With nothing to share
A mere fact

To be *there as*
Is a power to share
The inner with the outer
A virtuous snare

And every so often I felt that *just thereness* oh so acutely. In isolation. Even more so with the departure of Charlotte. Thereness as hers not here. The virtuous snare. Trapped by being only mine. Disbarred from the holy of holies by the mother. Defrocked from the sainthood by her accusations and her new opinion of me. Not that I had a frock to show for it. Though the mother had one for me at the dinner table. What then can a poor sinner do? He keeps knocking on heaven's door and nobody's in. Knock on Hell's door? Just like when I called for my best friends. I was sure that there was someone in, but they never answered the door. It put me in a mood, briefly. Being ignored. Unwanted. *What's the matter with you? Are you in a mood?* the mother would ask. That made me angry. She of course knew all about moods. She was always in one. If she was in a quiz, her specialist subject would surely be moods. Or dirt. Concealing herself in the mood always. Concealing the dirt. All covered in a mood.

What was the *in* of a mood anyway? Does coming *out* of a mood make the world see us? Does it reveal us as we are in our plainness? That means the mother would have been nearly always hidden. But there are *good moods*. So, you are always in a mood of one sort or another. Just that when the word mood is used when you are said to be in one, it means that the mood is bad. *Throwness. What's thrown you into a bad mood?* the mother would say if she was in a good mood.

*

Parked in the attic, in my mood, a mood that prompted hallucination, I felt like practising my backslider sermon to reverse the sense of approaching weakness. In a smooth, truly evangelical style but without their substance. Something very personal. The reversal of the saved by God's grace testimony. How near you can get to spirituality in the pure imagination without invoking God Himself.

The most dramatic testimony to God's power unto salvation is when the sinner is at his lowest spiritual ebb. To the evangelical mind, the lowest ebb is a drunken, gambling, whoring, fighting, disrespectful, swearing, blaspheming, Bible bashing fucker. Though, in communication of the holy message, the language has to be restrained for a sensitive evangelical ear. Inferences have to be drawn from respectable but limited language. So, what is spoken doesn't actually seem to refer to anything that bad, but it has to be bad to show how the work of Christ can reach right into the most base and barbaric of human lives and transform action and thought in the single, unexisting, divine instant.

Or you have to possess the language of the literary imagination, the ability to embellish the facts of circumstances. Truth, however, is in great danger of being a casualty. Preachers are the best embellishers of all and they have the best testimonies. That's why they are preachers.

I listened to the outrageous Ulster evangelist Willie Mallon in the packed Ulster Hall. Flanked by the parents and a throng watching in hypnotic awe. The awe of the holy in a place accustomed to the musical movement of Bach, Beethoven, Mahler and Mozart.

Oh how I was trapped in sin, with the Devil in person, hovering over me to claim me as his own. Out of a hovel of whoredom and gambling and drink, like in a dream I was led to a country lane, then to a field in the middle of nowhere, then to a ditch, a deep hole, a muddy ditch hole, a trench like the Wars had never seen, in the filth of the earth, in a grave, the created filthy earth fouled by the Devil's brigade marching in hobnailed boots to the beat of soul destroying sin. There on my knees in the filth, feeling the heat of hell just below me, I had on the one side sin and the Devil, and on the other the cross and the Saviour and the spirit of the almighty God. How I trembled, and in this trembling, I reached out a hand and placed my trust in the Almighty. In the cross. And oh the joy that thrilled my soul. This, saint and sinner is my profession.

Indeed it was. He was a good as his word. I could spot a liar when I heard one, and if the likes of Willie Mallon could lie, I could lie in my own cause. The people listened to Mallon and willed his tale to be true, as they willed their lives to be part of that truth. And the myth of the Mallon field of salvation left the Ulster Hall that night to be broadcast abroad as truth, and the fools all flocked to that truth. I knew the liar and his lies, but it was only revealed to me in time. And the revelation was slow to come.

CHAPTER 34

I didn't know the slopey Shankill or the fading Falls that well. Mostly seen from the attic window and the high imagination. Both were high up, heading towards the hills. The Falls was alas initially merely a name. People from the mother's side lived up there. So slightly more than a name when that information seeped through. In an imagining there were other streets there. A fairly good walk away. Vegetationless thoroughfares. Thoroughfarely unfair. The mother was born in the dingy arse hole of a communal habitation that was Cupar Street. It was Cooper Street in my head. Like *Do not forsake me oh my darling* Gary Cooper street. The mother was the father's darling, in whom the idea of forsaking was to be abandoned. Nobody I knew lived in the Shankill. Protestantism lived there. But there was an imagining there too. A picture. A Protestant arterial road. The word kill was in the name. Something to do with slaughtering. The killer Shane. Shane O'Neill. No, the wise father said the name was Irish for old church and was once ruled by roaming wolves and boar before men made their church there. Savages now roamed around the old hunting grounds. Protestant savages dancing and growling up and down their narrow streets. Marching savages. The Markets area was low lying, beside the Lagan river. I knew it also as a place of slaughter. Squealing pigs trotting to their place of death. It was

also the father's place of birth and early growth. Reared amongst
the swine. His old mother lived there in a hovel. I saw the word
love in hovel. A lovely hovel. It was lovely in a way that clean
council housing, into which hovel people wanted to be moved
to be rid of the hovel living, was not. Compressed and confining
streets with black cobbles. Rising black bricks straight out of the
earth. All shiny with damp from above and below. Pulsating with
activity from Cromac Street to the River Lagan. No place to plant
a flower. Or pick one. Even a weed had its troubles. There was
little of the Irish greenery in those streets whose people lived for
the idea of green. Filthy flowerless window sills. Fish market, ab-
attoir, the gasworks, the big bakery sucked in a thousand people
to labour, the hovels built around it. Little bare feet massaged
by the cobbles. Gas lamps with a homely glow lit up filthy faces.
Corner huckster whores sold shamelessly high-priced produce.
Day and night. High prices for pleasure for the lowly and low
paid. An unholy hive of so much striving. Striving to be, striving
to be something in someone else's mind. Striving to be sly and
slippery. Joy in anything goes. Immoral moves maketh the man.

The cousins from The Markets were all immoral movers, skivers.
Of diverse kinds. Wanting to know what you had and how to get
it from you. On my early visits in my small years, I learned the art
of evasion. They saw that I had decent shoes and clothes and that
I was clean, and so they smelled the promised land. The mother
in her holy lovingness called them Fenian skitters with bad habits.
*And don't you learn those bad habits from those skitters! Their das
are all no-good skitters. They'll all die of their lazy badness.* But, I
wanted to control the skitters. I didn't like their dirt. Nor their
touch. I smelled a bad smell. I wanted to teach them better things.
Introduce them to higher forms, new varieties of skiving. To have
them at my beck and call. In reality, they were weaklings. Artful
weaklings who desired to be led. I let them know they could not
pull the wool over my eyes, especially their filthy wool. But they
were unaware that I could and did pull it over theirs. Their little
beady eyes did not take much material covering. *Do you want this
and that?* I asked them, and they'd nod furiously. I said, *No harm in
wanting,* and saw them squirm in their wanting confusion.

Then I asked them to do my dirty work. My bidding. They learned my bad habits. They learned that a look from me was sufficient for them to know what to do. I sent them into the huckster shops to steal sweets for me. I praised them for their daring and then I tossed them a few as a reward. And I said, *Fuck the hucksters,* and they laughed and repeated it like a rallying cry. I was like the vicar of vice to them. They saw goodness. They fell down and worshipped me. They were afeared of my wrathful mind. I devised a look to give them if I was displeased. And when they saw it, they saw my wrathful thoughts. My chin veered off to one side and slightly protruded so that my bottom teeth jutted out of my jaw and almost touched my upper lip. I closed my eyes for a second and then sighed when my eyes opened again. The sigh was to be like the breath of God in the Old Testament, where it denotes His power and dominion over things. I had them swaying perpetually between hope and fear, living in the pursuit of shadows for novelties. Their lives were left open to deceit, to extreme emotional impulses, to easy anger and hatred. They gloried in the misery of others Encountering my look, they scurried about like frantic little rodents looking for a hole to slip into. Like the writer who writes to arrange the thoughts of the reader, here I was the author of their worlds. I said to them, *Here is my mind. Read it! I am your story.* In my presence, I kept them away from the authorship of their own acts and all their wilful modes were harnessed, though they thought they were of independent disposition. When I finally let go of them for good, when I did not return to those confined Market streets, what form of life did they come naturally to inhabit? There was no doubt in my mind. They would be the boys who would take the oath, affirm the cause and do the dirty deed that they were told to do. I could see it all out of the smudged glass of my bedroom window. That marked market world that traded lives. Out there. So close. On the hazy horizon. As for me, I would commit no one else's crimes So, I was the perfect material for a backslider.

*

The father and the mother did not go out together anymore, not hand in hand with the love and friendship that bound them together in their early romance. No joy left. Mostly sorrow, so there was a transition toward destruction. A conversion that condemned them. There was no contact with laughter and the ideas of each other as loved. Not a kiss in sight. Or a kind word. The only kindness is silence, for a word between them was rarely pleasant. Words were always for the administration of anger or annoyance. Was there a romantic period in their lives that lasted into marriage, and a language that went with it, when they knew affection and the words of affection? There were times when they took out their bikes and went cycling together. Before we had a car. Then there was something.

I had no adequate understanding of their times cycling together. Just an imagining. I had the vague idea that they went up to the Castlereagh Hills, on the southern edge of the city, and into the countryside, on the roads that took you quickly into the pleasant flat landscape of County Down. The mother on a bike was an uncomfortable thought to have. They went out and came back and I never had a thought of them in their absence. Out in the late afternoon after work and back just before it got dark. The door opened to the street as they parked the bikes in the hallway.

Does this reflect a reality or a dream?

The dream may have been that, in pursuit of little amounts of happiness and contentment, the father wooed the mother head on in the direction of the delights of hedonism. After initial success, these small sensual delights soon led to large scale emotional outbursts. The mother had a sweet tooth, so much so that the sweetness had in short time done away with her natural endowment of gnashers, and the father made efforts to tease out general sweetness through the administration of this particular sweetness.

As money was tight, this practice was limited to a Saturday night after the rigours of shopping which always left a bitter taste. The father gave us a lift to church in the evening and bought and brought her sweets on the way back. She had ordered the preferred type to suit her immediate taste but in his absence her contrariness got on its high horse, which bucked and bucked until, for no apparently good reason, the contrariness was overthrown and simple anger took to the saddle.

Perhaps the anger was inspired by the particularly acute awareness of herself as a woman of no importance. Sitting there by the fireside, watching television waiting for a small sack of sweets to be deposited on her lap. So, when he returned, she invariably turned her nose up at the treat before launching into silence with the prospect of an unsavoury pre-retirement exhibition of frustration which carried on through sleep into the next day.

The mother excelled at turning her nose up at things. It was not just snubbing, but the facial manifestation of the snub was a rare sight to behold. It drove the father insane but he kept that madness inside somewhere. Somehow. Her snub face was a screwing up of the upper lip towards the end of the nose. The lower lip being pushed up towards the upper lip by the upward stiffening of the chin.

In response to her claim that she was treated as a woman of no importance, the father sought out other areas to incline her upwards in people's estimation. He thought that this could be found in friendship and the different surroundings that friendship could bring. So, people came round to try to offer that friendship but she turned her nose up at them. People from the father's work came and the mother would snub them. Jimmy Cherry and his wee wife came around one night, all dolled up. Jimmy was a boss in the big bakery where the father worked. He had flat greasy hair, jet black, sunken cheeks and scary bulging eyes. His smile revealed big buck teeth and his complexion was white as flour. His wee wife thought his ghostly looks were lovely. She looked up at him admiringly. It surprised me to know that she wasn't the only one with this opinion. He frightened the life out of me. He came round to the house once when I was watching *The Pit and the Pendulum* and when he left I couldn't separate the fear I felt as a result of the goings on of the mad Don Nicholas Medina and the idea of Don Jimmy Cherry's greasy smile. They could have inserted the bakery man into the film with ease, to a decent enough effect.

I didn't know the time, or how much time had passed. Was it six o'clock yet? Trotter time if it was. Chomping on their precious pig's feet they'll be. By the fireside and the TV. Sitting, looking, chomping. Ripping the rubbery flesh off with their choppers. Tinned pineapple rings with ham slices waited in the kitchen for afters. Monstrous appetites manifested in munching. Savage inner mouth smacking. Annoying to the end. With ill-fitting falsers making you ill. A sickening sight. The older sister had generous dental gaps— tombstones—Stonehenge—memorials to inheritance. Mouthology. The mother and father had no such natural memorials. I often wondered what their original gnashers were like. No photos around to reveal the truth of the tooth, the whole tooth and nothing but the tooth.

Me here by myself. Beside myself. Assigned to self. A posting to the frontier. To speak alone. Fleeing to soliloquy. On my lonesome ownsome. Owning myself in play. Attending to my ownness. A pleasant free fragrance perhaps. Out of the windy ways of the cankers down below. Canker wankers! Stinkers. Slobs and sluts to goodness. Goodness knows what. In my high outpost. The dead time of a Saturday evening. Between coming home and going out. To a rendezvous with drink and smoke and banter and laughter and purposeful fleshful encounters that linger into the day of rest. If I glanced out of the window there might be… there, again, way down below…the little shoes pacing past. On little dainty feet. They would soon pass without me seeing. The fancy of mine. Little Charlotte.

There was between us a misunderstanding. Over an event at my school, a disco event. I asked her to come but she shook her head. But there was a smile there too. A sorry smile that was the loveliest smile. That's OK. She was a little female Fenian and that was it. Her will was tied. The Fenian bondage. But the asking and the refusal was intimate and soft. On a soft windless summer evening, the breathing was relaxed and familiar. Two timid minds in a most pleasurable misunderstanding.

Go on… won't you go?

I can't.

I know you can't. But I thought you could.

That does not make sense. The whole thing didn't make sense. I thought she would deny her Fenianism for me. I would have become a Fenian to have her little cold fleshy hand clasped in mine. *That which is born of the flesh is flesh.* She was born in my mind as flesh. But she would not have wanted my fake mercenary Fenianism.

I wanted nothing more than her. Still. More than eternal life. Just to be with her. More than spirit. More than soul. More than new birth. More than regeneration. More than salvation or of heavenly things. Nothing more mattered more than the flimsy flesh. The dying flesh. The corruptible flesh. Dying together. There was truth in flesh. Feeling in flesh. Fulfilment in flesh. This was the message of flesh, the love of flesh. The love of lovely flesh.

There's the wise flesh and the foolish flesh. There is the flesh that seeks continually to deny itself. It can because it has its idea of itself. The church people wanted to deny their flesh, everybody's flesh, but all they succeeded in doing was drawing attention to it.

Small dress, so small a dress, lightly encasing her fragrant flesh. So there was the empty Saturday evening street before my eyes. Fleshless. Dressless. Charlotteless. The bare side of a house wall across the street where I kicked a ball. And downstairs they were full of pig. The foolish awful flesh. The miserable flesh. And the hospitals were full of that awful failing flesh. Old flesh and young flesh seeking to preserve the flesh. At all costs.

I felt that pain deep in my flesh returning. My very own pain. A crippling stomach ache stimulated in crippling thought. To the Royal Hospital I went from time to time but they couldn't take it away. But I didn't want to hang around there. I wanted to take my pain away myself.

I soon saw it was all a misunderstanding with Charlotte. There was truth in the misunderstanding. Charlotte was there! Waiting.

CHAPTER 35

I was still up there waiting. In the everlasting anticipation. And I was anxious. And getting impatient. And I was not knowing. I was playing with my not knowing. Just saying things. Differently to the norm. I leaned, I lay, I limbered up. But it was still all waiting. Forms of waiting. And in waiting I began to think about waiting. Like waiting timidly in old doddery Dr. McSourley's waiting room. That was waiting alright in that room! A room made for waiting. Even the dust waited in mid-air. Until the door opened. Everyone waited for the wee Scottish woman in the white coat to come in and call their name. Then she called a name that wasn't theirs, and some annoying person whose name it was got up from their waiting and went out of the room and up the stairs in the hallway to see old McSourley who waited.

An appointment time seemed to mean nothing. But your name would come at some point. In the meantime, everyone sighed and shifted about in their creaky chairs, uneasy about more waiting. In their waiting they thought about the prospect of more waiting and the time spent waiting with their annoying complaints yet unseen to.

I never liked entering the waiting room. Opening the big door at the bottom of the stairs to a universal stare. Finding a chair as they all stare. As they sighed and tutted to tell you that you were just a nuisance name which might get called first even though you came in after them. And if you are a name before theirs you feel their stare stabbing you in the back as you left. In fact, some names waited outside the waiting room, in the hall, or in the street, just to avoid the room. I'd worry too much that I'd miss my name, and I'd be there until the closing time, waiting. In the old Victorian parlour waiting room that is not welcoming for the Irish, I sat and waited for my name many a time. Fitted for waiting only, with posters about vaccinations, leaflets defining diseases, and pictures of birds. But most waiting was done in impatience, in restless, timeless staring at the other waiters, where you got to know all about shoes and coats and hairstyles and sometimes other people's business that was whispered that bit too loudly. But mostly you learnt about the ways of waiting.

I continued to wait in the upper room, my very own room, my very own waiting, for tidings from below and the pain in my belly to go away. Bending over made it slightly better. As did leaning to one side. I thought of waiting in all areas of life. I waited impatiently for the father when he talked to people he knew when he met them in town. I waited over-excitedly for the next football match. I waited for the bus to school. I waited outside somebody's door for them to come out to play. I waited for that girl Eva to sit beside me in church. I waited for God to chastise me for all the thoughts that I entertained about her. Mammon, mammon, effing mammon she was in my mind. The ineffable mammon.

> *Mammon mammon,*
> *How I luv ya, how I luv ya,*
> *My dear old mammon!*

The thoughts just kept coming, never seemed to run dry, like they were drinking from   bountiful supply. I imagined myself sinking, sinking and sliding to hell whilst in the midst of the soundly saved. Like my sodding little church seat was in quicksand or like my bottom was on a tipping up slippery slope of a fairground seat. The waiting continued. And so did the thinking in that increasingly wayward manner. All evident in my fast wrinkling young brow. The thoughts were just over the brow.

When you're waiting on something, the thing is not in your possession. It's beyond you for a time. If we never had to wait we'd have everything we want, but that's not the nature of our lives. We're always waiting for something. Not wanting to wait, but wanting the waiting to end. Time is waiting, waiting and expecting the next thing to come along. Out of the horizon of things. Waiting for people to make their minds up, to do things. The freer people are, the more waiting they have to do.

Nigel was a friend who you always had to wait ages for. He could never make up his highly rational mind. It was infuriating to wait for him to weigh up all the pros and cons that were involved in a course of action. But, that was Nigel and the waiting for him was nearly always worth it. However, you had to know Nigel to know that.

The Bible tells us to wait patiently for God, but the saints in the church were like children with the impatience of children. (Yet the Scripture also says that we must be like children.) They couldn't wait. We'll *always* have to wait for God. That is the secret. So, you have to be patient. In a way you've never been before. For you can never possess God. The churches are only full as long as people believe they can possess God and empty when they have given up waiting. The truth is, God is simply too much to have. That's the lesson of the Bible. And that's fucking patience, alright. Waiting for nothing. But waiting has its merits. The anticipation of something itself can be pleasurable. And waiting for the ultimate is the ultimate pleasure.

I would settle for waiting for Charlotte, if I simply knew that at some point my going out was going to meet her coming in. I intended so many things with Charlotte. I placed her with me in a host of different circumstances. I'd say crazy anythings as long as the utterance had her name in it somewhere. I saw her laughing at my senseless expressions. She flooded my mind in a way that made me feel that I had no way of stopping her entry into it. Her presence was there with me even when she was not there, or was not even thinking of me in any way. And that was what I waited for. The particular real emptiness to be filled.

The men in the church waited for the women all the time. In a more rudimentary fashion where fashion was foremost. They

damned John Calvin and his damning necessity and waited in
their Arminian freewill to take them to the Promised Land. They
waited for the promise, waited for the promise of women, to see
them before their lusty eyes, and willed themselves towards them,
for them to admire their flushed fleshy manliness. The women
in the church were not supposed to dress to get the men excited,
all flustered to flushness of flesh. They were told endlessly by the
Pastor and his henchmen elders not to present their womanhood as
a temptation. Like parents told daughters not to look like hussies.
The women obeyed the holy instructions to a degree, but even
though their dress spoke the language of modesty, the excitement
generated amongst the brethren suggested a more lively vernacular
was at work, blazing a trail right up to their spiritually-protected
loins. Their palms sweat at the thought of the womanly flesh and
the flutter of light feminine raiment all over it.

To cover a women head to toe is not to deny the imagination
anything and the imagination is notoriously good at deception.

The closer you are to God, we were repeatedly taught, the
greater your temptations. Oh, how sorely were the men of the
church tempted. Of course they all claimed closeness to God, and
thought their lusty leering went unnoticed. They had access to
the language of womanly dress, which consisted of the expression
of thoughts that were intuitively grasped—and grasping itself was
much in the masculine mind—because they were the thoughts of
ordinary thinking.

The women themselves had thoughts and expressed them in
dress and the men had their thoughts that found their precise
correspondence in the Sunday service fashion parade.

Understanding clothes is like understanding a conversation…
and to understand a conversation one has to know the language of
which it is a part.

The language of dress was part of the language of the church
but it was also a part of the language of the mind-body drives,
the conatus that endeavours the mind-body to persevere. And
the language of sex was a real frontrunner in the church and was
subtlety made manifest in the behaviour of men to whom the spirit
of God was given as a hard cock.

Nothing was missed. Nothing of the Devil. Those stiletto heels, high and almightily firming up the smooth calf, the sacrificial calf, ankles shackled by straps, and finally, on the downward journey, feet squeezed tightly into slender leather sheaths. Ankles, calves, thighs. Hair falling on bare necks. Sweaty palms on sweltering summer evenings searched for cool silky satin slips upon which to unharness their blessed holiness. The laying on of these searching palms soothed their troubled spirits.

The Bible says that the spirit of God appears in many forms, and the feminine form is a favourite of the interpreters of godly forms.

And lo! In the midst of raving sermons my mind wandered. In and out of raving and ranting that terrorised the attention. It wavered. It wanted not to hear the condemnation of the competing promises of meaning. So the wandering was partly the presence of mind to avoid the more unpleasant truths. Midway through the sermon came the holy Battle of Midway. All at sea, drifting, until an internal inspiration fired up an alternative line.

I opened my Bible, giving the impression to all in the vicinity that the boy was being attentive to the message, that he was in saintly servitude to the Master, but on his mind was an augmentation of thought in amusement. He made a beeline to the prophet pages and the desperate men in church were bestowed with suitable Biblical Christian names.

McMorrow was heard shouting, *Praise the Lord,* and he became Habakkuk McMorrow. Baldy Hosea Fisher was begat next in the mind. The Philistines had some good names. Abimelech McCurley had an appropriateness to it for the specky-bearded elder. A mixture of saints and wrestlers and my eyes watered with the waves of humorous distraction rising to the surface. Pretty Boy Haggai Spencer. Jackie Pallo Obadiah Conlon. Beelzebub Balthazar Bradshawn. It was such a theatre.

Isn't that what religion has become in our day? Even in the days of the straight-laced. The theatrical is in man as much as the religious. The actor as much as the zealot. Indeed the actor zealot.

I saw the whole spectacle before me as a wresting match, the saved wrestling for the Lord Jesus. Leotarded and sweating like a pig, Pastor Two Rivers Millin is leading sinners to the Lord whilst having them in a Boston crab, maybe a figure four, or a half Nelson. *Yes, yes,* shouted the sinners one after the other thumping their hands on the floor, *I submit to the Lord. Save me sweet Jesus. Save me!*

The pulpit was a wresting ring in my inspired imagination. With the Pastor's spiritual excitement cup full to overflowing, he sprinted to the ropes and bounced off them with almost miraculous momentum, thus enabling him to leap from the platform   into the congregation, who variously spluttered out panicked *praise the lords and hallelujahs.* He forearm-smashed a couple of believers in the outside aisle seats and demanded that they shout praise the Lord. *Say Praise the Lord, brother! Say hallelujah, sister!* In their dizzied, disorientated embarrassment, they obliged. The Pastor laughed like Burt Lancaster right into their reddening God-fearing faces.

I told Linus what it was like if the imagination was applied and he immediately wanted to come to the church to see for himself. I wanted him to get saved so he would come with me all the time and we could laugh at the holy comedy show together. We would live in the light of holy laughter. He knew my mind and I knew his.

I heard the water drain from the bathroom sink one flight of stairs below. Dirty sink... I assumed the mother was probably setting about it with a Brillo Pad, diverted to the bathroom on her way up to see me for another session. She swore by the Brillo Pads. She performed a vicious Brillo Pad rub on grease like it was a personal vendetta. She gritted her false teeth and took to it with a fat hand and firm forearm. Like she glorified the act of inflicting pain on dirt. Holy warm water and detergent.

The mother pleasured herself with little acts of cruelty. In my younger days as a toddler she declared war on my head when washing my hair, taking particular delight in wringing out the wet strands with excessive force and gouging deep into my delicate scalp with her powerful fingers. Or trawling a fine tooth comb through my hair like a combine harvester in search of nits. She called me a wee baby and a slippery skitter when I tried to escape. It was not at all clear if my punishment in exile for the theft was a source of pleasure for her and that the crime had become incidental. Was she being the power of God unto my salvation?

I was beginning to feel peckish. I knew that nothing would be offered to the criminal. Even the condemned man got a last meal, I thought. They thought they could starve the truth out of me. I thought that this was in fact said earlier: *You'll starve until you confess.* Not so much a punishment as a torture. Or both. The Nazis. The Japs. Red Indians burying cowboys up to their necks.

Even the pig trotters entered the mind as an appetising morsel. A delicacy. My innards spoke. I thought of the starving Africans. They'll eat anything. A slug slithering across the yard wouldn't be safe in its slime. I felt thin. I hated thin. Like Les Buttocks' thin limbs. Bony. Like in the morning when I rose from bed. Thin. Weak. Thinweak. Marius Thinweak, a good Dickensian name. How would I ever get revenge, if I was weak? Revenge against the injustices. All the injustices that had befallen me as a boy. The things your elders told you always amounted to good advice. All learning they said. All learning! They said that the teachers of learning could mete out the stick to us at will. And that it was good for us. That was how we learnt. For fear of a beating. Like a dog. That was the lesson of life. Strife.

Next person to speak gets the cane. Tap tap tap of cane on teacher's hand. *That's not fair, Sir,* I said. *Out boy, hand out. But that's not fair Sir.* Whack! The pain ran up my arm and to the back of my eyes where it pushed out the tears. One boy in the class had his tears shoot out like bullets. The pain that pushed them out must have been enormous. But I once saw him crying when someone said he was a queer, so what was pushing out the tears? Was it also pushing out the queers?

I could dash down for a bite to eat to do away with the thinness. Cereal and milk. Didn't like it, but it swelled you up nicely. Big bowl of it until I felt like expelling a fart. The bowels worked well after a big bowl. No doubt they'd be giving the dog their pig scraps whilst the son starved to death in his outpost. There was no hope of death down there. Nothing near to it. They had swollen themselves up to life. I could hear the plates, scraped and emptied and stacked. The thin delft sound. Foodless food for thought. Jesus, I could do with a mouthful to swallow. A quarter pound of cooked ham sliced thinly. Sliced into shopkeeper's hand from the slicer and then onto grease proof paper. That noise of the slicer machine scything through meat. A crunchy pineapple ring accompaniment to meaty slivers.

They'd all be laughing in a minute, full belly laughter that was brought on by the fullness. Weakens the will to seriousness. Like a belter of booze. That's what the old cod Hughie the lodger called it. A belter. Some called it a swig. A swift kick of alcohol. He licked his greasy lips at the very idea. That old wanked-out wino. He wanted a swift kick up the weak arse, if anybody did. And I would give it to him. Except your foot would get lost in his over-sized shiny grey gabardines. Full of sitting shininess wiped shiny by a wooden chair. Shitting shininess. Chronic diarrhoea. The arse itself must be shiny as he always sat on the toilet seat. The arse of the trousers was akin to a shapeless sack. A mail sack. A male sack. Royal male, except he was a republican which he thought meant publican. He got his mail in his sacks. Slack sacks. Slacks, what a name that was for trousers. You bought slacks and old men's jerkins in Marks & Spencer's. You'd never be seen dead in an old man's Marks & Spencer's jerkin even if you imagined yourself as an old man.

The Carltin family menagerie lived at the back of us and the biggest son of the Carltin horde, in the hordes of sons, we called Jerkin Carltin. His real name was Gerard, but Jerkin served us well. *Seen Jerkin about?* sounded so much better. *Saw him in his Jerkin.* The Carltin family members were a nest of nothings to be respected, so they were fair game to treat with as much contempt as the mind was given disdainful unction. They oozed out of their council house abode like foul sewerage from a cracked pipe, spreading their toxic natures in all directions. The mother's main complaint was their smell, but that was a minor fault compared to the ghastly goings on in the mental apparatus of them. The mother gave the Carltins up as evidence that human kind was in fact made from the shite of the world and she gave herself special dispensation to use the word *shite*. But shite said softly and reverently and a lingering scoff made us feel part of it. *Softly and reverently the shite word is calling, calling for you and for me.* I sang that to myself from time to time. The mother would see my mouth moving but couldn't read the lips.

The Carltins came strongly to mind. In my new church of the backslider I would denounce this family for their badness. Not the sort of badness we wanted in our midst. Then all families would be unwanted. Denounced in many rich words with the full backing of my congregation. Avoiding circumspectness and venerability. Whilst the church of backsliders was still in innocent youth, I would declare the family dead in my head and transmit the idea to the faithless. Faith itself needed to be re-thought. Faith infected with doubt praised. No faith in fellow man. Treat him with the mistrust he deserved. Stay on your toes.

I was leaving and going... going elsewhere where life was better and truer to life where I was up to life and life invited me to its high table. It asked me what I wanted at the high table and I said, *Lord of life lead me*! Fat Granny died and everyone mourned and cried. Her delft po was full of black crap.

Death demands damned more respect than it is given.

*

The window was begetting boringness. Just looking to weariness. Nothing coming back. Leaning out. Leering. Like McAteer. The queer McLQueer. A seer in a different way. Unholy, irreverent. The very irreverent McLQueer. Steer clear of McLQueer. On account of his words. He said he liked the word *allure*. He said it over and over again because he liked the sound. The allure of the sound. But he said *alyour,* and the rest of us laughed in his face. And then he wrote it on the pavement with a stone. *Look at it, so alluring that word,* he said. *Isn't that funny?* Somebody remarked that he wasn't alluring in the least and that his pocked and pitted face was the only thing that was funny. He looked down on such unimaginative expressions, even though he had to look up at the insults coming down to where he had been thrown into the dirt. *Mere insults are not going to hurt me,* he said. That got the biggest laugh. That was his way. The way we knew well. This way. That way. Up and down. All around. An all-around thinker and joker.

Up there, looking up to the sky, at still and streaked with stretched out thin clouds. The sky was eating up the clouds. Unlike me who

was eating nothing. No wind. Unmoving. Blue patches sneaked in
on their weak wispy fringes. Meek clouds. My knees hurt like fuck,
kneeling on the cushionless chair that always sat under the window.
Just there for kneeling on. My neck ached looking up. Outside
nothing seemed to be happening. No one passed and I hated the
idea of waiting and waiting for nothing to come from the future
into my world of now. What if there was nothing coming in that
direction? What if it had all stopped coming my way? I wasn't going
anywhere. Nothing coming from anywhere. Unless everything had
changed in the way it happened.

But there was bound to be something. Not for me, for somebody
else, but it would pass me by and not make me part of it. I did,
however, feel wonderfully weary. Loose and rubbery. Daydreams
made the body even more forceless. The empty belly withdrew the
surface skin to the ribs and rumbled. I was doing all this thinking
about how to be bad, but with all the thoughts of badness I didn't
feel at all bad. Or not bad enough. Momentarily, with a thrust of
distinctive desire, I wanted to be like Albino Bad Bob in *The Life
& Times of Judge Roy Bean*. He just rode into town, shot a man's
horse and then said with complete economy of intellectual effort
to the shocked owner... *Cook it!* Bad Bob could drink boiling hot
coffee straight from the pot spout. He spouted badness. He was no
one's friend. Could a cultured man, a good man countenance such
physical crudity?

Justice is the handmaiden of the law, said Bean. *The law is the
handmaiden of justice.* It didn't matter a bean. Bean sought to lighten
his load with a formula. To spread the weight on the backs of all
with an idea that was outside all. Bad Bob searched for power only in
himself. In the end Bean and Bob were both alike because Bean *was*
justice, and Bob *was* his own law. So where did I find my own badness?
In a law? The mother said that I thought I was a law unto myself.

Les Buttocks was so firmly connected to something. Out of me
came the laughter at the buttocks, but it all really stemmed from
the tensed buttocks of Christ. Always presently tense. If I walked
along the thin line to Linus, and cut it behind me, I might escape.
But I really wanted Linus to crawl along the thin line to me and cut
off his escape route back to his world.

How did Saul of Tarsus become Paul? Why? Saul, slaughterer of Christians, becoming Paul, the Saint of Christians? The epileptic persecutor to ecstatic prosecutor of their cause? How? What sort of a leap was that? Over that seemingly unbridgeable chasm. A new man. It's that geometric leap. Linus to Sinus, I thought. But he'd still be Linus. Something else had to happen.

One window in this most motherly prison! Set in the roof betwixt two sloping ceilings. Under each sloping ceiling was a bed. Underfoot was a length of brown oil cloth. Aged and cracked. In the centre of the room was a sturdy table for games. Window, ceilings, beds, oil cloth, table, games. The words and things were a daily acquaintance. Now, this most binding word cell. Sealed in by the word. Even the non-word…the silence. I could hear a pin drop, or a pin could hear me drop. Almost. To sleep. The fact I did not jump from the window when I saw my prison all around me was a mistake. Was it? Was it even possible to act in that way? A complete denial, a miraculous escape. A leap. That would have been an act outside the convention. The convention is king. But it would be great to be the king of convention.

Own me. A whispered thought. A wilderness idea. *Own me! Bitch cunt fucking whore bastard!* I swung wildly, with words scything through the anger and the silence. The words they never wanted me to say. Old McKeown said them. Those words just spilled out, and I felt their body-warming effect. As I did in McKeown's. Like a warming venom coursing through my veins. Cursing my veins. Body tightening, I recognised their other worldly attraction because their source was that other world. Their life-giving force drifted into my orbit. The words inspired a form of laughter. *Bitch cunt fucking whore bastard, where is thy satanic sting?* I spun around and spat out the prohibited words in swifter and swifter succession. With the greater speed, they were thought all at once. They were sprayed with zeal and a joy that made me feel free. But I felt I needed someone else to say them to. Not someone daft like Impy Godthorpe. Then they would celebrate a greater reality. And I needed a cigarette to puff, needed to take within me its warm smoke.

CHAPTER 36

Harnessed ox. I felt constrained and heavy after the light-headed spinning. Unusually so, as I had an awareness of lightness most of the time. The heaviness was the process of bondage and slowing. Had you heaving. But it was mighty hard to kick against the pricks. I could quite imagine it. Mainly due to the fact that I misunderstood the pricks idea.

The Pastor said *pricks* with a great and powerful spitted *p*. He hissed the *s* before groaning gutturally whilst the word was hitting his audience between the frontal lobes. They all knew the idea of the pricks and the kicking against them. The idea itself was a prick. The prick of all pricks that kept us in harness. The fundamental harness. The evangelical pricks. It wasn't easy just to release one's self from the bridle, to take off somewhere, bridleless amongst the unbridled.

Backsliding begets a sense of hellish isolation. A powerful condemnation of the saint-sinner hiding in the midst of believers dispenses the isolation.

I was in a private prayer of forgiveness and a plaintive plea for acceptance, as the Pastor denounced the double-dealing, chameleon-like backsliders. I shuddered at the idea of a chameleon. The Pastor described the wilful sneakiness of the creature, its slipperiness, the darting eyes, aware of every opportunity to gain an advantage.

Then he asked the chameleons to come out in the open, cast off their disguises, roll their all seeing eyes in the direction of the true all seeing one, and in the simplicity of their sin, seek the gracious arms of Christ. It all seemed so simple but I had been there before many times. Forwards, backwards, forwards, backwards. Up and down. The anger built within me. Why couldn't I resist that eternal temptation? Why? But in the blackness of concentrated prayer I saw before me, almost outside me, my own will acting without me, choosing without me. The wilful me seemed to be more me than me. The identity in separation. It looked at me and said, *Where are you going?*

Then the shock. That question. *Where are you going?* Was backsliding actually going anywhere? I tried to see it as a creative move. But it came back to me as only a movement. The backslider was called evil, his will evil, and the evil was that of the Devil. So that backsliding might not be a change at all, for it was all a part of the same world. It spoke in the same language. It was merely a *response*. The Devil and his hell and destruction occupied the same world as Christ and his heaven and his salvation. Backsliding itself was fixed and determined by that world. The world that claimed all of me. It even claimed my crime. Was there no place of separation?

I was separated with Linus, was I not? It seemed that Linus was safely outside it all. He didn't understand a word I said about it. He laughed at the ideas I presented to him and proceeded to treat them as a joke. How could I ever be something else if I hated him for laughing at it? I looked at his laughing face and quivered with anger, though he saw not the quivering anger. He saw simply a pleasant, passive and confused smile. I reserved open quivering anger for family members but I also seethed at his senseless insensitivity. Neither did he see my seethe in my teeth. I must have looked like a total joke to him, presenting him with such a pitifully confused and frustrated countenance. An open mouth. Pleading eyes. All one to him, one he laughed at but didn't really understand. He made it all conform to some other set of ideas. His. And I could not see how that could work. Surely there was an understanding on the precarious margins? There simply had to be.

I was wavering in my forced state of seclusion. I wanted out. And Linus was in my sights. Out there somewhere. I felt that I must deny him and his laughing world also where nothing existed but things to laugh at. A world full of funny curiosities and a world empty of certainties. A comedy where the affirmation of the self was to laugh at something. To laugh at everything. Even the precious notions of a religion. I reconsidered my decision to make him a recruit in my church of backsliders, which was itself seriously in doubt in my increasingly doubting mind. He would make a mockery of it. Make it the object of fun. As he walked, home he was probably laughing his balls off at what he had just seen. The trial in the kitchen. Would he like it if I told him that people were wetting themselves in laughter at his silly pocketless trousers?

What frequency did he frequent? What tune did he sing but mine? I thought it was mine and I thought it was as precise as mine as I thought I determined its limits...a very narrow band difficult to tune into but once in, it was as clear as a Belfast bell. He would listen to me and act accordingly. I thought it was I that tuned him in to it, turned his dial for him, and once there he was mine, but was that true? Did he not just permit me to think so? He was a receiver deceiver. Was he indeed? It's the oldest trick in the history book, but one that Purvell the history teacher didn't teach us. The power behind the throne. *Yes, sire, no sire. Your ever so humble servant, sire.* And all the time they were conniving and scheming and laughing and mocking. The sire was in blissful ignorance thinking that it was he, the stringless one, who pulled the strings of all around him. I thought I was his sire, the sire of Linus, generating a world that he could serve in, he my sidekick, following my lead... but, in essence, I was his lackey. I was the sire alright, but one of those impotent sires, siring my own stupidity unable to beget the desired behaviour.

I always called for him at his door. He never ever called for me. The one exception being when he needed his door key. And then he just stood there gawking, probably laughing inside at the whole sorry spectacle. The evangelical interrogation. No! It was I who needed him. It was never really evident that he needed me. He fired me up. Got me going like a little mechanical toy. He wound me up and set me on a slope down which I had to walk. His little mechanical jester. A bloody buffoon rising in the morning and running around to his house with a big happy skip in my step. The joy that accompanied my idea of me and Linus changed to sorrow, in the instant I thought that series of thoughts. The idea of me there, in prayer. How it all hung on the hinges, how it was all either harmonious or chaotic on the basis of a thought. I felt myself pass swiftly from a state of relative composure into one of panic as if my whole world was unsure and unsteady. I saw a threat. I pounded myself with pity where before there was no such compassion. I suddenly despised my body like I despised the body of Les Buttocks. I hit my body in an act of self-punishment. I slapped my face and the idea pleased me. I thumped my thighs with firm fists. A pain with the idea of me as a deserving weakling as cause. I saw myself departing from the idea I had of myself. And I saw Linus as stronger and more powerful than me, but not just that. In the nature of his strength, I saw the nature of my own destruction.

*

The old creaking stairs were a dead giveaway that someone was on them and the precise identity of the personage on them was given away in the nature of their footsteps. The weight, the pace. Each of us had our own way of ascending and descending them. I tried to defy their creaks by knowing exactly where they were.

I loved impersonating the steps of others. I called it step stealing. A form of deception. A part of backsliding, I thought. Presenting myself as another member of the family. Identity fraud. I thought of them sitting in their rooms thinking that someone other than me was on the stairs. I loved doing old Hughie's gait outside the mother's room.

The old skitter Hughie came down from his high perch with a slow heavy stride, each step on the stairs revealing him in a lengthy creak. The mother knew it and hated it and slowly simmered inside at the very idea. Him and his feet on her precious, clean carpet. He was down for tea, that was his mission, with a mug in his trembling arthritic hand. The hands that I despised as much as he in his total being was despised by the mother. The total annoyance was made up of smaller annoyances: his annoying manner of step, his annoying holding of an empty mug. His humble apologetic hunch. His inability to receive into his hearing the first thing you said. He was a man of insignificance on the road to destruction. The mother cursed him to hell and wanted to see his destruction as payment for his malignant disruption. *Hell roast you, ya useless git!* she gargled out of the depths of her despising being. Hell awaited the unwanted.

It was undeniably the mother on the final steps to my room. Heading upwards full of food. But what was her fancy now? Her step was a shuffle. A pushed foot, hardly even lifted above each worn carpeted step. The threadbare bits threatened her sanity. Her mountainous hips swayed. Her pores pumped out sour sweat. Her heavy hand, with a slight moisture of sweat on the palm, slid up the banister and squeaked on the highly polished wood. I had heard her before fart with the effort. Mostly near to the summit. When the effort was huge. High octane. But I put that unpleasantry away. There was a pause. Always a pause to pick fluff up from the carpet. Or to run a finger along a dusty section of the paint work. Then the shuffle re-commenced with her cursing the dustmakers. Then she cursed God, I thought.

I suddenly wanted the comfort of church. To be in the midst of the misty-eyed with the presence of holy spirit anointing. Numbered in the company of the numinous. To be there in the morning time. In the bright sunshine, with the warm rays passing through the windows to the altar. The Sunday morning service. The communion of saints remembering. It wasn't a sinner service. That was in the evening. The gospel for the sinner. Grace for their sins. Grace abounding. Big busted sin busting grace. A graceful thing, thrusting out, eclipsing their dark imaginings, drawing their souls out in directions new. All in the midst of the soundly saved.

Just as I am without one plea. What a powerful little evangelical ditty. It weakened the sinner's resolve so that he denounced his sinful will. His being was not his own. He disowned himself. The sinner wanted to rid his soul of that one dark blot.

The Pastor pleaded with the sinner every Sunday night. *Come as you are,* he said. *Poor, wretched, blind, crippled in spirit.* He had the power of the word at his disposal in this setting. I needed the provider of power and freedom and life that was the church. It was a power to rule out any wavering. The power to boost the power of the will over the spirit. I desired the surrounding sense of spiritual idiocy over which I could preside as an intelligent interpreter of the foolishness. I would be like an ancient *nabi* nabbing their mad mental meanderings in mid flight. I would come back to God and give up my backslidden ways. I'd pray with such intensity and fervour that nothing would interfere with my aim. I would exclude all but the evangelical idea. The Christians chattered always of the new. A new creation. The new wine. They whined and droned, upright and prone, of a new heaven and a new earth. They rejoiced with hands raised to heaven when the preacher told them of the new. Oh, how they loved the idea of the new.

The mother despised the old, so she loved the idea of the new. She wanted a new house and hated the old abode that housed us. But what of the old? What of the old creation? What of the old wine? The old heaven and the old earth? Yet they talked of the old time religion that was good enough for them. But was it? They just repeated words. Always looking for the new points to a weakness of mind, a continual disappointment in that which they had. They wanted every possibility, every door to remain open. They were still children in their openness. And their selfishness. The old time religion was nothing to them, because there was no such thing. It was a dream. Couldn't they see the old was really the new, that which never faded?

The idea of the old being the new presented me with a firm excited erection. It pressed upon me and created an uncomfortable dilemma: to wank with a religious idea in mind. I took to wanking in a big way in my backslidingness, and the ideas that inspired the wandering hand were not far from the idea that inspired my submission to God. The hand that descends to hell and the hand that rises to heaven were one and the same hand. The worshipful limb. I raised it to God in his temple and I beheld the firmness.

The rock is my cock. The rock of ages, as I liked to take my time. I sowed to the flesh and reaped the flesh in abundance. Flesh upon flesh. Fabric upon flesh. Corrupted?

The mother renewed her threat at every meal. The food and the flesh. The threat that inspired the doing of the right thing. It was love that was in the threat it was claimed. *Eat or I will put you in a dress to sit at the table. Behaving like a little girl. You whimpering skitter. Then you'll be dressed for dinner, alright,* said she. That was love right there. There was an irritating laugh in accompaniment that told me that she indulged herself in such a humiliation. It was love right there. And she would describe the most girlie dress, with dainty buttons at the back, a bow at the waist, and satin frills on the neck and cuffs. Love in the detail.

The threat was however, more than a mere humiliation. More than a Pavlovian technique to get the animal to learn a way of life. The importance of *dress* in this evangelical context was well known. The power of it was known. I know it and knew of it from an early age. About as early as six years old. Fear abounded with the idea of a boy's flesh being shrouded and enshrined in a dress. Placed in a dress was being placed in sin. The mother placed me in sin. And the Pastor thundered out many a time from his big Bible: *The woman shall not wear that which pertaineth to the man, neither shall a man put on a woman's garment, for all that do are abominations unto the Lord thy God.* Being an abomination to the Lord instilled a particular fear. The mind itself was shrouded in a fear of the abomination of the dress. The travesty of the transvestite. More than the tight vest, dressed in the vestry, an investment rather in submissive sorrow.

There was chastisement in the air. Chastisement making chaste. I felt it, the strength of it, even in its coming. The index of punishments had changed. There was that hand in punishment. That hand again. When I was a toddler it was the hand. The mother's hand that left lumps on my legs for being in possession of nothing more than an unlit match. She chased me around the kitchen table until I felt the breeze of her wheezing breath on my neck. Then the flat of her hand on my naked legs. I lost my breath with all the bawling. The father was better at smacking the legs. His whacking hands were powered by massive muscles in his arms. He smacked me in bed that night for not letting the brother sleep and I feared him doing it again. My bawling entered a new dimension under that hammer hand. I tried to wriggle away but every new position met his chopping hand. Worker's hands. Thick fingers. I wanted good whacking fingers like that. I loved the name Whackford Squears in Nicholas Nickleby. He whacked all his pupils.

The smacking soon stopped and new lines of punishment were introduced. Locked in the glory hole under the stairs. Wearing the satin smock dress to general ridicule. Wearing the dress in the glory hole. Starving. No TV. All depleting to the strength that was in self-respect. Oh if Linus could see me in such a diminished state. What would he make of it? He'd laugh like a hyena. In the blinding blackness of a hole, feeling the smooth satin wrapped about me, I wanted to know if I had any strength at all and if I did not, I needed to achieve my own strength to see the weaker assemblage of endeavours in me to whom I could show my power.

In truth, the mother and father were plagued by weakness and only applied their superiority to their children. Others outside the home applied theirs to them as if they were the children. The whole set of encounters was not kind to them. Their particular destruction was inevitable though they firmly held to the belief that God would make them eternal. They lived in the brutal world but conceived it, in general, as the best of all possible worlds. And it was not a world to denounce, as it was a godly creation. On particular occasions, it was not conceived as such and they let the belief slip by accusing the impositions placed on their existence as being unfair, but they always returned to the belief that it was as it should be. It had to be fair. How else would they get up in the morning at all? And go to their dismal workplaces. The mother worked in a madhouse, the father in that bakery complex by the river that baked the Ulsterman's precious batch bread of life. The mother laughed at the feeble-minded loonybins from the vantage point of her best of all possible worlds and told us tales of their God-given antics. *God love them,* she said.

One time, when the father picked the mother up from work at the madhouse, I went with him just to see the mad people and their antics. The car glided through the gates and slowly along the thin winding road in the green grounds of the madhouse. A pleasant world for troubled minds. There they were. They appeared alone in all this space. They wandered and stood and stared. The rejected. They followed the car with their stares. They looked at me with their bulging watery eyeballs. They had loose chattering mouths. There was no fitting them into the world, so they were sent there to a world that they could fit into. They didn't seem to fit here either. It was not a fitting place. There wasn't an ounce of fitting to do. Except for the ones that had fits. I didn't want to consider the details of their appearance. The idea made me uncomfortable inside. The mother got big tubs of ice cream from the canteen where she worked, but I couldn't eat it because the nice idea of ice cream was spoiled by the idea of the mad people and their loose slobbery mouths. They ate their dinners in the canteen, so maybe a loose slobber from a loose-gabbing jaw had flown into the tubs. I wondered if there was place here for old Hughie. The mother said he's not mad. The father said he's not mad enough.

From behind the steering wheel the father confided in me about madness—with a not insignificant amount of venom in his tone—as he looked ahead at the road and then at me. One hand was off the wheel, flapping around in all sorts of directions tracing the flow of his thoughts. *Hitler murdered mad people in their droves,* he said, *just because they were weak-minded.* He told me that the idea of keeping them in a mad house to help them with their own madness was not the sort of idea that Hitler found appealing. The ideas he did find appealing were the manifestations of his own madness. The ones that sprung to life when he had all the mad people he could find crammed into specially-built camps where they were all bumping into one another with their madness and looking at each other from close quarters with their mad looks, not knowing that they would be in mad Hitler's head as we are in God's head. For a moment, I entertained the idea of God being mad. It made no sense, but it troubled me that I thought it.

This was where the father had a mad look in his own eye and

nearly spat out his false choppers from his angry mad mouth. His disgust at Hitler's ideas was made manifest in the tightening of his jaw, and his words were forced out of the tiny slit that his mouth had become. I thought of the black suffocating glory hole and being in there in the dress with hordes of mad people, all struggling for air and space. I held my breath to see how long it would take to die if I had no more air to breathe, just what's there in me. It was only a few seconds before I started to panic. And compounded panic at the idea of the mad people seeing me through the blackness in my girlie dress.

But what you have to remember, said the father in a calmer disposition, *is that there are different degrees of madness, from the total loonybin who doesn't know the very day of the week, to those who are hardly mad at all, and if you met them you'd hardly be able to tell that they were mad. They look normal but they are suffering inside.* So, I wondered if any of my family had that madness you couldn't see.

Hitler must have been a right madman, I said, *which meant he should have been in the mad camps himself.*

The father said a big *No!* in a big quivering voice. *Hitler wasn't mad at all, he knew the day of the week and the hour of the day alright.* But what actually was madness? I asked myself. Who was mad? And what drove you to madness? Where did it all start and where did it finish? What was the madness that didn't look mad? Did he know any?

We drove slowly on around the narrow winding path in the big Vauxhall Velux to the canteen car park where we waited. The mad people around and about were zombies heading in no particular direction. They never congregated in pairs or groups, they stood or walked alone. Their thoughts were all directed inwards so there was no external goal. Their consciousness was a witness to all the things going on inside them but had no understanding attached. Someone would come and collect them like cows being herded in for milking. Their minds were like meadows and they grazed there perpetually ruminating on the same old thoughts. But who could ever know what they are thinking?

When the subject of madness came up the father always repeated his joke. *They said that Napoleon was mad. They said that Beethoven was mad. They said that Hitler was mad. They said that Stalin was mad. They said that Uncle Fred was mad. Now he was mad!* He launched into laughter at his own words. He always clung to his own words, the words that he knew well. And he repeated them endlessly for his own sanity.

I needed to pay attention to my own words.

CHAPTER 37

At last, the soft slipper Mother shuffled onto the landing out-side my room. She opened the door and entered with her closed mind. The entire space was annexed with her look, which took in the wall space and floor space and object space until there was nothing apparently substantial left but her and me. Her pink nylon overall was all over me, inside me, a smothering garment. She was ready with her own smothering words, to speak them for me to listen and take heed. The words then took up the space in a way that ideas took up attention.

Tell me the truth! she said, in her most inconsiderate scratchy voice which provoked in me intense inner rage. If she knew the truth why did she want me to tell her? To have me confess it, that's why. *Confession is good for the soul,* she said all the time at other times, but not this time. She simply left me to think it, which I did. I thought of the soul in me and wondered how it was. Was it good? How could one tell? So, she wanted the confession out of my mouth and on my sweet submissive lips—not just giving lip service—to brand me as a liar and for the victory to be seen to be hers. My confession was good for her selfish soul. I prepared myself for the sermon in Mount Attic. And it came to life like Lazarus.

God is watching us. The liar cannot follow Jesus, and if you can't follow Jesus you cannot be saved. The liar can only follow the Devil

to hell where all the liars are shouting and screaming their confessions
but they can't be heard. It's too late. And the Devil laughs at them in
their desperate state of confessing. The Devil is the father of lies, and if
you are a liar, the Devil is in you, like the father is in his son. You are
possessed by the most evil of evil spirits, Satan himself. And you know
what tells me that you have the Devil in you? Not just the lie but the
self that lies. The self lies to be more important than God. He deceives
to deceive God. Not me but God.

I believed it all. I did. Heaven, Hell, damned sinner, saved souls, abounding grace, irresistible grace, falling from grace, the inescapable sinfulness of man, the supreme interfering God, His anger, His love. So why did I resist confessing? The discomfort of one little confession against an eternity in torment. So why did the eternity in torment never seem that impressive when the lie was in you? I didn't feel the Devil in me, but what was the feeling you had if he was in you? Just like the soul. Maybe not a feeling, but an experience. An experience of badness? A awareness of a foreign voice within? Was I to confess my evil in confessing my crime? *I am because I am*, I said to myself, *part of the community of believers in evil with the power over confession*. The evil articulators. It all went back to the idea of evil, the guilt, the confession, the discovery of the good. All crime was a sin and all sin was the expression of evil. The religious guilt stands above all guilt.

The mother, standing with stout arms folded, demanded that I articulated the evil done and in doing so, if I did so, she would condemn me. If I did, she said, it would signify to the Lord that I was his again. *Signify*—the word out of all the words stuck to me and would not be forced into the wilderness of words. There and then it seemed, without me knowing why, to give me strength. There, then, it was between me and her. Her, the whore, maybe McKeown's whore. The Devil in me told me to hate her, the whore. The whore that humiliates. The whore who lay down to life and allowed it walk all over her. Who sold her mind for cheap half-truths. Whore who called this life that walks over her, the divine way, the godly way. She was the whore who thought it right to say that the Devil was in me, possessing me. Making me steal a fiver and not confessing it. Making me see the action as a right action or as an action that is neither right or wrong. So, the Devil within told me to hate her life and her lying down to it and the waking to it every day possessed by it, which was a meekness that was to be hated.

This evangelical meekness is like nothingness, the closest thing to it. It does not affirm life. It is passive to it. It signifies the passing away of a soul. They say it does not resist the will of God. It relies and rests itself on the weak imagination to inspire it but the inspiration is only to further meekness.

The mother was the high priestess of low esteem. She revelled in her lowly status. She was a million miles away in my mind from the woman in Harry Black's, with all her cool silks and satins and perfumes swirling about her and all over me. That was no meek woman, for she had an effect on me that was powerful. That was a *she* alright, who possessed the attributes of a woman who endeavoured to persevere in all her womanliness. A whore to visit to spend time with in thought. And so real that it made my head spin and my loins go to the borders of beatitude. The mother was not of the same species as the graceful Mrs in Black's shop who had the grace of the Devil in her. I despised the female line of the mother but loved the female line of the silky smooth Mrs. I could take to myself the sheerness, in thought, and feel erect and upright and in command. And to take the material sheerness to myself was a profound pleasure that dominated me. A noble domination. At that moment, I was obedient to the idea of the Mrs. Where was that Mrs?

It was that Mrs that I would search for all my life, a quest for her yet unfulfilled. Her absence was my pain. I peered over the head of every conversation to see if she was there beyond them, and I feared that I may miss the Mrs as she flitted by in the Belfast shadows.

You don't want to end up like him in there, do you? That's where badness gets you. The mother was present to me again. Her head flicked to the right, indicating the adjacent attic room in which old Hughie O'Kelly the lodger was incarcerated. Prisoner of his own poverty. There to slip into bed and sleep without a peep. A borrowed existence, spent in his lazy bed, when the money and booze ran out, tightly rolled up in his sheets like a mummy dreaming of another richer life, free from begging and borrowing. As far as the mother was concerned, all that summed up sin. His array of filthy habits recommended him to her as an emissary of evil. Her vocabulary of life took significance from the language of filth. The highest crimes were the crimes of filth, knowingly and unknowingly carrying filth, transferring filth, depositing filth. Bad language was filthy language. Sex was the filth of the deed. Sex talk was the filth of the word. The meaning of the Christian Gospel to her was the Gospel of cleanliness. The fall of man was his fall into filth. He was the dust of the earth and the presence of dust before man's creation was an eternal annoyance to her. Old Hughie O'Kelly would never be an evangelical because of his nature as filth. Damned by filth. The Catholics were more comfortable with filth, so he could stay there. His body wasn't a temple to the Lord. More like a cesspool and the Lord didn't say that a cesspool was acceptable.

The idea of turning back into dust at death was the mother's greatest fear. She saw her dead body decaying into filth and it scared the filthy shite out of her. She saw someone picking her up as a piece of dust and despising her. My petty crime was not a crime to her because of the stealing but because it was a dirty act, a filthy act with a filthy over-thought. It involved filthy thoughts, like sex thoughts were filthy. My friends were banned from the house because they would bring in their filth, in their heads and on their bodies. When I sneaked friends into the house and up to my room she could smell them.

I hope there's none of your friends coming today, she'd say. *I'm cleaning the place and they'll just walk their dirt through on the soles of their feet.* Her case was largely to do with her opinion about the outside world and her inside world. The outer and inner. The soul within and the sin without.

Friends were filth and filth was sin, therefore friends were sin. Therefore, there were no friends of the father and mother. That was the sinful outside. The mother turned that nose of hers up at any attempt of the father to make a friend of his own, and together as husband and wife they had no friends and they were not even friends to each other. Fear of friends was fear of filth. Contamination. I saw all that in her eyes, her hating little eyes.

She had fluff between her finger tips, picked up from her travels up the stairs. I saw beneath her tight perm nothing but a head full of dancing dust. Ideas on the fluffy side. Where did she pick up this feebleness? Picked up on her imaginative travels like she picked up loose dust on her cleaning sorties.

From within me a new Devil made himself known. A laughing Devil to take back the room. On his high horse, a pale horse prancing and rearing up in defiance. The appearance of her quite suddenly became comical. The laughter got her going alright, she attributed it to the madness of the Devil in me, and she was soon shouting for the father to give her assistance to dampen it, to exorcise it. In the meantime she rallied to accuse me of being possessed by a bigger devil than she had thought, the devil of disrespect and the devil of disrespectful laughter. That simply inspired me to louder laughter and I strained to stop it but I was finding it impossible to do so. It was indeed like a devil inside me. I felt under the control of something powerfully other than myself.

I saw before me the comicality of her small slippered feet, her short legs, her tight mouth, her big sprouting chest that heaved in anger. She had in her tight twisting mouth a favourite sweet, a Riley's Chocolate Toffee Roll, which was circulating via tongue pressure and sticking occasionally in the loose dentures. She often said that it was her only pleasure, to suck sweets. To the father it was said, never directly but always within his hearing distance, something that sorely tested his patience. The particular sweet was a cursed thing in his mind. The whole absurd nature of it all seeped into me in a random fashion and the limb weakening laughter was forced out like the free-flowing semen in a boy's first raging orgasm.

Signify! If I had the Devil in me, why didn't it scare the shite out of her? Surely a devil would be the worst thing to have in the vicinity of a normal mind. An idea yelled at me within with great volume: *kill her, kill her.* The convulsing pliable body stiffened. Take the meat cleaver to her. That would show her the Devil in me, and she would be sore afraid when she saw her death coming at the hands of her possessed son. I expected to feel weakness and meekness at the idea but no, it seemed right and fitting and I felt strong, as if I could actually do the deed. Was that the Devil in me? The excitement drove right through me like a physic of salts. Right to the loose saliva in my mouth. The wetness soon became a harbour of dryness. The tide had turned. My tense rectum loosened as a world opened up. What was striking was that there seemed to be no interfering notions to block the suggestions that raged before my mind. Interfering notions were always a terrible barrier to action. No sooner had I decided firmly to do something than a notion not to do it lurched into being. Instead, ideas were lining up in a disorderly queue to strengthen the initial notion. A plan and not a plan. Ideas that followed and those that did not.

The meat cleaver would settle the matter. I could kill her stone dead and blame it all on old filthy Hughie. Two old birds with one stone. But Hughie wasn't a bird, even if I dressed him up in the wee frock the mother had for me. Only an affecting movement of mind took it from idea to actuality, to reality. Throw her down the stairs. A dead rolling mother gathering no dust. Push her rather, just as she shuffles towards the top step on her way out and down. She would surely bend there to pick up some dust. Place my foot on her arse and shout hallelujah. And laugh from the depths. Laugh at the tumbling mother. What an idea. An evil notion. It seemed that fear of anything departed from my mind. And I knew the importance of fear in the life of a mere created creature. I thought of all the fears and they seemed like nothing. Making my way up to my bed at night, on those damned creaking stairs, in the dim light, in the shadows, far up to the distant, frosty attic, disposed me to imaginative weakness. The clinging cowardice of dependency. *Christ save me from the forces of darkness!*

What a weak tool the mind is when it is crushed and assailed by cold, dark ignorance. The factory for idols rumbles into production. Ghosts.

Embryonic courageous ideas that may have been there needed an accomplice. They slumbered like damned-up lumber in inactivity. Dependency lorded it over me. Like the Lord God himself. *My help cometh from the Lord. The help of his countenance. The Lord was my help in time of trouble and vain is the help of man. I looked up to hills from whence cometh my help. The Lord shall preserve thee from evil, he shall preserve thy soul. He shall preserve thy going out and thy coming in.* I had a tendency to reach for support from all places until the places blotted me out. Love of the Lord was the source of weakness, not of strength, as it was open to great variation and had nothing of the character of clarity.

Without that clarity there is hatred and contempt, sadness and false joys, and wars and woes. If there is no mastery of the idea of self, there was no mastery of the self that thought it. The longer the mind endures in this state, the shorter its endurance. But there comes a point when you don't know whether you are in control or being controlled. If you think that, then it is the latter.

So, my courageous ideas were eclipsed by that idea of God, the inadequate idea of God that the imagination called up to renounce true virtue and enable the mind to chase the shadows of temporary advantage.

All that follows from such a quest is pain. Pain, pain, pain. Driving the sensible to the insane.

I trembled. There was a real idea of myself bursting forth that required nothing else to sustain it. No deception. The trembling spirit. The shaking in my foundations. Shivering with the crisp cold proximity of Jehovah. Shuddering to a halt with an idea of devastating clarity. The crucifixion at Calvary caused the Christian to tremble, but it was the risen Substance of God that I saw before me that caused me to quiver. The intellectual love. No badness. No deception. No lie.

If a thing is acting through its nature alone, then what is badness? Just when ordinary life seemed futile... I felt...

*

...I felt the nice money in my pocket. The nice weight of it. I grasped it and held it and it was mine. I took possession of it. I massaged the Royal countenances and figures and ribbed rims and the sum of it was not being given back. I could toss one of those coins to determine what I should do. Heads or tails? But there was no need, for there would not be any confessing to anything. No repentance. No begging for forgiveness. She would have to wait it out. Wait for her time when all would be clear. The mother withdrew with her dissatisfaction heaving in her empty accusing bosom, after telling me in her final words from her very own denouncing tight mouth that I was a bad egg. That I was rotting with evil. But I killed her alright, with my steadfastness. Neither with a meat cleaver nor with my foot in her fat arse that would take down the stairs to her doom. No church that night either. No pleasing prospect of evaluating Eva, or humming my *Ave Eva* in her presence. I was left to condense my thoughts into a state of sorriness, left to stew in my own sinful juices, but it was the night I saw the light, in a distilled shaft of illumination, and the sight of it was mighty to salvation. Not the salvation that was *slavation*. All things passed away alright, all previous certainties, and a new uncertainty was born.

The mother shuffled out into the landing, freely sliding off the brown oilcloth completely browned off by my stubborness, onto an unfriendly-for-shuffling, thick carpet that covered the landing and stairs. Her going came as a relief. And my coming attention focused firmly on the old dosser Hughie O'Kelly in the next room. He shuffled too. He shuffled in his flapping gabardines and worn black shoes to the dole office and then to the pub and then he shuffled full of booze all the way back to his lofty bed place. He said to me in a waking moment, a moment of agonising forced sobriety, that he'd tell the mother if I mocked him for the sake of laughter any more. Out of his state of forced abstinence, sprang intolerance. He was almost active in the world, in the house in the world. But did he think he was too good to be laughed at? How absurdly arrogant of him. Arrogance out of living insignificance. A trivial example of a being. He was absurd. I felt like throwing the informer bastard out of his very own attic skylight. And laughing at his descent. Rolling down the tiles, passing the gutter, falling, falling, falling out of sight into the concrete yard. His old egg head splitting open on the concrete. I despised his smelly piss-beer presence. He'd take it with him. All that would be left were his massed ranks of relics. I'd look at them and then pile them all in the bin.

Jackie McMaster and I once stood on him when he was asleep. We wanted to look out of the skylight that was just above his bed, but we needed the extra inches the bed offered to get our heads out in order to get a decent view of the entry below. I had smuggled

McMaster in one rainy Saturday, and the mother didn't smell him, even though rain gave off a powerful stench when combined with a boy's natural stink. We hadn't considered the old lodger's presence in the bed. I thought he'd be out boozing. It was just a mess of material. His paraffin stove was cold and his door was open. He was a cowlraift being and needed the heat constantly, so I assumed his absence.

So, we were on the bed on tiptoes holding open the heavy iron framed skylight, looking at the land of tall houses, shouting oddities at passing strangers, laughing, when out of his sleeping sack, in a modification of sleep that is called waking, the old dosser grasped a bare leg like he grasped a pint of porter on a Friday night. And since it was McMaster who squeaked out, it was the McMaster leg that the icy, greasy, sinewy hand took possession of.

McMaster wasn't used to being attended by some old life form that resembled death, so his face was an image of fear of such a thing and his body was strenuously in stiffness trying to deny the onset of trembling. I had seen that old face before on many a dark night when he appeared to me from behind the waxy flame of a candle on a mid-stairs encounter. I often dreamed of that waxy white face and it made me sweat. I woke in a sweat. The bed seemed to sweat. It was both unknown and familiar. Silently out of a deep shadow and in a weak connection, came a slender disembodied hand that searched for another body to cling to. I wouldn't have that form near to me, near enough to touch, and I withdrew from it to find concealment in the shadows. And behind me out of sight, I heard it say, *Help me, help me. Give me succour. God help me.* The word *succour* was unknown and caused great mental upheaval. It had vile associations. Intimate. Offensive. Aggressive lip succour, with his livery lips sucking me in like his favourite tinned spaghetti. Help? No help could be given to such ugliness and inferiority. Help to what? To beauty, to nobility? Impossible. Or perhaps I misunderstood. It lingered within me, and caused me on occasion to rise rapidly out of even the most almighty slumber. *Jesus! Jesus! Jesus!* I would say to that but found the way back to sleep blocked.

Tread we did, McMaster and me, on the messy bed like looney grape stampers, with the old sod below us wriggling like a

snake. Soon he was hissing, like the serpent, and then disturbed
sufficiently by the stamping to utter his ultimatums and insults.
Mother of Jesus, your own mother'll hear of it. Bloody bastards!
Admirable for the old wretch.

The words rose rapidly and burrowed deep into my ear. *Your
mother'll hear of it.* The old shitbag was toying with my temper
with those words. My treading became frantic as I searched with
my feet for his loose bollocks. I wasn't certain whether the public
growls and groans that I heard from him were rooted in his crushed
privates, but me and McMaster soon shifted ourselves off the
iron bedstead and leaped out of his cell-like quarters. *The mother
hates you, you ugly swine,* I murmured as I shifted myself at speed.
McMaster was in tow, still white as a sheet, laughing in a serious
fashion like a loon, and squeaking and twitching in all manner
of ways indicative of deeply rooted psychical fear. His chronic
sinus problem seemed to suffer badly to this sort of fright, the
heightened sniffing and snorting resembled a whinging child. The
great fear had triggered an increased opening of his nasal passages.
His scruffy bobbly woollen sleeve glistened with long strands of
the ghastly nose matter. Funny to a point, then serious after that
point as he sought comfort by hanging on to me. All the stuff of
normality for McMaster. And down the stairs to safety we leaped
in alarmed laughter.

*

The people at large spout off about respecting old people and
praising the charms and the wisdom of old age. In the films,
the wise old head is solemnly dishing out the profundities that
long experience has endowed. In reality, they do neither this nor
that, and the ones I know and have known, are blind and deaf to
knowledge.

The old dosser Hughie O'Kelly of the preposterously omnipresent
O'Kelly clan had no connection to an enlightened nature. Wise
oldness did not ebb and flow from him. Only a sea of ignorance. The
O'Kellys carried their world in suitcases preferring not to have an
O'Kelly abode in bricks and mortar, enjoying instead the freedom

of bestowing their presence on the solid foundations of bricks and mortar of others. In relative solidity. Fuck all of a valuable character was to be encountered in and around Hughie O'Kelly's heedless head. He still possessed his primordial scavenging instincts in total tact. He had little tact. In fact. I thought he'd be better dead and in the ground. Dead and gravestone read.

I wanted him dead and gone. I prayed for it. I asked the Lord to intercede in his life by removing it from his body. I jumped out from hidden corners to frighten him to death with mad loud shouts. *You'll be killing me one of these days,* he would say. He told the mother that such jokes weren't funny and that the death of him would wipe the smirks off all our faces. The mother herself continued to hand out strong laxatives to him in the form of chocolate squares just for a laugh. *The Lord is thy keeper* came suddenly and actively to mind and, just as quickly, passively exited it. The old lodger, I thought, was being kept for higher ends.

CHAPTER 38

*D*ear *God! Hallelujah! Say Hallelujah! Praise the sweet name of Jesus. Adore Adonai. Yell like hell for Yahweh!* I couldn't help myself. I uttered the unutterable about the ineffable. I said in a further mad spell of saying, *I am that I am! You are that you are! It is that it is. It is what it is. I will be what I am.* The mother, who was what she was, was now out of sight, slipping down the stairs partially on dust patrol, and partially preparing herself to explain my badness to the others. She left saying that I, a son of hers, disgusted her. That I was no more to her than the dust.

Meanwhile...the peculiar and sometimes painful world of decisions spread out before me, decisions I knew were in my power to take. However, it was a power that could often lead to paralysis, with freedom in necessity, sometimes the necessity necessitating that nothing could be done. Then, the whole world outside would seem, to the paralysed mind, to be performing in hyper-activity. Nature coming alive.

My life was in my own hands, that is, in my own mind, the mind that governed the hands that took the money and committed the crime and committed to life. The deceptive life of virtue. The virtuous life of deception. It is, it was, it came to pass. Knowing courage to be indispensable. A place to be, with minimal internal conflict. It never quite turned out that way for sure. It seemed like a fever had taken hold and all confidence and certainty were there, but as an illusion.

The reigning mother, a woman never to be deposed from her disposition to forgive easily, nor with the ability to see the follies of a young mind, continued to call me a bad backslider with her tight mouth. On her death bed, pinned to it by the throat cancer and with partial vision of eternity before her pin hole sized eyes—an experience you'd think would loosen any stiff jaw to a kind or forgiving word—she still had her tight mouth for me but not for anyone else. There, her hold upon me was vice-like.

The higher intuition, directed inwardly in self assessment, told me that I was a waiter in matters of wilful movement. Most of it was anxious waiting for it was always waiting for something, something that I desperately needed to be firmly in my grasp. A higher sense of withoutness within. What I *did* have was the perpetual need, so I had something. I also at times had the look of the needy.

The preacher, in an enlightened philosophical moment—he was usually dismissive of the philosopher, insulting him and his reason week in week out with a hating tight mouth much like the mother's—said that our relation to God, our fundamental condition when all else was discarded, was in our waiting for him. With his big black Bible opened to the Psalms he bellowed, *I wait for the Lord, my soul doth wait. Waiting to have him, to know him, to see him. To have him in salvation, to know him in our discipleship, and to see him in Glory*, he said. He became inordinately excited about the word glory, it made him dance, like an intoxicated red Indian war dancing, when he said it. That often led me to consider his dancing and the traces, not his words. And all around were affected in the same way, as they were moved to dancing in his wake.

But I thought, as I sat and listened to his message, week in week out, of abiding and possessing, that despite what he said about waiting, he wasn't waiting at all, for he said that he possessed God and that each of us can have God in our hearts. His waiting was over. How can we ever *have* God? is what I was always asking myself.

Like a spoilt child the preacher simply couldn't wait and declared, whilst holding his big black Bible aloft, that he possessed God, and that you could too, and that made him shout a bigger *praise the Lord*

and caused him to dance even more in an irreverent joyful knees-up
up the church aisle. He possessed God and he sparred with the Devil,
who he didn't possess and who might yet possess him, throwing right
and left hooks and uppercuts at the invisible evil enemy. *I have him!*
I have the Lord, he shouted and laughed. The two things he definitely
had, was a mistress, and a made mistake. The mistress was a mystery,
the mistress a mystery woman, and the mistake he made was to think
that God was to be had like a mistress.

*

Rest in the Lord and Wait patiently for Him, but there is no resting
and no patience. Like my uncle Paddy asking me in my infancy if I
wanted a penny now or sixpence later. The way of being is the way
of the furious desire to having.

In a certain class of thought, the weak evangelical class, I wanted
to have God more than anything, but in another form I knew
perfectly well that I never really had Him. I was submissive to the
idea of Lordly possession, instead of being obedient to the Lord.

It is a world of modes from the weak to the strong. The
evangelical mode is the mode of mad having - nothing less than
religious materialism. The spirit they worship is merely another
form of matter for they seek it to touch their material beings, and
to provide all things that matter in this world. Their miracle is to
turn spirit into matter. They are most impressed with the physical
miracles. Healing, the parting of the seas, the water into wine.
They even had my mind as one of theirs, but in reality all they
wanted was my body. My body in their body, one of their number,
the body of saints all praising themselves for what they had. Their
Gospel was the message of acquisition, of God and then of converts
to God and the things God rewarded them with here on earth.

*

I had my knees on the chair under the roof window and in that
preferred uncomfortably comfortable kneeling pose. I liked to
strain. To feel the body. And so, the world. Hold my breath, and

slowly let it out. I closed my eyes and saw the coloured clouds float by against the blind blackness. Going nowhere, I looked out on the street that had its lovely dusk time emptiness and stillness. Not a soul coming or going. Like a Sunday after dinner. The Lord's peace attended to. There was the slightest of friendly breezes blowing in from the solid black Cave Hill; that hit me like soft whispered words telling of the sweet and peaceful. The shopping souls had returned from their hectic day of acquisition. Saturday was acquisition day. The people I had seen around and about in the morning had all come home. The plume of smoke had long disappeared. So, I waited there, in my upper room, waited in a state of hunger, not having had the pig's feet, not merely for a God that I did not know, but for a time that will be my time to know. To know that I was a being, worthy of life. If I was not, if I failed, I would perish. Perish the notion.

Necessity demanded that the Larkin family moved away to England, but with a promise from Linus on his last day that they would definitely return in a year or two. I waited for that return. I waited and waited. Watched and waited. I waited too for Charlotte, to come my way.

It is now time to say goodbye to waiting. Life is now soft and smooth. I feel it all around me.

ACKNOWLEDGMENTS

Special thanks to my agent Pamela Malpas for her friendship, patience, perseverence and endless endeavour in the business of acting on my behalf.

Gratitude to Steve Gillis, Dan Wickett & Matt Bell at Dzanc for their significant contribution to the development and final production of this book.

I am indebted to Eileen O'Neill, who, through photographic detective work and memory, re-engaged me with Belfast memories that long separation had almost erased.